The Zamora Project

H. Marie Indigo

H. Marie Indigo

<u>The Zamora Project</u>

Copyright © 2024 by H. Marie Indigo

All rights reserved.

No part of this publication may be reproduced, distributed, or transmitted in any form or by any means, including photocopying, recording, or other electronic or mechanical methods, without the prior written permission of the publisher, except as permitted by U.S. copyright law.

First published in 2024

ISBN (paperback): 979-8-9898243-1-1

ISBN (ebook): 979-8-9898243-0-4

The story, all names, characters, and incidents portrayed in this production are fictitious. No identification with actual persons (living or deceased), places, buildings, and products is intended or should be inferred.

Contents

To all the cats I've loved, lost and held – and to my husband for helping make my book writing dreams come true.

Chapter One

"Friscuit!" I yelp and Mother throws her hands in the air, pulling the needle back and shaking her head.

"I've told you girls to stop using that word," she says, and I have trouble hiding the small smile her agitation brings up. She's been trying to get us to stop for years, but the swear word I created with the other hospice girls eventually became unstoppable.

"Sorry, you tied my arm too tightly and it hurts," I tell her, poking at the thick rubber band around my forearm. She rolls her eyes and continues working when I hear the swishing noise of Father's lab coat as he enters the kitchen.

"Dani, you are not above the curfew rules," he says, his voice cutting in from across the room. It's hoarse and gravelly, and sounds like he's been awake since before dawn as he adds, "This is your own fault for being out past curfew last night."

I scowl at him, but keep my mouth shut. While Mother may have kindness locked somewhere behind her blue eyes, Father's eyes are unyielding black doors that lead to even darker places, and it's always been an obvious fact that I am not one of his favorites.

I've already endured his lecturing this morning and watched in stunned horror when he systematically burned every one of my art journals as punishment for being out late. Now he's making me give extra blood for today's experiments, even though I've already given six vials this week. I don't have much else to my name, but am still nervous about what else he could be capable of.

Breaking curfew last night wasn't even worth it: chasing the swirling stars in the sky only earned me a cold, hard night in the storage shed and nothing but the charred remains of what took months to create. Perhaps if I had caught one, I could have proven to everyone that what I saw every night in my dreams was a real thing and not a figment of my imagination.

This was all very bad gravy, another one of our favorite swears, but I don't dare say that out loud. Not now, at least.

"Ready?" Mother asks and I nod, even though I really want to say I'm too tried and weak and hungry, too worried about the illness that's supposedly working its way through my body, and too unmotivated to play their games anymore. Every girl here is going to die in this hospice no matter what they do, so why bother with all these rules and tests?

I should be out living what little life I have left instead of here being poked at with needles and having to smell Mother's overly strongly perfume. She's put too much on today, and the smell of sugar and pine trees is making my eyes water.

Keeping my arm on the table for her, I turn my palm facing upwards and watch her gently swipe a wet cotton ball against my skin. The table is cold and smooth, and the stainless steel has been cleaned to a mirror finish so that a somewhat distorted and tired version of myself stares back at me; pale skin, brown hair, light freckles. I listen as Mother hums a song I don't know and stops just long enough to jab the sharpened needle into a vein.

Father leaves the room as soon as he's sure my samples are well on their way out of my body, but I can't bring myself to look at them myself. I don't like watching the blood climbing through the plastic tubing, and like seeing the little filled vials even less. But the procedure is over quickly and, before I know it, Mother is pressing another cotton ball to my arm and securing it with tape. The sharp smell of antiseptic hangs in the air when I finally turn my head to look at her.

"Thank you, honey." Her frowning gaze lingers on the vial for a moment before she stores it away and begins prepping her instruments for someone else. "I think this will be helpful."

"For the cure, right?" I ask her and she nods absently.

"Yes, for a cure," she mutters in response. Her gaze intensifies on the two filled vials now sitting neatly in her case and I catch a glimpse of how they each shimmer softly in white and gold hues, the same color that my naked skin glows in the moonlight. The glowing is a side effect, I'm told, of the very same illness that brought me and the other girls into hospice care.

Everyone has a variation of the same purple and red glowing skin except my golden self and another girl named Tara, who shines bright green. The glow is striking in the moonlight, but you would never notice it under normal circumstances. That is, unless you're looking directly at vials of our blood; then you can see the telltale shimmer of our poisoned bodies.

I sit for a moment longer and watch while Mother works, scribbling notes in an old journal and occasionally letting her gaze drift out the window towards the dusty horizon. A shaft of sunlight glimmers off the gold-colored brooch she has pinned permanently below her collarbone. The nesting bird stares back at me with flashing crystal eyes and looks old. Perhaps it is a family heirloom—I wouldn't know because we're not actually related—but looking at it has always brought me an unknown sense of peace.

Doctor Leonard Zamora, Father, and Doctor Martha Zamora, Mother, run a home for dying girls called The Zamora House. There are eight of us living upon a lonely hill far enough away from anyone to take notice of our undisclosed ailment. The Zamoras keep us mostly a secret, and while a handful of people know we're here, no one outside of the house knows we're capable of outshining the moon.

Back when the entire world functioned differently, the property we live on was a golf course. Then, when it was needed, it turned into a graveyard. But that was a long time ago and now it's just a house filled with sick girls and two doctors working on a cure.

I've never once considered the pair of them as actual parents. In the almost eighteen years I've lived here, the power they hold has always been more clinical than parental and it's easy to distance myself from them emotionally.

I've tried to remember the two people who actually created me; every girl here has tried at some point. But there is nothing to remember and they normally appear only as clusters of stars pulsing in the black night of dreams, shapeless and even a tad meaningless. Sometimes, their starlight spells out my name in the sky, but the glittering letters of "Daniella" always wake me before I can find who brought the moving stars to life. So, whoever brought me into this world, while tempting, has always been more of an afterthought.

"Get some fresh air, Dani," says Mother, pulling me from my thoughts. The comment feels like a gentle dismissal, and after giving her what I hope is a genuine smile, I hurry out the kitchen door and escape into the gardens.

Once outside I take in big gulps of air, savoring the crisp morning smell, the essences of wet earth and damp leaves filling my senses. The sun, newly risen in the sky, has yet to warm the dirt below, and I walk barefoot along the cool ground towards the garden's edge. While much of the space is taken up by anything we can grow and eat, there is a small area covered in the pinks and oranges of chrysanthemum bushes. They glow brightly when the sun's first rays hit them and look like fluffy blankets covered in dew.

I would say it's all a very pretty sight, but Tara, my friend and fellow sick girl, is bent double over them and vomiting her breakfast into the flowers. Beside her is my closest friend, Lily, rubbing Tara's back and offering soothing words.

So even though it feels like my feet are moving through the literal mud and my head is spinning from exhaustion and blood loss, I hurry over to them.

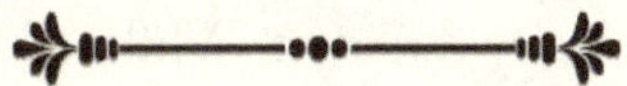

Lily looks up when she sees me and smiles. "I saved you a muffin from breakfast. You really should make sure to eat something after blood draw, you know that." She hands me a muffin laced with strawberry jam and this morning's vitamins stuck into the crumbly exterior like sprinkles. I let out a long sigh as I take it from her.

"I wanted to get out before it got too hot," I say back, suddenly realizing how hungry I am and taking a bite from the still warm pastry. I know I shouldn't let Father get between me and breakfast foods, but his eyes seemed extra volatile today and I didn't want to risk staying around too long. "Is she okay?" I add, looking down at Tara.

"I'll be fine!" Tara says brightly, springing up and causing both Lily and I to stumble away from her. "But you won't be if you pass out in the garden after samples and wake up a roasted tomato from the hideous sunburn." She wipes her mouth with the sleeve of her shirt and smiles widely, even though her face remains sunken and pale.

Lily pulls another small muffin from her pocket and hands it to Tara, who begins to nibble on it with a thoughtful expression.

"Why'd he make you give another sample today?" she asks. "Didn't you already do it yesterday after Prim?"

"She was out past curfew," Lily answers for me, and Tara nods in understanding as a faint breeze kicks up. She tucks her loose golden hair behind her ears and Lily's black locks drift over her shoulders. My own mousy brown strands stay limp behind my head, but a few delicate hairs slip out and tickle my nose and I swat them away.

All three of us are very different. While Lily is the tallest of the house girls, I am the shortest, and where Tara's eyes shine like dollops of honey, mine are an unsettling pale blue.

Every girl here is unique in many ways except for the illness that brought us together in the first place. Each of us was given up one way or another in this decaying world to come live in a house atop a graveyard and be spooky little girls together.

"Father is such a stickler for rules," Tara grumbles between bites of muffin, the color slowly returning to her cheeks as she brushes crumbs from her skirts only for them to land on my own. I flick them away from the wool and grimace at the rough texture. Another thing Father is a stickler about is how we dress, all long skirts and long sleeves even on the hottest days of summer.

I finish my own muffin in two more bites and contemplate going back inside for another, but the day is passing quickly and I need to pick up our weekly supply order. It gets dropped off outside the Zamora House's border along the nearby highway and is a short drive from the main property.

Normally, we're not allowed past the iron fence surrounding the gardens and chicken coop, but Tara and I had been given special privilege because someone needs to pick up the weekly deliveries, and there was no way Father or Mother would have time to do it. Though to be honest, it's a one-person job and I have a feeling Father only chose me to accompany Tara because he considers my life expendable. That it wouldn't be such a loss if the highways swallowed me up and no one ever saw me again.

"We should get going," Tara says and Lily gives her a long look.

"Maybe you should stay in the garden, I'm sure Dani can handle it."

"I feel fine. Just a stomachache from Sara's cooking again," Tara says, linking her arm with mine as we make our way out of the garden. "Besides, I want to drive the golf cart."

Lily stops before the garden's edge and watches as we walk on ahead. "Just be careful!" she calls after us.

"I always am!" I shout back.

"I'm more worried about Tara!"

"I'll make sure she pretends to be."

"How does one *pretend* to be careful? You're either careful or reckless, honestly..." Lily's voice fades the further we slip away from the gardens, laughing the entire time. I love Lily as if she were my real sister, but sometimes she could act more like a real mother than actual Mother ever could.

There are only two ways out of Zamora House's property lines: the main southern gate that attaches to a long driveway and the smaller northern gate that stays locked since it's actually closer to the highway than the main. The gate key is kept secure in a small tin case in Mother and Father's room on the house's first floor, but luckily Tara has already grabbed it and saved me the trouble of going back inside.

Once we're further out, I look up. There are no clouds above so the sky looks impossibly tall, and I stand still for a moment staring up until my neck begins to hurt. It makes me feel small and I enjoy the feeling, the knowing that I'm insignificant to the world. It takes the sting of being meaningless at home that much easier to handle.

Beyond the garden and tucked beside the iron fencing is an old path that stops near a storage shed, which holds the oldest, rustiest golf cart there ever was. I have no idea what golf is, even after Lily tried to explain it to Tara and me by reading passages from a book.

The fields around the property have long since grown wild with grasses and occasional trees, and are dotted with sunflowers as big as the sun itself, and sometimes, if you are lucky and don't sprain your ankle, you can stumble on an old, hidden headstone or, luckier still, find the remains of more ancient and rusty golf carts.

Somewhere in the distance away from home is the city of Bitterwater. Lily read in one of her books that it was once a dinky town, but turned into a bustling city when people displaced by The Dusting flocked to it. Towns just like it popped up all along the long stretch of Highway Five, which runs the entire length of this side of the country. But even with the new cities, the book said there are still huge stretches of land with nothing but desolate wasteland filled with the kind of waist-high bushes that scratch up your legs, pointy cactus, and desert wolves. They are called "the wilds."

"I like being out here," Tara says, opening the shed door and running her fingers along the cart's side. "It feels so, I don't know, mystical? Intriguing? Old? I wonder what it was like before The Dusting? I bet it wasn't as pretty."

"I bet it looked the same, but with fewer weeds," I answer.

The Dusting, which we all considered a terrible, on-the-nose name for a major event, happened almost sixty years ago and shaped the country into what it is today. A period of severe drought brought on by some serious changes in the climate, it decimated the country's croplands and left what was said to be nothing but dust in its wake.

"Are you sure you're okay?" I ask Tara as she slides into the driver's seat and starts the cart by pressing a button to better angle the installed solar panels bolted to the thin roof. She still looks horribly pale, her cheeks sunken. No number of muffins seems to help.

"Never better," she answers, gesturing for me to take a seat before we pull out into the sunshine.

I bend my face into the warmth and feel a stab of shame at how liberating being outside of the home's expansive property feels. How free it is not to have Mother and Father always watching us, breathing down our necks, counting the days till we die off. Sometimes, it feels like they want that day to come.

We pause briefly to unlock the gate, and then it's just a few minutes' drive until we see the highway peeking through the trees and our supply crates nestled beside the low stone wall dividing us from the highway and wilds beyond.

"Awe, we missed Carl," Tara laughs, scrambling out of the golf cart to pull open the closest crate. "I always love seeing his sour face behind the wheel."

"You're acting like something new will be in there," I murmur, watching her dig around the contents. She grabs the crumpled supply list from her pocket and begins to check off items as she smiles.

"There might be. You never know!"

I'm leaning in to help when something from the crate catches my attention and I pull it free: a newspaper, probably used as crate lining, but it isn't ancient and yellowing like normal and looks fairly recent. Tara bends over to look as well, a can of beans dropping from her hand and back into the crate as she lets out a low whistle.

"Martin Apollo? He looks dreamy, what did he do?"

I scan the words written below his black and white photo, my eyes opening wide. "He crossed The Dusting!"

"Really?" Tara grabs the newspaper and begins to read through it quickly. "Is that even possible?"

"Not according to Father," I say. "It's too far by foot and too dangerous by air, but it says right here that he leads land trains through the worst of it for a lot of money."

"What do you think a lot of money is?" Tara asks.

"I don't know," I mutter in response. None of us have ever left the hospice or had need for our own funds. Mother and Father took care of everything for us.

"And why would Father keep saying it's impossible? Looks like someone does it, and makes a living from it," Tara says, chewing on her lower lip.

"Let's talk to Lily about it later, maybe she can make sense of it," I say, loading the few crates into the back of the golf cart and tucking the newspaper back in its spot. Tara goes to help, but I notice her hands have begun to shake, so I take over.

"Thanks," she murmurs, wiping sweat from her forehead.

"You don't look so good," I say and help her to sit in the passenger seat.

"I'm fine, I just need to lie down."

But the closer we get to home, the paler Tara's skin becomes and then just as we approach the shed, all the color and warmth from my vibrant friend disappears in an instant and she slips from her seat. I nearly crash the cart into a nearby tree after she loses balance and topples into the packed dirt.

"Someone come help!" The plea rips from my throat so violently it leaves a lingering scratchy feeling and I have trouble keeping my own balance from the trembling terror of Tara's face, as she twists and convulses on the ground.

Luckily, Rana and Lily hear my screaming from the nearby chicken coop and Rana runs over to help. Lily arrives only a few moments later with Mother in tow, but at this point, I can barely register what is happening because I'm shaking so much with fright. Tara lays face down in the dirt, and I can barely see the rise and fall of her chest.

It's only as Mother takes over, barking orders at us in a voice gone thin with worry, that it actually hits me. No matter what we're told, it's never felt real, the possibility that we were not long for this world. But as Tara is lifted limply into Mother's arms, it finally sinks in: Tara is going to be the first of us to die.

Chapter Two

Mother warned me and Lily about giving names to the chickens, but we didn't listen. It's why I know we're eating Gus tonight and can only summon up enough courage to eat a few bites of his fleshy pink skin.

Lily always had it in her head that her real parents were animal lovers and it was her idea to always eat what was served, even if we knew who was on our plate. She didn't want any living thing dying for nothing; Lily was full of ideas like that. And since I always listen to her, even when she tells me to honor dead chickens, I went along with it.

No matter how sick to my stomach it makes me.

I don't know how she came to this conclusion about her family because we both have no idea what the people were actually like, but I think the narrative gives her a sense of peace because she hopes to find them one day.

Looking at her from across the table, Lily catches my eye and nods sagely before taking a bite from her fork. She brings a hand to her heart and sighs so loudly that Prim shoots her a disapproving glance and Sara giggles. She then delicately takes her vitamins one by one from a small container and pushes her empty plate away.

I am stunned she's able to eat right now. I keep thinking of Tara, and it's almost hard to stomach anything; however, I dutifully take small bites to honor Gus.

Father, at the end of the long table, drinks from his mug of coffee. He and Mother never eat with us, always too busy in their basement lab, but they often bring their pungent mugs of black coffee with them to the table. Lily said it's as if they are trying to force a bit of normalcy into our lives.

Mother sits across from him and along each side of the table sit the other house girls and I, four on each. No, not four...the chair next to Lily's is empty. Tara's chair. Even now I can see her eyes darting to it occasionally as she puts together a plate of Gus for her. Poor sweet Gus who used to peck at my toes is now being served up with stewed green beans and cornbread. It's like I can almost hear him clucking.

While we eat, Father drones on and on about how food was better back when he was just a boy, the light from a scented candle lit earlier by Sara illuminating his face as he rants. Friscuit, does he miss beef burgers for some reason! About every other day we hear that, according to him, ground chicken patties are nothing compared to their beef counterparts and that it's some massive insult to consumerism that he can't get his hands on anything but chicken meat now. The vast number of crops killed in The Dusting were sourced mainly for livestock feed, and with nothing to eat, the country's cattle began to die. Soon, only small pockets of privately-held cows remained and they became heavily protected. So even if he found one, it's not like he'd be able to eat it.

Chickens, on the other hand, had adapted to the climate changes from The Dusting and became the primary source of animal-based protein, so there are plenty of them to go around. Lily and I read once in a book that beef allegedly tastes better than chicken, like Father tells us, but we have no way of knowing if this is true. Neither of us has ever tasted a cow and honestly, I don't think we ever could after seeing so many pictures of their big, sad brown eyes in Lily's books.

Sometimes I wonder if eating all those cows are what made Father a very bitter man.

"Dani," Mother says. "Will you bring this to Tara before you go to bed? And please make sure she brushes her teeth; you may need to help her."

"Of course." I jam my own little collection of vitamins into my mouth just before she slides the warm plate into my hands. Cait elicits a strained sob when I stand to leave and Mother turns towards her, her blue eyes soft and comforting.

"Cait, dear, we talked about this. You're comprised enough as is, you need to stay away from that room for now."

"No one will miss Dani if she gets sick and dies," Prim snickers. "Let her gather up all the germs for you so you'll be safe."

Cait lets out another strangled wail and Mother, after giving Prim a sharp look, reaches over to pat Cait's hands as she hunches over, her shoulders shaking with quiet sobs. Cait and Tara are actual sisters who came here together as small glowing babies. They are the only two people here related to each other by blood.

"She won't die, she won't!" Cait sniffs into her napkin.

"Just like the chickens," says Prim.

In an instant I see Prim's smug face go bright red and what I think is her knee jerk against the table with a sickening thud. The jolt sends Sara's candle toppling over and Vera splashes her cup of water onto the small flames erupting from the table cloth.

With an animalistic growl, Prim jumps from her chair and glares at Lily, who leans back with a satisfied smile.

"Lily kicked me!" she screams, slamming her palms on the table.

"I did no such thing, you must have bumped a table leg," Lily tells her sweetly, taking a long sip from her water glass. Sara is doing a poor job trying to hold in laughter, but Vera and Rana busy themselves smothering the singed table cloth.

"That's enough," Father's stern voice rumbles, and Prim turns pale.

Prim and I have never really gotten along. She has a drive in her that aims to please Mother and Father as if they were her real parents, and her simping nature has always gotten on my nerves. Mother and Father may be the only parents any of us can remember, but it doesn't mean we have to think of them as such.

"Yes, sir." Prim slinks back into her chair, her eyes downcast as she turns a blank stare to the burned tablecloth.

The room has taken on a tinge of acrid smoke, but the air purifiers set up around our house make short work of it and I barely notice the smell anymore as I get up to leave the kitchen. Clutching Tara's plate of food, I use my back to push open the kitchen door and happen to catch Lily's eye. She gives me a bold wink and I have to suppress a small laugh. Prim deserved that kick.

I make my way up the wooden stairs to the second floor. Our home is ancient and vast and no one seems to know what came first: the house or the graveyard. Two stories of mostly dark wood on the inside and an exterior of wood bleached white by the sun.

It's the perfect place for two eccentric doctors to open their doors to a brood of dying girls, and houses a basement large enough to hold their various supplies and gadgets needed for their supposed good work.

Tara and Cait's room is at the far end of the hall, next to the one I share with Lily, and has a door painted bright red. The door Lily and I share is violet.

I knock lightly and hear Tara's mumbling reply when I step inside. She's draped across a chair looking out the window, her bed on the other side of the room with its sheets rumpled and unkempt. Cait's bed sits like an empty husk in the opposite corner, already stripped of its bedding. It's a depressing sight, but Tara's face glows softly in the fading light and she looks almost happy.

I walk slowly to her, and the sparkling sunset catches my attention before I think to place her dinner plate on the table beside her.

"Dani," she says slowly, turning her head towards me. "Just looking at that plate makes me feel worse. I don't think I can eat Gus; he was such a nice chicken."

I perch on a nearby chair and we stare at the food together. "Lily would want you to try to eat something. How are you feeling?"

"Tired and uncomfortable. Mother changed out my mattress and it feels like I'm sleeping on a bag of sand now."

"You'd think she would be set on making us as comfortable as possible," I say with a dry and humorless laugh. "She and Father are always talking about how we're all going to die young—that is, unless they find a cure."

Tara nods, looking back out the window. "I think I'm going to be the first."

"Don't talk like that," I say. "Even if what they've always told us is true, it doesn't mean it has to be tonight or tomorrow or even the next day."

Tara has been my friend for a long time. Losing her doesn't feel like a real possibility. Nothing has ever changed around here, so something like this, even this predestined early death, feels out of place.

Perhaps none of us thought it would ever really happen.

Tara sits up slowly and I have to turn away to keep from looking at her arms. The veins, snaking so close to the top of her skin, crawl through her body and look as if they're pulsing with every heartbeat. I can't help but wonder how she can even move without being in torturous pain, the nerves shooting all the wrong kinds of signals to her brain.

I take a deep breath before saying, "There's another batch of chicks ready to hatch soon, and Cait told me she wants your help naming them, so you have to get better."

Tara's face goes slack when I mention Cait, and with some effort she takes a few small bites of cornbread, the crumbs falling into her lap. She carefully brushes them away by flicking each one by one with her fingers.

"I don't know if that will happen."

A slow, burning sound rumbles in the distance and I look towards the vast horizon. The world seems so much bigger when I look at it from the upstairs windows, but once I'm down in the gardens or running through the old headstones, it shrinks and becomes so small I might as well be back inside these walls.

But I know there is more. Bigger and brighter things down the highway, cities that sparkle like a million fallen stars in the night and great oceans of blue water that glisten in the heat of the day. Lily read about them in her books.

"They always come at the same time," Tara says, interrupting my thoughts. She nibbles on a slender green bean and brings my mind back to the streaks of distant light before she continues. "I like to pretend they're dragons hunting in the night. They eat at the same time we do, for dinner, but there are a few that come for breakfast at dawn."

"I think they're only land trains crossing the wilds." The use of so much hurried scientific trial and error with genetically-manipulated dirt to combat The Dusting left the environment even more inhospitable than before, and the poisoned earth started to fight back. The resulting dust storms, fires, and tainted water led to a lot of people dying and a whole lot more of them relocating from the now inhabitable lands to either the east or west coast.

While giant land trains connect us together on the western side, they only run from north to south, and never cross the vast, dead lands between coasts.

"No." Tara's gaze is glassy as she looks out the window. The light reflects in her eyes, and for a second that's all I see: two round and shining orbs. She lifts a pale hand and points a finger in the direction of the distant speeding blur. I notice she's shaking a little when she says, "Dragons hunting for food. The daylight is too hot for them, so they only come out after the sun goes down. I wonder what it would be like to ride one."

"I don't think dragons really exist," I tell her, leaning over to pull the thick shades over the window. Tara's eyes widen briefly and color flushes her features in a flash as I fuss with the blinds.

"You can believe anything in your head and make it real," she says. "It's what's in there that counts and makes things true or not true. That means anything is true if you believe it." She shrugs at her own thoughts and continues to pick at her food.

I wonder at the stories she and Cait must make up in their evenings together. Lily and I had our own stories to share, but we had never come up with mysterious fire-breathing creatures in the night. Not that Lily would protest. In fact, I think she'd secretly love it, but only after she was finished telling me about all the different types of seahorses that live in the ocean. The stories we share aren't guesses about the unknown, but rather the adventures we would have there if we could.

Tara lets out a low moan and pushes the food away. "I don't think I can stomach more. Would you help me to the washroom? I need to brush my teeth. They feel like bad gravy."

"Sure," I mutter and curl my arm around her shoulders. "I still need to brush as well."

I try hard not to let her see my wincing face when she wraps her hands around my arm. The pain she feels must far outweigh my mild discomfort, but it's hard to summon the courage to truly face the fact that once Tara dies, someone else will be next, and so on until there are none of us left. Until all the spooky, glowing girls on the graveyard hill are gone forever.

Chapter Three

It's that time of the year between spring and summer, when the days are warm and the nights have a tendency to frost over. Last night I lay awake after Mother gave us cups of milk laced with her specialty drugs to help us sleep. Lily was asleep in moments, but the walls and shadows were speaking so loudly they kept me aching for hours in a living nightmare.

The moon whispered and told me she would take care of Tara after she died. I wasn't sure if I believed her, but the moving stars appeared, as they so often do, and spelled my name in the sky. They were only the brightest that could compete with the full moon's glow, and told me my real family said the moon could not be trusted.

The next morning, Mother and Father say they had to place an additional supply order that I need to pick up from the highway, so I quickly take the key from its place in Mother's nightstand and shove it deep into a pocket, where it weighs down heavily. I'm glad to get out of the house, if only for a moment, to take my mind off Tara.

Someone has tied three small, cylindrical weights to the key to serve as a keychain, and somewhere in my memory I remember there only being one, then two, and at some point, three. I never really had a good memory for these types of things and have never gotten around to asking Mother or Father about them, but it didn't seem to matter much. They are just keychains.

I'm patting my hand absently against my pocket, feeling the key's weight and turning to leave when I see Father standing in the doorway and freeze. He's watching me closely and blocking the only way out.

"How do you feel today, Dani?" he asks, striding forward on his long legs, his coat clean and heavily starched around his ankles. I don't have any space to move away from him.

"Um, fine. A little tired, I guess, but I think I'm fine," I stammer. Grabbing one of my arms, he jerks it towards his chest and looks closely at my wrist, twisting it painfully to each side as his dark eyes examine it closely. I know better than to make a sound and instead bite the inside of cheek until the sharp taste of blood fills my mouth.

"Head feed good?" he asks.

"Yes." It's a lie, my head is pounding from lack of sleep.

"How about your arms and legs, everything feels normal?"

"I guess they do. Nothing feels abnormal." One more lie: my left foot itches.

"I want you to tell me the moment anything feels different. That's an order, just like I'm ordering you to behave. Do you understand? Do you think you can handle it?" He lets go of my wrist and fixes me with an intense glare.

His hands leave my skin stinging and red and I back away from him with my head down. Friscuit, he's been in a darker mood these last few weeks and I know well enough to leave him alone. If you make him mad, which isn't hard to do, and you're lucky, he'll just assign you extra chores. But I've also known him to lock you inside the work shed for the whole day without breakfast and lunch as punishment.

"Yes, sir, I do."

He dismisses me with a flick of his wrist.

My shoulder clips painfully on the doorway when I hurry out and rush into the gardens. I can't remember what he was like when myself and the other house girls were younger, but I have been able to notice his increased unpleasantness as we've grown older. The less time spent in this man's presence the better.

I practically run out of the gardens to get to the shed, and then drive the golf cart a little too recklessly in my hurry to distance myself from not only Father, but the hovering shadow of Tara's death—as if I could ever escape something like that.

I skid to a stop by our property's outer edge where the land clears of overgrown trees and makes way for Highway Five. Only local deliveries use the highway. The bigger and more economical land trains avoid it and make use of the wilds, the sprawling, empty stretches of land between populated areas. It's easier to travel when things are desolate and barren and they are like shooting stars in the deserts—or dragons, according to Tara—and can go anywhere they want.

On the other side of the highway's asphalt is only smooth grasses and pressed dirt, places I assume cows and land trains would love. A low and sturdy gate separates our world from the more exciting one beyond the wilds and it's here that I park the cart to wait.

The world is noisy with life, birds chattering and squirrels dashing across the ground, their bushy tails fluttering in the breeze. Even the air breathes differently, a sort of freshness that only exists in small amounts in the garden. As if even being near Zamora House saps it of life. I lean back in my seat and close my eyes, tasting the wild wind.

But soon my attention catches on an incoming truck, groaning down the highway with great effort. There's no need to get out of the cart because Carl always does the same thing and I know his routine by heart: slow the truck down, kick the box through the passenger door, and speed off down the highway.

Maybe he knows who lives here, or maybe he doesn't, but Carl seems to think everyone here is a threat and he'll try to spend as little time with them as possible. Or maybe we're just not worth his time.

Which is why I'm so confused to see the truck slowing down and even more troubled when it comes to a complete stop in the middle of the highway. I bolt upright, body tense and alert, when I hear the passenger door open and a stranger walks around the hood.

"Are you from Zamora House?" A tall, broad-shouldered man comes into view. I'm just about eighteen years old, but he looks a few years older and could be in his early twenties. His casual smile catches me off-guard, and I stare a little too long into bright green eyes hidden behind his thick tortoiseshell glasses. He gives a small wave and I nearly fall out of the golf cart.

"Yes, um, that would be me. I'm Daniella, but you can call me Dani."

"Heh, just like the batteries," he replies.

"What? Um, where's Carl?"

"Don't worry, he's still here," the stranger says and gestures with his thumb towards the truck where Carl grips the steering wheel with white knuckles. The mystery man moves backs to the truck and lifts a large crate with ease and sets it down.

"Oh, I mean, I guess I've just never seen Carl have anyone with him."

"Never?" he asks.

"No, I don't think so." I look at the ground, at the fence, the sky, back to the ground, anywhere but him.

"I needed a ride, and Carl said he'd give me a lift if I helped him with the delivery." He gives me a lopsided grin as he brings the crate closer and sets it on the fence between us. I can't help but stare at his intimidating figure.

Carl is an old man with eyesight so terrible I'm certain he drives the highway half-blind, but this new guy has my head spinning. He is taller than even Lily, with brown wavy hair cut close to the sides of his head, and a face that looks a few days out from a shave. His eyes are a green so vivid they could be emeralds.

"Well, okay then," I say weakly, my hands clumsy against my sides because I suddenly don't know what to do with them. I finally settle on placing one on my hip and the other resting awkwardly on the fence.

Father has rules about speaking to anyone outside of the house, especially without his permission. He says it's to keep us safe from strangers, but for the most part, people avoid us anyway, too unsure of the unknown. Speaking with Carl is allowed because I may need to talk to him about the supply order, but it's not like he ever had the urge to speak to me. Maybe this isolation has left me a little rusty with my, um, social skills.

"You can call me Evan, by the way," he says, standing back so I can inspect the supply crate's contents. He watches closely as I fumble the order list from my pocket.

"Thanks," I mumble, not sure if he can even hear me when I hold the list to cover my face.

"Kind of a big order. You taking all this home yourself?"

I nod.

"Lots of fuel rods, don't you have your own sets of solars? I thought everyone in these parts had some."

"We do..." I pause because I don't know what to tell him. How do you explain that the pair of mad scientist doctors you live with go through fuel rods like they do cups of coffee?

"You also didn't order any toothpaste. Don't you need it?"

"What?" I shake my head at the strange question, still trying to determine why someone from the outside world would even want to talk to me. "I live with doctors. They say the stuff people buy from stores is full of chemicals that'll turn your teeth blue, so we make our own."

Evan stares at me again, his mouth hanging open like he wants to say something, but his eyes crinkle and he lets out an awkward laugh when he taps the side of the full crate. "Everything there?"

"Looks like it," I lie because focusing on the list is too hard when I can hear him breathing so close to me. Friscuit, he's cute, and I'm too nervous to figure out how to talk to him. I wish Tara was here right now to help.

Evan loudly whistles and I watch as Carl and his old truck peel off down the highway, leaving us alone. As soon as it's out of sight, he turns to eye my cart and lets out another whistle, but this one is low and appreciative.

"I haven't seen one of these in years. I used to fix them up with my younger brother when we were kids and we'd drive them all over our dad's golf courses." His eyes go distant for a moment before he brings himself back. "Did you know there's a hidden compartment under the seat? I read about it in a magazine. Used for smuggling extra booze under the limitation laws back in the day."

He turns back to look at me and I can see his face has gone bright red. With a smile that is more of a grimace, he holds his hand out as if he would like to shake my own.

"Sorry, I just find old stuff like this interesting. Good thing this is a single button start, your keychains look a little heavy and those could put unneeded weight on the ignition. Did you know they still make golf carts? That sport never went away, but they don't look like this anymore, much sleeker. My dad hated it when we drove around these clunkers."

"Do you...play golf?" I ask and immediately regret it.

"No."

"Oh."

There is a slight breeze above the fence between us, scooping up tiny leaves and twigs, carrying them down the fence tops and dancing them around Evan's outstretched hand. I finally take it and feel my insides melt when his warm hand encloses mine. We stand there for a second, not moving, and somewhere in the back of my mind I realize there is a fence separating us and I wish there wasn't.

"Anyway," he says. "Your teeth look pretty good for someone who uses homemade toothpaste and you drive a nice golf cart, so your parents must be proud."

I am frozen in the moment and when I don't release his hand right away, he clasps his other one around and gives me a firm handshake before letting go himself. I can't concentrate much on it because all I'm doing is thinking of how rough and big his hands are and how I can under no circumstances look up into those eyes again. But there is a tiny spark in my mind, like a shooting star, that launches from my mouth without warning.

"Why would you want to come all the way out here?" I ask. "There isn't anything around for miles."

"Secret passion of mine, something even more fun than fixing golf carts. Here, I'll show you." He grins and reaches into the pockets of his coat. I lean in closely and see he's brought out a small metal disc. He cradles it in his hand and holds it up between us so it catches the sunlight.

"Doubt you've seen one of these before," he says and I shake my head as he flips it up in the air. I jump back, amazed as small wings launch from its smooth surface and the disc hovers in the air overhead. It is a silver droplet among the clouds and I watch as it zips through the air, over the treetops and then down again, skimming the highway like a very tiny truck.

"It's so fast, I can barely see it," I breathe.

"You can see these better at night, like little shooting stars everywhere."

"Moving stars," I breathe, my remembered dreams bubbling to the surface and disappearing with a pop.

I feel rather than see him smile and look up just in time to catch him walking down the highway with his back to me, whistling the same song I heard from Mother earlier in the day.

"Need to get some work done, but I'll see ya around, Dani."

I let out a breath, feeling like it's my first in ages. There is a stupid smile on my face, but there's no one around to see it and I don't care as I jump in the cart to hurry home. Lily is going to love hearing about this.

Chapter Four

The sun dips low in the sky when I finally make my way back through the gardens. The hand Evan touched tingles for reasons I'm not certain of and I have to concentrate on keeping the smile from my face. No one, especially not Prim or Father, can know there is a boy wandering the highway so close to home.

Sara and Rana are waiting for me and rush to help carry the supplies inside. A few early rising stars pop through the deep blue depths of sky above us, twinkling in their own steady rhythms, and watch silently as I lock the gate and follow the girls inside.

"There's some new journals in here," Sara says as she begins to sort through the crate's contents. She hands one to me and smiles sadly. "Blank ones, though."

"Blank for now," I tell her, taking the new book and flipping the pages through my fingers. The fine white sheets whisper against my fingertips and bring warmth to my core. These will be perfect to draw inside, so I tuck a few extra books safely against my chest.

"Don't Mother and Father use those downstairs? Won't they notice some are missing?" Rana asks, drumming her fingers on the countertop while she scans the supply list.

"They never notice anything we do," says Sara, opening a bag of brown sugar and sniffing it. Rana pulls it away from her.

"He owes me," I say, digging through a nearby drawer for a new pencil. Finding one, I also grab an apple from a countertop bowl for later. Sara and Rana busy themselves putting everything away and I sneak out of the room so I don't have to help.

The house is quiet today and I could almost pretend I'm the only one here. It feels like one of Lily's stories, a lone girl living in a cabin in the woods or marooned on a tropical island, just me, the house, the trees and sky outside, and nothing else. Well, maybe Evan could be around to keep me company. I don't think I'd mind.

But I know everyone is either sleeping or outside in the sun, in reality. It's very hard to be alone here. Most of the girls spend as much time as possible in the sunlight, either physically or in our dreams. Being inside meant you had to face facts, give blood, or be tested on, but elsewhere held possibilities, even if they were only ever in your head.

I find Lily in our room, and true to her nature, she isn't sleeping. She's propped against the wall, sitting under the window with a lamp nearby. Several books lay discarded around her, rejections she went through before finding the perfect afternoon escape.

She sits under artificial light because the window behind her is locked tight. Father said it was all in the interest of safety and air purity. Still, it would have been nice to open it once in a while, if only to let in some fresh air.

Lily sits amongst her collection of small plants, each in their own colorful pot, and they glisten like crystals having just been watered. Most of the girls keep them in their rooms to bring a little of our gardens inside, their little leaves bending towards the sealed sunlit windows. The collection Lily and I have amassed is by far the largest, of course.

The plants survive with just a little sunlight and the same purified air pumped through our rooms. Every window on the second floor is shut tight, except for the bedroom next door, Tara and Cait's room. I noticed the lock had been broken some time ago, but never told Father or Mother. I'd whispered my secret to Lily and she made sure the window coverings concealed the broken hinge and it's been that way ever since. It was just another small act of rebellion, especially after I noticed Father locking our bedroom doors after we'd fallen asleep. Another so-called safety measure, I assume.

Our room today is bright and cool, but Lily's face looks red and swollen and when I come closer, I see her crying softly.

"Lily, you okay?" I ask, sitting beside her.

She turns towards me, her eyes soft and misty. "Yes, I'm sorry. I was just thinking about Tara. I overheard Mother speaking with Cait this morning and she doesn't think Tara will get better. She's going to be the first of us to die."

It's a fact I realized ages ago, but it doesn't hurt any less, however little I try to think about it. "Poor Cait," I murmur.

"Poor Mother," says Lily. "I think she's taking it really hard. And Father...Something just feels off with him. They've both been even more on edge after they locked her away in her room, you know?" Lily is quiet for a moment, then looks at me sideways and a small smile creeps onto her face. "While you were gone today, I remembered something."

"Remembered something?"

"From a really long time ago. Do you remember when we used to play hide and seek with Cait and Tara, when we were kids? We could never find them and I think I figured out what they were doing. Come over here!" Lily wipes the tears away and an eagerness catches in her voice and carries me with her to the elongated dresser under our window. It runs the length of the entire room and is covered in a long, tufted cushion to be used as an extra seat. She moves to the far end by the wall where Tara and Cait's room lays just on the other side. I set the blank journals on the floor and lean towards her.

"This is where they would hide, but we never found them and I figured out why," says Lily. "There's a loose panel inside, a secret entrance to the room next door." She opens a cabinet door and reaches in to knock on the wood. Pushing her body inside, she quickly pulls the panel out and lets me gaze inside to see a long tunnel leading to the corresponding cabinet of Tara and Cait in the next room.

"Friscuit, those filthy cheaters!"

Lily snickers and slides the panel back. She holds a finger to her lips, but her giggles spill over. "Shh! Tara might be sleeping. I was thinking we should visit her tonight after dinner. Mother mentioned she's been preparing special meals for her, so I don't know how anyone is going to see her. We'll sneak in tonight and bring her a new plant or something. I bet she'll like that."

"It's a lovely idea." I give my best friend a big hug and wipe a few tears from my own eyes.

"Oh! You got some new journals!" Lily excitedly grabs them from the floor and, pushing them towards me, laughs loudly. "Are you going to fill them up with drawings of vases, or going with my idea of nothing but Prim's fat face?"

"Shh, you said Tara might be sleeping! And no, I have something much more interesting. You're never going to believe what happened today when I went for the supply pick up."

Lily sits down on her bed, her attention rapt and eyes wide as she listens to the description of my day—well, actually I mostly describe Evan. I pace the room, pent up nerves controlling my every motion as I gesture my hands along with the story.

When I'm done, Lily lets out a long sigh. "You cannot tell Father about this."

"I don't plan on it," I mumble idly, picking a blank journal and sitting at our shared desk. I open to the second page because I always skip the first one. That page is specially designated for only one thing, my name in swirling script like I could be the main character of my own story.

It starts with thin pencil lines, two circles for eyes set apart from each other on the paper, and then even thinner lines within, the dancing lines that lay hidden along the iris. I take extra time to sketch the glasses, making sure they don't obscure anything important, and then I pull a pallet of watercolors close. The hues in the container are muddled from overuse, but still saturated with pigment and the perfect color to reflect Evan's eyes.

Lily bends close and watches as I blend neutral tones for skin that blend into darker shades for eyebrows. Then, I finish with forest and emerald greens for his eyes. It's not a complete face, just what I seem to remember most.

"Yeah, you definitely can't tell Father about him. I also can't believe you remembered his eyes with that much detail." Lily giggles and bats her eyelashes. "Can I keep this?"

I throw a pillow at her.

Tonight's dinner is leftover Gus and being enjoyed without Mother and Father. Vera said she saw them head into the basement earlier in the day and the only indication they were still around was the occasional kitchen visit for fresh coffee.

Dinner is always better without them, even with Prim being her usual annoying self, and I wish I could have stayed to enjoy it longer. The company of the other house girls has always felt more like family than two imposter caregivers could be. So, with great reluctance, Lily and I wash our dinner plates and quickly head upstairs to our room.

After brushing our teeth and changing into our night clothes, we spend the next hour waiting in silence. I pace the room waiting for the floorboards to stop creaking and the soft voices beyond the walls to become whispers, then snores, and Lily reads a book until I collapse next to her. My eyes fight to stay open, but she squeezes my hand and I spring back to life.

Finally, when the house is still, Lily and I creep through the hidden crawl space. She goes first, like everywhere we ever go, and I pick my way carefully behind her.

I'm still excited to see Tara, even if we couldn't find anything to bring her, but my breath catches painfully in my throat when we emerge into the next room and look at her. Only a small amount of light from the moon bathes her body, which lays quiet and still on the bed. I think suddenly that she might already have passed on, but Lily is braver than I could ever be and checks. Padding over on bare feet, she lays her hands on Tara's shoulders.

"She's still breathing," she whispers and my heart beats hard against my chest.

"Are you sure?"

"Yes, I'm sure. Come here." Lily pulls me to the bedside and we stand together looking at Tara. I can hardly believe how much smaller she looks from last I saw her and can barely keep my eyes on her frail form. Veins pulse beneath her pale skin and push her blood through a million small pores. It's as if her blood is trying to escape her body and it glimmers softly, giving her skin a shimmering green glow that feels brighter than usual.

The air around her has a metallic tang to it, as well as the lingering aroma of Mother's sugar and pine perfume. Lily must smell it too because she makes a face before looking at me.

"She looks worse than yesterday," I say and Lily takes my hand, her brows creased with concern. "She asked me to help her brush her teeth and she was unsteady, but still walking. This is bad gravy; she doesn't even look like she could hold a toothbrush right now."

"I wonder why it was so sudden," Lily muses. "Everyone else seems fine, so what's the difference between Tara and the rest of us? Why do we have more time than her?"

"Or we don't," I say softly. "Any one of us could suddenly drop dead. Maybe she's just the first."

"I don't feel it, I'm sorry, I just don't. There has to be a reason, there's always a reason. If I can just quiet my mind and listen carefully, I could figure it out."

Lily's voice trails off and she begins to walk around the room, occasionally examining Tara's meager belongings with a deep frown. Now that I've looked, I can't take my eyes off Tara. As sickly as she looks, her face is peaceful and her lips almost form a soft smile and I wonder what dying feels like.

Something falls sharply to the floor and my breath catches in my throat as Lily and I stare at the small jar she dropped, waiting in awful silence to see if anyone in the house heard. When it remains still and quiet, I turn back to Tara and have to swallow the scream in my throat when I find her staring back at me with huge eyes.

"Lily!" I hiss and she is by my side in an instant. I reach out and take Tara's hand. Even though her skin leaves mine smudged with her brightly-glowing blood, it feels like the right thing to do.

"My fingers are on fire. Am I dying?" she asks us and I turn toward Lily. Lily always has the best answers, but how do you even answer that?

"We don't know," she says and smooths Tara's hair against her head. I notice she shies away from touching her bare skin.

The inside of Tara's mouth is dark and black and I know without needing to check that it is slick with blood. Some dribbles down her chin and I reach over to wipe it with a corner of her blanket.

"We thought you might be bored and lonely," I tell her softly and another soft smile spreads across her face. She looks upwards, as if she could see through the ceiling into the night sky and perhaps beyond.

"I feel like a dragon," she whispers. "There is fire in my blood and I feel as if I could fly." She turns to look into my eyes. "Don't take the vitamins. I think Mother and Father are making us sick. Oh friscuit..."

"Shh, just rest, you know that's ridiculous and they're just trying to help," Lily coos and continues stroking her head. "Dani, can you open the window for her? Maybe some actual air will help her feel better."

"Good idea," I say. I give Tara's hand a small squeeze and could swear I feel her squeeze in return. Turning my back on them I cross the room to the one big window at the far end.

I was just here. Right here watching the dragons streak across the distance with Tara, and it only feels like moments ago that the four of us—Tara, Lily, Cait, and I—were playing together in this very room. Then we grew up and innocence faded to a song playing in a different room.

In a different house.

In a different world.

And while I remember there being games, my memory is too addled to remember what we played. Only that we were together.

Ducking under the blind, I throw my shoulder into the window to work it loose and am rewarded with a satisfying sucking sound as it pulls away from the sill. There is a rush of cool air against my knuckles as it glides under the window covering, making it flutter. I admire my bloody and glowing hands before I pull them back inside.

Lily falls backwards onto the floor with a muffled scream, but I barely notice her scrambling back up after Tara captures my attention.

What begins happening is soundless only in the way that nature is soundless, where nothing is said but the rustling of wind and grasses and dust scatter across the sky like well-versed poetry. Tara's body convulses and withers against her bed. Lily, her face white, hurries to me and we stand there, clinging to each other.

The blood that had been oozing from Tara's skin now truly flows free from every pore. But where it touches the sheets, the mattress, the floor, her pillow, each drop blossoms into a spiked, crystalline flower. Every petal pulses and dances and then, as if some silent command is given, they burst into their own separate flame. They are a thousand birthday candles gleaming in the glowing room and Tara's body is their cake altar.

I feel Lily's legs give out beside me and I crumple to the ground clutching her, my fingernails boring into her skin. Lily doesn't flinch, though, because neither of us can move.

Like any candle left to burn out its short life, the flames began to extinguish one by one until we are left in darkness and total silence. Then, slower this time, Tara's body begins to shake again. First her toes, her legs, hands and arms, until her back arches so quickly and violently that it looks like she is sitting up in bed, her spine unnaturally angled.

Her head falls back as she again bursts into flames and becomes the sun itself as Lily and I shield our eyes.

As quickly as it began, her body snuffs out and slumps over. Where each fiery flower had just come alive, a tiny green tendril snakes out to cradle her. The ones that don't find a place to rest weave together and grow and grow until they begin to cocoon the whole bed, crawling their way across the floor towards us. Lily regains her senses moments before me and I feel her pulling us towards the cabinets.

"Now this is bad gravy, we need to leave," she hisses into my ear. My legs are sluggish with fear and confusion, and my mind isn't completely certain what to do, but Lily brings me with her anyway and when one of the tendrils finally touches my left foot, reality collapses in force and fear grips my heart.

We scurry back through the crawlspace and Lily grabs the divider just as one lone tendril trespasses into the safety of our room, creeping towards us inch by inch.

But she slams the panel shut, slicing it clean through. It twitches in front of us a few times and then falls still.

Chapter Five

There is a sudden and violent rainstorm later in the night. I tell Lily I think it's the sky crying for Tara, but she insists it is nature restoring balance after such a loss. We stay huddled together on the floor under a blanket and eventually fall asleep to the echoing sounds of thunder. My dreams are full of dancers walking on tiptoe along sturdy, leafy vines and stars appear above their heads spelling out my name. I think I see my real parents silhouetted against the night sky, but their forms are shapeless and their faces are nothing but starlight.

When I wake the next morning, there is a gnawing horror building in my stomach and it makes the pain in my back from sleeping on the floor seem insignificant. I stand and stretch, the blanket falling off my lap in the still and quiet room.

The blinds have been pulled back and sunlight streams into the room as if nothing happening at all. Everything is in its place as I pull on an old summer dress and thin yellow cardigan, and the world seems ready to continue on without Tara.

Thinking of her brings fresh fear to my belly and I double over in the kind of phantom pain you feel more in your gut than your body. What was that last night? The ropes of veins twisting and turning, blood turned into green vines…It was as if a jungle had erupted in the room next door, born from my friend's blood.

My bedroom is suddenly too bright and too silent and I nearly stumble in my attempt to escape and find someone, anyone. I'd even welcome Prim. I need another living person to prove I'm still alive, that I can still breathe.

When I scramble out the door, I find Lily in the hallway.

She is standing in front of Tara's room and I turn slowly to her, as if she were a rabbit I could frighten away. But Lily is not like that. She is brave. She is fearless. Lily knows everything. Maybe she can explain what we saw last night and only needed to think about it for a moment or two before deciding, but when I get near, I see her face is white.

"Lily…" I start and she turns to look at me, her brown eyes distant.

"They locked the door," she says.

"Mother and Father?"

"Yup, and now they want us downstairs to talk about Tara." Her hands curl into fists by her sides.

"Maybe they'll be able to explain what we saw," I say. Lily spins towards me and grabs my hands so firmly it hurts.

"You saw nothing. *We* saw nothing. Whatever they say, just look down and go along with it. Something is not right. What we saw was not natural and certainly not normal. I know we're all going to die, but that…There is something very, very wrong with what we saw and they can't know we were part of it."

"You're scaring me, maybe we could…"

"No!" Lily stamps her foot, and the childish gesture takes me off guard. She notices my reaction and her cheeks flush.

"All right, I won't say anything," I say softly and she sighs.

"It was like watching life itself," she says. "Life, death, and then life again. Are we dying, or are we something else? Tara said she thought Mother and Father were making her sick. She said so, right before she died." The brightness returns to Lily's eyes. "She said to not take the vitamins. What if she's right?"

"We've been taking those our whole lives. I don't think—"

"Exactly! But why..." Lily trails off and looks towards the stairs just as I turn to see Sara approaching us.

"There you are," says Sara with her hands on her hips. "Mother and Father are waiting for you." Her face pales when she sees where we're standing and she freezes, her eyes misty and red. Lily lets go of me and walks to her. Taking her hand, she smiles encouragingly and starts to pull her downstairs.

"Everything will be okay," I hear her saying. "We'll get down there before they send Prim after us."

I follow after them, my palms sweaty as they glide down the railing. I stop to wipe them before ducking into the kitchen, but something catches my eye through a nearby window. There are people in lab coats constructing a big white tent outside, struggling in the rising sun. It must be hot out there, as I watch them wipe sweat from their brows. I've never seen so many people before and a chill speeds down my spine. This can't be good.

The other girls are already gathered in the kitchen, sitting soundlessly at the table. Sara idly picks at a cranberry muffin but the rest of breakfast remains untouched. When I take my seat around the quiet faces, it is a stark contrast to the muffled grunts and shouts from the commotion outside coming from the tent's construction.

Cait is noticeably absent, as is Mother, but Father stands solidly before all of us. He doesn't spare me a glance, but I notice he isn't wearing his usual white lab coat. Instead, he's put on a black jacket that looks pristine, crisp and dark. It seems to mirror the dark expression on his face and in his eyes.

Rana drums her fingers lightly against the table and Prim's focus rests on a pencil she's twirling around her fingers, her eyes occasionally darting to the window. She catches me looking at her and frowns.

"Seeing as Mother can't be bothered to help with this, I must be the one to make the announcement," Father starts. He remains standing and I'm reminded of how tall this man is, how imposing a figure he can be when not hunched over a cup of coffee. His hair, a mess of brown and white, looks wild, and there is an iron gleam in his eyes when he turns towards the door swinging open to let in Mother and Cait.

"I'm sorry to be late," Mother says. Unlike Father, she sits down, leaning over to pull Cait into her seat as well. The crumpled look on Cait's face is enough to tell me that she knows about Tara. The other girls must sense it too because they shift uncomfortably in their chairs, dreading the confirmation on what we already know.

"Tara has died," Father says curtly. "Succumbed to the very pathogens assaulting your own blood as we speak. The result is that her room will be sealed off until we can learn more of the acute condition that ended her short life so quickly. Another resulting causality"—Father stops and takes in a labored breath, rubbing his eyes with the palm of his hand before continuing—"is that we will be hosting members of the scientific community on the property.

They are here to observe and report, nothing else, and I except you to avoid them at all costs."

Lily and I look at each other with wide eyes, and I notice Prim's attention is back on the window, her frown deepening. Rana raises her hand and without hesitation whispers loudly to Father: "Do they know about our glowing?"

"They do, but please stay away from them all the same," Mother answers and everyone at the table lets out a small gasp.

Rana's face pales. "But they were already in the chicken coop this morning and asked me questions. I told them I didn't know any of their answers, what do I do if..."

"Ignore them," say Father, rubbing the bridge of his nose.

"But they wanted to know—"

"I said ignore them!" Father shouts, his fist slamming on the table. Prim jerks in her seat, her pencil rolling across the table, and the rest of us shrink down in our chairs. Mother's eyes are narrow slits of blue ice when she stands up to face Father. They stare at each other until Prim's pencil drops to the floor with a loud clacking sound and time stutters back into rhythm.

"Chores will be put on hold today," Mother says, smoothing her lab coat against her legs. She takes a breath and smiles at us. "Take the day to rest and reflect, and please, keep your distance from anyone you don't recognize."

There are nods of agreement as, one by one, the house girls begin to file out and I stand to clear the table of barely-touched plates of breakfast. But before Mother can escape from the emotionally charged space with them, I watch Father spin around to face her, his eyes narrowing dangerously.

"I hope you're happy," he says, leveling her with a cold glare that she ignores and lifts her chin when she addresses his comment.

"I am, actually. This course will provide the quickest results, as well as the proof needed for any additional funding from our sponsor, so don't turn your aggression on me, Leonard. You're letting your past color the future's potential and it's not the best look on you."

"You would let others taint our progress," he responds, looking down his nose at her. "We don't need anyone's help, especially not from that fool of a man and his hired goons."

"It's not fair to keep prolonging the pain of these girls. They've suffered enough, and if his methods can produce results faster, then I'm for it. They shouldn't have to live like this."

"This is *our* project," he retorts and his voice comes out in a high-pitched whine.

I step soundlessly back so I'm pressed against the wall. They haven't noticed I'm still there and my palms begin to sweat expecting them to at any moment, but they luckily seem to only have eyes on each other.

"And it still is," she whispers, placing a hand on his chest when she turns to leave. It seems to have an immediate calming effect because he takes her hand in his own as he follows her from the room.

I release a long, slow breath. Dumping the rest of the breakfast dishes in the sink, I wait a few unsteady heartbeats until I know they have secured themselves in the basement, and then bolt out of the kitchen.

Lily is waiting for me by a window in the hall, looking bemused as someone outside struggles to affix a tent corner into a long pole. They keep falling on their backside.

I watch for a moment with her as a tall man with a tan-colored coat comes to help, though he ends up just standing to the side and yelling instructions. His broad shoulders remind me of someone, but before I can get a good look, Lily yawns loudly and turns to look at me.

"What was all that about?" she asks. "Father in another bad mood?"

"I don't know exactly, but he seems upset about all this," I say, gesturing out the window just as Lily lets out another huge yawn.

"We'll talk more later." She leans in close, a humorless glint in her eyes. "I'm exhausted and need to take a nap, but find me later, there's something I want to show you."

I nod, give her a hug, and leave the house as quickly as possible.

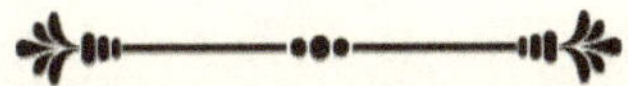

I pass through the quiet kitchen on my way out the back door. There is still a platter of leftover muffins sitting by the stove and I take one before heading outside. Someone even left a little brown envelope with this morning's vitamins for me, but once I'm near the gardens, I make sure to tuck them safely in my pocket. I'm not ready to make a decision on taking them or not. The muffin, however, gets devoured in three bites.

I take a deep breath of fresh air, free from the walls of Zamora House. There is something strangely fragrant about the world after it rains. Lily said books often talk about how nature comes alive, that no matter how small the raindrops the earth will make use of them, but none of her books speak of how it smells. Maybe because there isn't a word for it; Lily and I checked two separate dictionaries and came up with nothing. Or maybe it's such a distinctly personal thing that no one could ever attempt to write it down.

The sky is crisp and white and cloudless, and there is a cooling breeze not uncommon for this time of year. When I pass through the main garden area on my way to the shed, the droning of bees can be heard against rustling grass. A floral pinch in the air brings a lightness to my chest knowing that, even though I'm not long for this world, the time I do have is spent in a pretty place like this.

My head starts to spin as I think about possibly finding Evan out here and I take another breath to ground myself in the steadiness and predictability of nature.

Thinking of him is like a guilty distraction, and Tara probably deserves a better friend the day after she died. To be remembered and thought about, not a memory pushed aside for someone cute.

I find my legs moving before my mind can catch up with my thoughts and suddenly find myself by the shed. And as if I conjured him up myself, Evan is there, standing with one hand resting on the sun-bleached hood of the golf cart with his back to me.

I freeze, every instinct in my mind telling me to turn around. That he shouldn't be on this side of the gate, not this close to home, not in this special place. My head screams to run back to the house, to return to safety and obey Father's warning. But the bigger part of me, the part that wants desperately to seek out trouble, glues my feet to the ground.

My voice catches and feels foreign when I ask, "What are you doing here?"

He doesn't turn around, but I can hear him chuckle. "Hmm, let me guess who it is by the smell," he starts. "The smell of salty grass by the ocean sweetened by honey and...dust, maybe? No, too similar to dirt and not flattering at all, maybe the flying things you see reflected from the light through a window?"

"Do I smell?" I ask, edging around to face him, fighting the incredible urge to attempt discreetly smelling myself.

"Everything has a smell, just like everything gets old, wet when it rains, or glows in sunlight and moonlight. It's all nature." He finally looks over and grins.

"I don't know what the ocean smells like. And you didn't answer me: why are you here?"

"You've never been to the beach?" he asks, raising a perfectly brown eyebrow over his perfectly green eyes. He folds his arms against his chest and I have to advert my gaze to keep from staring. "It's a must-see, biggest tourist attraction this side of our small world. You'd have to wear a swimmer, though, can't swim in country girl dresses and little sweaters."

"I've never been anywhere but here and home," I say. "And this is all I really have to wear. Father isn't one for originality, so we all pretty much dress the same."

"Here and home," he repeats and his gaze returns to the golf cart.

"Why are you here?" I ask yet again, putting myself in his line of sight as he swings himself into the driver's seat of the cart.

He gestures for me to join him in the passenger seat but, when I don't move, he slides over and pats the driver's side instead.

"If you drive me around, I'll explain on the way. But for every question you get, I get one in return."

I sigh loudly and he only smiles sweetly in return.

"There aren't enough interesting facts to make me interesting, but I'll answer what I can." I sit down beside him, power on the cart, and back out of the shed.

There is a moment when I have my neck craned behind my shoulder to see where I'm going and the sunlight slowly slides from behind the roof and drapes over the cart as if it were a silk table cloth, or maybe melted butter over a cake. I close my eyes and savor it for just a moment, and when I open my eyes again, Evan is looking at me.

For a moment longer than a second, I wonder why I'm trusting him. For all I know, everything he's said could be a lie and Carl could be in a ditch somewhere. Or, as Prim says, he's heard stories of the spooky little girls living on a hill and wants to see them for himself.

Or worse yet, the problem is me. Maybe there is something wrong with my brain, and I'm too much of a risk taker.

"You know your face glows in the sunlight?" Evan asks suddenly and I slam on the brakes so hard he grabs the seat to keep from falling out.

"Friscuit, what did you say?" I gasp, feeling a trickle of sweat down my back, making the country girl dress stick to my skin.

"Sorry, the sun looks good on your skin tone and, um, friscuit?" He laughs awkwardly and clears his throat.

"Oh, yeah, it's a made-up word we use around here. Just don't use it around Mother," I explain and he laughs.

With narrowed eyes, I continue backing the cart out and coasting it towards the dirt paths skirting the iron fence. I purposely keep the cart against the wall, far enough to be hidden from the eyes of anyone out in the gardens.

"First question," I blurt out. "Why are you here?"

"I work here now and recognized your cart. It's why I came out yesterday, had to scout the land for the perfect place to set up the tent, those things are monsters. And I thought I'd wait for you here in case you showed up today. Happy to know I guessed right."

"You work there?" The words sputter from my mouth as my mind frantically tries to make sense of things. It has to mean he came with all the new scientists and doctors.

"My turn." He smiles wide. "What's your favorite color?"

"That's your question?" I sigh again. "I don't think I could pick just one." And it's true: when I tried to come up with an answer when Tara asked the same question years ago, my mind came up blank.

"Okay, fine, do you have any hobbies? Like what do you do when you're not driving around in a golf cart?"

"I feed chickens and sometimes I eat chickens," I tell him and look over to see him nodding deeply, putting a finger to his lips in thought as I continue. "Oh, and I like drawing and painting, mostly watercolors, and I'm really good at it."

"Will you draw me sometime?" he asks, and my vision goes twitchy for a moment as I return to the dirt road in front of us.

"It's my turn for a question," I tell him, stopping the cart. We sit still under a canopy of trees, the sunlight streaming through them to create shifting patterns around us, as if it were all a giant moving puzzle board of light and shadow. It's cool here, and the smell of crushed grasses and wildflowers carries in the air.

Evan nods and leans back, eyes closed and mouth partly open. If I didn't know any better, I'd say he was asleep. I can't help but notice his muscled chest as it moves with his slow breathing. Finally, the breeze quickens and brings close the sounds of clinking metal and rustling fabrics, of an army of people setting up camp nearby, of my life changing again and probably for the worst.

Evan hears it too and opens his eyes as he leans forward in his seat. For a moment, or an eternity, we lock eyes and stare.

"I'm not stupid," I say softly, gesturing towards the sound as it drifts through the trees. "Who are you?"

"My name really is Evan," he replies, his eyes not leaving mine. "My father has me working here, for now at least, so I'm here with the scientists."

"Is that who was setting up the big tent?" I ask.

Evan nods.

"Why are they here?"

"Let's say the tent owner doesn't like to be left in the dark about his investments, but it's my turn now. Will you draw me?"

I look down and notice Evan's thigh is pressed against my own. I pull away and twist in my seat to face him, ignoring the sudden coldness against my leg.

"Yeah," I start. "I can someday, but why are—"

"Great!" His face is bright. "How about now?"

"Huh, now? I don't have any of my—"

"I have some pencils, let's go now," he says, grabbing my hands and placing them on the steering wheel. "I mean, I know this thing isn't very fast, but we should go. Now. Don't want anyone getting any ideas."

He winks and it's my turn to nearly fall out of my seat.

Evan's hands are still on mine, glued to mine on the wheel, and he doesn't remove them until I press the pedals of the cart and we start back down the road.

"This way," he mutters, pointing towards the back of the big white tent as it appears like a great beast among the trees. "We need to sneak around the back, then I promise we can talk more."

Chapter Six

We go the long way, skirting the iron bars and luckily passing none of the other girls, even though I hold my breath the entire time.

They've set up the tent within the garden's perimeter, but I notice it's far enough from the house to be considered its own separate entity and close enough to the main gate to control who goes in—and who goes out.

Up close, the tent is no longer just a beast, but a great monster from a fairy tale. I stand beside its leathery hide and run my fingers along its scales, the white exterior heaving with breath and vibrating with unseen energy. I think this may be the closest thing to an actual dragon that I will ever see. Tara would have loved this.

Evan punches a code into a monitor hidden among the dragon's scales and ducks through a narrow door set in the monster's belly. He beckons me to follow and I slink after him, jumping from my skin when his hand touches the small of my back to gently push me forward. But even after the rush of adrenaline from his touch, the room we come into leaves me subtly disappointed.

Stacks of boxes line the walls, some of which have peeling yellow labels and others looking crisp and freshly painted. Piles of printed documents and the remains of someone's lunch sit on an antique desk. A few papers have fallen to the floor, and by habit, I pick them up and stack them neatly on top of the nearest box. The half-eaten sandwich I leave alone.

A sharp popping sound brings my focus back to Evan as he hands over a bottle of bright blue liquid. He holds another in his other hand and I notice the bottles are full of the tiniest bubbles I've ever seen and the blue is brighter than I could have ever imagined. On the side is a picture of a blueberry in the same vivid blue and my fingers itch to recreate the color in watercolor.

He takes a long drink from his bottle, so I do the same, the tiny bubbles tickling my nose. I think they taste like blueberries in the same way a picture of a strawberry tastes like real fruit. But it's still the most wonderful thing I've ever drank. Sweet, tart, and unnatural.

"Wow, I don't think I've ever seen someone look that happy with a soda before." Evan's laughter grounds my thoughts quickly.

"Father never put any of these on the supply orders before." I take another drink and savor the little bubbles on my tongue. "Besides, we make our own toothpaste; I think it's obvious that junk food is also off limits."

Evan chuckles and pulls up a few crates to sit on. He ignores the old leather chair behind the desk. I gingerly take a seat across from him by perching on the edge. We're so close that our kneecaps touch, and I fidget with the hem of my dress to keep from making eye contact.

He clears his throat and waves a hand around the room.

"This isn't the most interesting room here, not by a long shot, but it's out of the way and the primary scientists don't come here.

It's too, um, beneath them." He laughs harshly, takes a long drink from his glass, and then gazes at nothing in front of him.

"It's, uh, nice," I lie.

"Anyway, time for some answers." He drains the rest of his soda and sets the empty bottle on the desk. Then, as if he thought better of it, places it on the floor instead.

I take another small sip and let the bubbles linger on my tongue while I wait for him to finish. I set my own empty bottle next to his and my arm brushes up against my pocket with the vitamins tucked inside. I still haven't taken them.

"I know you all are sick," Evan finally says, his eyes finding mine. "And I'm, well, actually, *we're* here to help." His face tells me he wants to say more, but something keeps him from it, and when he doesn't continue, I cross my arms over my chest and hunch in my seat.

"I don't think anyone can help," I say and it makes my mind wander to Tara laying prone on her bed, covered in blood, glowing light, and green leaves. "We all have to die sometime; it just comes sooner for some people."

"That doesn't have to be the case for you." The words spit from Evan's mouth with an acid I haven't yet seen from him, but he smothers it quickly and asks, "How often do they test your blood?"

His words make my arm itch and throb and I absentmindedly rub it, not wanting to answer. Then without warning, he reaches over and takes my wrist in one of his rough hands, the crate sliding beneath me and knocking into his own. The movement forces my body to twist around so we're directly facing each other.

My breath catches in my throat and I think I see him give a little shudder as he pulls back my sleeve. Before I can yank my arm away, he's staring at the tender and bruised skin of my inner arm.

"This looks like a lot of tests."

He trails his fingers along my skin, and it tingles like the tiny bubbles. When he swipes his fingers along my flesh, I feel a shiver travel up my spine.

"Dani?"

"Hmm, what?"

"I asked how many times you get tested?"

"Oh, um, it's once a week for most of us, sometimes more for me, but Tara got sick recently so Mother and Father will probably increase that soon. They need fresh blood for testing." I pause and have to take a deep breath before adding, "Tara died yesterday."

He lets go of my hand and pulls back, a surprised but thoughtful expression on his face. "I'm so sorry," he says.

"Yeah, me too."

"Do they ever give you anything? Any medicines to keep you and however many of you there healthy?"

My hand hovers protectively over my pocket.

"Just vitamins," I say, tapping the pills. He nods slowly and holds out his hand. If I haven't taken them by now, I probably won't later, so what difference does it make if I give them away?

So I do.

Evan empties them into his hand, turning them over and over, though I'm not sure what he's looking for. He holds them to his nose and makes a face as he sniffs.

"Can I keep these?" he asks and I look at him surprised.

"Father said I should take them, but I haven't today." Despite my words, I don't find myself stirring to take them back after he tucks the pills into their little sleeve and secures them in his own pocket.

"Do you always listen to what he tells you? Somehow, I doubt you do." He laughs lowly and my attention goes back to how close we are.

"Why do you say that?" I find myself whispering because it feels absurd to speak normally with our bodies this close.

"Because you wouldn't be here talking to me if you did," he says roughly, and the plug is pulled suddenly from my braveness, leaving me breathless and nervous.

"I guess so." I lean away, pulling my legs to the side. "The whole house does whatever he says."

"Families are like that, too. You should try actual siblings."

He inhales as if to speak when the door slams open and a woman who looks to be in her late thirties with dark hair darts into the room, slamming the door behind her.

"That's it, Evan!" the woman grumbles, running a hand through her wild and frizzy hair. "I can't work with that snarky little—" She stops mid-sentence when she notices me, her eyes darting back and forth between me and Evan. She clears her throat and straightens her spine as she looks at me, a glint of compassion peeking from behind her eyes.

"Is that one of them?" she asks and Evan shifts his body in her direction, putting attention solely on her as he stands by my side with a hand on my shoulder.

"One of the girls, yes."

"Does he know she's here?"

"No," Evans says and his grip tightens almost painfully.

"Good, let's keep it that way," the woman says. She sits heavily behind the desk and pulls the half-eaten sandwich towards her. She nibbles on it thoughtfully and it's silent in the room until the sandwich is nothing but crumbs. At last, she extends her hand towards me.

"Lacey Kerrigan, I'll be doing your blood work soon. Well, me or that imbecile Milton, but I don't think this even bigger imbecile here has told you about it yet." She shrugs, picking at the crumbs left behind on the desk. "I expect you'll hear all about it at dinner tonight."

Evan's grip lightens on my shoulder but blossoms into a tug and I let him pull me towards the outer door.

"We'll talk about this more later, Lacey," he says. She grins and waves him off, already leaning back in her chair and settling into it with closed eyes.

It takes a moment for my senses to register the sunlight when we emerge back into the world and the belly of the beast is closed off behind us.

"She's nice, you'll like her," he mumbles, leading me back towards the golf cart. "You can trust her."

My head swims with the enormity of the day and I barely feel it when Evan pushes me into the seat of the golf cart. He leans over the side, his hands braced on the cart's frame and his face only inches from mine.

"You can trust me, too," he says and his breath covers my face before he leans in and presses the start button for the cart. "See you later, Dani. You'll have to draw me another time."

Lacey was right. Our evening dinner is a sheet of ice so thin the barest glance could crack an opening wide enough to swallow us whole. Father's face glows with a cold hatred as he tells us the scientists are here to assist his research and we'll be going to the tent for additional testing. He doesn't say when and he doesn't say what kind.

Sara tries to ask who these people are, but he silences her with a murderous glare and demands no further discussion. Mother causally tries to turn the conversation towards my upcoming eighteenth birthday, but is unsuccessful when we all remain too nervous to say the wrong thing in front of Father.

Later, after a dinner of steamed tofu featuring none of our feathered friends, Lily and I seal ourselves in our bedroom. She had already checked the hidden cabinet panel and assured it was sealed tight on our end, so we wouldn't need to worry about anything creeping past the threshold, but I make her check again before we settle between our two beds, facing each other in thought.

"Dani," Lily starts. "Did you take your vitamins?"

"No," I tell her, my hand clamping my empty pocket before I remember that I gave them away to Evan.

"How do you feel today? Any different, like extra sweaty or dizzy? Anything like that?"

"All of that, but I don't think it was from not taking the vitamins. Or maybe it was? I don't know. Lily, you have to promise to keep a secret."

She brightens, her whole face alive. Lily has always been a lover of information, and secrets are the best kind of information to have.

"You know I can, and besides, I have a secret to share with you, too, so we'll trade, okay?" She's wiggling in her seat now, her eyes bright and gleaming in the dim light. For a moment, I'm reminded of when we were children and sharing stories in the gardens, but the memory is too hard to hold onto, slippery and ephemeral.

"Do you want to go first?" I ask.

She nearly knocks me over jumping from the floor and I watch her dart to the window plants. They're all so very different looking, some curling together in tuffs of green furry veins and others pointed and sharp. Lily moves them around until she uncovers the smallest one tucked neatly in an empty can of creamed corn and brings it close.

My eyes open wide. "Is that the one that..." I trail off, pointing where I'd last seen it.

"Yes, it's one of the vines from last night. I wondered what would happen if I planted it, kind of like a cactus, I guess. It seems to be doing well so far." She holds it to her face and my stomach cinches painfully at how casually she handles it.

"That thing was made from Tara's blood," I say, feeling the knot turn into a wave of sickness, and with nowhere to escape, crashing into my chest.

"Well, it's just a plant now." Lily pouts, her lips set in a firm line. She drums her fingers on the can and the little plant waves with the motion. "I think it must be harmless now and it doesn't bleed when you poke it, if that's what you're wondering."

"I'm wondering so many things right now and I can't even make sense of them." I sigh and do my best to forget about the plant in her hands. "Did Mother and Father mention anything else today, about Tara or her room?"

"Nothing. I've seen them coming in and out of the room a few times, but it's so quick and I haven't been able to get a good look inside. And if they're taking anything out, I haven't noticed. Her window is covered up with something, so you can't see in from the outside either. I checked on that." Lily cradles the little plant against her. "There is one other thing, though."

"What?"

"A few of the people from the tent knocked on the front door today, but Father drove them off. He looked furious, he was screaming and yelling at them and I didn't understand what about. Something about privacy and protections and infringements, it didn't make a lot of sense—not like any of this does—but he was so angry. He then spent a long time outside just staring at Tara's window. No one has gone near him today."

"Did you hear him say any of their names?" I ask.

"Why would I listen for their names? Just a bunch of people in white coats." Lily laughs, but pauses and tilts her head towards me in thought. "So, is your secret better than mine?"

In a moment of bravery, I reach out to run a finger down the fuzzy exterior of the Tara plant and think I feel a humming response, but maybe I'm imagining things. I snatch my hand away just in case. I don't know how this thing came into existence and it creeps me out.

"I'm not sure," I say and watch as Lily sets the plant gingerly back by the window, making sure it rests in a beam of sunlight behind the bigger plants. She joins me between the beds again before I continue in a low whisper: "Remember how I told you about Evan?"

Lily nods enthusiastically.

"I saw him again today, but he wasn't out by the highway. He's with them, the people outside. He took me to the tent, to a little storage room in the back, but I don't think he was supposed to. Someone caught us inside, but it didn't look like she really cared at all. It seemed like they might be friends."

Lily's head tilts to the side and her gaze shifts to the floor.

"So, he's with the scientists? You said he had one of those flying things. I wonder if they've been using them to watch us."

"What do you mean?"

"Well, think about it," Lily says, her face lighting up as she meets my eyes. "This guy, Evan, shows up out of nowhere and has a little flying disc. I looked it up in a book this morning, it's a drone. Often used for surveillance, you know, spy stuff and simple map charting, they even put lights on some and do whole performance shows with them. It would make all the sense in the world that he was scouting the area for the rest of them, so I'm sure they could have done that in past as well. And now there is a tent full of people with a connection to Father and Mother camped right outside our front door."

I think back on when I first met Evan and how he was flying his little drone when he walked away that day. Was that what he was doing? Spying on us? And these drones, are they what I've been seeing in my dreams?

"Do you think something more is going on?" My voice quakes a little when I ask. Lily has always been the smart one and she is always, always, always right about things. If anyone can look between the cracks and see something out of place, it would be her. Her thoughts are terrifying, and as I sit in front of her and watch her eyes shimmer with a type of dangerous curiosity, she looks more alive than I've ever seen her, which is even more frightening. She holds up her right hand, palm towards me and fingers spread.

"Listen," she says, tucking a finger in as she makes each point. "One, you suddenly run into someone new around here, and you and I both know nothing like that ever happens. Two, Mother and Father are obviously hiding something about what happened when Tara died. Three, in case you missed it, there is a giant white tent filled with scientists and doctors in lab coats now residing in our backyard. And four, Tara's warning about the vitamins. There's more to this, I just know it. And maybe—" Lily sighs and closes her eyes, "Maybe if Mother and Father are hiding something from us"—her voice catches in her throat— "maybe they know things we don't. Friscuit, what if we're not dying after all? Or worse yet, what if they're doing something to all of us?"

My blood rushes past my ears and collects in my core. I've always been doomed, that's what Father and Mother told us every day. It was also something I came to terms with at a very young age, and thoughts of the future were always just fantasies. Maybe this is why I question so much, that I demand to understand what I can before I go and take more risks than I should.

So now the thrill of life dances in front of me like tiny bubbles, the ones that just fade away before you can pop them, and I look away, the braveness all but deflated.

"I've made my peace with dying, Lily. I don't think you should get your hopes up."

"Dani, something is happening here." I watch my best friend close her eyes and ball her fists by her sides. She stands to her full height. "This is something bigger than both of us, I believe it in my gut, even if you don't. Promise me you'll keep an open mind. Promise me you won't give up, even if we're both are already doomed, and promise me you'll continue to skip the vitamins until I can figure this out. Please?"

Lily holds out her hand for me to shake, and although I take it without hesitation, because you always do what Lily says, I'm unsure if I truly believe her. "I promise," I say all the same. "You're my best friend, Lily. I'll always trust you."

Chapter Seven

It is just after dawn when Father's rough hand pushes me from bed and I awaken to his indifferent stare before he turns to Lily. She wakes with a startled yelp and shoots me a worried glance.

"Wake up and meet the others out front," Father mutters before tossing Lily her robe and leaving the room.

Lily and I scurry to obey and I can hear the shuffling of the other house girls as they rush to do the same. Outside our door we file downstairs with quiet thoughts and hushed voices, gathering in a group before the front door.

"We must be going to the tent," Lily whispers and receives a few tired nods from the group.

"Friscuit, but why does it have to be so early?" Sara sighs, clutching a blanket around her shoulders.

Lily shrugs and looks around. We notice at the same time that something seems off and her worried look returns as she scans the room.

"Where's Prim?" I ask Vera.

"I don't know." Her voice is small as it comes from the dim hallway and her voice sounds nervous. "She wasn't in her bed when Mother came to our room."

"Where would she be?" Lily begins to ask, but silences when Father's shadow creeps upon us.

"Outside and to the tent. Someone will meet you there," he says simply before turning away. I can hear the door to the basement lab slam in his wake.

Lily is the first out the door with Sara following boldly behind and I bring up the rear with Rana, Vera, and Cait.

We stop in front of what we think is the front of the tent, a large opening created by two flaps pulled aside to reveal a thick plastic door. Bright lights shine at us from posts dug tight into the ground and the shadows elongate and distort our features. Lily halts before it and her head tilts back as she takes it in.

"I suppose we knock?" she asks no one in particular.

"I wish Father was with us," Rana says, kicking loose pebbles in her path. "He could at least have walked us inside."

"I'm glad he isn't here," Cait mutters from behind her.

"Same here," Sara chimes in. "Father's been in a bad mood since these people came; he wouldn't be very pleasant."

"Like anything around here is ever pleasant," I say, nudging my way towards Lily.

"After you," she snickers and I roll my eyes.

"Well, let's get this over with," I sigh and reach towards the handle, but it swings open before my fingers make contact and out walks a wiry young man. His beady eyes take us in, scanning each girl from head to toe as he shifts uncomfortably from foot to foot. He pushes a pair of thin glasses farther up his nose and lets out a snort.

"Which one of you is Rana?" he asks and Rana swiftly raises her hand. He hooks his finger towards her and gestures her to follow.

"Come on, you're with me." He holds the door just wide enough for her to slide through, and after giving us one final grimace, lets it slam shut behind them.

"Ladies," Lily mumbles. "It's going to be a long day."

There are murmured agreements all around, but my eyes stay glued to the plastic door. I hadn't noticed before, but now the embossing catches my attention and the feeling of familiarity stirs within when I try to read the name. I'm turning to Lily to ask her opinion when the door pops back open.

"Dani?" A tired voice captures my attention and I turn to see Lacey Kerrigan staring back at me. There is a small twitch at the corner of her mouth, but she gives no other indication she's met me before, and as with Rana, she pulls me through the door just as quickly. The last thing I see before it snaps shut is Lily's stunned expression.

"Dani, Dani, Dani," Lacey repeats musically as she considers me with dark eyes. "Short for something?"

"Daniella."

"Just like the batteries." She laughs and pushes me in front of her. "Well, Daniella, since this is our first meeting, today is going to be relatively simple. Just some basic information entering and documenting, that kind of stuff. Just need to establish a few baselines. You can call me Lacey, by the way."

She stops and brings her hand to my shoulder, and the hard way she squeezes feels like a warning, so I keep quiet and nod. She smiles in return and we continue again down the hall.

Lacey leads us past more plastic doors, some sealed tight and a few open and empty, and we travel under the high vaulted ceiling of the tent. I look up as we pass its center and see the center steeple stretching up high.

We finally come to the end and enter a small room. The walls here are made of the same hard material as outside, but there is no ceiling and I can look above and see the great white canvas breathing with the wind. If I were very tall, I could look over the edges and see into the other rooms.

Lacey gestures towards an examination table and watches as I struggle to climb up and perch on its edge.

"You're on the short side, aren't you?"

"So I've been told."

"Well, sit back and don't move, there's a scale built into that thing and it'll throw off your weight," she tells me and I do my best to get comfortable as she starts opening drawers and placing containers on a metal tray. She sets the tray over my lap and pulls out a small, portable scanner, which she holds over my chest.

"Do me favor and touch each of these," she says, gesturing with her other hand towards the tray. "Both at the same time and just with the fingertips of one hand."

The two containers sitting on the tray each have a tiny flowering strawberry plant and I wonder at how perfect they look with their pristine green leaves and tiny white flowers.

"Just touch them?"

"One with each hand, please." She leans forward, watching as I gently prod each plant with an index finger. There is a gentle hum from each when I feel the life brimming within, but nothing extraordinary happens. She looks pleased and scribbles a few notes into a small black journal.

"What did you think would happen?" I laugh. "I spend a lot of time in the garden touching plants and I've never noticed anything strange."

"Give me your hands," she orders and I obey, if only for the sharpness of her tone. In one swift and deliberate moment, she's pierced a finger on each one with a sharp needle. Blood immediately begins to dome on the tips and she holds firmly when I try to yank away.

"Don't move," she snaps. Then, maybe remembering herself, she smiles gently and lets go. "Touch the plants again, please. Don't worry about the blood."

When I don't move, she raises an eyebrow and nudges the tray with her elbow while standing back. I raise my hands towards the plants and hear her suck in her breath. Tension is thick in the air as I reach for the plants and Lacey hovers the scanner over my heart.

Her face falls when I pull back my fingers from the plants, leaving blood smudged on their tiny white flowers. The only difference is a slight bend in the leaves as they twist upwards.

"Okay, okay, okay. This is okay," she mumbles and scribbles more notes in her journal before snapping it shut and holding a hand out for support. "Come with me."

I slide off the table and follow her out the door. "What did you think would happen? Aren't you just going to test my blood? Why are you even here?" I can't stop the questions from bubbling over like a pot of water Sara left boiling on the stove.

"So many questions," Lacey muses as we pass by the same doors as before, all closed now. "Dr. Zamora's work has been called into question and we've been sent to access his work."

"What's wrong with Zamora House?" I ask her and she doesn't turn around when she answers.

"Nothing is wrong with the house itself—well, except for the fact that it's built on an old graveyard." She laughs and nearly trips over the corner of a headstone jutting from the ground. She stops and looks at it, a blank and careful look on her face that reminds of me of equal parts curiosity and horror.

"That's not what I meant."

"I know," she says, shaking her head before moving on to lead me to another plastic door. This one has a black square printed on a thin sheet of white paper tacked on it, and the sign flaps haphazardly as she pushes me inside.

"Dr. Zamora seems to be taking good care of you all, considering the circumstances. Everything looks fine, chart-wise and even head-wise."

I eye her warily. "Except we're all slowly dying."

"Sure, that too."

"Are you here to help?"

"We're here to chart his progress, so yes, we're trying to help."

Lacey has let the door snap shut behind us and I'm thrown off in the dark room. When she switches on a light, I realize this particular space has a low plastic ceiling hovering just above her head and a metal grate providing a stream of fresh air from the corner. There is also a light in the corner made to look like a full moon.

"Stupid Milton has to crouch when he comes into these rooms." She laughs and points to the medical table taking up the bulk of the space. This time she helps me up before handing me another tray containing two more strawberry plants. I reach to touch them but she slaps my hand away before I can make contact.

"Wait one moment," she orders and takes a deep breath. "Comfortable?"

"Um, yes?"

"Good," she says, reaching by my shoulders and pulling out a pair of thick brown straps, which she crisscrosses over my chest. I try to bolt from the bed when I realize she's strapping me down, but Lacey is stronger than she looks and her hands pin me down while she secures a lock near the side of the bed.

"What are you *doing*?" I scream, tugging uselessly against the harness.

"It'll be fine, it's just a precaution so you don't hurt yourself. Try to breathe normally."

"I don't think I feel comfortable with this," I stammer but the words feel useless once they leave my mouth.

I'm about to say more but I'm cut off by a terrible, human scream that cracks out of the metal vent. It is primal and guttural, and feels like a warning. Lacey stares at the vent, her eyes distant and only coming back into focus when she turns towards me again.

There is only one person I know of who can scream like that.

"What are they doing to Prim?" I push against the harness and feel the table wobble beneath me, but the straps do not budge. My eyes water with frustration as I arch my back against the restraints.

"Just hold still," Lacey says, swallowing hard. "This will be over soon enough."

"Why is Prim screaming? Where are Father and Mother?" I thrash again, the leather biting into my skin.

Lacey doesn't respond and instead grabs my left hand tightly. I can't see her face as her other hand grabs a long surgical knife from nearby table and runs it cleanly down the middle of my palm.

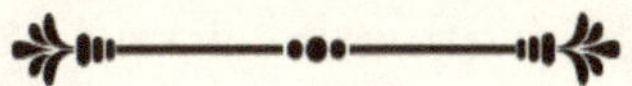

This is a pain I've never felt and deep down I know it is one that I will never forget. The knife retracts from my hand as smoothly as going in, but the torrent of blood and agony it unleashes are almost too much to handle and my mind tries to react by shutting down. Before I can black out, Lacey slaps me hard across the face.

"Sorry, but that had to happen," she says, dropping the knife onto the table and setting the strawberry plants within reach. I'm bent inwards as much as the straps will allow and clutching my hand, trying to stanch the bleeding, but Lacey peels my arms away and holds my palm up to her face, examining my blood closely. Her eyes dilate slightly as she marvels at the way my blood shimmers slightly against her hands.

"It's going to get dark in here, but it will only be a moment. I need you to look at the plants, and when the primary lights go out and the moon turns on, just touch one with the bleeding hand. Doesn't matter which plant, but make sure you only touch *one*."

Then, maybe as precaution, she pushes one of the little plants to the side and waits till I take a deep breath and look her in the eye.

"Why?" The word comes out raspy and gritty, and she lets go of me.

"Like I said before, we're here to assess Leonard's work." She shrugs and points to the plant just before the lights in the little room click off and the fake moon springs to life. It must be drawing a lot of power from somewhere behind it because I can hear the electricity buzzing inside.

It takes a while for my eyes to adjust to the new light, and if it weren't for the soft hissing from the air vent and the electrical hum, I could almost forget everything and imagine I am at home and safe in bed with my eyes closed. But my collarbone is bruised and raw, my palm is slick with warm blood, and Prim's primal scream rings over and over and over again in my head.

"Whenever you'd like to start," Lacey says quietly and I think to myself that I might as well get this over with. That maybe if I play their games, I'll be able to get out of here quickly.

So I touch the plant. At first nothing happens, but as more and more of the room comes into focus, the plant begins to shimmer and shake and glow brighter than even my blood. And then my skin is glowing along with it and I happen to notice Lacey's full attention is on the plants and not my skin that glows as brightly as the artificial moonlight. I pull away from the plant slowly and feel an uncomfortable tingling in my fingertips when they lose contact with the leaves.

"Fantastic," she murmurs, reaching towards me and removing the plant from my shaking hands. It continues to grow slightly, newly budding flowers forming almost perfect looking strawber-ries, but slows to a stop when she takes it across the room.

I feel the connection crumble like a dry cracker and a wave of exhaustion swells in me. Lacey comes back and waves her scanner across my body, humming another song I've heard from Mother. My eyelids are so heavy I can barely keep them open and I have to blink several times to bring her back into focus.

"Friscuit, are we done?"

"Almost," Lacey says, her back still towards me. "Just one more thing."

Lacey returns to my side with a long syringe that she taps her fingernails against. She studies the light green liquid inside the tubing as it catches the moonlight and glows as brightly as the fake moon.

"What is that?" I ask, suddenly alert and shifting my body as far from her as the straps with allow. "You are not sticking me with that!" Her eyes follow me but she makes no move to back away.

"Sorry, sugar, you've lost way more blood than I would have preferred and I'm sure you're confused and dizzy right now. This here is just something to speed the process up and get it over with quickly so you can feel better." Her eyes look up at me as she points the needle tip towards the second plant. "After I give this to you, all you'll need to do is touch the other strawberry plant and we'll be done for the day. Sound good?"

"You mean I can leave after this?"

"That's correct, right after this. Well, a tech will come in and clear you, patch you up and all, but that'll only take a moment. No more tests today." She taps the syringe one last time before snapping on a pair of tinted eye coverings and smiling widely. "Ready?"

I nod.

"Remember, just reach out and touch the plant with the same hand." She points to my damaged palm, which still pulses slightly with fresh, glowing blood. "And listen, I know you won't remember this later but, well, I'm sorry about this."

I don't have time to respond before the needle slides painlessly into my skin. Unlike the stabbing pain in my palm, this newfound pain starts in my toes. It travels up my spine, bone by bone, vertebra by vertebra, gathering strength as it crashes through my blood, trying to push and shove every cell free from the inside out.

I scream, and it is a scream so loud it rivals the one I heard from Prim and I hear it echoed back at me from the vents, one by one until I think I've heard the personal torment of every one of the other girls. Even Lily.

"Touch the plant now!" Lacey's voice cuts through the hazy waves that threaten to shatter my entire body, but lifting my hand is complete agony. When I swallow back the worst of it, I'm blinded by how brilliant I'm glowing. Squeezing my eyes shut, I can still see the burning light seared into my vision.

"Now!" Lacey screams again and, somehow, I find the willpower to place just one finger against a single leaf.

But that is enough.

That is all it needed from me.

Because once blood escapes from my glowing skin and comes in contact with the plant, everything changes and the world collapses in on itself. A spasm shoots up my spine and lances into the base of my skull, the force of it throwing my head back and creating stars against the blackness of the plastic ceiling. Now I am rising from table, looking down at Lacey and my body laying prone on the medical table, the moon flickering magically by our sides.

I am floating free from my body's defective shell, but when I remember that the moon cannot be trusted, I let the stars swimming around my head guide my senses back to the table. And as they slowly blink out one by one, my mind relaxes into the green void and all is still.

Chapter Eight

I wake slowly, as if it was any other day, as if I was in my own bed, and as if nothing at all had happened. The straps are gone and I'm instead imprisoned by a stiff blue blanket. My skin burns when I move and discover a spiderweb of bruising over my chest.

It's still the same plastic room, but someone has turned the moon off and it sits grey and empty, the buzzing power quieted. And yet while the moon remains unchanged, the rest of this prison cell is almost unrecognizable. It is green and lush and covered in leaves, and when I swing my legs to the floor, ripe strawberries squish between my toes and give off a sickeningly sweet scent. I've also left behind a perfectly human-shaped outline against the mattress. The stark white fabric looks foreign against the jungle blossomed beside it.

"Whoa," I murmur, my heart throbbing as I take in the explosion of life all around me.

Someone must hear me because the doorknob turns. The door opens slowly as leaves and vines and strawberries all bend against it until I eventually see Evan standing there. With wide eyes, he takes in the room before he turns those enchanting green eyes on me.

"Definitely worth the wait."

"Wait?"

"Yup," he says, closing the door behind him. He sets a basket of supplies on top of a mound of strawberries and looks me over. "You're the last one to wake up, everyone else already left for late breakfast."

"I don't think I could eat anything right now." I cross my arms and bend into myself. "I feel like I'm going to be sick. What time is it?"

"The nausea is natural and will pass." Evan sits down next to me on the medical table. "But I'll tell you what's not natural."

"What?" I say and look at him. He's very close and I realize our knees are pressing together again. His hand rests behind us, almost as if he could pull it upwards and wrap it around my waist. He is all I can see and the vines, the pain, and the million strawberries are distant pin pricks of memory from a forgotten book.

"The reason you don't seem surprised by any of this." He gestures around the room, breaking the spell. "Most of the others cried, one of them danced naked in her room, and one was so overly enthusiastic I could have sworn she was faking it. You, though, are sitting here with a sour look on your face as you make strawberry jam between your toes. In my humblest opinion, I think you've seen this before."

Thinking quickly, I turn away and pull my knees to my chest. I don't know if I can trust Evan—I don't even know who he is—but I have enough instinct to know he's caught on. Of course the other girls reacted like that, Lily and I were scared out of our wits when we saw what Tara went through. Of course this isn't new to me, and I was stupid enough to let that show. Lily would be so disappointed. I'm sure she pretended well enough to convince anyone.

"I've seen it once before," I whisper and he leans in to listen. "I watched Tara die. Father doesn't know."

"I'll keep the secret." He winks and slides off the table. Standing in front of me, he takes my hands and grunts a few choice words when he looks at my injured palm.

"Looks like a smooth incision that should heal fairly quick. Lacey's brutal, but she's careful about her work. I'll give you something for it and the bruising. You won't even remember they're there," he says, his eyes going distant for a moment before he pulls bandages and ointments from the basket he brought with him.

"All my life, I didn't know any of this could happen," I say and he nods slowly. The words feel comfortable coming out, as if holding them in would make my skin itch. He listens quietly while dabbing something cold into my brutalized skin and hums a song that catches on a distant memory.

"What are you humming?"

"Hm?" He barely looks up as he wraps a long white bandage around my hand.

"The song, I've heard Mother hum it before."

"It's that song, *Snowbirds*. One of my favorites. Use it for all my passwords," he tells me and I shake my head at him. Evan looks at me and tilts his head in a very Lily-like way. "Don't tell me that crazy Leonard doesn't let you listen to music."

"Nothing made in the last century." I wince when the bandage tightens to its final fit.

"You'll have to change that someday," he says with a smile and turns to get something from his basket. He brings a pad of paper and hands it to me with a pen. "Need to make sure you have your motor skills up and running again, and since you did promise to draw me..."

"I guess I did promise." Truthfully all I want to do right now is sleep, but my body betrays me and drops my legs away from my chest. Taking the pad, I stand to turn around and use the table to spread the pages wide before I put pen to paper.

The lines come out shaky at first, my hand barely able to keep hold of the pen and my legs struggling to support me, but years of practice can teach someone how to turn mistakes into more deliberate flows. Before long the paper has eyes, a nose, hair, and a chin. I leave the mouth for last because I have to look up at Evan to make sure I get it just right, and something about staring at his lips makes it hard to concentrate.

Evan lets out a low whistle when I hand it back to him and the way he studies the drawing makes my face flush with embarrass-ment. I watch as he folds it neatly and tucks it into his pocket before returning to the basket.

"Does this change anything? This, um, power we have...could it be helpful for a cure to whatever's killing us?"

Evan is quiet for a moment before turning to look at me. "Your blood seems to be more powerful than nearly all the other girls."

"You're not answering my question. How is making strawberry jam helpful in finding a cure so all of us don't die?"

"That is a complicated answer, and one I hope to elaborate on when we see each other again, but just know that I'm trying to help. None of you should have to live like this."

His words remind me of something Mother said the other day, but before I can ask him for more, he looks down at me and sighs.

"One more thing and then we can talk more," he says quickly and, with a firm hand, pushes my shoulders back into the bed so that I fit perfectly in the indentation from before. I see his other hand holds a new syringe, the liquid this time glowing a bright yellow.

"What now?" I ask, barely able to suppress a yawn as my body, now in a more comfortable position, tries to fight falling asleep.

"Another shot," he says, tapping the needle. "Some vitamins to help with the blood loss. It won't hurt, I promise."

And for some bizarre reason, I believe him.

"Just get it over with," I say, looking away, but the shot is quick and too painless to even feel.

"You're more powerful than you realize, Dani," Evan whispers into my ear as the world again closes in on itself and I slip away into the dark. Suddenly, all of this early morning's events float lazily down long dreamy rivers and disappear into a lingering sunset that quickly turns to the dark void of night.

The smell of pancakes wakes me from a fitful sleep. My body aches and protests rolling out of my bed and I realize with a shock that I've nearly slept through breakfast.

Bolting from the room, I race down the stairs, gripping the banister for balance as I run. There is a sudden and sharp sting that shoots up my hand as it glides across the wood. I slow to inspect my hand and find a paper-thin cut on my palm. The cut breaks open when I press my finger into it, and a sliver of blood smudges against my nails, but I can't remember where it came from. I'm walking into the kitchen so concerned by my hand and a numbing sensation along my chest that I nearly run into Prim, who sidesteps from me with a scowl.

"Watch where you're going!" She flips back her curls and glares at me.

"Good morning to you, too, Prim."

"Morning!" Rana says absently from behind the table. With hands on her hips, she studies Sara's movements as she carefully mixes a bowl of pancake batter. Turning to me, she whispers urgently, "Please just try her pancakes. I swear I've been helping her make them and not to...*experiment* with flavors again."

"Again?" I question, but she ignores me and points to the table where Prim has taken her seat and now rolls a mint leaf between her fingers absentmindedly.

"Are you sure it's a good idea to let her make food?" I ask Rana when I finally sit down at the table.

Rana has always cooked for us, ever since Mother provided us with some basic instructions when we were young. Rana took to it naturally, but her closest friend and roommate, Sara, was a different story. She is, well, not the most talented cook.

"Smells wonderful!" Rana ignores my question and turns her attention to Sara's bowl. "What did you just mix into the batter?"

"More butter!" Sara answers, vigorously stirring something into the bowl that is definitely not butter. Rana looks at me with a grimace and even Prim turns a shade greener.

I can't stay I'm especially excited for breakfast today and not just because Sara is making it. Ever since waking I've felt dizzy, as if the whole house were moving in slow, agonizing spirals that leave me winded and confused. I'm also so exhausted I can barely think straight. I mean, what else could explain how I'd be willing to subject my stomach to Sara's cooking?

Everything was normal yesterday, expect Father letting us know we'd be going inside the tent soon. And I don't think Lily and I stayed up too late discussing everything that's happened recently. But feel like I haven't slept in years, and judging by the yawns around me, I'm not the only one sleep-deprived this morning. I'm starting to wonder why we all seem so tired at the same time when I'm jolted from my thoughts by Sara dropping a steaming plate in front of me.

"I call them spicy cakes! You'll have to tell me what you think of them." She beams, and from the corner of my eye I catch Vera stop in the kitchen doorway and step wordlessly out before anyone else notices. Sara also passes me a small packet of vitamins, which I tuck wordlessly into a pocket.

"Thank you! I think I'm going to take them upstairs so I can share with Lily!" I grab the plate, which burns my fingertips, and hurry away from the table as fast as I can, leaving Rana and Prim to their fates.

When I get back to Lily, I've already nibbled on a tiny bit of pancake and find it surprisingly, shockingly, good. Lily is exactly where I expect her to be after waking: perched cross-legged on her bed with a book in hand. I climb up to sit beside her, the hot plate on my lap.

"Friscuit! What is that?" Lily wrinkles her nose when I offer her a bite.

"Special of the day, Sara's Spicy Cakes!"

"I see." Lily takes the forkful of cake I offer and chews thoughtfully before shrugging. "Could be worse." She places the fork down and considers the spicy cakes for a moment before shaking her head.

"How do you feel this morning after not taking your vitamins?" I ask.

"I feel fine, but we can't totally say it is due to the vitamins, or rather, lack of them. I am a little tired, though. I can't believe I overslept; it must be late morning already!"

"Don't feel bad, everyone else slept in this morning, too. Have you found anything helpful in your books?"

"No," Lily says slowly. "All these books take place ages and ages ago. We don't have anything modern. It's all so bland and I've never noticed before. It's funny, I've always loved these books, the science ones, the histories, but now...I don't know."

"We could ask Father and Mother for new ones?" I say before really thinking it through. They would never do that and Lily must be thinking the same thing as she frowns deeply.

"I think our best bet is any information we can pick up from the people in the tent. They have to know something! Why else would they show up after what happened to Tara? Father mentioned we're going there soon, so we can ask them questions when we do. There's also got to be something in this house that I'm missing. Something! Anything!" She shoves her hands through her hair, then sighs and looks at me again. "We'll figure this out together. Just remember to ask all the questions you can think of when we finally go in the tent."

"I will..." I start to say more, but the words clatter in my head and fall in a heap. I shake my head and flex my injured hand before continuing. "Everyone had such a late start this morning, I wonder if we're going inside tomorrow."

Lily's frown deepens, so I try to smile reassuringly and hand over the cold spicy cakes, which have now conjured a slick sheen of greasy butter flecked with what might be dried chives. "Well, dear friend, you'll need your strength for all that research, so eat up! I'm going out for some fresh air."

"I don't think I can eat this," Lily moans and flops backwards onto her bed, the cakes almost spilling to the floor, but she isn't so lucky.

I leave her alone with the rest of Sara's cooking and make my way downstairs. After pausing to check my hair in a hallway mirror, something I never do, I'm just closing the pantry door with a granola bar in hand when I hear Mother approaching from behind me.

"Dani, darling, do have a moment?" she asks. Her freshly-washed hair lays damp against her lab coat and the bird brooch looks recently polished.

"Of course," I say, walking over, the lightness having fled my feet and replaced by the heaviness of duty.

"Thank you, dear." She smiles and pats my shoulder. "I'm hoping to grab a quick blood sample before you leave. I just want to make sure you're still healthy."

"Didn't you just take one?"

"It'll only take a second. Come on now." She traps my shoulder with a gloved hand and gently steers me towards the now clean kitchen table.

I have a sickening feeling in my gut that says giving blood this soon would be a risky thing, but Mother is the scientist and doctor,

I guess she would know better. An anxious feeling blossoms in my chest, and I wonder if she'll ask Lily for blood as well.

Mother guides me to one of the chairs. With practiced precision, she swabs my inner arm and inserts the needle. With nothing much in the kitchen, I find it hard to distract myself from watching the blood make its way through the plastic tubing. Finally, my eyes land on the small collection of empty glass vials sitting on the table by Mother's hands.

Unlabeled, they look pristine in their little wooden holder. Each clear, unblemished glass shines in the sunlight streaming through the kitchen windows and I don't think I've ever really looked closely at them before.

Usually, they are filled to the brim with blood so I try to keep my eyes turned away, but today the little empty vials sparkle. They aren't actually smooth, but have a small design set in the middle of each one, a cloud pointed at the top like a triangle. I find my hand moving of its own accord, but just as I'm reaching to examine one, I feel Mother pinch my skin with a clean cotton swab.

"Perfect!" She beams at me. "This'll do nicely."

I stare at her, wanting with everything inside me to ask why she needed this sample or what she plans to do with it, but nothing comes from my lips when I open my mouth to speak. She stares back, her brown eyes serene.

I stand and swing my arm around a few times, the pain from the needle already subsiding. Mother begins to collect her things before giving me a small smile.

"You always were the bravest at this. Ever since you were a little girl."

"At what?" I ask.

"Vaccines, blood draws, anything involving a needle, really. You even helped calm the other girls when you were little. You were such a brave little glow worm. Just something you've always had in you, I guess," Mother says, her eyes misting and darting around my face. She smiles sadly, lingering just a moment before turning back to her instruments.

"I don't remember any of that. This is just routine."

"I know you don't remember; you've been with us a long time." Mother sighs, rubbing at one eyelid, and I notice how deep the darkness spreads beneath her eyes. I can't help but wonder when she last had a full night's rest. "Thank you, dear, you can leave now."

"Thanks," I say to her and try my best to mean it. "I'll see you later."

Mother smiles at me and turns to leave. As she picks up her tray of vials, one of them catches the light and shines a small rainbow on the wall. But I hurry so fast out from the room I barely get a glimpse before the door slams shut behind me.

Now her words swirl like oil on water in my mind, and I can't help but think on how I was too scared to confront her, to ask her questions, to really understand what's happening to us, to Lily, to the other girls, or to even be brave like Mother says I am. Now the feeling of helplessness weighs heavy on my chest and makes me feel even more useless.

Chapter Nine

Outside is sweltering and the sweat trickles down my back in the worst way. It's enough to remind me that summer is just around the corner, if not already upon us. Even the breezy air is tinged with heat and the spring chill a thing of distant memory.

I'm only too happy to duck under the shady trees by the back gate and run my fingers along the damp iron, the pillars cool and comforting. Resting my forehead on them, I breathe deeply in the still air. I'm straightening to pull my shirt away from flushed skin when a stick cracks from behind.

"I was wondering when I'd see you again," I say to Evan when he walks over. He stops suddenly, turning to look back the way he came before speaking up.

"Out for an early stroll before work," he says with a smile, "but I didn't realize it would be so hot out here."

"It's been hotter," I say. He leans against a tree and sets his backpack on the ground between us.

"Here," he says, pausing to reach into the bag. "You look like you need it."

I roll my eyes but can't pass up the sparkling glass bottle he hands over. The bubbles and bite of the dark liquid burn in the most delicious way down my throat and help to clear some of the mugginess from my head. They also make it easier to remember the first soda we shared together and I drink it quickly so he won't see the nervousness in my expression.

"Thanks," I gasp after drinking nearly half the bottle. He winks and I think I would blush if my face wasn't already on fire from the warm weather.

"Come on, let's get out of this heat," he says and holds out his hand.

I stare at his outstretched palm, unmoving. Something about this seems strange or familiar. But there is a greater piece inside me that pushes me forward. Forward and towards Evan's outreached hand.

"I brought my own transportation today," he says when he pulls me along the iron walls. "Thought you might like to see how a golf cart built well after The Dusting handles."

"Don't talk about my rickety piece of junk like that. She's just got character."

"No, she doesn't," Evan says almost too matter-of-factly as he points to a pristine and sleek cart parked behind. I turn to look and have to nod in approval; it does look a lot better than my piece of junk.

Evan coaxes me along, and before I know it, I'm seated in a comfortable seat next to him. The cart starts without a hitch and we're off, riding in silence under the sparkling foliage. The rushing air on my face feels good so I close my eyes and loose myself in the moment. Only when we slow to a crawl do I open them and find we're beside the behemoth of a tent again.

Evan climbs out, swinging his bag back over his shoulders before he offers his hand for me, but I swing myself out instead. He grins as we enter the same room as yesterday. Someone has cleaned up a bit, but there are still breadcrumbs on the desk that he sweeps away with his hand.

"Here, why don't you try some of this?" he says, holding a small yellow-tinged jar filled with something that jiggles. He takes a little knife and spreads some of the thick gooey jam onto a biscuit.

I pick it up, flashes of Sara's cooking streaming through my mind. "What is it?"

"Chicken jelly!" He smiles broadly and pops a biscuit into his mouth. "It's really not as bad as you'd think and, well, you're looking a little pale. Probably lost all your electrolytes from sweating so much, so you should eat. Just don't think too hard about what it's made from."

A small bit of the jelly drips off from the biscuit to the desk and glistens in the dim light.

"Can't be worse than what I had for breakfast," I tell him and try a nibble. It crumbles in my hands so I have to shove my whole palm against my face and eat the entire thing in one bite. Excess chicken jelly sliding between my fingers, spreading against my cheek and staying there.

Evan is laughing, but it at least sounds good natured. Living with Prim all these years has taught me to notice the difference.

"Here, let me help with that." He takes a clean napkin and before I can say anything, he's raised it to my face and wiped the corners of my mouth. My laugh that escapes is both awkward and forced as I push his hands away.

"I'm not a child!"

"Are you sure? You eat like one," he says and puts the napkin down. "See, just by eating a little something, you already look better. Interesting…" He considers me up and down. "Are you sure you're okay?"

"I think so? Maybe. I'm not sure. I've felt off all day, but whenever I eat something, I seem to feel better. I think I'm just tired."

Thinking about being tired makes me crave sleep all the more and I find myself stretching my arms up high overhead and yawning deeply, the initial excitement of being alone with Evan worn away to exhaustion and a small amount of unease.

"I'll pack you some samples to eat on the way back," he tells me, returning my yawn.

"You look a little drained yourself," I tell him.

"Just working too much." He shrugs. "I've been asked to stay contracted here a bit longer, which I didn't plan for. My brother isn't around, so everything is landing on me again, and my father is of no help." He pauses and frowns. "Well, he's never much help."

"I see."

His face brightens again, though the light doesn't reach his eyes, before he says, "Don't worry. I'll be around for a while more."

"That's a shame." I chuckle and look away, hoping he doesn't notice the slight tremble in my hands. Looking for something to draw away his attention, I grab one of the glass jelly jars and peer at it closely. Something about it twists within one of my flimsy memories and I hold it up in front of Evan.

"We got a case of them this morning, fresh from the processing plant," he says in answer to the silent question. "They send us stuff like this now and again, promotions and such."

"This picture on the bottle, what is that?" I tap the jelly bottle's label and it brings him back up. The coldness that appears in his expression makes me shiver and I silently regret the bad gravy I've put myself in.

"Our endeavor's sponsor, the Cloudspeak Corporation," he says flatly and shifts away. "Biggest company this side of the country. They're literally everywhere and you've probably seen that logo on everything. They own the world, or rather he owns it all. It's not so much a family-run company as it is controlled by just one man."

When he says it, I look around and he's right. Little mountains and little clouds are everywhere I look, the same logo as the glass vials I noticed this morning.

"Do they do more than just food?" I ask. "Would they do medical supply stuff?"

"If Tobias Cloudspeak owns a company that makes it, he makes a lot of it. He's ensured a little bit of himself is everywhere." Evan closes his eyes for a moment and when he opens them, a gate has been closed. He grins at me and stands up. "No need to worry, though."

"Worry about what?" I laugh, sliding off the desk. "That the Cloudspeak Corporation somehow owns and controls my life as well as half the world?"

"Something like that," Evan says, rubbing the back of his head. He smooths out his shirt without looking at me. "Just be careful in that house. Everything is pretty controlled out here, but in there, well...I don't agree with Tobias about much, but that Dr. Zamora seems a little off and we know nothing about his new wife."

"They're both mostly harmless, just like to take our blood a lot for testing," I say, but catch on to the second part. "New wife?"

"Martha is his second wife; I believe the first died at some point. Came up in the news some time ago and there was lots of talk about it. In any case, just be careful."

It's surprising that Father could get one person to marry him, let alone two. "I always am."

"And better get back home before someone finds us in here," he laughs. "Oh hey, I almost forgot, I got you something!" He reaches into the desk and pulls out a cylindrical white and blue box. He hands it over with a lopsided grin.

"Don't be offended, but I got you some real toothpaste. Home-made stuff tastes terrible," he says lightly, pressing the small package firmly into my hands as my face burns in embarrassment.

Friscuit, I've never left a room more quickly in my life.

The air outside the tent is much cooler, but still the start to a warm day and I walk slowly to give myself time to wipe all the confusion brought on by Evan. I'd rather carry these emotions secretly than have to explain to anyone about them, and there is even a hesitation that grows with each step when I think about telling Lily.

At first the cooling air feels good, but then I feel the tree shadows prickle at my skin and it's as if the air bites like an animal. When I step back into the sun, the sweat trickles into my eyes and heat creeps up my spine. I take a moment to stand still, willing the deep breaths to still the warring feelings within.

Letting my eyes drift to the side I realize I'm staring directly through two of the iron fence bars. I can just barely make out the highway beyond as it stretches in either direction for miles and miles and miles, as if maybe it goes on forever.

Unwelcome thoughts begin to settle in my mind. Thoughts of bigger towns filled with more Cloudspeak logos, more people, more tents, more buildings. Even the ocean is out there some-where, though I have no idea what it actually looks like and will never get to see it in person.

By the time my tired legs bring me to the garden's edge, the sun has started its descent and I find Lily waiting for me near the chicken coop. She is haloed by the radiant light, but her skin still looks sallow and dull. I know without asking that Mother also took blood from her today. She smiles at me and I smile back because, no matter what, we will always be the light each other needs.

"Tell me more about this chicken-flavored jelly," she says to me after I am through telling her of my day, of meeting Evan and eating snacks, but leaving out my secrets.

Her skin glows faintly as the sun disappears and reminds me that we need to be inside soon. When the sun has sunk well below the horizon, our skin casts pale light around the hens and roosters. As ever, the chickens seem oblivious to us because, for all they might know, all humans glow like the moon.

"That wasn't my question," I laugh, letting her take the broom and continue sweeping the second half of the chicken coop for me. "Do you think this toothpaste will be better than the stuff Mother makes?"

"I don't know," she giggles in return. "That jelly is just too dis-tracting. It could be a complete meal if you added some chopped vegetables on top, or maybe some cream? I bet Tara would love it."

Her light laughter cuts off and I see her tilt her head to the side and stare in the direction of the distant front gate.

Her fingers fumble and the broom falls from them, scattering the chickens. A sleek black car screeches to a halt near our front door. A cloud of dirt swirls in its wake as the driver exits and opens the passenger door for someone. I only have time to see polished black boots stomping down from the passenger door before Lily tugs at my sleeve.

"Let's get inside," she whispers urgently. "I'd rather not be caught talking to anyone we shouldn't."

Kicking the broom aside, we hurry into the house through the back door leading into the kitchen, slamming it shut and causing Rana to jump in surprise. Lily takes off to one side of the house to find Father and Mother, and Rana and I run through the other rooms to tell the rest of the girls.

"What do you think this is about?" Rana whispers and Lily, having just returned, shakes her head. We wait in the hall, stone-faced and silent. Even Prim hangs in the back, her palms pressed to the wall she leans against.

Mother is the first to arrive, her face remarkably free of any emotion, and it isn't long before I hear Father hurtling himself through the basement door. His imposing figure stiffens when he enters the room and he cracks open the front door to look into the driveway.

He gives Mother a searing look, and something unspoken and frantic must pass between them because she suddenly straightens her posture and looks around the room, seemingly only just noticing us.

"Well, girls, looks like we're to have unexpected company tonight. Now I know it's been a while since we've gone over our etiquette lessons, but I have faith and trust in you to remember how to act and what to say, yes?"

There are murmurs in muted reply and I catch Lily's wide eyes. Sara shifts from foot to foot and Cait nervously fidgets with the sleeves of her shirt. We wait to see if more will be said, but Mother only walks over to take Cait's hand and smooth down the back of Sara's hair. We're so much older now but the gestures, while childlike, are comforting all the same and the faces around me begin to relax. Except mine and Lily's. Even Prim's mouth remains in a tight line.

"Is the testing going to happen tonight? Are we finally going into the tent?" Sara asks and Father spins towards her.

"Why would you be tested this late in the day?" he snaps, slamming the front door shut and coming to stand in front of us.

"Everything will be okay, just remember your manners," Mother says, her tone much more even.

"Yes, remember them," Father repeats, his glare passing over us all to linger just a tad longer on my face. He straightens his lab coat and gestures for Mother to do the same.

By now I can hear the chickens going mad with the newness of it all, and I don't blame them. My own stomach twists with anticipation and makes it almost impossible to line up with the other girls against the wall. Being the tallest, Lily is at the front of our column while Prim stands next to me at the end.

"Who do you think it is?" I whisper to her, but she stays quiet even though I can feel her shaking beside me.

Father swings the door open before anyone has a chance to knock and bellows out a greeting in his deepest voice. "Tobias Cloudspeak! You old fool, great to see you!"

A man even taller than Father strides in. I want to see the person responsible for bringing chicken jelly into the world and look him over. He wears a crisp green suit that illuminates his dark eyes, and when he smiles at Father, I can see his teeth are perfect and straight. He clasps Father's hand in both of his and smiles broadly, a dimple forming on the side of his cheek.

"Leonard! It's been too long!" he says warmly, eyes blazing as he surveys the rest of us with a bemused expression.

Since we were very young, Father and Mother had instructed us on what to do should we receive visitors. They stressed the importance of their research and our illness, and pounded into our minds that secrecy was in our best interests. That people fear what they don't understand, and the less they knew about us, the better. As such, our job was to remain silent and still and as much a part of the wallpaper as anything.

And while we receive these instructions on a weekly basis, this is the first time anyone has ever been invited inside. My mind twitches back to the group Lily saw trying to come inside after Tara's death, and I can't help but wonder why this man would be allowed in when they weren't. Why would Father be so quick to let him into our world?

"And these must be your wards," Tobias says brightly to us. "And a prettier group of girls I never did see! Ladies, it is a pleasure to finally meet you in person." Cait and Sara giggle softly, but I can feel Prim shrink beside me. He pats at his suit pockets and produces seven lollipops covered in iridescent plastic wrap.

"Now, let's see Lillian?" he asks and Lily steps forward, her face neutral as she accepts the treat and stands back quickly. He names us off one by one and hands a lollipop to each girl, his expression serene the entire time.

I have to fight the urge to roll my eyes when he finally arrives on my name. We're basically adults now, almost eighteen if not already, and here he is passing out candy as if we are children.

"Ah, and you must be Daniella Starling?" He grins when I reach out for his offering. He pulls it back at the last second and looks to Father with an arched eyebrow. Father's face reddens, but before he can say anything, Mother steps in and plucks the lollipop from Tobias. She hands it to me, but doesn't take her eyes from him.

"Martha," he purrs, "it is good to see you so well. I hope my surprise visit isn't an intrusion?"

"Not at all." She beams at him. "We would be delighted if you joined us for dinner."

"Oh no, no, tempting but no," he laughs. "I was just hoping to have a frank word with you and your husband. It shouldn't take more than a moment of anyone's time."

"Of course," Mother says and turns back to us. "Girls, run along and tidy up before dinner. Give us a moment to catch up with Dr. Cloudspeak."

Lily nods sweetly at Mother and turns smartly on her heels, the rest of us following close behind. I'm almost to the safety of the stairs when a large hand leaps out and lands on my shoulder, holding my body in place.

Chapter Ten

"Aha, she looks just like her," Tobias croon, his fingers digging into my skin. "And she's much too pretty to be named after a third-rate brand of battery."

I keep my eyes on the floor, staring at his polished black shoes. Something in way he compliments my looks creeps under my skin and warns me to keep quiet.

"She goes by 'Dani,'" Mother says from beside me.

"Dani," he repeats slowly, letting me go. "I'll try to remember that. Well look at me, Dani, let me see that cute little face."

When I don't look up right away, he stamps his foot so suddenly it releases a spring of nerves and I jump back startled. My eyes dart around the room and land on the wall, on a lamp, on Mother's shoes, anywhere but the man standing before me. That is until he reaches out with a smooth palm and gently lifts my chin to look into his face.

His eyes bore into mine and they are the kind of dark and muddy woods Lily reads about in her fantasy books. The kind of forests where monstrous beasts and dark fairies reside. For a moment, I stare back into their depth and am lost in the questioning familiarity I find there. Then he throws back his head and laughs so loudly his grip loosens and I'm able to stumble out of his reach.

"Oh dear, oh my poor Leonard, oh dear, oh dear." He pulls out a white piece of cloth from his pocket and has to wipe away milky tears of mirth. "I would recognize that look anywhere! And I still can't believe she's named after batteries. You should have changed it when you took her in."

"Recognize my look from where?" I ask, catching his attention and cringing away from the look he gives me. He smooths his suit against him and looks down his nose. He ignores my question.

Under normal circumstances, Tobias Cloudspeak would be an older but very attractive man, yet the way his eyes linger in places they shouldn't and the coldness locked behind his smile makes my spine tingle with unease.

"Spitting image, I tell you!" He chuckles before loudly clearing his throat and waving me away. "Anyway, we have much to talk about. Sweet Martha, please lead the way and let's get down to it, all right?"

The instant their backs are turned, I scramble silently up the stairs to safety. Out of reach and out of sight, I lean against the wall and slide down it to the floor. I have to hang my head between my knees to steady my breathing.

"I've seen him before." Prim's voice carries above me and I look up, expecting to see her peering down her nose at me. Instead, she's looking towards the stairs, her face an unreadable mask.

"When? I've never seen him." Lily appears, extending a hand to help me to my feet.

"This isn't his first visit." Prim's voice is dark. "It was a while ago, but I'm *sure* it's him. It was late last summer, during the windy days, and Father brought me to him in the middle of the night. I think he was trying to take Vera, but you know her, she can sleep through anything. I don't think he could wake her."

"What happened?" Lily asks softly and Prim looks like she is searching hard within her memories before she responds.

"He took me outside and we stood by the door until this man just walks up from the shadows. He looked me up and down, and then left as quickly as he appeared. But I remember those eyes."

"Friscuit, at night?" Lily gasps. "Do you know why?"

Prim shakes her head, and I stare at her in confusion. Lily just looks thoughtful.

"I can't forget the look in his eyes when he saw my skin glowing," Prim continues, closing her eyes and balling her fists in a very Lily-like way. "I didn't know what else to do, so I turned and ran as fast as I could back upstairs. Father didn't follow, but Mother brought me some milk and told me I did well. The next day, they acted like nothing happened."

"Did you ask them about it?" I ask and suddenly the Prim I know snaps back into place.

"Of course not, I'm not stupid enough to bring up something Father doesn't want to talk about."

"Why didn't you tell us?" Lily whispers and Prim has the decency to look ashamed before she flicks her hair back and moves towards the door of her room.

"I think they wanted me to forget it happened," she says, one hand on the door handle. "A few days later, Father came to me and said that if I talked about it with anyone, he'd drain me of every last drop of blood until I was dead."

Lily gasps and clutches my arm. "Why would he want to keep a visit from that man a secret? He's probably just another doctor, maybe he was here to help."

"He's no doctor," Prim says, her voice hard. "And because that's what Mother and Father want. They want us to forget."

"How and why would they do that, and why are you just telling us now?" I breathe and watch Prim's shoulders sag before she walks into her room.

"Because it seems like this round of testing is done and maybe you'll stand a chance at remembering it this time."

The door closes firmly behind her, and Lily and I are left alone in the hallway.

"What did she mean by the testing being done? It hasn't even started yet," Lily says and I shake my head in response.

My mind feels heavy as Prim's cryptic words take their place among the other jagged pieces of broken memory. It's like a shattered mirror, and each piece reflects a different chapter, but the only way to put the chapters together to form a full scene is to pick them up—and they are too sharp to handle.

"He said I look like someone he and Father seemed to know," I whisper and she takes my hand, her head tilted in thought.

"Did he say who?" she asks, following my lead. Maybe her mind is just as jumbled.

"I don't know, but apparently I'm named after batteries."

"Batteries?"

I shrug, any answer I could give her disappearing in a flash.

"I wonder what they're talking about down there," Lily muses, creeping back towards the stairs and distant murmuring voices.

"It's not like they'll just invite us down there."

"You know, Dani, I have a better idea," Lily says, her eyes bright. "Did you notice? Father came up so quickly, he didn't lock the basement door behind him. Let's go take a look!"

"Wait, Lily!" I yelp, but she's already gone and I have to scurry to catch up with her.

The voices from the kitchen feel louder than they should as Lily and I creep down the stairs, letting only the tips of our feet slide down each step as carefully as possible. We slip by the kitchen without being seen, and just ahead the basement door beams with slivers of light around its corners, glowing like an enchanted picture frame.

Lily pushes me ahead because my feet don't seem to want to move forward anymore. But even with her help, my whole body jerks to a stop in front of the doorway.

"We shouldn't do this," I hiss. "This is bad gravy, what if we get caught?"

"I don't know because it won't happen," she says, opening the door just wide enough to slip inside. Being alone in the hall is even more terrifying than actually going in so I quickly follow her.

None of us have ever been in the basement before. Mother and Father simply do not allow anyone inside and keep the door locked for "safety." Too many chemicals and breakables and possibly dangerous things, so we just stay away from it. No one has ever thought about going in because it was just never done.

There is also this deep-rooted fear of what Father may do if he ever catches anyone trying to venture inside. He must have been really rattled by Tobias for him to leave this room unguarded, and maybe he was counting on everyone following the rules. You'd think he would know me and Lily better by now.

Lily tiptoes down the metal stairs and I follow after, pulling the door shut behind us. The room we come into is bright and windowless, and while I notice a similar ventilation system as the one in our rooms, the air feels unnaturally cold and sterile.

One long metal table divides the room and every inch is covered with small glass vials, some full and some empty, stacks of paper-work and various metal objects and framing I can't identify. The walls are lined with white-sheeted panels, and in stark contrast to the clean feeling of it all, a few leafy green plants hang from the ceiling, dirt scattering the floor and nearby tables.

I look around, unsure of where to begin, while Lily immediately begins to rummage through stacks of paper, humming quietly to herself.

"What are we looking for?" I whisper.

"I'm not sure. I just assumed something would be obvious." She sets the papers down and moves to another stack collected on a metal table by the wall. The chipped surface looks old, almost as if it had been here long before the basement became whatever this is. On its worn top, eight glass vials sit in a wooden container. They look out of place, and I wonder if Mother or Father had set them down in their rush upstairs.

I come to inspect them and only need to read a few to know they are blood samples. Lily sees them, too, and curls her lip in disgust as she moves away to continue searching somewhere else. I watch as she passes by the old table again and something catches my eye on the hanging plants. She turns towards different papers, her head bent down over something she found, so I peer more closely. I have to rise on my tiptoes to see them clearly.

"Lily, look!" I say, pointing at the smallest of the plants. She sets the papers down and comes to inspect the plant with me.

"This is different from the one in Tara's room," she says softly, gently caressing the small leaves. "But wait, it has purple veins running along the edge. Wasn't the one in Tara's room orange?" She jerks away quickly and I move to her side.

"What is it?" I ask and see her eyes water and shine, as if she could cry, but something in her refuses the emotion. The plant sways gently from her touch, the only movement in the room. Lily reaches out to steady it.

"What if someone else's blood made this?" She carefully pulls a tiny vine from the back of the plant and tucks it in her pocket before moving off again, her determination increased and her face pale and unflinching.

Small white flowers have started to bloom in the center of the plant, circling the vines like a crown of daisies. I begin to run my fingers along the petals when one of them dislodges and floats carefully to the table, landing on an old, worn journal. It's covered in dirt from the plants above, as if no one has looked at it in some time. Water damage puffs the bottom corner of its spine, and I have to open it carefully so it doesn't break apart.

"Hey Lily," I call and she looks up from across the center table.

"What did you find?"

"I'm not sure, but it has our names and everyone's photos." I carefully flip through the pages, finding an entry dedicated to

Rana, a baby picture of her with the smallest smile, and another of Prim with narrowed eyes. Even as a baby, she looks too smug for the world she found herself in. But there are more pages, more pictures, more information, more names. Lily comes over with color and excitement back in her face.

She is a much faster reader and I let her take the lead. Turning to a file of a child, a little girl with curly brown hair, I hear her breath catch suddenly in her throat. She pulls the journal from my hands and flips to the next page, her eyes bulging. She flips to another and another and another. Then, with shaking hands, she jams the whole journal down her shirt to keep it snug against her chest. I look at her and see her face has gone green.

"We need to go. *Now*. Did you move anything else on this desk?"

I shake my head as she moves another older and dirtier book to cover the missing gap left by the journal. She then grabs my hand and pulls me back towards the stairs.

"What did you see in there?" I ask quietly, just before slipping out the door. Lily's face is grim and her eyes hard when her gaze finds me in the last of the bright basement light.

"I don't like this, Dani," she whispers, her voice pitched low and excited.

"What did you see in there?" I ask again. I'd reach for the journal, but it's tucked securely in her shirt.

"We need to get out of here first." She swallows, her eyes closing for a moment. "Come on, let's go."

She stops speaking when we emerge from the basement, so I stay quiet as we step slowly out into the hallway, closing and locking the door behind us. We hear Mother, Father, and Dr. Cloudspeak in the kitchen, and a spark of warmth encircles my gut, knowing we made it both in and out of the basement unnoticed.

As quickly as we can, we hurry up the stairs and slip into our room, the lavender door shutting securely behind us. Lily drops the journal onto her mattress as if it were a plate too hot to handle and I stand there staring at her, waiting for her to explain what she found. Dread pools in my stomach like spilt milk and before she speaks again, she glances at me, a look in her eyes like she's fighting the urge to spill tears. But Lily won't cry. She's too tough.

"That journal has a record for more girls," she finally says. "I saw us listed, but towards the back"—she swallows hard— "because we're listed after the *real* Zamora daughters." Lily looks through me as if trying to see beyond the wall, all the way to the valleys and deserts beyond, maybe even to the sea.

A heavy silence climbs into the room and waits, and the only thing I can hear is the rushing of my blood as my heart beats too quickly. And then there it is, the twisting in my stomach, the building of something both intriguing and awful, and the knowledge that even Lily doesn't have all the answers. Even Lily can be scared.

It feels like I'm someone else, someone entirely new and separate who is not Dani, but who is listening and watching Lily and Dani speak together in a faraway place. Other worldly anxiety spreads behind my eyes and I speak because I don't know what else to do.

"But where are they now?"

Lily's eyes find me and she pulls from her pocket the tiny purple-veined vine before resting it next to Tara's little plant. "I think they're dead," she whispers.

Chapter Eleven

My head pounds as I watch Lily pace our room and, after taking a moment to remember to breathe, I push my emotions down my throat before asking for more.

"What else did you see in there?"

She stops and cautiously picks the journal up. She hands it to me and I hold it for a moment before opening. It's heavier than it looks. The leather bindings weigh it down. It must be a better quality than my art journals. A quick look inside tells me I won't understand much of the scientific secrets it holds, but I do find a few letters tucked deep inside a back pocket.

I hand them to Lily, watching her eyes widen as she reads before she hands them back. She tells me they are love letters from Mother to Father, dated much before we were even born. Fourteen total letters, some much more graphic than others, with a few scientific notes and formulas thrown into the mix. Gross.

I turn to a random page in the journal, and even though my world has been flipped upside down these past few days, I find myself cracking a small smile at the first picture.

"It's you! Baby Lillian May," I breathe excitedly and turn the photo of a small, pink Lily towards the nearly adult one. She stops her pacing and leans in to inspect it closely. We turn to the next page and see Prim, "Baby Primrose Helena," her smirking face already too good for everything around her.

"You and Prim look almost identical," I say, to which Lily grimaces.

"What do you think these numbers and letters are under the photo?" she asks and I shake my head, too unsure of what to make of them. While I recognize much of the information listed alongside each picture—weight, date of birth, hair color, eye color, the shade of each girl's glow—the whole page is filled with abbreviations, scribbled notations, and collections of confusing numbers. If this gibberish is impossible for Lily to understand, then I have no chance.

"This part right here," she says suddenly and points to a boxed area towards the bottom. "It reads 'carrier' information, but it's just a string of numbers?"

I let out a small gasp. "It's shipping information! They're a little different, but I've seen numbers like this before on the supply orders."

"Could they lead back to whoever shipped us out in the first place?" Lily asks. And then, in a very quiet voice, she adds, "I wonder if they could lead us to our real parents?"

I nod, thinking carefully on her words. Apart from the scattered and faceless dreams, I know absolutely nothing about my real parents. They gave me up, or so I've been told, and I never wanted to waste the little time I have in this world wondering about them. But with this information, their enigma is going to have to wait, because what we see in this journal only poses more questions.

Lily continues to turn the pages while I look over her shoulder, taking note of the different shipping patterns and how the numbers for Tara and Cait are the same while the rest vary wildly. There are also notes about something called bioluminescent algae, which Lily explains is from the ocean, and how each baby relates to both it and some rather complicated scientific notes.

"This bit makes sense, at least." Lily points to a section circled by pen a few dozen times over, as if someone knew of the importance. "Blood-Type. I read about that once, everyone in the world falls under one of the major blood types. It must be important to their research."

We flip through pictures of Sara and Vera, then land on Tara's page where we have to remain silent for some time before summoning the courage to read. In tiny, neat writing, her date of death is listed just under her picture along with the phrase of "accidental overdose of..." Then it's a complicated string of numbers and letters. While this formula means nothing to us, the weight of our friend's death hangs heavy in the air.

Then we finally land on my own page: "Baby Daniella Starling." Lily's eyes narrow, and it takes me a moment to see why.

It's just like the other photos, a small, pink-faced baby laying prone on a yellow blanket with stars, but a smudged line points up from my head. It's the ghost of a pencil mark someone tried to erase and is just barely legible along the journal's seam. We can't read it entirely, but there is one word that slices through my heart as if it were a knife and I warm butter. One word written so forcibly that it refused to be erased from this world.

"'Dangerous'?" Lily questions, taking the journal from my hands and holding it close to peer at the word. "Why would your head be labeled as dangerous?"

"I don't know," I say. Lily looks like she would say more, but changes her mind, though I can see she's thinking hard on the word.

"Nothing about you is dangerous," she finally says.

"Thanks, Lily."

We take a collected breath and my shoulders tense as Lily turns to the beginning pages. After a collection of confusing handwritten notes, four more babies are listed, all with similar information but no shipping codes. Lily runs her fingers along the first girl's name, a tiny baby named "Dylan Zamora."

"It's so strange we've never heard anything about them," she mutters, flipping to the next girl and studying her picture. This girl, Rebecca, is older, maybe about four years old. The following girls, Chelsea and Andrea, are older still. Andrea could even be our age. The page listed afterwards is dedicated to a woman named Victoria, who seems like she could be their mother. Something about her smile pulls on a string of familiarity, but the quality of the photo makes it hard to tell.

All the girls bear a small resemblance to Father, the same dark hair and tilt to their chins. Chelsea even has his eyes. Each one stares up from their photo with pale faces and vacant looks, save for Andrea. There isn't much detail to the photo, but she wears a white dress with a bird shaped brooch pinned neatly to a black sweater. She has on the same dark expression Father takes when his anger boils to the surface.

"They all died," I say, tracing my finger along the dates written under Andrea's photo.

"They were also very young," she says softly, looking up at me as she sets aside the journal. "Even younger than us. I wonder if they're buried out in the graveyard? Tucked away and forgotten." She looks towards the window, as if she could see them playing out in the garden.

"We don't know that."

"There's a lot of things we don't know." Lily sighs, tucking her long legs to her chest and wrapping her arms around them. "Such as why Mother and Father never mentioned they had daughters who suffered from the same things we do. Maybe they don't want us to know they failed once before."

For the first time in my life, I can hear a small hitch in Lily's resolve. A tiny crack visible in her defense. And as much as I desperately want her to accept our fate like I have, a part of me breaks alongside her. But before I can say anything, there is a sharp rap on our door and the shrill voice of Prim, calling us to dinner.

Lily rips the journal from my fingers and shoves it deep under her mattress. When she looks back at me, I see the fierceness I've always known.

"I'll read through it all later. Just stay quiet about it and don't say a word unless I do, not even to Prim. This needs to stay between us. And whatever happens, don't worry." Her eyes bore into mine as she takes my hands in her own. "We'll always have each other. I will never let anything ever happen to you."

Her words tug at me in an ominous way, but my response comes from deep within my heart: "And I will never let anything bad happen to you."

When we arrive downstairs, only Mother sits alone at the table sipping her strong black coffee and staring silently at her empty dinner plate. Father is nowhere to be seen.

When I wake from a restless night, the world swims like a bowl of soup threatening to spill and it takes a moment for my heart to beat normally. I'm still sweating when I look at Lily draped across her sheets, her face pressed into her blankets as if she were dead. A touch of jealousy rises to the surface at how well she is always able to sleep.

I try to wake her, but she mumbles something unintelligible and tucks even deeper into the sheets. A scattering of memories from the day before tells me I'm wasting time, so I'm grateful when she moves just enough that I can retrieve the journal from under her mattress.

There is only one person I can think of who can help us understand the strange wordings and codes and numbers peppered throughout the journal's pages.

I take the journal downstairs, clutching it so tightly it leaves an imprint on my collarbone, and I don't let my grip slack until I'm well into the garden, past the golf cart and just under the shade of the iron fence.

The journal feels like an unwelcome guest. My fingers tremble as I begin to open it and I notice instantly that Lily has removed the love letters. Which is probably for the best, because thinking about the romance between my two caregivers makes me queasy—or maybe it's just the lack of breakfast making me ill. A wild raspberry stalk twines the fence beside me and I cram a few berries into my mouth, but spit them out quickly when their sour taste overtakes my senses. I'll have to ask for some chicken soup when I get back, maybe that will help.

I'm about to turn to my entry when voices carry through the trees and I nearly drop the journal. Crouching low in the overgrowth, I peer through the tall grasses with my head thumping painfully from my headache.

A man stops some distance away, and it's easy to recognize his booming voice when it cuts through the trees.

"It is disappointing and infuriating," Tobias Cloudspeak laments to someone and I gasp when I see Evan just a few steps behind him.

"What is?" Evan asks and they stop only a few paces away, their backs, thankfully, to me.

"That Leonard is as stubborn as I am!" Tobias barks in shrill laughter. "I can admire the man's ambition, but it'll only take him so far. History or not, I will not suffer him. I simply will not do that! Martha, maybe, but not that simpleton."

"What are you going to do?" Evan asks slowly, edging around Tobias and gazing towards the fence. His eyes open wide for all but a moment before the mask is pulled back on, and I know my cover is blown.

"It's not your concern and not why I brought you here," Tobias answers. "Your job is to do what you're told and report back to me. Are we clear on that?"

"We are," Evan replies, watching intently as Tobias brushes past him and back towards the property's front.

"I'm glad to hear it," he calls out over his shoulder. I wait and watch as maybe a minute goes by, or an hour, or an eternity, but after a long silence, Evan approaches my hiding spot.

"Hello," I squeak.

"Morning, Dani," he says. "Did you try the new toothpaste yet?"

"I have it hidden in my room and promise to try it soon. Is everything okay?" I ask, tilting my head after Tobias Cloudspeak. The slight movement brings a flash of pain to the base of my neck and I think my headache may be getting worse.

"Just a performance review of sorts. It gets harder and harder to be a good employee these days," Evan says with his usual bright smile. "Maybe he's just upset his order of pineapples didn't come in. He always was a big fan."

"Pineapple is the tart stuff, right?" I ask, having to swallow a little bile at the thought of food. "Yellow label, tin can?"

"The tinned stuff is garbage. The smell of real, fresh pineapple is something worth living for. Did you know that some places even use the whole thing to hold drinks? They just hollow out the fruit, mash it with liquors, put it back in, and stick a straw in it!"

"I have no idea what a real pineapple tastes like, but I'll ask Lily to look it up later." I stand and brush grass from my shirt.

"It's hard to remember how sheltered Leonard keeps you," Evan says with a smile, reaching out and swiping away an errant flower from my shoulder. I give him a small smile but find myself stepping away from him.

"Hey, I was wondering..." I start, my fingers drumming the journal's cover while Evan frowns at me.

"Wondering what it would be like to taste a real pineapple?"

"Yes, no, well, can we talk in private?"

His spine stiffens and he glances at the journal clutched in my hands. I rub the back of my neck to ease some of the pain creeping into my spine and muster a small smile.

"I think so," he finally agrees. We walk together in silence until the white tent pokes its great head from the trees and I realize we're headed back to the storage room.

My face flushes when we enter into the cool interior. He's just turning around to face me when I press the journal towards him, using it as a barrier between us. I'm on a mission and cannot allow any distractions, even confusing ones like him.

"We found this in Father's lab," I begin. "There are things in here we don't understand and I think they might be important."

He opens the journal and scans the first several pages, his eyes opening wider and wider before he snaps it shut and gestures for me to take Lacey's chair behind the desk. "Where did you find this?"

"We stole it from Mother and Father's basement lab. You seem to know a lot about the world, so I'm hoping you understand what's written in there."

Evan looks down from across the desk, and I can sense how much bigger he is. I'm fairly certain he's not that much older than me, but I still feel like a child sitting this close to him.

He hums as he flips to the first page again, then the second. I don't know if he is only skimming the details, but his brows furrow the further he reads. He's probably gone over the first several entries a few times before he rubs his eyes. Opening their forest depths slowly, he takes a deep breath and looks at me.

"Well, it's a bunch of medical facts. You probably recognize some, I'm assuming?"

"Some, but in the bottom box, is that what I think it is?" I ask.

Evan examines the "carrier" information on someone's page, then flips to Sara's page and nods to himself. "Shipping codes, probably related to transportation from when you were brought here."

"Do you think they could lead us to our parents?" More so for Lily's curiosity than my own. I may dream of my parents, but I'm not eager to learn more about them.

"They could point in the right direction."

"I see."

Evan sets the journal down, leaving it open on my page, and braces his hands against the table. His head hangs low and his shoulders tense in thought. I lean over to peer at my page and notice he was looking at the date printed neatly below my photo.

"My birthday is coming up," I say. "Will you still be around?"

He looks directly into my eyes. "I was here for your birthday."

"It hasn't happened yet."

He winces and asks, "How old?" ignoring my statement.

"Eighteen," I say slowly and his eyes narrow.

"No wonder the project's been moved up. Leonard won't be able to keep his secret project going after you turn eighteen."

I blink. "What are you talking about?"

"Eighteen is when you're required to sign up Required Industry Service for two years."

"The what?" I ask, even more confused now, and Evan is silent a moment before continuing.

"The Required Industry Service, the RIS, is mandatory public service from the government where you get your first job dealing with the general public."

I frown. "Father and Mother never said anything about that, and Lily hasn't read about it in any of her books. She would have told me if she did. This is something everyone has to do?"

"You can actually get it out of the way at sixteen, but eighteen is the deadline. You'll need to sign up for something like working in retail, a restaurant, or maybe parks and recreational jobs if they're available in your area. Basically, any job that makes you deal with the general public. The government thinks personal experience with customer facing jobs makes everyone get along better. They supplement the income you earn, though, so it's been fairly good for business in general. It's also nearly impossible to get out of and as long as you can physically work, they don't care if you have three arms or glow like a table lamp. If you can't prove you're actually dying, you have to do it or risk them getting involved in your personal life."

"There's nowhere to work around here."

"Rural kids move to the bigger cities if there aren't enough jobs in their hometown. The RIS helps fund that kind of thing to make it harder to get out of it."

"But...we're all dying."

"Is that what Leonard told you or what you believe?"

Lily's voice echoes in my mind, small and triumphant, full of the possibility of more life to come.

I shake my head. "This is a lot to take in and it still doesn't explain why you can't remember what day of the week it is."

"You're the one who can't remember," Evan says softly, his eyes turning back to misty forests. "It's all part of the project."

"What project?"

Before he answers, Evan lets out a deep sigh, the kind that comes from your core and makes you shut your eyes as if you're in pain. "I'll show you," he says. "Move that chair back against the wall, I need something from the desk."

I try to stand, but my legs wobble and my head spins. Evan doesn't notice my stumble, so I force myself to swallow the discomfort and terror as I push away from the desk.

He pulls open an ancient desk drawer. Inside is a collection of wadded papers and old food wrappings, which he deposits on top of the table.

"Despite Lacey being a brilliant scientist, she is not known for her cleanliness," he explains, cleaning the drawer out completely. He then raps his knuckles several times along its side until a small tab pops up. He pulls on it to reveal a small cubby containing a pristine white folder embossed with the little peak-topped cloud of Tobias Cloudspeak.

"Before I show these to you, I want you to know that I never took any advantage, and that there are people—myself included, and Lacey to some extent—who are working hard against all of this." Evan takes a deep breath and hands me the folder.

His face looks unsettled as I open the crisp bindings to reveal a stack of paper. It's the nice kind, thick and smooth, but not blank. Someone has already drawn on each page and as I go through them, I slowly realize what I'm looking at.

Each is a portrait of Evan, some more shaky than others and some so beautiful they look like a photograph. One is nothing but flowers and green leaves covering the entire page, and another is of me crowned with a halo of strawberry plants with even more flowers spiraling from my bleeding fingers and toes. I would know my work anywhere, but find it difficult to recognize the dates printed by someone else's hand on each one because the last one is the seventh of July. My birthday.

"Friscuit, are these mine? I don't remember any of them," I say, dropping them on the table and rubbing the back of my neck. The pulsing pain beats painfully under my fingers, and I close my eyes as the frustration of my poor memory causes tears to burn behind my eyes.

"One for every testing day," Evan says. "I had to make sure you regained your motor functions and weren't still sprouting flowers before sending you home. You have this amazing power in your blood that breathes life into the botanical world, but you don't remember any of it. Just like you don't remember your birthday happening already. The drug I gave you at the end of each testing day made sure you forgot it all, and I'm sure Leonard and Martha had their own concoctions for the years prior."

When I see the depths of his green eyes wandering and coasting along these uneasy statements, I feel faint. He reaches out and grips my shoulder. I feel him tug, as if he wants to pull me in for a simple hug but I don't, or rather can't, react and stay stiff and unnerved.

That's when the realization of everything hits me, punches me and rips so many holes in my chest that I'm surprised I can still breathe. The world and everything I thought I might know, or want to find out, collapsing around me in a mountain of weedy thorns.

How much of my life has someone taken by erasing my memories? And, more importantly, why was I born with such power in my own blood?

Evan repeats my name now, over and over and over again. But I don't respond and I don't see him. I can't think or see anything at all except a suffocating darkness as black as Mother's coffee.

Chapter Twelve

acey's sharp intake of breath makes the world snap into place and I open my eyes to see her staring down from above. She produces a small pencil-thin light that she shines into my eyes before saying, "She looks like crap."

"Dani, can you hear me?" Evan asks from somewhere next to her.

My tongue feels swollen to the roof of my mouth and I can't answer him, so instead I roll over and press my throbbing head to the cold ground. My forehead meets something hard and flat and I absurdly wonder if I'm lying on a gravestone. After a moment, I push myself up and feel, rather than see, Lacey takes a step back.

"Keep your head down," Evan mumbles. He leans down and passes another scanner across my chest, but I meekly push it away.

"This is not good," says Lacey. "That's a nasty head wound, too. We need to return her to Leonard before she jeopardizes everything or he goes ballistic, neither of which would be a pleasant experience."

I struggle to stay awake and find it hard to focus on Lacey's voice. Every bone in my body aches and the urge to vomit grows with each breath. I try to slow my breaths, but my body rebels by sucking in staggering amounts of air. Evan sits beside me on the ground.

"This is going to get ugly fast," he says, "so I think it's best I say goodbye now and Dani...I'm so sorry. Talk to Prim when you can, she will explain more."

"Prim?" I start but anything else finds escape from my mouth impossible.

"I'll see you again, I'm sure." Evan leans close, and I think he says something more, but I've run out of energy to focus and drift off once more.

When I come to again, it is to the kind of yelling and anger that sparks from within and comes out in nightmare inferno. Father is yelling from somewhere nearby, but sounds as if he may be moving from inside the house and then back out again to yell some more. Someone mentions something about the fence and someone else says something about finding me.

Then suddenly someone is carrying me upstairs. They have a hard time holding my weight, and I feel more hands touching me and know instinctively some of them belong to Lily. Rana must be there too because it smells sweet, like frosting and bread from the kitchen.

My eyes have trouble focusing, so there are only quick flashes of faces and murmured voices and then I'm abruptly alone on a bed. The back of my head stings from a deep cut at the base of my skull and a fresh headache pours into my brain like freshly-squeezed juice, replacing the nausea with searing hot pain. I touch it gingerly and my fingers come away with red, glowing blood.

Forcing myself up onto my elbows, I look around the familiar room. The area is clean, sterile, and cold. The bed once freshly-made has been thrown apart and the blankets lay haphazardly to the side. The walls seem newly painted and a fresh lock system shines brightly against the window, cutting me off from everything in the outside world. Even the mattress is new, but is lumpy with an earthy smell to it. It also feels like I'm lying on a bag of sand.

I recognize everything and nothing in here, but achingly accept that they've brought me behind the red door. They've brought me to the room where Tara died because I'm sure they expect that is what will happen to me.

I will be the next to die.

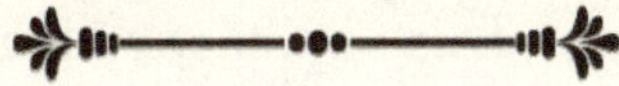

No one comes to see me for the rest of the day and the loneliness is so consuming that, for a time, it is the only pain I feel. Slipping in and out of sleep, the ache in my head flickers around like the paper dolls Lily and I once played with. The tips of their toes tap endlessly at every nerve in my joints and they wear medallions around their necks in the shape of birds.

At some point the door creaks open and light so bright it hurts my eyes fills the room. Mother is there, humming another song I don't know while the stinging sensation of a needle slides under my skin. The song she hums plays softly inside my head and the unknown words remain indistinguishable from my own breathing.

Something cool speeds into my veins and seeps into my muscles, racing and tingling all the way to my shoulders and finally radiating tendrils of ice into my skull. It makes the dancers in my mind stoop and fall, crumbling in small stacks of pink tulle, their hair sticking to their faces with sweat. They let me welcome the blissful grip of sleep.

Sometime after that I wake and stand, woozy from not having had anything to eat in some time, and the room sways before me. But while the floor threatens to take me, I stand my ground, my hands gripping the bedframe with white knuckles.

I will not give up that easily.

I try the door first, but find it locked.

I try the window next, but find it locked as well.

The strength it takes to try to pry them open leaves my body strained and I can barely keep standing, so I brace my hands against the wall.

"They locked it," echoes a familiar voice from behind me. I turn to see Lacey in a chair against the wall. She's leaning back and regarding me with tired eyes, and I wonder how long she's been there.

Somewhere beyond the window, a dragon bellows in the distance. I lumber to the window to see it breathing fire from somewhere far away. I stand there, watching and waiting in the stillness, until Lacey speaks again.

"Where is that word from? Friscuit? You said it as you passed out."

"We found it on a headstone once. Tara thought it was a funny name and it just never went away," I tell her, crossing the room to sit back on the bed. "We use it as a swear."

"Funny," she muses. "This is such an odd place to build a house, on top of an old graveyard. But regardless, you should get back in bed, they've taken too much blood from you. You're weak."

"I'm not weak," I tell her and she raises an eyebrow at me.

"I don't suppose you are," she says, and I think she is going to say more, but we're interrupted by the door unlocking and Evan walking in.

"We're leaving," he says, not looking at me. He runs a hand through his hair, and I can see purple rings under his eyes. His shoulders are slack with exhaustion.

I cross my arms over my chest when I look over at him. He is still a good-looking guy, even beaten down, but the initial thrill I had when seeing him is gone and replaced with something akin to discomfort. Evan's tendency to water down the truth has long since washed away the silly little crush I once had on him.

"Why would we leave so soon?" Lacey asks and I turn to look at her, only just realizing that she has the same defeated and sagging look to her.

"Depends on whom you ask. The company wide email says we've collected enough data and are going back home for in-house trials."

"And what do you think?" Lacey asks, regarding him with a grim smile as she stands, stretching her arms up high.

"Tobias is up to something new and I think he's planning on re-locating the girls, so we need to move up our plans," says Evan, then gestures towards the door. "We need to talk more on it tonight, but for now, could I have a moment alone with her?"

"I guess, but only because I like you better than Milton." She yawns and pauses in the doorway to rest a hand on his shoulder. Her face is barely level with his chest when she tilts her head to him and whispers, "We'll regroup soon. Hopefully it won't be too late."

She leaves, locking the door behind her so we're suddenly alone, watching each other until I find the courage and strength to speak.

"Why didn't you tell me you've been drugging us?" I ask, the acid in my voice surprising me.

"I told you several times," he says, perching on the edge of the bed. "You just don't remember."

"Was it the same for everyone?" My legs twitch as if they want to pace the room, but blood runs cold through my veins and I don't have the energy. They do, however, carry me towards the bed so I can look directly into his eyes for a full confession.

"Yes, and no." A small, twitchy smile speeds through his expression. "It never worked on Primrose. Milton even tried several dosages, but the drugs didn't work on her like they did on the rest of you."

"Why is that?"

"I don't know, she must have some immunity," he says, leaning back with a thoughtful look. "Leonard, or maybe Tobias, must have threatened her with something serious if she never told any of you. Or maybe it never mattered and she did try to say something. It's not like you would have remembered it anyway."

"She remembers it all?"

"Everything."

"But I don't...Was it really that bad?" I ask, thinking of Prim and trying to hide the tremble in my voice. Maybe I mistook her actions as part of terrible attitude when it was really just defeat and frustration. And pain. Was this what she meant by the testing already being done? She knew it was because she remembered going through it.

"It was bad for her," he says, and for all that I've ever thought of Prim, I marvel at the bravery for having known what each day would bring and continuing to get out of bed.

I take a breath and refocus on Evan. "I think you owe it to me to tell me who you are and why you're really here."

"I've never lied to you," he says and I choke back a bitter laugh, irritation simmering within.

"But you've been known to drug me into forgetting what you have told me. So now you get to tell me everything," I say, trying not to grind my teeth against every word.

Evan runs a hand through his hair and stares at the floor. "Are you sure?"

"Yes," I tell him.

Without looking up, he nods. "Well, Leonard and Martha are well known for this so-called home for sick girls. What's not widely known, though, is their partnership with The Cloudspeak Corporation, and as if that isn't bad enough, that the three of them are responsible for the origins of the girls' so-called disease."

"It's an anomaly we were born with," I interject. "They don't know anything about it."

"That isn't true, Leonard created it. He manufactured the disease in a lab using a concoction of bioluminescent algae, hence your moonlit glowing, and tested on his first family before it all ended horribly. Then he and his second wife purchased another set of children for their experiments. A new set of girls genetically manipulated in the embryonic stage by Doctor Martha Zamora, experimented on by Doctor Leonard Zamora, and funded in secret by Tobias Cloudspeak."

"*Purchased* new girls?" I whisper.

"Paid a lot of money to some desperate people, then legally adopted the lot of you. Leonard's a smart man, he must have known the government would come looking for you once you turned eighteen and hadn't signed up for the Required Service. It's possible he didn't expect any of it to matter if his experiment succeeded or you didn't survive that long."

The strength flees from my legs and I sit down heavily beside him, unsure of what to do or even think as the room loses focus. I don't even feel how tight my hands have become until I uncurl my fists and see the red and angry marks my nails have dug into my palms.

"What was this experiment?" I ask, unable to keep my voice steady.

Evan laughs without humor. "What does this dried-up crust of a planet need more than the healing touch of an angel? With the power in your blood, the entire world could become livable again. For a price, that is. That's the official story at least, but I personally think it's all because they want to revitalize more farmlands for cattle ranches. Tobias and Leonard sure love their beef, but that could in itself be massively profitable." He pulls a folded piece of paper from his pocket and spreads it on the bed, pointing at what I recognize to be one of my drawings. The one in which a literal forest seems to sprout green life from my very touch.

I let my fingers trail across my halo of strawberries. "I was created so Leonard Zamora could eat burgers again?" I mutter, the fear inside ebbing into an empty void deep within my body.

"Maybe, but it's more about money and power. I also think Martha's intentions may have originally been about curing the environment before her husband's experiment twisted her emotions."

His words remind me of Mother staring out into the wilds with the wind blowing hair in her face.

"Neither of them has shared how they did it with anyone, not even Tobias," Evan continues. "But with that information, or even with just you and Prim, The Cloudspeak Corporation could make enough to buy a whole new country and do this all over again."

I jerk my head up to look at him. "Wait, we can't all do this?"

"Only you and Prim have shown potential. You're actually the two youngest, so there was more time to perfect the process, which means the others aren't nearly as effective. In any case, there are people within the scientific community who take issue with this kind of human experimentation. Lacey and I had a plan to stop it, but we ran into some issues. Leave it in our hands, all you need to do right now is rest. I'll talk to you about it more in the morning. I'm looking to make sure a few of us stick close to your, uh, family."

Evan sighs and closes his eyes for a moment before he stands. He looks like he may want to say more, but he crosses the room quickly to wait by the door. He knocks once and it opens to let him out, then locks loudly behind him.

I stare in disbelief at his quick departure, my eyes glued to the door as if he might come back at any moment, but the stillness and quiet fester in my mind and flush my face scarlet.

"I'm not weak," I repeat to myself, stalking to the other side of room towards the long cabinet. Hope swells in my chest that while Father and Mother may have fixed the window, the secret crawlspace will be untouched. I fall to my knees in front of the cabinet's door and find myself too flustered to do anything more than stare at it.

It takes a resting pause, and then every muscle screams in protest and bile rises in the back of my throat as I focus my effort into this single moment. Determined to get through to the other side, I'm able to raise my arm enough to knock on the wood, but my loose knuckles give way to fingernails feebly scratching down the panel's surface.

And then I see my arm, stretched to the limit in front of me, looming long and lean in the fading light. Any temporary courage I had summoned from within escapes in every breath, out of every pore, even bleeding from the hot tears that roll down my cheeks.

When I see the lines creasing across my body, a whimper escapes from my lips. Veins pushing their way up towards the surface of my arms, pulsing with glowing blood that is determined to escape my skin.

The shine surrounding my skin is brilliant, but anything but peaceful. This is how Tara looked before she died and now there is no question and no number of answers that can prove it otherwise.

I am going to die.

Chapter Thirteen

"Dani!" Lily hisses in my ear and I bolt upright, the movement sparking pain in my neck. Last night's nightmares are still fresh in my head as I reach out to touch her face, just to make sure she's real.

"Umm, how are you feeling?" Lily asks through my hand, one finger partially up her nose.

"Lily?" I rasp and find my throat sore and dry. She hands me a cup of water from the nightstand and watches as I gulp it down.

"You look better." She laughs, taking the empty glass to place it gently on the table next to a plate of plain biscuits.

"I don't feel it." I stuff one biscuit into my mouth, barely chewing, and have to wash it down with more water. My stomach cramps painfully from hunger, which surprises me after everything that's happened.

"Well, you do. We've seen all sorts of people coming in and out of here with all kinds of bottles," Lily says. "They've probably got you drugged up on something good."

I hastily bring my arms in front of me for a good look, but while my skin is covered with goose pimples and cool to the touch, it is otherwise one pale, fleshy color with no veins seeking to escape.

"What happened to me?"

Lily leans back on the bed, tilting her head up to look at the ceiling. "I don't really know. I was outside with the girls when we saw a small truck speeding up the road. We ran over when we heard Mother screaming for Father to help and saw a man and woman pulling you from the back seat. They said they found you outside somewhere."

"I don't remember any of it," I whisper and Lily takes my hand as she turns to me.

"Cait and Vera were faster and made it inside first, but I lagged behind to see who brought you." She smiles. "I had a feeling you would want to know."

I smile back and think how lucky I am to have a friend like her. "You know me well."

"The woman got back in the truck too quickly, but the man looked just like one of your drawings. I recognized his eyes and think it was Evan. He looked at me funny and seemed to know who I was. He very quickly told me to tell you 'It's under the seat,' but I'm not sure what he meant. I was about to ask but Father came up, and it was all yelling after that, so I got out of there."

I nod. Father's temper is not something to be witnessed in person.

"Did you show him the journal?" Lily asks next. "Is that what's under the seat?"

"It must be," I say, rubbing my temples. Small remnants of a headache remain lodged in my skull, but I can at least form full, functioning thoughts. My mind works quickly to decide on how much to tell Lily.

"The numbers I recognized in there...I was right, it was shipping information."

"So we could find our parents!" Lily whispers excitedly.

"Theoretically, yes, but there's more," I say softly, a light headed feeling passing behind my eyes as I try to remember everything Evan told me. "He said we're all in some big science project, that Father and Mother somehow gave us this supposed illness before we were even born, then purchased us from our families and have been experimenting on us our whole lives, then giving us drugs so we don't remember any of it."

Lily looks right through me. She doesn't even tilt her head this time, but the stiffness of her posture and the wild look in her gaze unnerves me. Her eyes twitch visibly and I can almost see her mind working, as if she's playing a card game and has one last move before an end that will determine all our fates.

"I believe you, we need to escape," she states so matter-of-factly that I'm too stunned to agree or disagree. "I always suspected something was going on, something not right about this place." She laughs harshly and rises to pace the room, and while she's keeping her voice low, there is an urgency I've never heard from her before.

"Where would we go?" Even though I may be thinking clearly now, there is a large part of me that doesn't want to believe or even *think* about these new revelations.

"We'll follow the highway." Lily stops in front of me. "I bet we can find someone to help us."

"Evan said he would help," I say, but Lily shakes her head.

"Can we trust him? The man who has been drugging us every day for who knows how long? We can't trust anyone but each other. What is this experiment even for, anyway?"

"Something about revitalizing the planet for a profit, but only Prim and I can really do it."

"Profit!" Lily spits out. She crosses her arms. "It explains so much. The secrecy, the way Father and Mother keep us locked up here and as far away from outsiders as possible. We're a valuable *commodity*! All of us locked in a cage for their profit, and I bet this whole thing isn't even moral, or legal." She goes still, then looks at me with dread. "Maybe they were trying to speed things up and that's why Tara died so quickly."

I've never seen Lily like this and feel the urge to help her back down from this dangerous edge, but before I can say anything to her, muted voices from the hallway begin to drift towards us.

"I have to go," she quickly says and hugs me fiercely. "We'll talk more later."

"Please come back soon, being here alone is driving me mad," I tell her and she chuckles before diving back through the passage. I close it behind her and jump back into bed just as the doorknob turns.

When Mother enters, I'm not surprised, but when Father follows her, my stomach drops to the floor. I sit up in bed to watch him closely.

"Ah, you look like you're feeling better already," Mother coos as she sits beside me. "Darling, let me see your arm. We're going to do a few tests and make sure you're on the mend. You gave us a big scare!"

I let her grab my forearm and watch silently as she twists it back and forth, even bringing out a magnifying glass to peer closely at the skin of my inner wrist. She doesn't tell me what she's looking for, but it's easy to guess.

Father watches us, his arms crossed. When our eyes meet, it's like something *snaps* in him. His face is a mask of nothingness when he steps forward and brushes Mother aside with one big arm.

"How many times did you see him behind my back?" he demands, his face only inches from mine. His breath smells like something stronger than coffee.

"What are you talking about?"

"Don't act like a stupid little girl. You know who I'm speaking of, that Cloudspeak boy. What did you tell him?"

Icy fingers wrap their hands around my stomach when the pieces come together and form one name: Evan Cloudspeak. He'd talked about his family and his job, but knowing that they are one and the same—and that he kept that from me—drains the color from my face.

"I don't know what you're talking about," I tell him, my mind working to make sense of everything. It feels like an incomplete puzzle where I can see the whole picture, but am missing key pieces.

Snarling, Father rears back with an angry glare. And with a swirl of his lab coat, he marches towards the door.

"I believe you can finish up in here," he says to Mother, then pauses in the doorway to glare at me with cold eyes. She smiles sadly at him as he points an accusing finger in my direction. "Make sure this one stays in here and no one else comes in. We want to make sure she recovers fully before the move out."

The walls vibrate from how hard he slams the door behind him. Mother's gaze lingers on the wall, her chest rising, as if she wants to call out to him—and then she exhales heavily, as if fighting back the urge.

"Mother," I say. "What did he mean by move out?"

The question seems to grab her attention and she turns to me with a bright smile. In the past, I would have believed the smile she gives me, even craved it. Today I notice how it doesn't reach her eyes. Perhaps it never has.

"We're going to be leaving soon," she says, like I'm a child who can be placated with adventure. "Not tomorrow, but the day after. We're moving towards the coast." She gestures towards the window, as if she could see our way there. "I heard it's much safer by the bigger cities and I think you girls will love seeing the ocean."

Her smile disappears quickly as she reaches into a pocket and produces a syringe with a long needle.

"What is that?" I breathe, trying to back away, but her grip is too strong.

"Just some vitamins, they'll help you feel better. It'll make you sleepy, though, and it's okay if you take a nap. You can wake up later and brush your teeth, I brought you some toothpaste and your toothbrush." She nods towards the corner dresser before firmly gripping my arm in her hand. "Now just lie still..."

Moments later, or maybe hours—it's hard to tell the difference in the dark—I realize that Mother was not lying. I do feel better. The headache remains a small, blunt sensation at the back of mind, but if I make myself busy with other thoughts, I hardly notice it.

I reach over and turn on a small lamp to bathe the room in warm light. The floor is cool under my bare feet when I roll out of bed, and I make a mental note to find some socks later.

Someone left behind a plate of garlicky mashed potatoes for supper and I gratefully shovel the pillowy clouds into my mouth until I feel almost normal. My mind keeps wandering back to Evan and the queasiness that follows is too painful, so I choose not to think about his lies and eat through my emotions.

Pulling on a fresh shirt, I grab the toothbrush and the small green container of toothpaste Mother left out before making my way towards the window to watch for dragons.

The moon is so bright that it's hard to see much outside, but while it can't show me beyond the walls, it illuminates the aged window frame. The patterns in the wood grain glitter and gleam and shimmer in the light. When I tilt my head to look closer, they swirl together like a jumble of letters and my breath catches when I realize they form names.

From a cursory glance, the etchings might be simple impurities in the wood. I don't think anyone would have noticed them had they not been illuminated in just the right way. They seem to be mostly from Tara, since she's written her name and Cait's name over and over again. Then I notice another name gleams just below her own. *Andrea.*

But it doesn't end there. One etched line doesn't exactly fit with Tara's signatures, and I squint to make it out. As if to help, the moon shifts just right and light fills the creases of the etched words.

I read aloud: "Don't brush your teeth."

The strange advice makes me pause, the tub of toothpaste heavy in my hand. I set the unused toothbrush on the sill so I can lean against the window, pressing my forehead against it. The cool glass feels slick on my skin and I find myself taking slow, deep breaths when the emotions creep back up.

Why would Evan lie?

Am I dangerous?

What happened to the Zamora daughters?

Why would anyone not brush their teeth?

Who is Evan Cloudspeak?

Oh friscuit.

A dragon streaks by in the distance and I suddenly realize that, ever since Tara died, I've ceased to think of the moving lights as the land trains they actually are. Now they are just dragons racing each other in the night.

What would it be like to be one of them? To care for nothing in the world but chasing your shadow to the ends of the horizon?

I pass the night away in thought, picking at a small hole in the new mattress and letting the little seedy pebbles fall to the ground.

Chapter Fourteen

The morning dawns with one small but amazing change: the red door is unlocked. Jumping from bed, I grimace with the taste of last night's dinner. It's then that I remember having taken the strange and slightly offensive suggestion of not brushing my teeth. I'm unsure if it's a wise decision, but don't have time to think on it before Lily bounds through the door.

"You look better!" She hugs the air from my lungs. "But your breath stinks!"

"Thanks," I croak back, gently pushing her away. "Must be from the garlic mashed potatoes last night."

"Sara made those," says Lily with a grimace as she leads me out the door, "and I think we'll have to fend for ourselves this morning as well. Rana has food poisoning. She's been sick in her room all morning, so Sara took it upon herself to make breakfast for everyone, but so much has been packed away and she wasn't left with a lot to experiment with. We might get lucky and find some plain scrambled eggs."

I stop mid-stride and look at Lily. "What if it's not food poisoning?"

"I haven't heard much about it, but I wouldn't doubt it was something Sara made and none of the other girls have said anything." Lily taps a finger to her lips in thought, then tilts her head and looks at me. "I had an idea last night while you were having the time of your life sleeping. I need the journal, though, to see if it's true or not. We should get it now."

I look around the hall, at all the open doors and empty bedrooms. "Where are Mother and Father?"

"In the lab, same as always. Go out the front door. If you pass through the kitchen, the girls will never let you leave. I'll grab you something to eat and we'll meet in the garden."

I nod and slowly make my way to the front of the house. Sound leaks from under the basement door as I pass by: Father's deep voice and Mother's soft replies. I step slowly, unwilling to risk any chance they might hear me.

I'm almost to the door when Prim rounds a corner and we nearly collide. We make eye contact and she frowns deeply, but before I can say anything, Vera calls to her for her help in the kitchen so I take my chance and leave. All the same, I can't help but wonder if I should have tried to talk to her.

The air is heavy, and when I look up the sky stretches on for miles without a cloud in sight. I walk slowly and purposely through the fresh morning until I find Lily at the garden's edge staring at the house and chewing her bottom lip.

"I hope they don't say anything to Mother and Father about us not helping to pack. It might look like we're up to something."

"They're too busy to notice," I remind her, but then remember Prim's frowning glare. The revelation regarding Prim's memory has been heavy on my mind, but I can't think of any way to bring it up to her.

"I was able to get you the only edible thing," Lily says and dumps a handful of granola and dried strawberries into my hands. Shoving the entire fistful into my mouth, I try to smile with full cheeks and she giggles as we walk towards the shed. And yet, the further we walk from the house, the more nervous she looks. I take her hand, giving it a gentle squeeze that she quickly returns.

"Where under the seat would it be?" she asks when we enter the shed, leaning into the cart to peer under the seemingly empty space with narrowed eyes.

I examine the seats and when I do, the cart's model number along the edge catches the sunlight and glimmers. "I remember Evan telling me something about golf carts like this, that they were made for smuggling alcohol."

"Hiding alcohol?" Lily laughs, but when I don't join in, stops and tilts her head in consideration. "That was a thing a few dozen decades ago, so I guess it makes sense there would be a secret compartment."

"Exactly!" I jump in front of her and shove my hand under the driver's side seat. My gut clenches when I don't feel anything save for a smooth surface, but then my heart leaps from my chest when I try the passenger's side and a small, almost unnoticeable knob clicks against my finger. When it lifts open a fraction, I can slide my hand inside and am rewarded when my fingers bump against the warm leather of the journal.

"I've got it," I gasp and Lily leans in as I pull it out. She takes it from my grasp and tucks it securely into her duffle bag.

"Let's go!"

We make our way back through the gardens and are just passing the flower beds when Mother bursts through the front door. Sweat drips down her flushed face and she says nothing to us as she stomps off the porch. Cait appears next, her face scrunched in thought.

"What happened?" Lily asks, watching Mother as she paces the driveway.

"I don't know," Cait murmurs. "She came running up from the basement. I heard shouting from Father. I think they were arguing."

I look towards Mother. She's stopped walking, her posture so rigid you could almost think she wasn't real, just a giant doll. She faces the eastern horizon, her back turned towards us. One finger on her left hand taps rhythmically on her hip as her light brown hair flutters in a breeze.

I remember what Evan said and follow her gaze towards the distance. She's facing east, which means she's looking towards The Dusting, and although we're too far to see anything, the sadness etched along each line of her face says she's deeply troubled about something.

"Cait, why don't you go show her those drawings you found the other day?" Lily says, pushing Cait toward Mother. "The ones you and Sara did when we were kids. I bet she'd like that."

It seems to break Cait from the spell. "You're right, maybe she just needs a distraction. With everything going on lately, I think I do too."

As soon as Cait's back is turned, Lily shoves me inside the house. When we're secreted away in our room, we crouch between our beds with the journal between us.

"There!" Lily's finger thumps down onto Tara's page, her fingernail pointing at her blood type. "O Positive, and now"—she flips to Dylan Zamora's page and points again— "O Positive as well."

"And both are dead," I murmur as Lily flips the journal again and lands on my page.

"AB Negative, just like Andrea," Lily says, the excitement draining from her voice. "You said you and Prim were the only ones with power and Prim is AB Positive. Whatever they're working on has something to do with blood. Maybe they needed to test which type was the most compatible."

Lily leans back against the bed, her head tilted as she stares at nothing. I try tilting my head the same way, wondering if maybe ideas and thoughts would come to me like they do her, but my head is a cotton-filled mess. All I can think of is Evan and how I'm not sure whether or not I want to see him again, like he promised I would.

I sit that way until the thinking makes my eyes heavy and I almost drift off to sleep. Pulling the journal closer I open it again, but something flutters from it and slides under the bed. It goes unnoticed by Lily, but I dive after it.

"What was that?" Lily asks. I crawl out from under the bed, the paper clutched tightly in my hand. I spread it on the floor in front of us: my face with a crown of strawberries looks up.

Lily is quiet for a moment before she asks, "Is that what you and Prim can do?"

"Yes," I whisper and Lily moves the paper closer, studying it with wide eyes.

"It's so beautiful...but is that toothpaste in the corner?"

I look where she's pointing and notice someone has drawn a small tube of toothpaste, then circled it with a pen. There's even a little smiling face drawn next to it. Rolling my eyes, I snatch it from Lily and stuff it back into the journal.

"What happened with Evan?"

"Who? Oh, you mean Evan *Cloudspeak*?" I empathize his last name, to which Lily blinks in surprise. "He's a lying piece of..."

"I'm so sorry." Lily sighs, glancing back at the journal, as if his face is etched upon it. "But he does look a little old for you, anyway, and we know he's a liar."

I shove my hands through my hair. She's right, and yet... "I'm still pretty conflicted by it. He seems to want to help us, but like you said, I don't know if we can trust him, especially not now."

"Maybe this is a good thing, because I've been thinking—"

"Friscuit, Lily, you're always thinking. You think more than any of us. You probably think more than everyone here combined."

She laughs lightly and waves me off, her smile dropping quickly. "I have another brilliant, great, fantastic, out of this world idea and I want to run it by you," she says, taking a seat on the edge of her bed.

"Of course," I whisper right back, sitting opposite from her with a smile.

"Just be quiet and listen, something isn't right here. All the lies and all the tests, I just don't like it. It's not normal and..." She trails off, takes a steadying breath, and squares her shoulders. "I think we need to leave and get help, tonight."

Somehow, it's both a surprise and exactly what I expected to hear from her. "Do you think anyone would even help us?"

"They have to because this isn't right," she says softly and points to the journal. "We can't trust anyone here. Five people have already given their lives for this. Who knows when this will be over and how long it could go on? Once they figure out you and Prim are the only ones who can do this, what will that mean for the rest of us, and what will that mean for you? You have the same blood as Andrea Zamora and look what happened to her."

The realization that I will die is not new to me; it has been hanging over my head every night for as long as I can remember. I already thought it was coming last night, when I saw the way my veins pulsed. So when Lily's words reach my ears and travel their slow way to my brain, they land on a soft pillow of welcome familiarity.

Had I fully accepted death?

No, I don't think so.

Would I fight to prevent it?

I think I could with Lily's help.

"I'm not dead yet," I tell her and hold out my hand to her.

She gives it a squeeze before saying, "I feel a thousand years old, like I've been marooned on an island and stopped counting the days because everything is always just the same. But tomorrow night, after dinner, we'll get out of here. We'll bring help, we'll figure out what's going on, and we'll do it together."

And my heart believes her. It truly does.

The sun draws me awake in slow and torturous ribbons of undiluted light. Mother had insisted I stay behind the red door for the night and I mourned the feeling of never waking up in my old room again. And when Lily and I come downstairs for breakfast, the hallways have been stripped bare and cleaned to a glossy sheen. It's almost as if no one has ever lived here.

Lily's eyes dart along the barren walls and the overpacked boxes leaning against them. I look too, willing something to grab my attention that may help us on our journey. I catch her threading fingers along a purple scarf that sticks out like a tongue from one of the boxes before she winds it out and over her arm. With a grin, she stuffs it inside her duffle bag.

"Smells like pancakes again," Lily murmurs. "Let's hope they're out of the kitchen so we can sneak some food before it's packed up."

I inhale deeply the vanilla that wafts through the air. "Rana must be feeling better."

When we arrive, Rana is indeed bustling about from stove to counter and back. Sara stands nearby, giving her full attention.

"So what did I just say?" Rana asks her as Lily and I take our seats.

"That there are some things you simply cannot substitute and cooking is more science than art," Sara repeats. "But why can't it be both? I feel like it should."

Sara cracks an egg into a heavy bowl and pauses as the yolk drips from her fingers. "It could be, as long as you take into consideration there are some things you shouldn't swap out and remember that some ingredients are not suitable for breakfast foods."

Lily plucks an apple from a nearby serving dish. "I bet that's how the best foods were created. You have to get a little crafty sometimes."

Rana waves a spatula at her and batter hits the wall in splatters of beige. "Don't encourage her," she snaps. "Unless you want fish sauce in your pancake syrup?"

"We're having fish for breakfast?" Cait asks, walking in with a massive binder her in arms. She lets it fall loudly onto the table.

"Rana is teaching me how to make breakfast." Sara beams. "One day I'll be as good a cook as she is."

"One day, sure," Prim mutters, following behind Cait. She moves to the window and looks out.

"What do you have there?" Ignoring Prim, Lily leans over and inspects Cait's binder.

"It's a memory book," she says and I tilt in for a better look.

It's one of Father's old black binders, worn on the edges but sturdy. She flips through the pages and it's bursting with drawings, scraps of pictures cut from what look suspiciously like some of Lily's books, and every now and then an actual photograph of someone.

"It's perfect," Lily says, hugging Cait tightly. "Tara would have loved it."

Tara would like being alive better, but I keep that to myself as Cait closes the book delicately and looks in my direction. "Mother said you wouldn't be helping with any of the actual moving today, so I was hoping you would have time today to draw something for it."

My fingers twitch, and for a second, I imagine the book burning on the ground, Father's stern face shaking his head in annoyance through the flames. I feel Lily's eyes on me and know we have other things to take care of today, but don't feel I can decline.

"I think I can, but it won't be ready till dinner. Is that okay?"

Cait nods enthusiastically and the smile that stretches across her face reminds me of Tara. "Thank you," she whispers.

"She only has time because she's too weak to help with anything else." Prim snorts from her position by the window, still looking intently outside. "It's probably best to give her something to do, so she doesn't run out on us and get eaten by the dragons."

"What's your problem, Prim?" Lily says, stepping between us.

It seems to take Prim off-guard. Her attention snaps towards Lily, the mask slipping from her eyes. "No problem," she says, hugging herself, her fingers squeezing deep into her forearms as she looks at the floor. "Something just doesn't feel right about this sudden move, and I couldn't sleep last night."

She looks up to see us staring at her and her face turns crimson before she frowns and walks out of the kitchen.

"I'd say that was strange, but that feels normal for Prim." Rana laughs and resumes stirring her bowl. "Sara, get the flour out of the box over there, we need to add a little more."

Lily and I watch as the lessons continue while Sara follows her directions dutifully. They make the most delicious pancakes we've had in ages, glistening with the last of the butter and dripping in vanilla-infused syrup. Lily and I offer to clean up while Cait walks away with a plate for Prim.

With the others happy and full of pancakes, Lily and I finally find ourselves alone in the kitchen. We stuff a box of dry cereal, a plastic container of jerky, and as many apples as we can into Lily's duffle.

Before leaving, Lily stops to look at Cait's binder left behind on the table. "I'm glad she's making this," she says, running her finger along the book's spine. "Some things shouldn't be forgotten."

When we arrive back in our room, she deposits her bag on the bed and we rummage through our already packed boxes to find a few more skirts, some thick socks, and a bottle of sun block. Afterwards, our two duffle bags sit beside my bed, waiting to help us survive a few days' walk into the unknown.

"I wish Father would buy us pants," Lily says, holding up her favorite long brown skirt. It's the lightest of her skirts, with small pink roses dotting the tawny fabric.

"Traditionalist," I mutter and toss her a pale ivory shirt to match. "They'll do as long as we wear the thicker socks and our winter boots. Hopefully we can get to Bitterwater City before he does. What time do you think we should leave?"

"Early morning," says Lily. "Everyone will be asleep and we run the best chance of Mother and Father actually being asleep as well. I hear we're having a big dinner tonight, so maybe that will help everyone sleep better."

"Do you think we'll need anything else?"

"I'm not sure," Lily says, tucking our bags deep into the low cabinets. "But you should start on that drawing Cait wants you to do. It might look suspicious if you don't."

"I don't even know where to begin on that," I sigh. "Something to remember like skirts, dust, and chickens? Chickens wearing skirts in the dust? Or maybe just a chicken dinner?"

Lily laughs and tosses an empty notepad in my direction.

"It'll come to you, it always does." She smiles and leaves the room.

Once alone, I find myself pacing from one wall to the other. The occasional thump of heavy boxes being dropped and repositioned below is the only sound in the otherwise quiet and still room.

I gravitate towards the window, notepad and pencil in hand, and look out at the cooling desert. It's a western-facing window so I have a full picture of the sun setting peacefully in the distance, the colors bleeding into the last lingering clouds and making the sky a purple shade similar to the bedroom door.

In the distance, skirting close by the main road, a long slender dragon combs through the hazy light, and I marvel again how the smoke beasts are actually just land trains. I've never seen one in real life, so for all I know they really are fire-breathing dragons filling their bellies up with unsuspecting desert travelers.

Holding the empty notepad close, I leave the room and venture toward the red door once again. I take a quick look down the hallway to make sure no one has noticed and slip inside. This room lacks the warmth and familiarity of the one I shared with Lily, and I think I can still catch the lingering smell of mossy vegetation in its corners.

I make my way to this room's window frame and run my fingers along the grainy edges. It's bright and the sun doesn't hit the wood in just the right way, so I can't make out the names, but think I can see the phrase about brushing teeth. It makes me subconsciously run my tongue over my own and frown over the unsetting and dirty feeling.

How can I expect to concentrate on anything with this awful taste in my mouth?

Then I remember that little drawing in the corner of my sketch. Evan had given me a small tube of actual toothpaste, not the homemade stuff.

I leave Tara's room quickly and dash back to my own. The toothpaste lies hidden behind a loose floorboard and I chide myself for forgetting to add it to my packed bag. Grabbing my tooth-brush, I dab on a small amount of the white and green paste and proceed to brush my teeth in the slowest way possible, using only a small glass of water from our washroom.

It tastes like what I think snow would taste like and in no way tastes like the coldness of a desert night, but rather like the icebergs Lily reads about in her books. Where the homemade stuff had an effective but chemical burn, my mouth now tingles with an icy warmth I've never felt before. I close my eyes to savor the feeling, and in doing so, my head spins with images and ideas while my pencil catches them on paper.

It's an early summer morning in the kitchen and I see Sara, bending over a pot of boiling water, her face scrunched tight in concentration. Rana stands nearby with her hands on her hips, watching with a smile.

Cait carefully pulls off a piece of loose wallpaper from a nearby wall and tucks it neatly inside her binder of memories, and Vera is ready to cover the gaping hole with some tape. Prim sulks by a window, her gaze distant and far away, but she turns and smiles when she notices what Cait has been up to.

Lily sits neatly in a chair, several books spread across the table in front of her. She's pointing at one and gesturing towards Tara to look closely at the page, but Tara's busy feasting on a pile of pancakes.

From the doorway, Mother and Father stand with steaming cups of coffee, quietly watching the scene. Father is frowning deeply, but Mother has a fond smile on her face.

I sit back and look at the picture, my hand smudged black and my eyes hurting from the fading light. Every family member is there—except me.

There's only one space left that has enough room, so I find myself drawing my image there. Pale, small, and driving the golf cart towards the highway.

Chapter Fifteen

Tonight, we eat Sylvia, a plucky red hen that would always try to eat my fingers. No one but Lily and I care, and I watch as she takes slow and purposeful bites of her dinner, lingering on each a bit longer than anyone else. I eat slower, but savor each huge bite knowing it may be some time before another hot meal comes my way.

Cait chatters about the binder she's made. I know she has it hidden under the table because she keeps looking down excitedly. It's a move that would normally irritate Prim to a breaking point, so I'm surprised to catch her staring out the window again with a pensive look.

Mother and Father are with us tonight. They sip their black coffees and let the steam rise into their faces and fog their glasses. Mother's face is unusually pale, her eyes darting to the side as if she's nervous of the very walls and, like Prim, there is an unsettling sadness to her features. Can she truly be sad we're leaving?

Father's eyes are distant and calculating, as if he's going over something in his head. He gazes out the same window as Prim, and while the sun has long since sunk below the horizon, the sky glows ruby red and reflects in his eyes. It gives his already stern features an even more sinister look. The spell only breaks when he takes a sip from his mug and the lenses on his glasses glaze over with steam to cover his dark thoughts.

"Girls, I have a special treat for you," Mother says at last, getting up from the table. She sets down her mug and I notice she's left a small smudge of red lipstick along the rim. She must still be arguing with Father because he glares silently at her when she moves to the kitchen counter and returns with a red tin. Seven perfectly-shaped chocolates lay inside and she hands one to each of us.

"You've been working hard and I thought you'd like a special treat," she says before returning to the counter to refill her coffee. Her back is turned to us so I can't see her expression, but her voice shakes slightly as she adds, "Make sure to eat the whole thing."

Her words aren't needed, though: every girl, with the exception of myself, has already eaten their piece. Chocolate has always been a rare treat for us and whenever we're presented with some, it's usually consumed immediately. I'm still working through a mouthful of mashed potatoes and have more chicken to eat, so I set my piece aside for now.

Mother eventually turns back around and looks at us with misty eyes. I have to remind myself that this woman has her hands in the mysterious experiment happening here, but pity for her lurks somewhere inside me. She's always tried to be a good motherly figure—at least, I think so. She is the only one I can remember, after all.

Father clears his throat and sets his own mug down, but his coffee is only half gone. He turns his attention towards me, so I quickly push some chicken onto my fork and cram it in my mouth. But even as I chew, I feel his cold eyes watching me.

"Make sure to eat your chocolate, Dani," Mother says to me, sitting at the table again. I set my fork down and swallow the last of my meal before biting into the small square. It melts slowly in my mouth, and while it tastes creamy and sweet, it leaves the smallest amount of acidic aftertaste that itches the back of my throat. Disgusted, I set it back down on my plate and look at the other girls for their reactions, but no one else has seemed to notice the unfamiliar taste.

"Why bother with her?" Father huffs, and Lily and Prim turn their attention towards him. "She just does what she wants like the useless circus trash she is."

"Circus trash?" Lily blurts. "What does that even mean? You're not being fair and should treat her with some respect." The tone of her voice is icy and Father turns his attention towards her when she snarls, "You're always so mean to Dani."

I open my mouth to say something, stunned and a bit confused by the name-calling, but no words come out.

"I have every right to treat her as I see fit." He jabs his finger at me. "She might be an important piece to 'curing' you lot, but it doesn't mean I have to put up with her insubordination and insolence."

"You know, she's sitting right there," Prim snaps. "You don't have to talk about her like she's not in the room." My mouth falls open. I don't think she has ever come to my defense before.

"Not you, too," Father says and takes another long drink from his mug, not even looking at her. "Prim, I expect better from you."

"Let's not fight," Mother says, returning with a full cup of coffee. The steam rises so high it mingles with her hair, and for a second it looks like smoke encircling her light brown curls.

Father grunts, raising the mug to his lips.

"It's true," I whisper, looking down at the table. "You're always picking on me."

Father pauses, the cup only inches from his lips.

"What did you just say to me, Daniella?"

I raise my head and lock eyes with Lily. She gives me a tiny nod, so I take a deep breath and turn towards Father. The sun has set, so the reflection in his eyes is gone, leaving them nothing but two black voids.

"You've always treated me differently from everyone else," I say, my eyes on fire as I hold back tears. "Why?"

He laughs, actually laughs, and drains his mug before continuing.

"Because you remind me that even greatness can propagate mistakes in life."

Lily slams her fork down on her plate and Prim turns her attention to Father, her eyes wide. The rest of the girls shrink back, but Mother's body is alert and tense.

"You speak so highly of yourself," I spit at him, the words flying from my mouth like chickens let loose in the morning. "If Doctor Leonard Zamora is great at anything, it's being a mean and bitter old man with a strange vendetta against just one of his so-called daughters."

"Enough!" Mother shrieks and her outburst slumps me against my chair. She rarely raises her voice.

"I've had my fill of this," hisses Father, rising to refill his coffee. "We've given you what we can—life, and a chance at being a part of something greater than any of us—and all I ask in return is a little obedience, which you've never been able to give. You're a constant reminder of my own failures in life. I should never have brought you here."

The table is quiet, and all I can hear is the beating of my own heart and Mother as she tries to calm herself with rhythmic breathing. Her face is once against turned east, and I think she may be fighting back tears. I turn my gaze back to Father and keep my eyes locked with his until Sara's unsteady voice breaks the silent room.

"What do you mean by 'something greater'?" She looks towards Mother when Father turns his back on her to stare out the window. Somewhere in the distance, I can see a dragon streaking by.

"He means the cure for your illness," Mother says quickly and reaches out her hand to stroke Sara's hair. "Even though it took you from your families, it helped bring me the daughters I always wanted and I'll forever love all of you. But that's enough for tonight, I promise we'll talk more about it tomorrow. Right now, everyone should go to bed so we're ready to leave in the morning. Get upstairs and make sure to brush your teeth. I left out your toothbrushes and fresh pots of toothpaste for each of you."

There are murmurs of acknowledgment around the table, but she knows we'll all brush our teeth. We always have before. My half-eaten chocolate sat forgotten on my plate during Father's outburst, so I grab it quickly and store it in my pocket before rising to leave with the rest of the girls.

"I'm excited to see the ocean!" Sara trills and smiles broadly at Cait, who clutches her binder close as Mother hugs them tightly. Prim frowns at the window before leaving the room, a faraway look on her face, and Lily and I get up to follow, but Mother manages to grab us both in a bone crushing hug.

"Dani, my sweet, creative child, and Lily, my little bookworm," she gushes. We peel ourselves off her and follow the rest of the girls up the stairs. I turn to see her smiling after us and the reflection of Father's black eyes in the window before Lily closes the kitchen door.

My stomach sinks when we arrive upstairs and all the girls except Prim have disappeared into their rooms. I can feel Lily's disappointment beside me. This means we won't get a chance to say goodbye.

"Did all this seem strange to you?" Prim asks, coming close to us. "I still can't figure out why we're suddenly moving away, we've been here our whole lives."

I can sense Lily's internal struggle with the question, but the smile she puts on is believable. "I'm sure Mother will give us more information one way or another, despite what Father may think of it. But until then, we just need to make sure we're all looking out for each other. Just be quiet and listen, everything will find a way to work out."

"But don't you feel this unease?" Prim yawns deeply. "Trust me, I know something bad is happening here, but I feel like something even worse is going to happen soon. I've been having these nightmares." She shudders and rubs her eyes vigorously. "I think I need to talk to you about it...again."

"Okay Prim," Lily tells her, yawning herself. "Everything will be okay. We'll talk more tomorrow and make a plan, okay?"

"Yeah, that sounds...good, tomorrow then." Prim's words slur together before she vanishes behind her bedroom door. The last I see of her are fingers slipping across the doorframe.

Lily yawns again, and I suddenly realize just how tired I am, the leaden feeling creeping along my legs and rooting me to the ground.

"Lily, I'm so tired, how are we going to do this tonight?" I whisper to her just outside our purple door. Her eyes almost look sunken when she puts her hands on my shoulders. When she smiles, the fire that usually dances behind her eyes is muted.

"Go inside, brush your teeth, and take a quick nap," she says around a yawn. "We can't leave till much later anyway. I'll stay up and do some reading, then I'll come get you when I think it's safe."

I hug her and she returns the hug in her fierce and wild way.

"I'll see you soon."

The night is still and bright outside, and even though my window is sealed tight, I can imagine the sharp taste of the cool desert air. Stifling another yawn, I move towards the little sink to brush the taste of chicken from my mouth. Mother's toothpaste sits alone on the countertop, the black lid catching the moonlight and gleaming brightly. I am about to smear it on my toothbrush when a thought occurs to me. If I can't taste the cool air outside, then maybe I can taste something similar.

It takes a lot out of me to venture towards the cabinet and crawl inside. Pushing the loose panel aside, I'm able to reach my duffle bag and slip out the tube of Evan's toothpaste. There's no response from Lily on the other side, and I imagine she's engrossed in one of her books.

Taking the tube with me, I have just enough energy to move the toothbrush around my teeth, savoring the coolness and the fizzy taste of mint dancing across my gums. It brings me to life just enough to remember the half-eaten chocolate stored in my pocket.

I won't try eating it now, though, I just brushed my teeth. I don't want to relive the chemical taste of it again, anyway.

As each thought I make becomes muddled and fizzy like soda, I start to find it hard to think clearly, to hold onto a single thought before it slips away completely. But there will be time for thoughts after Lily and I are far from this place. Then we'll return and share all the good things with the other girls.

We'll save them all.

But now, I'm so tired my thoughts are jagged, unfinished sentences that scrape at my mind.

And all I need is sleep.

I barely make it to the bed.

Something breaks through the darkness.

Through the still warm night.

Footsteps, heavy and pacing.

Back and forth.

Breathing the heavy air.

Oh friscuit, I'm so tired.

It is the lack of sound that wakes me. Not the choking smell or the stinging air, but the quiet beating just outside the door.

My sluggish muscles make it hard to prop myself upright. The moving stirs my blood to pump quickly and painfully to my head, and I have to fight the urge to retch as the room comes into focus.

My heart thumps to its own song as I try to make sense of everything, but when I realize Lily never came to get me, adrenaline sweeps through like a windstorm and I leap from the bed.

A bright orange glow shines where the door meets the wooden floor, and tendrils of fire lap under the frame in long slender tongues. When they pause to gather strength, smoke snakes in to fill the room and my eyes water in the haze.

Landing heavily on the floor, I am absurdly surprised to find myself still dressed from the night before and there is a moment that I find myself thankful for the shoes tightly bound to my feet. A small mercy in an otherwise terrible situation as I crouch low to the floor, having remembered Lily once explaining that smoke always rises.

I can't help the bile rising into my throat and I vomit off to the side, my stomach heaving with the pressure. My mind tells me to lie down and wait for the sickness to pass, but that is not what Lily would do, so I crawl towards the window instead. It's sealed tight, locked with some unseen force probably on the other side.

As I turn and make my way to the door, my skirt tangles around my knees, so I take a moment to lay prone on my back and kick it completely off. I leave it crumbled on the floor and notice one pocket oozing with melted chocolate from Mother's gift the night before. Something looks wrong about its color, and I watch in horror as the brown starts to pop with sickly yellow bubbles as the temperature grows. I have to force myself to look away and crawl towards the door, my skin rubbing raw on the floor and leaving a trail of blood behind.

I'm only a few feet away when I'm forced to back up. The heat from whatever is blazing on the other side burns at my cheeks and

I make a hasty retreat backwards. I press my back to the wall, each breath coming in small gasps as I try to stay calm.

An iciness closes in on me, despite the heat radiating from the door, and it causes my limbs to shrink within themselves and every muscle bunch together in a ball. I wrap my arms around my knees, hugging them close.

I think of Mother and Father and wonder where they are, if any of the other girls made it out. The chocolates must have been laced with something to make us sleep, but why? I should ask Lily…

The crawlspace!

Leaving my discarded skirt on the floor, I make my way to the cabinet, desperately hoping that Lily will be there waiting for me. She would never leave me behind.

Every joint feels like it's disconnected from my body as I raise my arms to push through the loose panel. I'm starting to not feel like myself and maybe that's a good thing. The real Dani would be sitting in a pile of her own vomit, her skirt on fire and oblivious to the tiny spark inside her. A tiny hope waiting to ignite.

When I open the cabinet, I'm surprised to see the hidden panel has already been pushed to the side exposing a darkened portal into Lily's room. I don't remember moving it, and despite everything happening, I find myself frustrated again at my poor memory. Shaking my head, I push my sluggish body through the space, the duffle bags we packed last night spilling out before me.

I tumble to the ground and inhale large gulps of clean air as I shut the cabinet door against the worst of the smoke. It's easier to move without the weight of the skirt and I'm able to stand up. The act of doing so breaks the skin again on my knees and cold air pelts against the bruised skin. I glance down but don't have time to do anything. It could be worse. I could be burning to death next door.

"Lily!" I shout when I see her form curled on the bed. I rush quickly to her side. The room is still cool and when I look at her door, nothing yet glows under the lavender frame.

I shake her, my hand clasped tight on her shoulders. She's fallen asleep reading again, a book about the ocean laying open on the bed next to her. She was reading about sea creatures called dolphins and a bright blue photo shows them leaping through the air above water.

"Wake up! We have to get out now, the house is on fire!"

My fingers dip deep into her shoulder as I rock her back and forth, but she doesn't stir. Annoyed, both with her and the pounding in my head, I shake harder. "We have to go!"

She still doesn't move and something cracks sharply in the walls and makes me jump from her bed, my hand knocking the book to the floor. Another crack, this one longer and more urgent, sends me back towards the her with tears in my eyes, my hands and legs shaking so badly I can barely stand.

"Lily?" I croak once more, my hand going to her face and jerking away once I feel the coldness on her skin.

"Lily!" Her name burns in my throat. With a desperate cry, I grab at her arms with shaking hands only to find them stiff and unmoving. I feel for a pulse on her wrist and find none.

I think I say her name one last time, muttered so quietly I don't even know if I said it aloud, or if it was only a passing thought. Another snapping and creaking sound comes from the door and the menacing sound reverberates in my chest as wood splinters and cracks around me.

What do I do now?

"Dani!" a voice screams from behind and a hand jerks my shoulder backwards. "What are you doing? You need to get out, move it!"

I whirl away to find Lacey now in the open doorway, an axe in her hands and curly hair a massive heap upon her head. The remains of the door lay littered around her feet.

"What are you doing here?"

"Move!" she yells again, but I struggle to focus on what she's saying over the terrible sound of popping flames and cracking wood all around.

When I don't move, she drops the axe to the floor and hauls me by the arm, her long nails digging into my skin. She pales when she sees Lily and spins me quickly away.

"I can't just leave her!" I scream.

"You have to save yourself," Lacey says harshly, pushing one of the duffle bags into my hands. "Grab your things and *run*."

"I don't know if I can leave," I tell her and can't help the tears that spill down my cheeks.

"But you have to," she says, resting her hand on my shoulder. Something in the house shudders as we both fight to stay upright. "You've gone down those stairs more times than you know and faced much worse than a simple fire, even if you don't remember any of it. You're more dangerous than simple flames and you're braver than you think."

When the shaking settles, Lacey throws me into the hallway ahead of her.

"What about you?"

"I've got some business to take care of first," she says, picking up the axe and smiling as she strides down the hall, the flames leaping tall around her. "You go on ahead and maybe look for some pants outside, I'll be right behind you."

When Lacey is gone, I reach into the duffle bag to ensure the journal is safe inside and then run back to Lily's still body. I pick up her ocean book and carefully place it closer to her so she will have something to read in whatever comes next.

Chapter Sixteen

The hallway glows with fire burning so brightly it hurts my eyes. Clutching the duffle bag close to protect it from the scattering embers, I race down the stairs. The effort combined with the smoke burns my lungs, and I'm struggling to breathe by the time I've made it to the kitchen. Sprinting out the back door, I gulp down fresh air.

"Dani!" Evan yells and races towards me.

And despite everything that has happened, I suddenly remember I'm not wearing anything from the waist down and shift my bag to the front for more coverage. The pettiness of it rubs raw at my heart.

"What are you doing here?" I ask.

He is unnaturally silent when he takes me in, his eyes flicking over my legs and arms, and when I turn to look up at him, I see the moon full and bright behind his head. It shines like a halo around his perfect face and illuminates his features like a fallen star, but for all his glimmer, he seems enraptured by my own. I take a step back.

"I'm sorry," he stammers. "I've never seen your glow in real moonlight. It's beautiful."

Something must be wrong with me because I have to fight my body from going to him, everything screaming inside to seek comfort so that I am not alone. But instead, I take another step back. And back again.

"Who are you, really?" I ask before I even know the question exists.

The world burns brightly as he stares with wide eyes into my soul and when he opens his mouth to speak, I can pick up a faint tremble despite the deafening sound of fire.

"Tobias Cloudspeak is my father, but trust me that it's in name only. He's always felt everyone in our family should be involved in the business, and thanks to my brother, I couldn't get out of it this time. I'm so sorry for my part in this and I've been working to get you, all of you, out. I had a role to play and I'm sorry for it. Just know that I..." He lifts a hand to me.

"That you what?" I spit back at him, slapping his hand away.

He swallows as he lowers his hands and looks at me with those green eyes that seem to stay impossibly emerald, even at night.

"That I can't let him get you," he says. "Get out of here while you still can and before he gets here."

"Before who gets here, your father?" The question shoots at him, dripping with the kind of deep fear that knots up your insides.

His mouth moves around "Yes" but his voice is drowned out as something towards the back of the house snaps and breaks. It's followed by the sound of screaming chickens filling the air. But for all the sounds pummeling my ears, the only thing I can really hear is the ragged beating of my heart.

Another light catches my attention, further off in the distance behind Evan. It glows brighter by the second. Evan turns to look, and even with the fire reflecting on his features, I can tell his face has gone pale at the car speeding up the driveway.

"You need to leave right now," he says. "Take your golf cart and get as far away from here as possible! We'll find you." He goes to grab my arm but I jerk away. A part of me wants nothing more than to stumble into his arms and cry. To cry for my home and everything familiar, to cry for losing my best friend, and to cry for myself. But I force myself to be brave.

"It's what we were planning on doing, anyway," I snap at him, swinging my bag around and marching through the garden, uncaring of what he may see of me.

I turn one last time toward what was once everything in my small life. Evan stands before it, dark and silhouetted against raging reds, oranges, and yellows. He is a single spot against a raging sun as he watches me go, standing still among the flames.

I run to the shed and power up the cart, and I don't look behind me as I back out and drive the short distance to the iron fence.

I'm still swiping at my face for the tears that threaten to come when I leap out and pull on the gate door's handle, but my feet grind into the ground and dust stirs around my ankles in particles that sparkle like floating diamonds when the gate doesn't budge. Sudden coldness grips the base of my neck and tightens into my spine and I feel how much my hands shake as they try to open the gate again and fail. I need the key.

I don't even have time to think. There is only just enough time for me to act, so I take slow and deep breaths when I turn back towards the house.

I hear Evan calling my name, screaming it, actually, yelling after me as I bolt into the house crowned with flames. I don't know what he says and only a small part even cares. His screams cut off as I enter the house again and I close the door in his stupid face.

The hair on the back of my neck stands on end as I speed down the hall towards Mother and Father's bedroom and the fire raging above makes the house groan. I don't have a lot of time before the whole place collapses. Besides, whatever or whoever is behind Lily's death could very well be just around the corner.

I open their door slowly, carefully running my fingers along the frame as I push it forward. Standing still, I close my eyes to help my ears pick up the slightest sounds of movement from within, but there is nothing.

I step inside and immediately freeze. Muscles burn with the signals my brain sends them, telling them to flee or turn to the side and vomit. As if there is anything left in my system.

The contradicting messages push and pull at my organs and a deep and painful lump forms in my chest. I blink a few times to see if I'm dreaming or if there is perhaps the smallest chance I could wake up from this nightmare.

But this isn't the case because in front of me, laying with her hands clasped around Cait's binder, is Mother. Her face is pale and her chest unmoving.

It's absurdly one of the few times I've seen Mother not wearing the starling brooch. It's carefully placed atop the empty pillow beside her. Something overtakes me and I snatch it up, pinning it carefully onto my shirt for protection.

There is an angry shift in the house and I know my time is limited, so I run around the bed and grab the gate key. The gravity of the situation makes it feel heavier than normal when I clutch it close to my heart.

Just before I close the door behind me, I take one last look at Mother and find her almost smiling, and then stuff the key into my bra because I'm not wearing anything with pockets. It takes all my effort to concentrate on placing one foot in front of the other as I run back toward the kitchen, but somehow, I manage to keep moving forward.

My head swims as the reality of the situation blossoms in my heart and I'm so absorbed in my addled thoughts that I don't notice Father standing beside the kitchen table until it's too late.

"Where do you think you're going?" he asks, his eyes burning brighter than any fire.

Oh, friscuit.

"In case you haven't noticed, the house is on fire," I reply.

Father regards me with dark and narrowed eyes, his broad form blocking any chance of escape. There are singe marks across his face, and it looks like his fingers are torn and bleeding. Flecks of dried blood streak down his lab coat.

"You're not going anywhere." He slurs at me, taking a long drink from a dark glass bottle and uttering a wild sounding laugh. "Unless you want to tour around and admire Martha's charming work?"

My head spins as the image of Mother's still and empty face fills my mind. I have to force myself to keep my eyes open and on Father as he folds his arms over his chest and glares at me.

"Mother did this? It feels like this has your name written all over it."

Father throws the thick bottle and it shatters on the ground into a hundred amber shards.

"I won't take credit for her sedition. She did more than just this," he growls, running a large hand over his face and depositing flecks of blood along his jawline. "We were so close, in fact, I'd even say we were successful. We just needed a little more time and a few more girls."

"You sound insane," I say and he chuckles lowly.

"I'm not the one who drugged you unknowingly all these years with toothpaste, hiding behind lies and smiles and hugs, and then set you on fire to stop your 'suffering.' But I would have been upfront about it, told you what you were as soon as you could walk and talk and been done with it. Martha was the one who insisted on the 'normal family life,' bah! Thought it would be good for me to have some daughters again to help focus."

He's moved now, standing so close I can smell his foul breath and see the utter loathing in his eyes.

"Don't you dare give me that look. You look just like your foolish mother," he snarls, producing another bottle from the cupboard and draining half of it in an instant. "I should never have let Martha talk me into purchasing you from her."

"What does my mother have anything to do with it? Did you know her?"

He scoffs. "Everyone knew Scarlet, she was the star of her show just like you're the star of mine. But it's not like you would know that, we made sure you wouldn't remember a thing. You're nothing more than the product of my life's work, my ticket to immortality and fame and a better world. I must admit, though, I'm disappointed that after all this—" He pauses to work his wedding ring off and throw it across the room. "That after all this, *you're* the one who managed to escape. I would have preferred it had been Lillian, or maybe even that lunatic, Primrose. They were much easier to manage, but I guess I'll make do with you."

"Don't you dare say their names!" I scream. "Is this all we were to you? Just some experiments?"

"It's all you were to your families. They freely sold you. Bought and purchased. I have the receipts, if you'd like to see." He sneers and takes another drink from the bottle. "So don't be so small minded about this, Dani. Stop pretending that everything revolves around you. It's much bigger than that and you're going to help me bring my findings to the world. You might not have been my first pick, but at least your blood burns with all the real possibilities this experiment has to offer." He chugs the rest of his drink and slams it on the table. "So you're coming with me."

Faster than I thought he could move, he lunges for me, fingers digging painfully into my upper arm. I try to wrench away from his grasp and only succeed in flailing about, so I scream in his face, "I didn't consent to any of this, *none* of us did, and I will not give you my blood or my life just so you can eat cows again!"

His skin goes molten and he strikes me hard across my cheek after letting me go. Tears fill my eyes until I can barely see and I'm wiping at my face when I hear the front door slam open.

"Yoo-hoo!" A deep voice echoes through the house. "Leonard! Come show your slimy face and stop hiding like a coward!"

Father's face falls, his rage replaced by fear. Too quickly to resist, he grabs my shoulder and shoves me roughly under the kitchen table, wedging a chair against the side to help conceal my form. I don't have any time to slip out before the kitchen door slams open and a pair of polished shoes stomp into the room.

"Good evening," Father says, his voice surprisingly low and neutral.

"Time for your performance review," Tobias growls and stalks towards the table. "Can you tell me what is going on here, hmm? Can you explain to me why my investments are dead and on fire?" Father stays motionless and silent, but I can hear his heavy breathing as Tobias comes forward, their faces inches apart. "And where the *hell* is Martha?"

"Dead," Father answers simply, moving to the other side of the table to face him and I find myself trapped between them.

"Dead?" Tobias shrieks and I can see his fingers curl from my vantage point under the table. For a second, I'm afraid he'll throw the whole thing aside and see me, and I have to cover my mouth to muffle the scream that almost escapes.

"She started out so promising," Father says, "and that drive to cure this forsaken, poisoned earth was just the perfect kind of dedication I needed to move this project forward. Too bad she got so involved with the subjects." He laughs, humorless. "It really seems to have been her downfall."

Tobias blows out a stream of air through his nostrils and drops his hands flat to the table with a *thud*. Each word he mutters is coated with malice. "Where is she?"

"I left her where I found her in the bedroom," Father says. I can hear the creaking of the counter as he leans casually against it.

"How could you—"

"She did this to herself," Father interrupts, and the simplicity in his voice is frightening. "Killed all the subjects with her toothpaste idea, I bet. They were already weakened from the sleeping drugs we gave them after dinner, so all she had to do was overdose them with a little more. Everything was ready to pack up and move them to your facilities, but she finished them off before we could touch them, then destroyed our archives and took herself out of the equation. We lose, she wins."

I understand the words he says, but they refuse to sink in, even as all I can think of is the warning etched into the window frame in Tara's room.

"I never lose, Leonard," Tobias says, rounding the table toward Father. "I thought you might remember that by now." His words are punctuated with an earsplitting *BANG* so loud it makes my ears ring. It's the kind of sound that is so sharp you barely have time to register that it happened at all save for the ringing silence that fills your head.

Father's body crumples to the floor, his face turned away as blood starts to pool under him. I have to clasp my hands even tighter around my mouth to keep the overwhelming fear from escaping, but luckily Tobias leaves as quickly as he had barged in. I can barely hear him calling out orders to someone, but can't make out what he says over the fading ringing in my ears and my own shattered breathing.

Suddenly a hand reaches under the table and grabs my shoulder, and only then does the scream escape—right before another familiar hand covers my mouth.

"He's busy ransacking Leonard's research. If you don't go now, there won't be another chance."

Evan all but drags my unresponsive body outside. My feet stumble uselessly under me, so he finally gives up and picks me up and carries me like a child. There are no words as I feel him setting me down next to the gate. The smell of nature mixes with the overwhelming smell of burning wood and brings fresh bile to my throat.

"Did you get the key?" he asks.

My nod brings a fresh wave of sickness to my stomach. Scratching at my chest, I pull out the little key. It feels unfamiliar and heavy in my hands as I turn towards the gate and unlock it.

"Good, now go!" he commands and I look up to see him running back towards the house. I don't have enough energy to wonder why he's running back in there. I don't even have enough energy to care about it. The only thing I can do is force my body back into the golf cart and drive recklessly through the trees towards the highway.

Once I make it past the low fence, I see headlights shining in the distance, just close enough to outline an entourage of vehicles headed my way. Maybe they're just fire trucks or concerned citizens, alarmed at the billowing smoke behind me. But a nagging feeling in my gut says not to take any chances, so I cross the highway to the wilds waiting on the other side and drive blindly forward into the vastness beyond.

The rough terrain is unwelcoming to the golf cart's tires and the jostling it brings makes my teeth rattle, but the headlights grow dim and distant in my wake. I don't stop moving, convinced I may now run into something, or worse, *off* something because the wilds are unrecognizable this close. I'm far too used to watching it from the safety of the upstairs windows. Brush sweeps sideways in the wind, rippling like bathtub water. But the rabbits that dash madly out of way are not the kind I recognize from our gardens, and the shrubs and gnarled trees along my path twist in unfamiliar ways. I know it all and yet I don't.

I think I hear Lily's voice in my head telling me to keep going, so I don't stop until the sun has crept well above the horizon and the brightness of the new day begins to sting my tired eyes. Then, when it finally becomes impossible to see clearly, I force myself to slow the cart and come to a stop beside an overgrown and ancient Joshua tree, twisted and bristled.

"Everything and everyone is gone," Lily's voice echoes inside my mind. I know she's right, but I feel too numb to mourn right now. Fatigue soon overtakes my body and mind, and even though it's too warm and the cart seats are hard against my aching limbs, I rest my head on top of my bag and welcome a dreamless rest.

Chapter Seventeen

My eyes are crusted shut when I finally return to the waking world. Rubbing at them only seems to make it worse, but I manage to grope blindly into the duffle bag beneath my head and find a bottle of water to rinse them.

At first, I splash water haphazardly onto my face and the coolness is so refreshing it makes me sigh. Then I realize this water needs to last until I find more and quickly move to just sipping it with more restraint. Still, I feel much better—psychically, at least.

Afterwards, despite the protest in my arms and legs, I make myself get out of the cart and do a few stretches, but the simple movements make me double over from a coughing fit as I spit ashy lumps. I also rub my temples at a headache that just won't leave me alone.

Standing still to ease my breathing and the beating in my head, I turn west to find the sun is well on its way below the horizon. I must have slept nearly the entire day. Still, it appears no one has followed; all I see around me are gently sloping brown hills with scrubby bushes dotting their bases, not another person or animal in sight. I turn back only once to find a cone of black smoke rising high into the sky. I can't help but wonder how long home will burn.

"*But it isn't home anymore,*" I hear Lily remind me.

I check the cart's power cells and determine I can still go a little further today, then notice a grouping of wild strawberry plants brimming with mostly ripe berries. I pause and wonder if maybe I had something to do with their growth, then make sure to collect a few handfuls before powering up the cart and making my way deeper into the wilds.

Swirling in high and lazy circles above, I can barely make out condors roaming the skies as I continue bumping along the rocky ground, dodging fallen trees, hundreds of little bushes, the skeleton of some unknown animal. I feel like I could go longer, drive further away from the thoughts and feelings that threaten to overtake my mind, but the golf cart's power cells are fading fast and I won't be able to go much further until I can recharge them.

"Friscuit," I mutter to no one but myself, frustrated that I hadn't thought to charge them during my nap. Now it will take longer to charge by the moonlight.

Luckily, if there is even such a thing as luck for me anymore, I spot a cluster of oak trees not far away and make my way towards them, hoping the old cart will make it that far.

It doesn't, and I have to push it the last fifty or so feet. I'm out of breath when I finally stop under the largest center tree that points straight up to the incoming stars above.

The dirt swirls around my ankles as I round the cart to look through my bag to find something to eat, but something looks wrong when I open it, and I realize with a sadness that sinks deep into my bones that Lacey handed me Lily's bag. It takes every ounce of strength I have to force myself to take slow, shaking breaths as I sort through everything I have left of my best friend.

Tears well in my eyes and make it hard to see as I push aside the clothing that I already know will not fit my frame and find the bag of chicken jerky. The rest of the food, the cereal and apples, had been stored in mine.

Tucked within the folds of her favorite skirt, I find the journal. It might be the most valuable thing in my possession now—well, besides my own blood. I move to the side of the cart and stuff the journal, still wrapped in the skirt, into the secret compartment beneath the seat.

I can't bear to look for anything else inside, but I manage to summon just enough courage to find a button down top. The green and black plaid looks much more festive than I think I could ever feel again, but since I know nothing else in there would fit me, I tie it around my waist for some coverage, taking care to move slowly when I find the skin of my exposed legs raw and sunburnt. The weather had been kind to me today and the sun had felt good, but one thigh is the color of a ripe tomato.

I then tuck the gate key deep inside the duffle bag and ensure Mother's brooch is pinned securely on my shirt. The bird's cool crystal eyes seem to calm me, even if only by a little, and I want to keep it close.

Taking a big handful of jerky, I lay the bag on the seat next to me and stare at the roof of the little cart as I take small bites. The strawberries I picked earlier help round out the meal, but they settle oddly in my stomach and I find myself daydreaming of frosted cookies, sandwiches piled high with roasted vegetables, basically anything covered in cheese, and cold lemonade.

When my mind wanders to pancakes, the tears return. It wasn't that long ago that I was eating pancakes with the girls and looking at Cait's binder of memories. It crosses my mind that I should have taken the binder with me, if only to help my bad memory to never forget my friends, but thinking of prying it out of Mother's cold hands is unsettling. No, maybe it was better to leave it behind.

But what if I forget them? What if someone out here drugs me, again, and causes me to forget them all? I squeeze my eyes shut at the thought and find them full of tears when I open them. It hurts to be awake, so I let myself fall into another dreamless void.

The rhythmic sound of rain wakes me and I open my tired eyes to the blackness of night and the warm breath of an animal nudging its nose against my hair. It takes a moment for my surroundings to coordinate with my thoughts, and for a time I just stare ahead of me at the moving shapes surrounding my golf cart. Then, when the snuffling against my ear becomes quiet, I rise up and look around.

The moon creeps out from behind scattered rain clouds, full and bright above the trees and the dappled and shifting light on the ground makes it hard to see the creatures milling about. But one—perhaps the one that had nudged at my hair—ventures closer and peers at me with curious brown eyes, its breath foggy in the light mist of rain. It's a female deer and it nudges me with its velvety brown nose again. It's only then that I realize I'm glowing as bright as the moon. When I raise my gaze back to the doe, I'm suddenly reminded of the cow picture I saw with Lily and despite everything, I give it a small smile.

Although the other deer don't approach me, they remain close by, as if they are moths and I a light they can't resist. It's strangely calming to be surrounded by them—to not be alone—but the tranquility is shattered when a terrible sound rips through the air. It's a deep, commanding howl and it makes the deer take off into the night, leaving me alone once again.

I wish I could follow them.

The howls turn to growls and snarls and I leap out of the cart, a cold sweat breaking on my skin and dripping down my back as I lean up against the oak tree. The noises are coming closer and I catch the owner of one silhouetted against the bright sky: a massive desert wolf, maybe the leader of his pack, and he's looking directly at me.

Without thinking, I scramble on top of the golf cart. There are some low hanging branches just above and I barely have time to lay my hands on one when the wolves break into the small cluster of trees and begin circling the cart.

My voice finally finds itself and I let out a scream that makes the lead wolf cock his head to one side as he regards me with regal eyes. I scramble up the tree's side, the hard bark cutting deep into my sunburned skin, making me cry out. The rest of the pack pays me little attention as they begin nosing around the golf cart below me.

I find a branch big enough to straddle and look down in horror as one wolf finds the bag of chicken jerky and tears into it, its massive paws also knocking my storage of strawberries onto the ground to grind them into the dirt.

"Stop it!" I find myself yelling, but only the pack leader looks up at me. He shakes himself, the dirt of the wilds flying from his coat and returning to the earth, and sits down to wait patiently for his pack to finish off what little food I had with me.

Sleep pulls at my mind, but I know better than to fall asleep in a tree and risk falling from it, so I force myself to stay awake. Occasionally I scream at the wolves, but all they do is nip at each other and search for scraps of jerky in the dirt.

One of the wolves ushers in a group of pups who chase each other in circles around the tree's base until the lead wolf trots over and bites at their heels to get them in line.

"Don't you have better things to do?" I ask the wolf and, as if in answer, he lets out a long, baying howl that has the rest of them howling in return. I have to cover my ears at the noise, but to my relief, the howl seems to be a rallying call and they all abandon the golf cart to lope away from the trees and back into the wilds.

I watch carefully until I can't see them anymore. And yet, even when they're out of sight, I don't dare descend and stay glued to the tree with tight and tired muscles. The clouds regroup and rage in the night sky, but even through a downpour of warm summer rain, I keep to my perch as if I, too, were some wild animal.

When it's been quiet for some time and well after I hear the wolves howling again in the far, far-off distance, I gingerly make my way down the tree. I do my best to keep my burned and raw skin away from the rough bark, but it's difficult and I'm swearing up a storm of bad gravy by the time I make it to the ground.

A heavy weight settles on my shoulders when I search through my ransacked belongings and find all my food eaten or destroyed. At least they left my remaining water untouched, however little I had to begin with. Then in a panicked move, I check under the seat and feel a sense of relief wash over like the steam from newly cooked pasta noodles when I see find the journal safe and untouched.

I decide it's too risky to stay here so, to a distant hum of wolf song, I get in the cart and power up even though I know the solars did not have nearly enough time to charge. But even though I press both feet on the pedals, the cart will not budge from its spot under the oak tree.

I get out and prod at the wheels with my foot only to find them sunk deep into mud. I throw my shoulders at the sides and even try digging out the mud from around each wheel, but the ground is too soft and the cart too heavy.

I drop heavily into the seat and put my head down on the steering wheel, cradling my face, and finally let the tears take over.

When that ceases to feel like enough, I throw back my head and scream at the clouds and moon, then immediately cover my mouth and hope the wolves didn't hear. It still can't stop my sobs. My chest heaves with them and my ribs feel like they'll crack wide open with each shattered breath.

I cry until I have no more tears and it's just quiet shaking that makes my head pound and my throat parched. Then my body goes still and my limbs go numb from exhaustion, mental and physical. I lay my head on the steering wheel and let the numbness take over, as if I were Lily and dead to the world.

The next day is warm. Really warm. As soon as I open my swollen eyes, I find the sun already beating down on my battered skin and my cuts and scrapes feel like they sizzle in the direct sunlight. I don't want to leave the shaded cluster of trees, but I know I need to get out of here. If not to put more distance between myself and the smoke still curling lazily in the sky behind me, then because the desert wolves could return at any time. I'd probably be an easier kill than the deer.

The golf cart starts up fine, but still won't budge from its spot and the little engine groans with the effort I put into trying to make it move. I get out to inspect the wheels again, but find the once sticky mud has dried around them like hard clay, encasing each one within the earth. This thing isn't going anywhere.

"Friscuit!" I should so loud that the few birds in the trees above scream and take to the air. I have to go on by foot, there isn't any other way. I need to keep putting distance between myself and Tobias Cloudspeak. For all I know, he'll inspect the burnt remains of the house for bodies and discover one is missing.

I shove my hands through Lily's bag looking for the sunblock, but don't find it and a string of curses leaves my mouth again. Of course, we stored it in my own bag back at home, because one thing going right would be too helpful. Lily had told me once that mud could be used to slather on your skin instead—creatures called elephants used to use it—but the sun has already baked the ground hard and I refuse to waste my water to create some.

So, I wrap another of Lily's shirts around my waist and another over my shoulders like a shawl, covering every inch of skin possible, even though it leaves me a sweating mess beneath. I stuff the journal and gate key in Lily's bag and sling it over my shoulder. With one final pat of the golf cart's roof, I turn my back and walk away.

For hours, I do nothing but force myself to put one foot in front of the other and keep walking. At some point my stomach begins to growl, so I figure it must be well past lunchtime. But there is nothing to eat; the wolves had made sure of that.

I'm not used to skipping meals. Mother and Father always made sure our pantries were well-stocked, and we always had access to food. Looking back, though, I wonder if that was something they had to do for our "health." For the amount of blood they took from us, maybe they had to keep us well fed or we'd simply waste away, drained of every ounce of what makes someone alive in the first place.

Or, an even worse thought, what if some of that food was laced with the memory-altering drugs? What if it wasn't just the food, but the purified air pumped into our rooms, the bath water, or even the chicken feed?

Thinking about it won't help, so I try my best to push all thoughts of poisoned household items aside. All the same, I make a promise to myself to be careful of anything, especially food or toothpaste, presented to me in the future.

There is a nearly dead strawberry plant that I stumble upon in the evening and as I hover over its brown, crispy leaves, I consider opening one of my many leg wounds and smearing it with blood to make it grow. Even though Evan made sure I forgot the actual process, I know enough from seeing my drawings—from hearing Father's ravings that last night in the kitchen—that my blood might be able to revitalize the plant and create a few berries. I look from my legs, to the plant, and back, weighing the pros and cons. In the end, I decide against it. It might answer some questions, might at least take the edge of my hunger, but I don't even know if I could make the cut stop bleeding or if the smell might bring the wolves back. There will be time for my own experimentation later; right now, I can't risk any infections from trying to pry more blood from my already aching body. Maybe if I become desperate, I might consider it then.

There is a light in the distance that becomes brighter as I walk towards the setting sun. I put my hope in that it's a small town, tucked within the wilds and full of people who will help me, or who can at least spare a cup of water. But as the light and I approach each other, I get the feeling that it's something more, something far greater, that travels quickly through the wilds.

My head feels like it's in the clouds, maybe from not eating anything today, or maybe because my water has run out, or maybe from the heavy weight of the sun, and my skull continues to pound with my ever-constant headache. It only gets worse as the sun continues its descent and the bright light gets closer and closer, blindingly so. And yet, after everything I've dealt with since the only home I'd known went up in flames, it's hard to summon any fear.

The light's source hurtles towards me and brings with it a low rumbling sound making the little rocks by my feet dance. It moves quicker now that it's almost upon me, approaching so swiftly that I only have enough time to shield my eyes. When I throw my arm in front of my face, I lose my balance and fall unceremoniously to the ground, arms and legs trembling from exhaustion as much as fright. Only then do I realize it truly is a dragon, just as Tara always said, and the blinding light must be the fire it breathes.

"Please don't eat me," I whisper urgently and it responds with a low whistle as the light slows to a stop mere yards away.

My arms drop and I open my eyes. As they adjust to the blinding light, I can make out a tall figure silhouetted before me.

But it is not a dragon and the light is not its fire.

It's nothing but a giant land train, a bright and brilliant light shining from its core. Standing in front of this light is the tallest person I've ever seen. Her hair is the color of the crayons Tara and Cait used to play with, drawing on any surface they came across, and is a fiery combination of purples, red, oranges, and pinks that halo a face of smooth, dark skin. I'm conflicted for a moment, because I don't know which is scarier—speaking to this total stranger who has stumbled randomly across me in the wilds, or the desert wolves I know must be waiting for me somewhere in the distance.

Then, as if she teleported, she's suddenly standing before me, chin held high and tilted to the right, eyes the color of two full moons wide with fascination. Her voice is energizing, dramatic, and something I feel would be more at home on a stage and not commanding the empty wilds. She looks me over twice and asks, "What on earth happened to you?"

Instead of answering, I crumple to the ground and fight the urge to pass out.

Chapter Eighteen

T he woman who stands before me is the tallest person I have ever seen. A navy waistcoat tucks neatly around her slender, leanly-muscled frame and wide dark pants cover her legs. There is a brooch pinned to her chest that looks like it could be gold, but without light is nothing but a dull brown bird in flight.

"Everything okay, Magenta?" The question comes from the bright lights beyond and I shrink back, realizing I don't know how many people could be lingering nearby. I wrap my arms around my waist and look to the ground.

"Yes," she says. "We nearly ran this little rabbit over. Come on, Charlie, have a look for yourself."

The shortest person I've ever seen in my life saunters over to us, maybe about half my height. I can't make out his face, but he holds his head high and shines a flashlight straight into mine. My eyes water from the brightness but I'm glad for the light concealing my glow.

"You don't find these in the wilds every day. Well, I guess you do, but not alone and not at night," the short man says. "And most of them have pants. What's your take on it, Mag?"

Magenta blinks her yellow-colored eyes a few times and stands to full height. I crane my neck and lose my balance, falling further backwards and digging my palms into the earth to keep from lying flat on my back. I don't have the strength to right myself.

A long arm reaches down and an open hand with fingernails painted a deep blue appears in front of my face, but I don't take it.

"Troubled little rabbit," Magenta purrs, pulling the hand away. She looks down at Charlie, who peers at me from between her legs. "Bring Jack out here and get a blanket."

"Right, boss," he says, scooting quickly away.

I'm still looking at Magenta's face when her hand suddenly tucks a stray lock of hair behind my ear. Her eyes glitter when she peers at my brooch and I shy away when she speaks again.

"Look at that skin, hmm...Someone is sure is to be missing you. But who? There isn't anything for miles and miles and miles."

"There's no one left to miss me," I whisper, which isn't entirely true, but I keep my mouth shut for the rest. She waits, expecting more, and sighs dramatically when I stay silent.

"We miss the dead when they are gone, little rabbit, so who is to say they do not miss us in return?"

I feel my eyes betray me when fresh tears sting my lashes.

"Ah, the first puzzle piece," Magenta sings softly.

"Mags?" a deeper voice calls from the bright lights and I look towards the newcomer coming our way.

The blood clenches in my heart when he steps from behind Magenta and I fully see the way his brown hair flops over his head, the broadness of his shoulders, and eyes the color of forests.

He looks almost exactly like Evan, but it's not him. He's not quite as tall, he's younger, and there is a leanness to his frame with a face touched by working in the sun. A red scarf around his neck flutters in the nighttime air as he looks down at me.

"Ah, Jack," Magenta coos, her eyes lingering on Mother's brooch as she takes the blanket from him and tucks it around my shoulders. "We near tore this rabbit in two by running her over. Thank the Heavenly Starlings Jordan saw her on the radar in time or she'd been truly sliced clean through the middle."

Jack continues staring, regarding my bare legs and rising to meet my eyes. The urge to vomit comes suddenly upon me and I turn from him and heave onto the packed dirt beside me.

Unfortunately, I have nothing left to lose and my stomach pinches painfully with each convulsion. Between choking breaths, my mind has little time to process why this man looks like Evan or why I'm still alive.

Almost as if she can read my mind, Magenta stands on tip-toes and turns her attention towards the wilds. "Do you see that? Fingers of smoke in the distance?" she asks and Charlie, who has returned to stand beside her, cranes his neck to look. Jack looks as well.

"Jordan did say she spotted a fire somewhere east of here. Could be a standard fire in the wilds, but looked fairly localized," Charlie says, taking a moment to spit off to the side.

"That doesn't look like a typical wilds fire," Jack argues, coming to stand on Magenta's other side. "But I bet our rabbit knows something about it."

"Nope," I croak.

"Hmm," Magenta purrs again. "We'll ask again later, but in any case, we were behind before and more behind now. Jack, take her inside somewhere and tell Jordan we go in five. Charlie, you're with me. I need to look into something."

And with that Magenta charges off towards the lights with Charlie racing after her. Jack and I are the only ones left as somewhere behind me a desert wolf, probably the pack leader, wails shrilly and is answered by several more wolves.

He extends his hand towards me, but keeps his face neutral.

"I can assure you that we're the best of your current options. Unless you want to stay here for breakfast. The wildlife will no doubt be very welcoming."

The desert wolves shriek in reply and I consider the person before me.

"You look so familiar," I say, the words shooting suddenly out, and he pulls his hand back, his expressionless face now frowning. I stand on my own and notice again his resemblance to Evan. Shuddering at the familiarity, I look behind me. There is a barely noticeable cone of smoke in the darkening distance, shifting slightly in the wind so it bends and sways as it makes its way towards the evening clouds. Ash that was once my entire existence rises with it towards the sky in shades of pale gray. This remaining smoke is the last of Lily and all the girls as they rise up into the great beyond.

"Goodbye," I whisper, and finally turn my back to the smoky plumes of home.

Jack rubs the back of his neck in a very Evan like way and points ahead of him while walking forward. "Come on, little rabbit," he calls. "Time you got your first look at Magenta's Magical World of Circus Curiosities. We've been—"

But I cease to hear him as he goes on. In fact, I don't hear anything except Lily's voice speaking softly about things I can't understand. Something in me snaps from the pressure, bending to the breaking point, white and gold sparks dancing across my vision. And suddenly all I see are stars that are either above me or just in my head, and all I feel is the cool ground against my cheek.

"*Wake up*," Lily's voice whispers softly and something falls from above and smashes onto my nose.

"Friscuit!" I yelp and I sit upright to claw at my face to see what it was, only to find a bundle of note cards, yellowed with time. I push them to the side and rub my knuckles into my eye sockets, willing the grittiness to ease.

The ceiling above is a dazzling display of tiny white and yellow dots. They twine with green and blue swirls and form a repeating and soothing pattern that looks indented into the background. The small room sways slightly and a loose curtain to the side exposes the ground racing far below outside. I must be inside the belly of the dragon.

I rise and find my back aching painfully. How long have I been sleeping? It feels like forever ago that I was in the kitchen with Lily but only minutes since I found her lifeless body.

I next find a large bottle of water that I drink from greedily until I think better of it and pause to inspect it closely. But finding nothing abnormal about the container or the crystal-clear liquid inside, I continue to sip it slowly while looking about the room.

A thick layer of dust covers everything, and it's such a stark difference to the sterile environment I grew up in that my hands recoil whenever I touch something. Someone hasn't been here in a long time, but at least the covers on the bed seem new, even if the headboard has seen better days. The bed is low to ground, but I can still shift my body to sit upon the edge. My knees bend awkwardly against my chest.

I let the room sway and tilt until I can no longer keep my focus on the groaning walls or the sound of air rushing by. The emotions take over and, securing my hands around my body, the tears become a violent torrent that leave me empty and dry inside. I roll onto the floor and stare up at the ceiling until a new sound breaks the dusty air.

Someone knocks at the door, but I can't bring myself to answer it. Whoever it is starts to murmurs in soft tones, but I can't make out what they're saying until the door creaks open.

"Hello?" squeaks a young boyish voice, but I ignore him and stare at the bed.

"I brought you some cake. It's the only thing the cooks had left." The voice laughs in a stuttered and clipped way. "It's well past dinner, you slept the whole day and, well, you know how it is. I'm Parker, by the way."

When he makes no attempt to leave, I turn my head and find a slender boy, maybe only a few years younger than me, with brown hair cut close to his scalp and a familiar red scarf around his neck. He shuffles his feet, and after I don't respond, sets the cake on a stack of boxes before hastily departing, closing the door quickly behind him.

Pushing up and sitting with my back to the bed, I stare at the cake and it stares back at me, pink frosting and all. The ache in my heart has crept into my stomach and the pains of not eating are catching up, but can I trust it?

I'm suddenly so hungry that I decide to take my chances. I feel like I could eat every chicken in the coop and it makes me wonder if the chickens back home escaped their fate and are running free in the wilds, eating worms and dodging the desert wolves.

The way to freedom for them seems easy, just escape and survive. If they can do it, then surely, I can. I've already escaped a mad scientist and a house burning down, so at very least, I can eat a piece of cake without thinking too much on it.

Forcing myself to rise, my muscles ache as I work to feel the blood running through them again. I touch my toes, I twist and turn and do all manner of stretching exercises I remember learning with Lily, and once I'm satisfied and mobile, I make my way to the cake.

It sits on a small white plate and glistens in the light streaming from another window. There is a black emblem along the plate's edge that looks like a series of Ws and Ms and I can only guess it has something to do with Magenta's something or other.

I also find that Parker hasn't brought me a fork, but it doesn't matter much as I stick a finger into the frosting and tentatively try it. When there's no strange chemical taste and nothing happens, and I both stay conscious and can remember why I'm here, I stuff handfuls of it straight into my mouth. It's the sweetest, most wonderful taste in the whole world, but only dulls the pain a small amount.

Licking my fingers, I stumble back to bed and see someone has propped my duffle bag against the wall. Tears threaten to come again as I search through the meager belongings, dreading I may find something that reminds me too much of Lily.

Taking a deep breath and knowing I can't very well continue another day wearing just underwear with a few shirts tied around my waist, I find a skirt that I'm relieved to see fits my waist, even if I have to roll the top a few times to keep it from dragging on the ground.

The gate key and attached keychains fall from the bag when I shove it away, so I set them aside on a small shelf above the bed and prop the journal beside them.

I next find a small bowl of warm water behind a curtain with a clean towel which I use to scrub my face raw. Then I find myself scrubbing my neck, my arms, my fingernails, any place I can reach. As if I could clean away the fiery memories of flame and ash swimming beneath my skin.

With my flesh tingling and pink, I turn my efforts towards the cluttered room, stacking whatever I can lay my lands on and drinking from the bottle of water. Determined to keep busy, I then use the damp towels to wipe up the thick layers of grime. All the while, the outside terrain zips by in a hypnotic, soothing rhythm.

I'm finally nearing the end of my cleansing spree when I come to the stack of cards that woke me. Picking them up, I realize they are not cards at all, but old printed photographs, bundled tightly with a pink ribbon.

Having run out of things to clean, I sit down and untie the ribbon, letting it drift to the ground. The photos contain the stuff of Lily's dreams: animals I don't recognize, tall buildings reaching to the sky, long stretching oceans. I see amazing costumes with feathery plumed hats and one outfit made entering of little straps, leaving nothing to the imagination.

But it's the last photo that stuns me, both freezing my hands and coating them in sweat at the same time. One person in the photo is clearly Magenta; even after seeing her once, I could recognize that hair on anyone, but the other...

The women beside her barely comes up to Magenta's shoulders and she wears a red and sparkling suit. I check the back and find "Magenta and Scarlet," but nothing else to indicate who Scarlet may be. I flip it back over and examine the small woman. Her middle protrudes violently and looks as if it could be the most uncomfortable pregnancy in the world, but her smile only says she is happy. One hand rests causally on her belly, close to her heart, and above it sparkles a glittering brooch of a bird in flight.

The familiarity of the bird adornment and her name bring a fresh wave of confusion. Frowning deeply, I pluck the photo from the stack and remove Mother's nesting bird from my shirt. The flying bird in the photo is hard to make out in detail, but it looks startlingly like the one in my hand, as well as the one I saw pinned on Magenta's coat. Something tells me it isn't a coincidence. I decide to ask her about them later and tuck the pin deep into Lily's bag.

I then let out a heavy breath and curl up on the bed, holding my knees to my chest, and fall asleep almost as soon as I close my eyes.

I dream of wolves chasing me for hours through an endless desert, and whenever I look back at them, they disappear in the purple haze of Magenta's hair. The stars come out and once again spell my name in the sky, but this time they turn into golden birds and fly away into an oncoming dark and dreamless sleep.

Chapter Nineteen

I wake to the empty room and relieve myself in the small toilet I find behind another curtain and use the rest of last night's water to clean up.

The swaying motion of the train has left a mild state of discomfort in my stomach, and combined with only eating cake and some crumbs of chicken jerky, I'm left craving something more substantial.

I wait around a little bit, but it soon becomes apparent that no one plans to check on me or bring me something to eat, so I take it upon myself to venture outside of the now pristine cabin. Gripping my empty cake plate because I don't know what else to do with it, I take several deep breaths and crack the door open.

Stretching before me is an impossibly long hallway covered in a deep burgundy interior that feels more like plastic than wood when I run my fingers along its slick surface. It opens wide in either direction, filled with other cabins, each embedded with golden numbers above rounded doorways. I turn towards my own door arch and see the number sixty-seven gleaming softly from the pale light glowing in the panels above.

Still clutching the plate, I'm just closing the door when a trio of high-pitched voices descend upon me and I spin so quickly towards them that I almost drop the plate.

"It's the rabbit!"

"She doesn't look like a rabbit, though?"

"You're right, I thought maybe…"

"That's silly, you've been reading that comic again, haven't you?"

"It's not a comic, it's *facts*. The world is wild!"

"It's a comic."

"Well, there are comics in it."

"Why don't you ask the rabbit?"

Three girls bound up to me, looking like they couldn't be more than twelve or thirteen, and if I thought Tara and Cait looked similar, these three are exact duplicates of each other, from their faces to matching dresses. I only know I'm not seeing things when I notice each wears a different pair of colored shoes.

"Jack said they found you in the desert. Was it hot out there?" Green Shoes asks.

"Really? That's what you're going to ask her?" says Purple Shoes.

"Maybe you should ask how it felt to be carried like a baby by Jack?" Yellow Shoes sighs dramatically. "We all know he's as hot as the vent stacks!"

The three of them burst into giggles until Green Shoes falls over clutching her sides. I want to laugh with them, but nothing comes out. All I can muster is a slight smile as I ask, "Do you know where I can find Jack, or maybe Magenta?"

"Jack's busy with the cow," Purple Shoes says and grabs my free hand.

"He asked us to bring you. We checked earlier, but you were sleeping." Yellow Shoes joins in and takes the plate from my hands. Green Shoes takes my other hand and grins.

"We'll take you to get some food, Daniella! And then to Jack!"

"How do you know my name?" I ask, trying to pull my hands away, but their grips are surprisingly tight for their small size.

"Someone put it up on your door already." Yellow Shoes points and I follow the direction to where someone has already tacked on a small chalk board plate with my name printed neatly in the center.

A little bead of sweat drips down my spine. I can't remember telling anyone my name. "You can call me Dani."

"Let's get some cookies, Dani. I'm starving!" Yellow Shoes starts to drag us down the hall and I'm forced to follow.

"People in The Dusting were starving. You are certainly not," Green Shoes snaps.

"I guess you're right. Are you hungry, Dani?"

"Very, uh, what was your name?"

They burst into giggles again.

"We'll tell you," Green Shoes says.

"But you probably won't remember," Yellow Shoes continues.

"It gets terribly confusing and most people don't even try," Purple Shoes sighs and the others giggle.

I follow them along the hallway, passing by other cabins. We move too quick to read any of their names, but the sister in green shoes, Mindy, says they're mostly empty in this part of the train and the names have no meaning any more. Bindy, wearing the yellow shoes, explains that Magenta's Magical World of Circus Curiosities hasn't been the same in some time.

Cindy in the purple shoes mentions they don't have many main attractions anymore. Except the cow she makes sure to point out. An actual live cow that people can touch and pet for ten dollars. According to Mindy, though, having a cow isn't enough to pay all the bills.

They tell me they're triplets, born into the circus life. They enthusiastically point out that their parents are retired, fat, and happy, but it's nice they're off the land train because they took over their former spacious cabin on the floor above.

"Plenty of room for shenanigans," Bindy says with pride, but Mindy rolls her eyes.

"Nothing really happens around here," she whispers to me.

"You're probably the most exciting thing to happen in a while," Cindy agrees. "At least we're setting up for winter camp after the next show."

"Oh yes, we're going to The Salted Baths! I read all about it in Girls Weekly Magazine." Cindy winks at me.

"You just want to go there for all the boys," Mindy tells her, and even though she rolls her eyes, she smiles fondly at her sister.

Their laughter helps to lift the heaviness from my chest. There's a real connection between the three of them, and if I can't trust anything else, I can at least trust the bond they seem to share with each other. That will have to be enough for now.

We soon leave the rows of empty cabins and pile into a small lift no bigger than a standing shower that takes us to our destination.

The dining floor is located on the very top level of this train section and the girls say it's because the smoke and steam will have less of a journey to escape through the vents. The aroma of fresh-cooked pastries and bread becomes noticeable and when the doors finally creak open, I'm flooded with an overwhelming smell of grease and baked goods.

We stumble out of the lift into a spacious floor. Flanking both sides are long metal tables set as buffet stations and behind them are slender kitchen areas bustling with workers covered in crisp green aprons. While the buffet to my right is a wondrous display of food, the left side is barren and polished to a silvery sheen. Mindy explains it's because there are fewer people to feed and they don't need to have both sides open anymore.

"Open for breakfast, lunch, and dinner," says Cindy as she deposits my empty cake plate on top of a large metal trash can. "Let's grab some fresh cookies!"

I follow behind the girls, gripping a freshly-washed plate that is still warm and damp. Cindy, Mindy, and Bindy march quickly to the very end of the countertop and start piling their plate off with cookies. A lot of cookies. I even catch Bindy sneaking a few into her pockets and Cindy popping one in her mouth when no one is looking.

I stand there holding the plate to my chest as I wait for them and nearly drop it when someone's foot makes contact with the back of my knee.

"Get a move on, will ya? I hear we have bacon today and I'm not about to let the greasers make off with it all again," says the very large owner of the foot. She pushes past and the smell of hay and straw coming off her makes me homesick.

The food here looks amazing and my stomach pinches painfully in agreement, but I still watch everyone carefully as they serve themselves. I finally conclude that there is no way someone could have slipped something dangerous into this food if this many people are enjoying it, but I still decide to eat only what I see others eat first.

A loud clatter to my left scatters my thoughts and I whirl to see a slender girl dropping to her knees to pick up mounds of clean white napkins. Years of helping the other house girls with their tasks make me help her, no questions asked, and I kneel beside her, grabbing at the napkins before they can be stepped on.

Someone snickers nearby and the girl blushes. She's very pretty, but the look she gives the passing men is the ugliest I've seen.

"Thanks, I hate diner duty," she grumbles once I've handed her the last of the napkins. Then, after finally looking directly at me, her eyes open wide. "What in the world are you wearing? That skirt is huge!"

"Oh, um, I didn't come here with much," I say, feeling my cheeks flush crimson. She nods in understanding and puts a hand on one of my shoulders.

"Sorry, that was rude of me, I've known girls to come here wearing nothing but potato sack dresses. It's the way of the world. But I am right, that skirt is much too big for you and looks awful. Find me later and I'll help you out." With one last smile, she rushes back into the very crowded seating area.

"Don't mind Bluebell," Mindy says to me, having appeared so silently by my side that I jump.

"She's always a little grumpy, but especially worse in the mornings before breakfast," Bindy explains.

"And especially when she's on diner duty," Cindy laughs and pushes me forward. "You should find her later, she handles all the costumes and clothes and such, but food comes first! Follow me."

This time, they come with me to the front of the buffet and we work our way down, though the girls have trouble fitting any more food on their plates.

I notice many of the dishes are vegetarian based and Mindy explains Magenta won't eat meat, so it doesn't show up often on their menu. Though occasionally there will be something like bacon or fried chicken, which is always very popular and disappears fast.

Despite my stomach being unsettled from the constant movement of the land train, I find myself spooning a big helping of scrambled eggs onto my now cold plate, securing a hot, buttery roll, and even manage to grab the last apple before we arrive at the end of the line. I'm greeted there by a short man whose belly pokes out from under his pink shirt. He sits on a low stool and picks at his teeth with a plastic toothpick.

"Where's your book, girlie? Need to stamp it if you want food," he snorts at me and the color drains from my face as he spits an inky wad of sludge into a nearby bucket.

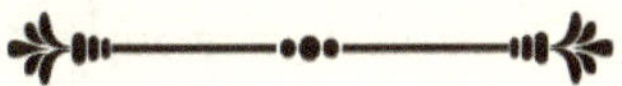

"Book?" I squeak and suddenly Cindy is beside me, Mindy and Bindy standing guard behind her. The short man springs from his chair, and even though he barely reaches Cindy's shoulders, he waves a long finger in her face as he snatches little books from them. In quick succession, he embosses each with an icon looking startlingly similar to the Cloudspeak logo.

Cindy takes back her book and sighs. "Beetle, she's a special guest of Magenta, so you have to let her pass."

Beetle slumps back on his stool. "No one passes without a stamp and I'm not going to believe anything coming from the mouths of you three. Not anymore." He gestures angrily towards the three girls with a hand missing several fingers. "Last time I trusted you lot, I got stuck with vent duty for two months."

"But we'll give you a cookie!" Cindy giggles and Beetle's face goes red.

"No book means no food," he grunts, making a grab for my plate, but Bindy is quicker and snatches it away first. She pulls her sisters to the side with a worried look.

Beetle regards me with little eyes and the realization of his name comes upon me as I imagine the black dots materializing and crawling away.

"Let her be," a low voice mutters from behind and I spin to see Jack. The piercing green of his eyes ensnare me in a web of memory before he looks down at the little man.

Beetle shrinks away with a scowl and returns his attention to the growing audience around us, furiously stamping their books without comment.

Ignoring him, Jack gently grabs my shoulder and steers me in the direction of the three sisters, who have now found an empty table and already descended upon their cookies. My own plate of scrambled eggs sits untouched between them, but I notice someone has placed a large chocolate chip cookie on top.

"For energy," Cindy smiles when I join them. Mindy's eyes are big as she takes in Jack, who sits heavily beside them. Wordlessly, Bindy offers him a cookie and he takes big bites from it, regarding me with his forest eyes.

"You look terrible," he says and I hear the girls holding in their laughter. "Eat quickly, I'm taking you to Magenta when you're through. She'll, no doubt, know what to do with you."

"Good morning to you, too," I mutter, grabbing a nearby fork and taking large bites of egg until they're completely demolished. I then set the fork down and pick up the roll, nibbling it between bites of the tart green apple, ignoring the way Jack stares at me. Cindy nods in approval when I finish everything more quickly than I would have liked and have to turn my attention back to Jack.

"Of course I look terrible," I tell him, licking buttery crumbs from my fingers. "You would too if you'd been running for your life half naked through the wilds."

"So, you really were naked?" Mindy gasps.

"She said 'half,' so maybe just topless?" Cindy inputs.

"No, I heard from Supper that she was missing pants, right, Dani?" Bindy asks and I feel my cheeks burn hot. Jack shifts in his seat and looks around us, his eyes scanning the small number of people leaning in to listen to our conversation.

"Let's go," he says, rising and reaching down for my hand. I smack it away and he glares at me.

"You don't have to drag me," I tell him and stand on my own. Mindy presses another cookie into my hands and smiles.

"For later," she whispers and I'm smiling back when Jack just walks away and I have to rush to follow him out of the busy dining area.

As we walk, Jack goes on and on about how the land train is put together. The diner car and kitchens make up the spine of the dragon, where we just were, and Magenta lives in the head, where we are going.

Anyone who is someone, he says, lives in the belly of the beast, and anyone who is not someone, lives near the lower decks of the tail. Which is also, he points out, where any resident animals are kept, except the cow who lives in a guarded room down the hall from Magenta's office.

I want to ask him where he lives, but based on the way anyone we encounter scampers quickly from our path, he is someone important.

The rest of the dragon is made of various rooms dedicated to storage or quality of life. Jack tells me one of Magenta's top priorities is keeping her kingdom happy and well-fed, and we pass through entire rooms dedicated to libraries, delicate gardens stocked with real butterflies for pollination, and even a water tank big enough to dive into for a swim.

We make our way up a steady incline of room after room until I don't think I can walk anymore. Breakfast has cooled in my stomach and I wonder out loud how long we've been traveling through the train. Jack, now standing at the end of yet another garden room, tells me this is the last door before Magenta's territory.

"Stay close," he mutters.

He takes a deep breath before punching a quick code on a discreet side panel. The door hisses open and he once again grabs my shoulder to lead me through. I let him this time, because my body has gone rigid in fear at the darkness that fills the room. It descends upon us like a blanket, and before I can bolt back out, the door hisses shut.

There is still the sway from side to side coming from the traveling beast and it makes it hard for my eyes to fully adjust to the darkened space. I can hear Jack move away and, disoriented, fling my arms to grab his blurry form, but am unsuccessful. I instead hug them close to my sides, trying to keep from falling over.

Another door hisses open, and for a brilliant moment, Magenta stands silhouetted against bright light. I know it is her because of her hair and the deep and silky voice that rumbles across my skin, reminding me yet again of the power she seems to emanate.

"Go ahead, Jack," she says. "Leave and turn it on from the other side."

Jack disappears into the light as Magenta joins me in the dark and the door hisses behind her. There is no more movement, no more sound, and the blackness that encases us seems hungry until suddenly it is no more but pale light and an electric buzzing sound takes its turn to consume me from the inside out. The light of a miniature full moon, shining above like a crystalline chandelier, bathes us both in a warm glow.

I don't need to look down at my skin to know I'm glowing as bright as a table lamp. I can see it written in every strand of Magenta's moonlit and mighty hair.

"Well, my little sparkling rabbit," she purrs as the door hisses open again. "Seems the little man living in my hair was right about you. You're going to be our guiding star."

Chapter Twenty

Magenta reaches for my shoulder and pulls me to the next room. I follow numbly, having given up trying to control my own direction today. The door closes again and I have to blink several times against the brightness of real sunlight cascading around her shoulders.

The room we're in is comfortable and clean, with dark oak walls covered in various trophies and knickknacks, collections from a life well-lived. A large couch lines the wall with another smaller one just opposite it.

"We're in the left eyeball," Magenta informs me. "The mighty beast has to be able to see, yes? So I felt it only fitting that I should be the one doing the looking."

"Who lives in the other eye?" I find myself asking and Magenta gives a throaty chuckle.

"The cow," Jack answers for her, taking a seat on the couch. He props one leg atop a knee and leans back, arms resting on either side of the cushions. His gaze drifts outside through a window, but I can tell he's listening intently to everything being said.

"Well, little rabbit," Magenta says. "Sit down and let me tell you of the pieces I've put together." She gestures to the sofa next to Jack and I wearily lower myself beside him. The land train lurches and my hip bumps into his own. He shifts further away. Magenta perches across from us, looking directly into my face.

"What do you know?" I ask.

"Why don't you help me complete the puzzle, hmm? What I got is there's a fire along the highway, smoke rising higher than birds can fly, a broken-down girl left abandoned amongst the scattered debris of emotion and tears, shining brighter than the moon herself. It all seems both a terrifying and familiar story, but I know better than to pretend I know someone else's tale best. So, enlighten me, little rabbit. What fairy tale did you crawl away from?"

I remain silent, not knowing what I can say that won't bring on the tears or sound like horrible lies, so instead I look around Magenta's room. It's built of the same highly-polished walls of the many hallways, but she has displayed multiple photographs of performers and circuses and animals I can't even name along one wall. Along the other hangs a collection of what look like weapons. A crossbow even hangs just above my head. I chew my lip in thought until Jack saves me from answering.

"It won't matter what you say, she looks like she already knows," he says slowly, uncrossing his legs. Magenta reaches over and slaps his shoulder hard with an open palm.

"Have a little compassion for the craft!" she sizzles.

"Oh, was it craft you were going for? Sounds like you're just poking fun."

"I can do both," she says, sitting up straight and patting her hair. "So, as his highness next to you has pointed out, I received a droll communication this morning from the vicinity's reporter. Seems a nearby hospice went up in flames sometime in the early hours a few days past. All lives lost, it appears."

"All of them?" I choke. I didn't think I'd still had hope that someone survived, but evidently I did, as my heart sinks.

"Apparently not all," Magenta says, her eyes boring into mine. "But what I find fascinating is what that house was called."

I glance at Jack, wondering if I should be wary of answering, but he only raises his brows, blithe. "The Zamora House?"

"There is a relation to a 'Doctor' Leonard Zamora, I assume?" Magenta asks and Jack's head whips toward her at the name.

I nod numbly and Magenta rises from the sofa to pace the room, appearing as if in deep thought. My heart clenches thinking of all the times I watched Lily do the same.

She stops near an ornate desk against the far wall and picks up a small square of red velvet, then grabs a small brown book from a drawer. She returns to give me the velvet square and the book to Jack.

"It's not hard to guess who you are," she says, her features softening. "Even without the brooch, I would know from your eyes, from the way you carry yourself, even the slightness to your build. Would it shock you to know that I knew your parents in a love story from long ago?"

"I never knew them, so I'm assuming someone else did, but what's the connection with Leonard Zamora?"

"Well, you see, I don't like to dwell on fairy tales without happy endings, and if you don't mind, I won't get into that right now. It is a story for another time."

My face flushes angrily, and glance at Jack for help, but his eyes are closed, his forehead wrinkled as if in thought.

I'm torn between wanting to shake them both by their shirts until they speak and simply crawling back into my new bed. There is empathy for Magenta, perhaps, creeping through my veins because I know what it's like to not want to revisit the past, but also frustration towards her cryptic attitude regarding my life.

My parents may be nothing but a hazy dream, but they are still *my* parents. I feel I have a right to know what they know.

"*Just be quiet and listen,*" Lily whispers.

I huff and turn my attention to the velvet. My breath catches when I unwrap the square and see the metal bird, forever trapped in a state of flight, the brooch's pin poking into my hand. It is the same one Magenta wore when she first approached me in the wilds and the same one, I think, worn by the pregnant woman, Scarlet, in the photo. It also reminds me deeply of the version Mother wore, tucked on a shelf in my room. It's almost like they are all the same bird in a different stage of life. Magenta is suddenly there, plucking the pin from my hand and attaching it to my shirt.

"We could use you here, little rabbit, and the man in my hair says to me that you have nowhere else to go. So will you stay and fly for us?"

"Yes," I breathe, my fingers closing in on the gift. "As long as you promise to tell me about my parents when you can—Wait a minute, fly?"

"I promise to explain everything in due time, but you will need to perform in order to stay with us," she says and I press back into the sofa.

"Okay, but fly?"

"Oh, something similar to what you did in the Midnight Room." She gestures towards the door. "That is what you'll do, and thanks to some creativity on my part, it'll also take care of your Required Industry Service, so it will be a win-win for everyone involved."

"Just stand there and glow?"

"Stand there and glow," she repeats and the weight of the whole dragon is suddenly pressing down against me. Lily and I had planned to get help, to tell the world about what happened to us and what was happening to the other girls. But what does it matter anymore? Everyone is dead and all I have left is myself to worry about.

Then again, perhaps making myself known will be the best way to tell the world.

"*You have to worry about him, too,*" says Lily, and the shadowy form of Tobias Cloudspeak streaks through my mind, clouding further thought with a gracious voice and sinister eyes.

"I can...but just so you know, someone is looking for me," I say softly and Magenta raises an eyebrow as Jack leans forward, his hands resting on his knees.

"Who?" he asks.

"Tobias Cloudspeak," I say and watch him tense.

"You'll be safe here. I have experience in hiding things from that man." Magenta sucks in a breath and casts a sideways look to Jack. "Been 'hiding' his son here for years. Sometimes the best place to hide is out where everyone can see you and no one can touch you. But you're tired, we can see that. We'll be in Greenfield in about a week and we'll set you up then. Jack, take her to get some food and maybe some new clothes. She looks like a sick puppy."

Magenta rises from the sofa and crosses to the window, her back to us. Jack rises to his feet and offers a hand to help me up, but I don't take it. He shrugs and holds out the small brown book from Magenta's desk.

I don't take it because I'm too busy looking at him. I think I knew he was related to Evan from the moment I saw Jack's green eyes, or maybe when Magenta mentioned Tobias Cloudspeak and I felt his body shudder against mine, so the revelation doesn't surprise me. All the same, the confirmation is unsettling.

"Don't lose this," he says, shoving the book into my hands. "Lose it and you don't eat."

"Has anyone ever lost one before?" I ask and Jack frowns as I run my fingers along the Cloudspeak logo embossed along its edge.

"No one still around," he says and walks away without waiting for me. I take one last look at Magenta, but when she doesn't turn back, I leave without saying goodbye.

The chandelier moon has been turned off in the Midnight Room and red glass lamps glow softly from rows lining the walls. Jack quickens his pace and we soon leave them behind and crowd into a small lift at the end of the hall. I think I catch the faintest whiff of something musty and earthen, and wonder if we're near the cow.

"That couldn't have gone any better," Jack says, releasing a long breath.

"Did you know my parents? Is Evan your brother?"

Jack studies me for a moment and seems to decide something, since he nods. "The Amazing Starlings died," he says. "At least, that's the story everyone knows. And yes, he is, but I don't talk to him very much."

My mouth is open, mere seconds away from asking more about the Starlings, but someone sticks a foot into the lift's door and the boy named Parker practically stumbles into Jack's arms.

"What do you need, Parker?" Jack asks, pressing a button on the wall to keep the lift from leaving. I catch a hint of annoyance in his eyes, but he covers it up quickly.

"Sorry, Jack, I was headed to the cow and wanted to tell you. Did you know they're letting me work with her? Supper is furious with jealousy." Parker laughs loudly and seems to notice me for the first time. "Hi Dani! Did you like the cake?"

"I did, but you forgot to bring a fork," I tell him and immediately feel bad when his face falls. "It was good, though. I still enjoyed it."

"Sorry about that. But hey, to make it up to you, do you want to see the cow?"

I glance at Jack, but he doesn't look back. "I've never seen one before."

"I don't know if we have time for that," Jack says, but Parker has already grabbed my arm and is dragging me out of the lift and back down the hall towards what I think is the dragon's other eye.

"Fine, we'll go see the stupid cow," I hear Jack grumble, stalking after us as Parker and I hurry down the hall.

The door leading to the cow's room is locked tight. Jack and I watch as Parker tries several times to let us inside. Each unsuccessful attempt comes from his sweating hands, and the nervous looks he gives over his shoulder at Jack are hard to watch. Finally, Jack pushes him out of the way and opens the door with his own code on the first try.

And just like that, I am halfway home as the earthy smell surrounds us, filling our noses with grasses, seedy water, and chicken poop.

I'm surprised to find the animals inside live in such luxury quarters. The room stretches far from us and I think it may have once been two separate areas long ago combined into one enclosed farm. Someone has even painted the walls with rolling hills and white flowers, and the smooth roof above is a lightened shade of blue.

"Over here," Parker says to me and I follow him carefully through flocks of chickens. No one here pecks at my toes—they don't know me yet—but they lovingly swarm upon Parker.

"This is impressive," I say.

"I don't have much in the way of talent, so I'm glad Magenta and Supper found a good reason to keep me around."

"Who is Supper?"

"No one of importance," Jack answers. "Least not for you, right now. You'll be reporting to me. Parker here, and people like him, report to Supper."

"You make it sounds like he's less of a person," I snap at Jack and he bristles. He opens his mouth as if to reply, then shakes his head and looks away.

"It's okay," says Parker. "This place couldn't run without people like me. And who knows, I hope to be as important as the next person one day. Unless I let another chicken die, and then I'm really in for it."

I look at Parker again and really see how much younger he is. I thought he might only be a few years my junior, but he must be close to thirteen or maybe even twelve, the same as the three sisters. Something about this life must age you terribly fast—or in Jack's case, make you sour like bad gravy.

"Let's take a look at this cow everyone is so excited about," I say to Parker and he leads me to the very end of the long room, Jack following slowly behind.

"Here she is," Parker says, opening a small wooden gate. Inside is the fattest and biggest creature I've ever seen. Black and white, with a big pink nose, she blinks at me with the now familiar sad, brown eyes.

I'm too stunned to move. "What's her name?"

"She doesn't have one," Parker laughs. "Everyone just refers to her as 'Magenta's cow.'"

"People pay good money to see her," Jack says from somewhere behind me. "She makes us quite a bit."

At the callous comment, I reach a hand up and rub the cow's leathery nose. She leans into my palm, closing her eyes and letting out a long sigh.

"She likes you," breathes Parker. Jack scoffs and reaches out to pat her neck, but the cow makes a low grumbling sound and turns her backside to him, and he scowls.

"Maybe you could help me around here, Dani. It'd be nice to have some company," Parker says.

"I'd like that," I say, my eyes misting a little at how familiar this place feels.

Something in me clicks into place, like one of those puzzle pieces Magenta was talking about. The hens mill about, pecking at seeds, splashing into their water dishes. One brave chicken even pecks at my heels. Their musty smell and twittering sounds bring me back home, and if I concentrate very carefully, I can imagine Lily and Tara here beside me.

Whether they mean to or not, the chickens remind me of what I left behind. As if some unseen force is guiding my hand, my fingers close around the brooch Magenta gave me. The cold metal presses into my palm. Maybe it's the brooch's mystery that clings to me, or Lily's voice that urges me to seek answers, but I decide to stay and find out. I need to complete this puzzle.

Besides, it's not like I have anywhere else to go.

"I've had a lot of experience with chickens. I can help," I tell Parker and he nods emphatically. I turn towards Jack, who appears to have lost interest.

"Show her the way back when you're done," he yells over his shoulder as he strides for the door. "I have work to do."

"Jack's an odd fellow, but he's always been nice to me," Parker mentions after he's gone, motioning me towards one of the feed bins. "I think people are afraid of him because he's just so...well, unlikeable at first. But he'll warm up once he gets to know you."

"I don't understand him at all," I say. "I don't know if he likes me or hates me."

"You get used to that feeling from him," Parker says, using a large scoop to gather the crispy looking chicken feed. "He's still the most stand-up guy in this place."

"Is that why you wear the same scarf?" I ask and Parker grins, coming back over.

"He gave it to me a while back, haven't taken it off since," he says proudly and I make a face.

"That explains the smell."

Parker laughs so hard the scoop wobbles and chicken feed scatters around us. We're suddenly up to our necks in hungry birds. Half laughing, half screaming, we run out the door.

Chapter Twenty-One

When I wake the next morning, still full of potato soup and sourdough slathered in extra butter, I find a parcel in front of my door. It's a package of neatly folded clothing, and while it's all very plain-colored and drab, the stitching is well done and everything fits well enough. The fact that pants are included is the best part. I push the heavy skirts aside and step into them, marveling at the freedom they provide.

I find a small note tucked inside from Bluebell saying Jack spoke with her. She promises she'll set me up with better clothes in the future, but it looked like I needed something now. Right now.

So it is with a fresh set of clothes that my days settle into a routine of chickens, chores, and food. The only thing new is the shape of my daily nightmares, which come upon me most nights when my room is at its darkest and I am at my most alone. I wake up screaming for Lily, then go back to sleep with her still, pale face in my dreams.

Parker is grateful for my help and I marvel at the speed in which he picks up on taking care of his feathery army. We spend our days covered in feathers while Parker speaks of how excited he is about our next stop after Greenfield, The Salted Baths. He promises he'll take me to lunch there.

Mindy, Cindy, and Bindy walk with me every day to the dining floor, and I sometimes follow along with them during their mundane chores, which they always make a game out of. And in between all the feedings and cleanings, they teach me about the lives of everyone in Magenta's care.

There are the tumblers, like the three sisters, who bounce around the stage in every color of the rainbow and were all born into this lifestyle. They pride themselves on their lineage and say the longer you can trace your circus roots back, the better.

There are the clowns, who mostly keep to themselves, so Parker couldn't say much of them aside from their keen interest in the Stage Girls, who also keep to themselves. Parker has tried to get to know many of them and failed horribly. Bluebell is one of the Stage Girls and they basically do everything from working backstage, to food services in the dining room, to concession stands, and to meal prep.

I ask the sisters about Jack, and they say being Magenta's most treasured act keeps him out of everyone's way. When I ask what he does, though, they simply say it's too hard to explain and then distract each other by telling me of their future plans.

Life goes on like this for a few days. Beetle starts to make eye contact with me when I pass him, and even Sally, the big lady who sees to the cow, sometimes saves a seat for me at breakfast. I haven't had time alone with Jack since my meeting with Magenta, no matter how badly I wish to corner him for more information regarding my parents. Every day, I wake up remembering everything from the day before. It's small, by all standards, but it feels so much like a triumph that I can't help but take pride in it.

In fact, I've noticed a big improvement regarding my addled memory, and the mundane activities that once slipped from my mind's grasp now stay locked in place. Maybe I never had a bad memory; maybe Mother and Father just made sure I thought I did.

The past, though, is another story, and I find it difficult to recall much of what happened in The Zamora House. Even the faces of those closest to me are hazy. Lily and Tara's faces grow fainter and fainter every time they appear among my dream wolves, and Lacey and Milton have become ghostly images. It's alarming, how quickly they go, but maybe it's a result of my mind recovering, my brain struggling to keep track of what it previously had not.

After a week on the train, I hear from Sally that we'll be in Greenfield tomorrow, and the excitement throughout the dining floor feels both energized and frantic. I realize that I have no idea what I'll be doing in the show tomorrow and try to ask the sisters about it, but rather than answer they hurry back to their room after dinner for what they tell me is beauty sleep. Parker disappears altogether. It makes the journey back to my room long and silent as I worry about what Magenta expects me to do.

I'm just opening the door to my room when I notice Jack approaching from the opposite direction. He carries a canvas bag, and dark circles ring his sparkling green eyes.

"You owe me answers," I announce while stepping inside my room and waiting for him to follow. When he doesn't, I shake my head and begin to tidy up. Most of the mysterious belongings have been packed away in an old storage trunk Parker delivered. It rests against the wall and serves as both a bench and place to store someone else's memories. I strung the photos up as garlands over the bed.

"I've been busy," Jack says, finally coming inside and closing the door behind him. Fidgeting with the bag slung over his shoulder, he looks around the clean room with a blank expression, his eyes darting over the shelf where I've placed the old gate key and then at the photos I've hung overhead. Whatever he's thinking he doesn't give voice to, and instead sits down on the far side of the bed. There's a foot of space between us, but it still feels too close.

"Friscuit, everyone here is always busy," I say and lean away as heat flushes my cheeks.

"And always will be," he mutters, then blinks, as if what I've said registers. "Friscuit?"

I ignore his question and take a deep breath, knowing this is my chance for answers. "You didn't finish telling me about my parents. If Magenta knew them, did you know them, too?"

"A lot of people did, even more so after they died," he says, plucking a nearby photo from the garland. "But I did not *know them* know them, since they died when I was barely a year old."

The photo he took is one I dismissed easily: an out of focus man standing off to the side as the woman, perhaps Scarlet, balances on a low-strung rope. Little stars spin around her head in a dazzling blur and I think the man might be controlling them.

"*Drones,*" Lily calls them.

"Your parents were Magenta's favorite act," Jack continues. "The Amazing Starlings. I don't know much, but I think the wife danced on a tightrope while her husband flew these little machines. It was all a big spectacle, like some story they told over the course of each show. She even preformed while pregnant, which Magenta hated, but the audience ate it up."

"What happened to them?" I breathe. Lily's voice suggests I would already know if I listened correctly: they died.

Jack lets out a long sigh. "No one knows. They disappeared just before she gave birth and Magenta told everyone they died during a rehearsal gone wrong. They were always a little crazy, so it wasn't a long shot that The Amazing Starlings could have somehow gotten themselves killed. Magenta never talked about it and everyone just moved on and forgot."

"Do you know their names?"

"Scarlet Starling and her husband, Stan, I think. He took on her last name when they got together," he answers, barely covering a yawn as he hands the photo to me. He leans back, stretching out along the bed and folding an arm over his eyes.

Scarlet! I can just make out a hazy memory of that name spilling from the lips of Leonard Zamora just before Tobias found us. I lean over Jack's body and pull down the photo of the pregnant woman in red standing next to Magenta. Was this my mother? I look at the photo Jack took down and run my fingers along the out-of-focus man in the corner. Was this my real father? I turn to ask him, but his soft snores break the quiet. I jab him hard in the ribs.

"Excuse me, this is my room. What do you think you're doing? I have more questions."

Jack moves his arm a bit and cracks an eye open to look at me. "We have a few more minutes until we need to leave, thought I'd close my eyes for a second."

"I don't think so," I say, even though I swear I hear Tara's voice urging me to let him stay. "And where are we going? It's already been a long day."

"And it's about to get longer." He grunts and gets up, looking down into my eyes. "You need to come to practice."

Flustered and only a little annoyed, I look away and sniff. "I don't know why I need to practice standing and glowing. You need to tell me what else you know about The Starlings."

He laughs and rises from the bed. "If I knew more, I'd tell you, but we need to practice. Magenta thought it best to let you rest as long as possible, but that cuts into our time on the ropes. Anyhow, you see that bag over there?" He points to the canvas sack he dropped on the trunk. "That's your costume for the show, so keep it clean. You won't need it tonight, though."

I feel the color drain from my face. I knew it was going to happen, but the thought of actually preforming, even if I just stand there and glow, in front of a lot of people is tormenting.

"I'll take good care of it, then," I manage as he opens the door to let himself out.

"Please do. This place isn't made of money. Get changed into something comfortable, sweats should be fine, and meet me in the hall." With that, he closes the door behind him. I can hear him shuffling outside my door and I wonder if he can hear how hard I roll my eyes at him.

No matter my nerves, the excited part of me, the part that carries Tara's energy, ushers me to look in the bag. Instead of clothes, however, I'm confronted with what looks like a giant nude sock with arm and leg holes. How am I supposed to even wear this?

"I don't hear changing in there!" Jack's annoying voice calls through the door and I groan so loudly I bet the whole floor hears it. I hastily slip on a pair of soft grey sweatpants and find a snug white shirt with long sleeves. After pulling my hair back in a high ponytail, I head out the door to see what kind of practice Jack has in store.

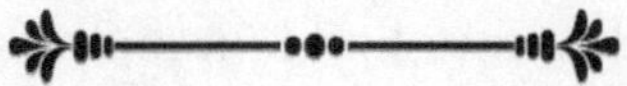

We take the closest lift, no matter that it's one of the smaller ones. Jack goes in first, but when I don't follow right away, he pulls me inside by my shoulders until my back is flush with his front. I swallow hard and am glad he can't see the heat rising to my cheeks, but he must sense the slight trembling in my shoulders because I can feel him laughing slightly behind me. Neither of us says anything until we arrive and bolt out of the confined space.

Jack runs a hand through his hair and straightens his shirt once we're out, but I'm too engrossed with the room we now stand in. It's the largest room I've ever seen. We're still inside the dragon's belly, but this must have been created by merging several dozen rooms together and I find myself marveling again at how big this beast really is. Groups of performers lay about on large mats, stretching and talking amongst themselves, and above them are a dozen poles rising up to a ceiling littered with a thousand lights that look like stars among the ropes and pulleys and swings that dangle from them.

"This is our practice room," Jack says, coming to stand by my side. "Do exactly as I say up there and you won't get hurt. Or don't, and fall to your death."

I don't have time to glare at him because a chiming sound begins to ring from a large clock on the wall and everyone remaining in the room starts to file out, nodding at Jack and giving me curious looks. We're soon left alone.

"Um, is this safe, to be here alone?" I ask, my voice echoing in the large space, and turn to find him pulling his pants off. I yelp and whip around to face the wall. "Friscuit! What are you doing?"

Jack laughs and taps my shoulder. "Turn back around, Dani. You're going to see my costume sooner or later, might as well get it over with now. Can't have you getting distracted while we're up there."

I turn slowly but refuse to let my eyes drift south. He rolls his eyes and walks away from me towards a nearby ladder, and I see him fully in his tiny little sparkling shorts and suddenly the nude sock makes much more sense.

He is all lean muscle and smooth skin with just a hint of a swirling black tattoo on his left calf. The shorts do cover the important bits, which I'm thankful for, but he could be naked if not for the crystals and small piece of fabric. I realize after watching him that this is as close as I've ever come to seeing a boy—well, I guess a man, since he's close to my age—naked. Suddenly reluctant to be caught staring, I hurry to catch up.

"All right, come over here," he says, pointing at the ladder. "You need to go up this."

"You mean *climb* that? No, it's too high." I gaze upwards at the ladder rising all the way to the ceiling. Looking that high up makes my head spin and my palms sweat.

"This is nothing." He takes my hand and sets it on the steel bars. "This is the shortest one we have, the real one is taller. Just go up and stand on that platform, I'll be right behind you."

I swallow and wipe my hands on my sweats before I begin climbing the ladder. After all, I told Magenta I would perform if she let me stay and eventually tells me how she knew Leonard and my parents. But I haven't seen her since that meeting and no other information has been provided to me. Maybe she's waiting for me to pull my weight before she's willing to answer any more questions.

"I know what you're thinking," Jack says after he's spent several minutes following closely behind me on the ladder. When I glance down at him, I gasp and clutch the bars tightly when I notice how high we've climbed already and how he causally swings by one arm while saying, "You're wondering about your deal with Magenta. She's been busy, but she did give me this to tell you and maybe it will help with tonight's practice. She said to tell you there were three brooches for three sisters."

"What is that supposed to mean?" I ask, my eyebrows drawing together.

"She's like this sometimes, but only if she likes you. My guess is that that she's being intentionally vague because she gets a thrill from her own dramatics. I'm sure you'll see her soon and she'll tell you more. That is, if she's willing to talk about it when you do. All right, that's the platform, step off there and hold on to the bar on the side."

"Okay," I say in a voice that shakes as badly as the golf cart going over the rocky slopes of the wilds. When I reach the platform at last, I find it's little more than a metal square, and so very high up off the ground. Gritting my teeth, I ease myself off the ladder and reach for the metal bar to keep my shaking legs steady as Jack joins me and grabs at a swing hanging just off to the side. He sits on the bar, which I can now see is wide enough for two people to sit side by side. He wraps one arm securely around the long cords holding it up and holds out his other toward me. I shake my head and stare wide-eyed at him.

"You're going to sit beside me on here," he says, patting the bar. "I'll grab your shoulders and hold you while we swing down. You're a tiny thing, so it shouldn't be a problem."

"I thought I was just going to stand here and glow," I squeak and he gives me an evil grin.

"More like sit here and glow."

I glare at his smile. "I'm not doing it."

"Are you scared?" he asks.

"More like *terrified*."

"It's not like I'm going to let you fall," he says, shifting against the rope. The lights catch the sparkles on his shorts and his crotch is blinding for a moment.

"How can I trust you?" I say. Anger at the situation helps me forget how far away the ground is.

Jack sighs. "Look, I'm not going to force you to do this. You're welcome to climb back down, but this is a much faster way of getting this over with. I'm not going to lie, your first few times doing this are going to be terrifying and nothing I say will help with that, but you can trust on how thrilling it is to swing through the air with me. It'll feel like we're flying. And you're a Starling, so it's in your blood.

"You have no idea what's in my blood," I whisper, but he somehow hears me.

"You'd be surprised," he mutters and holds out his hand again. I look from it to his face, then let out a sigh and take it. His palm is warm, but rough and callused, and he closes it securely around my wrist, guiding me to sit beside him.

Holding onto the thick cording with one arm, he loops his other around my shoulders and I can't help but turn myself into his chest, my hands gripping his waist so hard I think he might grunt at the contact, but I don't care. I'm not letting go.

Then he stands up and pulls me with him, my short legs leaving the safety of the metal platform, and I squeeze my eyes shut. With a mighty push, Jack launches our swing from the platform and I know, even without opening my eyes, that we're soaring through the air, picking up speed as the swing descends and slowly gathering strength for a downward thrust once we reach the apex. My heart launches into my throat while my stomach drops to my feet as wind whips at my face. But just as I'm getting used to it, we're flying backwards and I dare crack open my eyes in time to see the world far below me.

The feeling is both beautiful and, as Jack put it, in my blood. There is something exhilarating about this experience. And even though I know I'm clutching him so tightly I'm surely leaving fingernail imprints in his skin, I feel like I've returned to my home among the stars.

The swing eventually comes to a stop and Jack leaps off with me still clinging to his shoulders.

"You can let go now," he grunts, pushing my hands gently off him and setting me on the ground.

"That was fantastic!" I find myself saying, adrenaline making my hands shake. Without even thinking about it, I leap up and wrap my arms around his neck, which he returns stiffly. We stand there for a moment, breathing heavily as the exhilaration calms and leaves us mirroring each other's breaths. It feels somehow...safe, to stand so close to him, after I've just placed my life in his hands to fly through the air.

All the same, he is the one to let go first and pushes me to his front facing the ladder. His breath is warm in my ear and I can't help but lean into him slightly as he lays his hands on my shoulders. My small movement makes his fingers press just a little more into my skin.

"Glad you like it," he whispers. "Because we need to do that again about twenty more times tonight."

The smile drops off my face. "Wait, *what*?"

Chapter Twenty-Two

Greenfield isn't green at all. When the beast of a land train finally pulls into port, all I see is a scrawling town set upon a mound of pale dirt. It shimmers with the barest resemblance to the color green, but the pamphlet Parker slipped under my door early this morning assures me it's only temporary. During the driest and warmest of seasons, the city is mostly bare, but becomes a completely different world in the rain thanks to its dormant seeds making up much of the ground.

We've stopped next to a great empty field of the oddly-colored earth, and from my window I can just make out the dragon opening her mouth and spewing out a dining floor's worth of people onto the land. Everyone from the performers to the Stage Girls are busy hauling out boxes and equipment, and I'm in awe at the sheer speed in which they assemble a massive purple and white-striped tent surrounded by several smaller ones, everything connecting like some massive star.

No one can see me watching, since my room is too high up, but I can't help but only peep over the sills of my windows to watch. I feel like I should be down there helping, but Jack made me promise to stay here until he came to get me. Something about resting up for the big show, but it's left me feeling anxious and guilty to sit here while everyone else works.

Jack must have known I would try to break his rule because he even had Parker bring my breakfast and make me promise I'd stay put. Even if I don't care about breaking a promise to Jack, I wouldn't do that to Parker.

So I spend my boring morning dozing by the window and watching the performers practice their acts. Occasionally I make out the three sisters running among the different pockets of people, and I know without even paying much attention that they're pulling pranks on their fellow tumblers. One brave soul even tries to chase them away but is met with what looks like an explosion of glitter.

The sunlight streams into my window and the food Parker brought earlier sits barely touched beside me, my nerves too taut to eat very much of it.

It doesn't take long for my eyelids to close in hopes the nightmares would stick to their namesake and only haunt me after sundown, and I drift off thinking I'm a bee flying above the gardens back home. Mother chases me away but Father stands ready with a net. I'm so lost in the daydream that the sound of my opening door barely registers before Jack's deep voice brings me back.

"You're not dressed," he grunts, pulling the door closed behind him. "And you didn't eat."

"Oh, right..." I sit up and stretch, twisting my spine this way and that and willing the tiredness from my limbs, but when I finally look over at him, I nearly fall over in shock. "Do you just *walk around* like that?"

Jack looks down at his pair of skin-colored, sparkling shorts. He grimaces and marches over to the trunk, picking up the discarded sock dress and tossing it at my face.

"I wouldn't get too snarky, you get to wear this."

I feel the color drain from my skin when the realization I had been putting off finally comes crashing down.

"I really have to wear this thing?" I grimace, holding it in front of his face, and he nods, turning to face the door.

"Just hurry up, we don't have a lot of time."

I look to ensure he isn't peeking, and even though I'm embarrassed to try and get this thing on in his presence, I'm also extremely ready to get out of this room.

I keep my eyes on his back as I peel off my simple brown pants and try stepping into the sock, which is surprisingly more supple than I initially thought thanks to some incredible stretching abilities. I still have to take it back off again when I realize my old and battered underwear will not do, and against all better judgement, I take everything else off before putting the costume back on.

It leaves me feeling bare and exposed. My breaths come startlingly quick when I realize I will have to venture out wearing what must be considered practically nothing.

What I hadn't noticed before is that the suit has a few sparkling crystals against, well, my own important bits, and they remind me of flowers and leaves. I turn to grab a pair of shoes, but Jack spins around and stops me, his hand wrapping around my own. We might as well both be naked and his touch makes warmth flush through my body.

"If I don't wear shoes, then you don't either," he says, looking straight into my eyes. Our bodies are too close and his breath on my shoulders makes me shiver. I hope I turn away quickly enough so he doesn't see how red my face burns.

"We match," I whisper and he rubs his thumb over the top of my hand, almost like he doesn't even think about it, before letting go.

"Come on, we're going to be late and Sally hates it when I'm late," he says, holding the door open for me.

Setting my hand on my belly, I take a few deep breaths. If I can run out of a burning building, I suppose I can do this. I think.

The lift takes us quickly to the ground floor and we exit through a small lobby. Feeling the earth under my bare feet is a strange but familiar feeling, and I take a small second to squish the seedy dirt between my toes, marveling at the steadiness of the ground beneath me.

For as busy as the field seemed from above, we don't encounter a single other person as we make our way to the entrance of a tented tunnel that I think must lead to the main tent. My stomach swoops as we approach a plastic door displaying a familiar symbol, but Jack opens it quickly and we slip inside. Even though I hurry through, the embossed logo of Tobias Cloudspeak brushes against my shoulders and reminds me that he is always close by. One of these days, I'll find the chance to ask Magenta why the logo is everywhere despite her apparent distaste of him.

The corridor slopes gently downward until we arrive just under the main tent's center, the muffled noise of what sounds like hundreds of people drifting above and around me. We finally emerge into a smaller room with a large metal cage set in the middle of the floor, which rests on an even larger circular platform. The smell of grease and metal fills the room and Sally waits for us in its center.

"I was worried you'd be late," she says.

"I'm always on time," Jack says, pushing me towards her, but my legs lock.

"Wait, I don't know if I can do this. It sounds like there's a million people up there!"

"Would you even know what a million people looks like?" he asks dryly.

"Does it matter?" I snap, wringing my sweating hands together. I pace the room while they talk to each other until a light begins to blink on the wall and Jack looks at it with a curse. He comes close to me and sets both hands on my shoulders.

"What can I do to help settle your nerves?" he asks. Sally snickers beside us and he shoots her an annoyed look.

Truthfully, I don't know what could make this situation better. We practiced late into the night so my mind knows what I'll be doing up there, but I don't know if my body will corporate.

"I don't know," I tell him, my breaths starting to come in quick and almost painful.

"Okay, how about this?" he asks, pointing to a long scar on his arm. "I haven't told you about this, right?"

I shake my head.

"But you want to know, right?"

I am kind of curious, so I give him a small nod.

"Great, I'll tell you afterwards! Get in the cage!" he says, clapping me on the back and disappearing quickly through a side door before I can say anything back to him.

I stumble towards the doorway, but Sally begins to gesture me towards the open cage and I turn back to her instead.

"All right little lady, get on in and this thing will take you up to the main floor when it's your turn for the spotlight. Jack will come get you, go with him just like you practiced, and then it'll all be over."

"How many people are up there, really?" I ask her, unable to keep my voice from shaking.

"Enough," she says with a vague smile.

Panic grips my core and the trembling in my knees makes it hard to keep standing, but Sally comes to the rescue and swoops me up in her big arms and deposits me into the cage, closing it behind me.

"Where did Jack go?" I squeak as the floor beneath me begins to shudder.

"Don't worry, he'll meet you up there!" Sally calls, now standing across the room beside a control panel on the wall.

A buzzing sound fills the air. The floor hums below me, and I suddenly find myself and the cage rising above Sally's head. It climbs towards the ceiling that is opening above like a giant's maw as he yawns.

"Wait! What do I do before he gets there?" I yell down to her.

"Just stand there and glow, like you practiced! Oh, and keep away from the bars, they're a little rusty and I haven't had time to smooth them out."

"Why are you making this sound so easy?" I manage to scream back as the sounds of people above turn into a thunder storm and the lights dim and create a darkness so thick I can't even see my own hands. Below the noise, I can barely hear Sally answering me.

"Performing in front of an audience is easy!" she yells. "The cow does it all the time!"

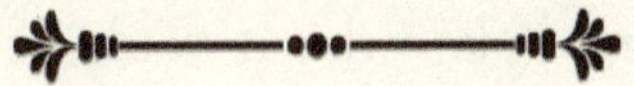

The floor above continues to open wide and the rusty cage makes its way through the spreading gates. It's too dark to make out the bars of the cage, so I do my best to stand still as the coolness of fresh air rushes past my nearly naked body. The audience must surround me on all sides, and I hear their excited chatter begin to calm as I raise upwards.

I have to clamp my hands over my mouth to muffle a scream when I realize the cage continues to move past ground level and keeps rising, all the way until I could be as high as the tent itself. The aching panic starts to return when a familiar buzzing sound startles me and I leap forward to clutch the rusty bars for balance. My left hand glides against smooth metal, but something catches on my right and the slick feeling of blood warms my palm.

A sound not unlike thunder claps from nearby and the source of the buzzing comes alive in what must be the biggest fake moon in existence. It hangs far above on a giant cable, surrounded by slow moving drones that circle in a swarm of moving stars. Unlike the audience below, I am mesmerized by the moon, but their collective intake of breath at my glowing skin makes me realize they only have eyes for the golden radiance that is my body.

I wonder what Lily would think of this, of these strangers staring at my glowing skin, like all I really am is a circus spectacle. I know Tara would dance around naked in the cage just for the thrill factor—which, to be fair, is only a step behind what I'm wearing. The nude sock is so sheer my entire body glows, and the parts that are covered in crystals give off what I guess is an alluring blur. I fight the urge to cover myself, knowing it would be useless to even try.

The audience gasps again and I look from my perch toward several smaller platforms set up nearby, each holding one of the performers hanging onto long suspended ropes. A tinge of jealousy rakes through me when I see their socks are solid black and much less sparkly.

They swing around for some time until a new platform rises and my counterpart appears opposite the cage, his tiny crystal shorts glittering in the moonlight. But what strikes me the most and just about freezes me solid is that his skin also glows.

Jack is *glowing*. And it's not just any glow, but a deep purple and red. The exact same shade as Lily.

I watch as the rest of the performers and Jack take to the air, swinging on their ropes and various suspended bars with an ease that must take a lifetime to learn. Even Jack seems like a natural as he flies through the air. I've never seen him practice his individual routine. I'm sure there is a story being told, but I have trouble following their patterns as, one by one, the other tumblers disappear into darkened areas of the tent until only Jack remains. He swings lightly to me and lands on the lip of the cage.

Still holding on to his rope, he flings the door open and holds out his hand for me to take.

"Ready?" he says through his smile.

"Um, no." I take a small step back.

"Everyone is watching, so just grab my hand and hold on," he hisses, smile unending, and waves at the crowd. They cheer back at him.

"This is so much higher than the practice tent." I whimper.

"I won't let you fall," he says, stepping close and grabbing my arm before I can register his movement. "I'd tell you if I wasn't sure you can do this, but I know you can. Just take my hand and trust me."

We stand at the edge of the platform, the audience below cheering and waving and laughing and crying and somewhere, somehow, a small voice breaks through and it's Lily telling me that I am Daniella Starling. I can do this. It's in my blood.

I let Jack grab my hand and feel lightheaded as he twirls me tight into his chest, one arm wrapped around my shoulders and my own arms hugging his waist so tightly I know he'll feel it in the morning. He drags my legs off the ledge and suddenly we're flying through the nighttime sky like two shooting stars. I shut my eyes through our speedy descent and barely notice when my feet touch the ground that squishes between my toes.

Jack lets out a breath and I do the same, thrilled to know we landed safely. Then Jack bends in a low bow, finally letting go of my hands. Without the added support, my knees give up and both my hands make contact with the dirt below. Blood from my cut palm immediately begins seeping into the waiting earth.

And that's when it occurs to me.

I do more than just glow.

I make the very earth flourish.

Which is exactly what happens.

Jack jumps back as the ground *erupts* in a circle of bright green grasses. Pinks and yellows and oranges of flowers I've never seen before shoot from the ground and rise up around our ankles and then our knees. There is even a tall plant that snakes up in vines around Jack's leg, covered in tiny purple grapes.

I yank my hands off from the ground when I feel the tingling sensation in my fingertips, but it's too late to stop the growth. I clutch my hands tight to my chest and stare wide eyed as the audience rises out of their seats in complete, stunned silence for a beat, then another. And then the entire tent cheers so loudly I cover my ears, no matter the blood I might be smearing against the side of my face.

Jack plucks a grape from one vine around his legs and pops it in his mouth, surveying the ground with narrowed eyes. They then shoot up to me, their green as bright as the grass. He grabs my hand again, possibly to keep me from falling and repeating the scene all over again, and pulls me so close I can feel his hot skin against my own. The reassuring warmth is comforting as he raises our hands to bow to the screaming audience.

"What was that?" he whispers urgently into my ear, still smiling and gripping tightly to my waist.

"I could ask you the same thing," I snarl in reply and poke the skin of his glowing arm. His grip on my waist tightens. It sends a shiver down my spine, causing my body to press against his uncontrollably. I think I feel him tense beside me, but relax a moment later.

"Seems like we both have some explaining to do."

"I guess we do."

Then Magenta is there, standing tall in front of us, and Jack pulls me off to the side as she begins speaking to the audience in her booming voice. I can't tell what she's saying, it's hard enough to summon the courage to walk as Jack leads us back to the cage, which has now lowered to ground level and starts to sink again once we're inside.

When I look up, I notice the drones are still swirling high above. I think they are spelling out a name as Magenta's echoing voice becomes muffled when the gate closes above us before I can read it. A wave of remembrance washes over me, and I can't help but wonder if the stars ever spelled out my mother's name.

After we're back underground and my eyes adjust to the newly dim light, I see Jack's stupid face looking down at me and the astonishment, wonder, and fear that filled me earlier wrings out like a wet sponge. Soaking up the rage and betrayal, my hands fly up and shove him away as hard as I can.

"You're a jerk! Why didn't you tell me you glow?"

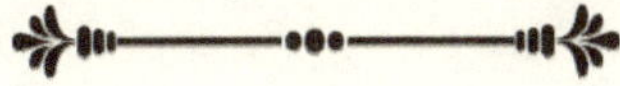

"Tell you that I'm freak as well?" Jack yells back, his face red. I stumble away at the name and he must see the pain in my eyes because he turns away quickly.

I won't let him escape my questions. "So why do you glow? Who are you? Were you experimented on, too?" The demands pour from my mouth as my feet propel my body from the cage with Jack flying out behind me.

"You just made a bunch of flowers and plants grow from nothing. I should be asking *you* the questions!" He moves in front of me and jabs a finger into my chest.

"It wasn't from nothing, there are dormant seeds in the ground. That's how plants work, or maybe you should read a book sometime!" I try to push him out of my way, but he's too big and solidly built and it feels like trying to move a house.

"Are you two okay over there?" Sally cuts in and I blush because I'm not sure how long she's been listening.

"We're fine," I tell her, slapping Jack further away from me.

"Better make up quick, or at least pretend to. Got the cubby all set up, then it's off to after show dinner. Good job, little rabbit, they seem to love you almost as much as the cow," Sally says, her face stretching in a kind smile. The honesty in her expression melts away some of my anger.

"The cow isn't magic," Jack grumbles.

"I'm not either," I snap back. "What's the cubby?"

Sally's smile falters and I can sense Jack shifting behind me.

"Ah, well," she begins, a bit awkwardly, and starts to walk backwards. "Just a little something the top performers do after the show, generates a little extra money and you get to split it. The rest goes to Magenta." When I don't follow her, she sighs and waves her hand. "Come on then, the sooner you're in, the more money you have a chance at making."

Jack only follows once I start walking with Sally down another long tunnel. After a few moments, Sally looks down at me.

"Not right of him to call you a freak, but that's what he thinks of himself," she says quietly, casting a look back at Jack who shuffles some ways behind us. "He's had a hard life. Got called that by his own family before Magenta took him in, and I think he resents that glow."

"I had no idea he was like me," I whisper.

She nods. "I bet that's true. Most of us here have something we ran away from and it's a kind of courtesy that no one brings it up, least not to your face."

I nod like I understand what's just told me, but find myself still struggling with the image of him glowing so brightly in front of me. Maybe I'm too prideful to forgive Jack for not telling me, but then again, I'd kept my secret from him as well.

Instead of exiting all the way to the grounds below the train, we turn and enter a much smaller striped tent. Sally leads us to a section closed off by a maroon curtain, and it takes another moment for my eyes to adjust to the almost complete darkness that surrounds us.

"Here you are," she gestures to a transparent cube about the size of a small bedroom. Someone has set up a little sofa and a short table covered in various snacks and two tall glasses of water. Jack pushes past me and sits down heavily, crossing a leg over the opposite knee and leaning back, as if nothing's happened.

"What do we do in here?" I ask.

Sally shrugs. "Whatever you want for the next hour."

She locks the door behind her and I turn to Jack, setting aside how angry I am at him for now. He must see the confusion on my face because he sighs and pats the sofa next to him in invitation.

"Might as well settle in, this is the boring part. We just sit here and people stare at us and we stare back at them." He points to a smaller fake moon in the corner of the room that begins to glow brightly. "They like to see things like us up close."

"They just watch us?"

"That's the idea. Supper's crew will make sure none of lookers get any other ideas."

The comment makes me shiver.

I don't sit by him, but instead find myself pacing the room before the first lookers enter. They mill about for a while, and although I can't make out what they're saying, they seem fascinated by our very existence. Couples hold hands and stare at us with shining eyes while children tumble over each other to get close to the clear plastic wall between us. One man leers at me for far too long before someone from Supper's crew hoists him away. Jack remains on the sofa, clearly bored.

We watch the people streaming past, and our water and food remains untouched as we try to ignore each other. Then, just when the silence between us begins to feel overwhelming, he opens his mouth.

"How did you do that?" he asks.

I don't have to ask what he's referring to. "I'm not sure. It's just a freak talent I recently learned I could do." Out of spite, I emphasize the work "freak" and Jack winces.

The stream of lookers has dwindled to only a handful of people nervously approaching the divider. I realize they're different, dressed in faded clothing, eyes a little too hungry and a little too haunted. But still they come as close as possible and watch me and Jack glare as if we really were two magical people from the sky.

"I can't do it," Jack says after a while. "But I don't think I'd want to. Something like that makes you valuable, and being how I am now has already been enough of a pain."

"Were you born like this?" I ask, staring back at the people staring at me.

He pauses, and for a moment I don't think he'll answer, but I can hear him rising again from the sofa and standing. "I was," he says softly. "But my brother wasn't."

"I see," I whisper.

"Our father always liked Evan better. I think it's because he hadn't been such a failure to him," he says in a quieter voice that makes me look over at him.

"Why would you think you're a failure?" I find myself asking.

"Because I can't do what you can, maybe. All the side effects and none of the action," he says, a hard and bitter edge creeping into his voice.

I think about his words and something occurs to me. He's been standoffish since we met; the easiness that I first encountered with Evan didn't naturally occur between us and it makes me think the brothers are two very different people. Still, he's been honest with me so far—a far cry from Evan—and there is something I want to know from him.

"I have to know, do you resent the fact that I can do more than you?" I ask.

"Wow, straight to it then." Jack laughs. "I mean, I have always liked a straightforward girl, but you really get right to the point, huh?"

"Friscuit, never mind." I huff and turn my back to him. He comes up behind me and places a hand on my shoulder to turn me around to look into my eyes.

"Look, Dani, I won't lie to you. I tried to get you out of my head when I first saw your glow because all it did was remind me of my past life..." He scratches at his jaw, glancing past me to the lookers, then back. "This scar on my arm is from when I was very, very young. They were taking blood from me and I tried to get away. Something broke and tore my skin, leaving me with a nasty wound. It was discovered soon after those early tests that my blood wasn't viable for their experiment, and I was just... forgotten. So no, I do not resent you for what you can do. I resent my father for making us like this and for what he's put us both through."

I let out a breath, and then my heart reacts before my mind and rest my hand on his broad chest. "Thank you for being honest with me. That's something I didn't have a lot of in my life before I came here."

He gives me a small smile and places his hand over my own. We stand like that for a moment, our two glows merging into the color of sunset before he breaks the contact with a sigh and returns to the couch, and I return to the people waiting to see us.

There are only a few now, just a single family. The husband is dressed in an old brown suit, his partner in matching grey. He holds the hand of a little girl who breaks away and runs straight to the divider, pressing her little palms between us. She's wearing what must be her best dress, an ill-fitting blue thing with a white collar covered in embroidered hearts. Her smile reminds me of Tara.

I kneel and scoop up a little dirt. There is just enough blood still oozing from my palm that it catches on a single seed and I'm able to produce a small white flower. I press it against the wall between us and the girl's smile could light up the entire night sky.

She's reluctant to leave, but Supper's people are ushering her parents back through the curtains and she has to run after them. All the same, she makes time to turn and wave to me. I wave back, watching her leave with her family.

"Waste of time, people like that never give good tips," Jack mutters from behind. Rage flares up and I whirl to grab my still full glass of water, then splash it onto his stupid face.

He reels away from me, sputtering, "What was that for?"

"For being a jerk," I say simply. I'm swiping off a bit of errant water from my shoulder when someone's deep-throated chuckle rings out behind me.

"He probably deserved that," a voice says from the open doorway and I turn, expecting to see Sally, but almost lose my balance when I come face to face with Jack's slightly older double.

Sally pokes her head from behind Evan to address Jack. "Sorry Jack, haven't see this guy since you both were little tykes and brought him around in case you wanted to see him, too. Seemed pretty interested in our little rabbit when I told him the story."

Evan grins at me and I do the only thing I can think of, which is grab the other cup of water and splash it onto his stupid face as well.

Chapter Twenty-Three

Jack and Evan exchange glances, and while they look like essentially the same person, standing next to each other makes their differences hard to ignore. Both are tall, much taller than me, and have brown hair that could be a wavy mess if left unkempt. Evan is clearly older and has eyes more like the forest hidden behind thick glasses, but Jack is my age with eyes that glow freely in an almost unnatural green and yellow hue.

I don't move out of the way quickly enough when Evan shakes water from his hair. "After everything I've done for you?"

"It's all part of the family business, secrets and lies and hiding things. What is with your family?" I avoid looking at him as I follow Sally from the plastic cube and into the darkened day. Evan and Jack trail somewhere behind us.

"Nice of you to show up," I hear Jack say to Evan, lengthening his stride to walk past him and place a hand on my shoulder, then gestures back to Evan with his thumb. "How do you know this buffoon?"

Pushing his hand away, I realize how little anyone here knows about me. Not even the triplet sisters know how I ended up nearly being run over by their beast of a land train. Maybe it's just the circus way, like Sally told me, not to pry because you never know when someone might be hiding from something or someone.

"He was the one who told me to run," I say quickly, wrapping my arms around my waist. We're far from the tent and while the dirt between my toes is warm and comforting, the wind bites at my exposed skin. Jack seems to have procured a brown leather jacket at some point, but his muscled legs are still bare. Sally slows to look back at us and frowns.

"Jack! You didn't bring anything for her to wear over that thing?" At least he has the sense to look sheepish under her hard gaze.

"I forgot," he says, his brows furrowing while Evan shakes his head at him.

"Wonderful," she mutters. I think she may also mutter a few choice names for him, but I pretend not to hear as she strips off her own plaid flannel and hands it to me, so she's in nothing but a simple short-sleeved shirt. I try to refuse because the shirt smells like a freshly-cleaned barn and attempt to give it back, but she says the years of hard work have made her skin too thick to notice something like cold.

We continue back into the dragon and the moon glows above us. To their credit, none of my companions stare at my glowing skin, and I think it might just be another example of the circus way. You spend all day and night having someone stare at you, so you don't need it from your fellow performers.

Evan's hand grabs my arm to slow me down, and Jack slows his pace with us. For a moment, I'm caught between the two of them as each looks at the other, waging some sort of war I want no part of. Luckily, I'm saved by the squeals and hollering of the few people here that I've begun to trust and consider friends.

"You were so good!" Bindy squeals, peeling Evan's hand off me.

"You must have been scared half to death, but you looked great up there!" Mindy says, shouldering Jack aside.

"We need to get you inside quickly. Can't be giving anyone a free show, especially these two!" Cindy giggles, grabbing my hands and pulling me along.

Sally chuckles good-naturedly and lets them take me, her job of escort finished. I don't even know what time it is, but it must be late because my body is weighted with exhaustion.

The sisters make sure to stuff me in a lift ahead of them and deny access to Jack and Evan.

"It's our turn," says one of them from behind me, though I have no idea who.

In a matter of minutes, we've emerged into the crowded dining floor. We must be the last performers to arrive because the noise is deafening, and to make matters works, Beetle rises to give me his own standing ovation that half the floor participates with. At least it feels welcoming, and not as if they long to stare at me like the lookers.

I stuff myself with stewed chicken over heaps of golden rice studded with chunky tomatoes. Someone has even made little loaves of bread shaped like bunnies with tiny capers for their eyes and carrots for their ears. The sisters clap in delight as they take turns making them hop about our table before cramming them into their mouths.

The world has gone dark outside the windows, but inside is warm and bright, the sounds of satisfaction from a show that went especially well. Even the smell of sweat and probably cow is dimmed by the giant cakes the cooks have wheeled out for us. The sugary icing laces the air with sweetness.

Someone had the foresight to bring in extra tables and chairs, but it's only just barely enough to seat everyone. The tumblers make room for the clowns to sit amongst them and some Stage Girls smile indulgently when Parker offers to carry food to their tables. I even see the girl from my first morning, Bluebell, take him up on the offer and smile politely when he trots after her like an eager duckling.

But for all the smiles and kind words, there is a feeling I can't quite shake from my skin. A haunted feeling deep inside that, while I may be a celebrity now, I might always be an outsider.

No one even notices when I slip away from the table, hugging an overfilled plate of jam tarts and crusty, dark pastries to my chest as I silently disappear into the nearest lift.

Everyone who is someone is on the dining floor and my footsteps echo in the lonely hallways. I'm almost to my doorway when an open door catches my attention, directly across the hall from mine. I feel almost certain it wasn't open earlier today.

I can't help looking inside.

"Looks like someone forgot to close his door on the way out." Magenta's smooth voice penetrates the still air and I find her staring out the room's one long window. My eyes became adjusted to the dim light on my walk here, so it takes no time at all to make out what lays before me. The room itself is bare, just a small bed and dresser holding an empty soda bottle, but the view makes the breath catch. I'm lured in like a moth, hypnotized beyond reason.

Beyond the window, the ocean stretches out into the flat line of the horizon. We're not especially close by, but near enough to see its distant rolling waves. It's a water so vast and enormous that it feels like it could go on and on forever.

"*It does*," Lily whispers in my ear.

I imagine setting thoughts of her free to follow the moon's bright path skimming along the water's rolling surface. But the wind brings them right back to me, so I tuck them safely back inside.

Magenta eyes me, kindly ignoring the way my hands tremble around the plate as I gaze out the window before us.

"That was some amazing trick, little rabbit," she says. "Luckily I'm used to amazing things, but others out there"—she gestures vaguely out the window— "are not used to such things because it scares them."

"I didn't mean to do it," I say softly.

"But I'm glad you did," she says, turning her back on the window to look down at me. Her golden eyes gleam in the dark. "This discovery will provide you with the thing you're so desperately searching for. A home, I think? Or perhaps it is just safety or purpose?" She tips my chin up, so I have to look at her. "Aren't you a lucky little rabbit, hm? No one can touch you now."

Magenta leaves me inside the moonlit room, and I remember too late all the questions I have for her. I rush for the door, but when I poke my head into the hallway to call out for her, she's already gone.

The next day is one of rest and relaxation—for the rest of the circus. Jack found me in the breakfast line and told me to report for more practice exactly one hour after I finished eating. I glared at him until he stalked away.

The dining floor is virtually deserted as everyone is sleeping in from the night before, but one familiar figure sits alone at my normal table, humming a familiar sounding song to himself while eating a biscuit covered in honey.

"Is that song still your favorite?" I ask, sitting across from Evan.

"Yup, Snowbird, and it's still the code I use for everything, too. I'm a simple man," he answers around a mouthful of food, voice garbled.

I take a deep breath and focus on my own plate of food. If Jack wants me climbing that ladder all day, then I'm going to need the energy. I'm considering returning to the line and stuffing my pockets with cookies when Evan loudly clears his throat.

"It's funny," he muses.

"What is?"

"That you ended up here, too. I didn't have a choice, since it's the lesser of two evils and I have to finish the RIS somewhere. But you could have ended up anywhere, in any town, with anyone. You could have been safe and living in obscurity, so the fact that you ended up back where you started is actually quite amazing."

"Nothing about what happened to me is amazing," I snap. At least he has the decency to look ashamed. "My entire life was destroyed in that fire, including the only family I ever knew, and you were there for it all. You know, with all your lies, I wouldn't be surprised if you had something to do with it."

He goes pale. "I had nothing to do with that fire. No one thought Martha capable of something like that off. Even Lacey had no clue about her plans."

"Then tell me your side of it," I spit back.

Evan's look softens and there is a sagging defeat in his shoulders. "We think Martha purposely used a fatal dose of her own blend of sleeping drugs in your toothpaste and maybe something else at dinner that night. She's fed them to you before, but always in small amounts. I think you were only ever mildly affected. If it makes it any better, we believe the girls were dead before she started the fire."

He's wrong, it doesn't make it any better. I don't think anything can.

"But why would Mother do that?" I whisper as my eyes well up with tears. I swipe them away because I don't want the few people around to see me crying.

"We think it was to spare you from what Leonard and Tobias had planned. I'm still unclear where they were taking all of you, but it definitely wouldn't have been a nice place. At the very least, it would have been a hospital of sorts. Tobias has access to a few abandoned facilities near the borders, but more likely..."

When he doesn't continue, I prompt, "More likely what?"

He sighs. "More likely it was a prison, or maybe an old asylum, somewhere to keep you bound so they could study you and keep you secure and hidden. They thought Martha's treatments were affecting results and wanted to speed things up."

"So why not let the other girls go? You said it was only me and Prim who showed any potential."

"Doesn't matter, you were all part of Zamora's little project. It's not about what you can or cannot do, it's all about what's in your blood and making more girls like you. At least Martha made sure to destroy all her notes with the fire."

"It's in Jack's blood, too," I whisper, casting a look to see his reaction. I'm not disappointed, Evan's face contorts, almost painfully, as he looks off to the side, refusing to meet my eyes.

"In Jack, but not me. They had to have a control for their first experiments, so I was spared."

I think about what life must have been like for Jack, knowing that his brother was perfectly normal, or for Evan knowing about Jack. Maybe it was lonely for both of them.

I suddenly want nothing to do with him and shove to my feet. "I need to go," I say and hurry from the dining floor while gripping my plate of breakfast food tight.

The hallways remain cool in the mornings and they raise bumps on my skin as I race back to my room. I make it there without Evan following or anyone else noticing and after the door closes behind me, I'm able to fumble my plate onto my bed before my legs give out and I slide to the floor. My body shakes from the strained torment of seeing Evan and trying to process everything that's happened between us.

The naive little crush I had on him makes me furious, and while I try to look past that, I still find myself feeling like an idiot. So sheltered that I'd reach for the first cute boy to show interest in me.

I close my eyes, cross my legs beneath me, and place my palms atop my knees, keeping my breath measured and calm as I work to empty my mind of every addled thought.

It's sometime later that I lift myself from the floor and make quick work of my now cold breakfast. Jack said I needed to wait an hour after eating, so I lay back down on my low-slung bed and close my eyes, drifting off into a restless nap.

When I wake sometime later, I see I've neglected to close the window blinds. Sitting up and rubbing the sleep from my eyes, I gaze out the window at the grounds below.

All of the circus has been wiped clean from the seedy earth. Everything is gone except the circle of deeply colored flowers that once circled the very center of Magenta's Magical World of Circus Curiosities. It is the only indication that we were ever even here.

Chapter Twenty-Four

The dragon travels quickly during the night, so we arrive at The Salted Baths the following day. Eager to see the ocean, I scramble to my window after waking but am disappointed to realize my room faces inland. But while the view lacks the picturesque beaches and sparkling waves I was told to expect, it makes up for in a sprawling city.

Up as high as I am, I can make out the tracks of homes, tall buildings that reach into the sky but are still far enough away to look small, streets and shops and vehicles and sidewalks and even people milling about, most gazing in wonder at the beast that towers over them.

As if on cue, I feel my window vibrate as the dragon bellows a greeting to the city itself, and the people below begin to clap and cheer. I sit back, stunned that a place this large could even exist, and think of how small the world on top of the hilly graveyard feels compared to this.

I'm barely dressed in the soft brown pants when the three sisters push my door open in one swift movement and their screaming enters the room with them.

"We're here!" Bindy sings in her highest and most dramatic voice. She is followed by Cindy, blushing furiously and calling over her shoulder.

"Sorry if we woke you, but you better get used to the noise. Not my problem you chose the room across from her!" She stomps inside and I peek around to see Evan standing in his doorway, looking tired and grumpy. Behind him the ocean gleams through his window, but I ignore him and close the door behind the girls.

"We're staying here forever," Cindy whispers into my ear. Her sisters clap and spin in circles, but her eyes hold mine for a moment longer as she confides in me. "People are saying this isn't just a stop over, but a permanent residence."

"Forever?" I whisper back and she nods, tapping a finger to her lips.

"Let's get something to eat, I'm starving!" Bindy wails, grabbing hold of my arm and leading our group right back out the door. Evan is just leaving his own room, but Cindy sticks her tongue out at him and skips ahead down the hall.

"What exactly are The Salted Baths?" I ask.

"Picture this," Bindy starts to explain. "It's gigantic and huge and *so big* it could fit at least *three* land trains inside. It has pools, snacks, shops, restaurants, photo booths, an ice-skating rink that I don't think is open right now, places to eat..."

"Bindy, shush, you're making me hungry!" Cindy pouts. By the time the lift has finally arrived, Evan has managed to catch up and squeezes himself inside with us.

"We're on our way to breakfast right now, so who cares!" Bindy retorts. "Anyway, it's mostly about the pools! There's slides and contests for the best dives, and shopping and maybe even famous people!" Bindy shrieks along with her sisters, and Evan and I both instinctively cover our ears.

When calm returns and the sisters have been consumed by giggles, Evan pushes his glasses further up his nose and looks down at us. "They're all saltwater pools. Pumped in from the ocean, filtered, and sent through a set of warmers."

When the lift arrives on the dining floor, Cindy, Bindy, and Mindy stop giggling long enough to roll their eyes at Evan before they scurry towards the growing lines for food.

The whole train must be getting an early start. I've never seen so many people packed onto the floor for breakfast, and even though I think I had my share of looks last night, there are now plenty of fresh faces available to shoot discrete glances at the new glowing girl. Well, the glowing girl with the incredible flower trick.

"Everyone's here today," Evan says, as if reading my thoughts. "A full day off is a rare thing."

"Makes sense," I mumble, picking up a hot plate and almost dropping it. Luckily Jack appears from nowhere and tips it back into my hands. Casting his brother a look, he steps between us, a lazy smile on his face.

"Want to go out there with me today? Couple of celebrities out on the town?" Jack smiles, and instead of answering, I seem to forget how to breathe.

"Ooh, Jack! Are you going to wear the sparkly shorts in the water?" Bindy hops to us, her plate spilling over with more than a few breakfast cookies.

"Please!" Cindy cries, swinging her free arm around her sister, the other holding tightly to her own plate of cookies.

"You three are terrible," Jack says.

"Well, I, hmm," I stammer. I've never been in anything bigger than a bathtub, and while leaving the beast seems thrilling, I don't know how to swim. There were no lakes or rivers near The Zamora House and building a pool in an old graveyard was out of the question. It wouldn't have mattered, anyway. Father would never allow us to wear something like a swimmer in the water.

Like Lily always said, he was a traditionalist.

"I don't have anything to wear, so I probably should just stay here." I laugh lightly.

I turn my back on them because I can hear them discussing something related to saltwater pools and I don't want to think about it. The thought of spending a day with Jack seems scary enough, and the thought of being in the water even scarier, but spending the day alone with the chickens and cow feels even worse.

"I can help with that," a soft voice says behind me and I turn to see the pretty stage girl, Bluebell.

"I'm sorry, help with what?"

"Getting something to wear. I know you haven't had much time, but you should have come to see me sooner." Her smile is polite, but it still brings a flush to my cheeks as I grip the sides of my plain clothes against my ribs.

"I'm sorry," I tell her and she smiles again. It seems genuine, at least.

"Come with me!" She grabs my arm and forces me from the chair to follow her. I don't even have a chance to grab a bite of food as she whisks me out the door.

"I don't think anyone has a swimmer to spare, but you won't need one," Bluebell says as the lift travels to what I'm assuming is the Stage Girls section of the dragon. "The Baths are run by some nutcase and everyone is required to wear the same thing. They basically issue you a swimmer upon arrival, as if it was some sort of boarding school, and they are terribly unflattering!"

A few of the girls in the lift already nod along with her comments and a tall blonde—Minty, I think—takes another arm so I'm sandwiched between them.

"Don't worry, we'll take good care of you," she says with a wink.

The Stage Girls are girls just barely old enough to be considered women who do almost everything on the train, from assisting the performers to working the concession stands, and even some light performing, if needed. Parker made sure to tell me they are a vital part of helping the train function properly, even if it doesn't seem like it. They come from all over: some are here for their Required Industry Service, since their towns were too small to accommodate them, while others were born into the life. A few are even runaways, who truly ran off to join the circus.

The majority of them have somehow managed to amass their rooms together to form their own small world. They make my hallway look like an abandoned graveyard in comparison to their colorful posters, dripping laundry hanging across the walkways and open doors inviting one and all.

Minty and Bluebell pull me into one of the rooms where we're met by a short man with spiky green hair and gold tattoos. The robe he's wearing seems old and shabby, but the embroidered Cloudspeak logo looks well cared for.

"Snuzzle, we need some help," Minty says, pushing me forward.

"This is the rabbit, you know, the glowing flowery one?" Bluebell says. "Seems like she's in a similar situation as we were. Came here with nothing to her name."

"I see." Snuzzle drags his words out, looking me over.

I cross my arms over my chest, feeling my cheeks flush. I sense a thin layer of scrutiny from him that makes me uncomfortable.

"I came with some things; they just weren't exactly *mine*," I tell them and Snuzzle gestures for me to stop talking.

"She looks the same size as you," says Snuzzle to Bluebell. "Get something from Butterscotch, too, but shoes would need to come from storage. None of you here have feet that small."

Minty claps her hands excitedly as Snuzzle crosses the room and pulls out a long, pale pink scarf for me. The soft fabric is almost hard to hold as it glides through my hands.

"This, too. I think you must have a brooch or pin to go with it, yes?"

I don't have time to react before the girls pull me out into the hallway.

"Oh, that's so pretty! I didn't get anything nearly as pretty when I first came," Minty tells me. "It's tradition that every new girl gets a gift, but all I got was a comb and a few hair ribbons."

Bluebell snorts. "I got a pair of socks. They were nice, at least. Snuzzle is in charge on this floor, so we had to get you approved by him." Catching my questioning look, she takes my hand and leads me down the hallway. "He's been here longer than anyone else, did his Required Service and never left. He has a passion for anyone who finds themselves alone in the world."

I want to ask more questions, but we've arrived at the only closed door in the hallway and I wait to the side as Minty pounds on it.

"Wake up, Butterscotch! You missed breakfast again!"

The door cracks open and a short girl, maybe only fourteen or so, with caramel colored hair steps aside as the girls lead me through the door.

"It's so dark in here!" Bluebell reaches over and tugs at the window blinds, bathing the room in warm sunlight. I almost think Butterscotch hisses like a cat before diving back into her blankets. Across from her is another bed that Bluebell forces me to sit on, ignoring the snoring lump across from us that Minty pokes at with a smile.

"This is our room." She gestures towards the two beds. "I have some old clothes I can give you and I'm pretty sure I know which ones Butter can part with."

"Don't give her my red dress!" Butterscotch's muffled voice calls out and Minty rolls her eyes.

Bluebell pulls items from a storage chest and then from a standing rack that holds more delicate garments. She talks excitedly the entire time about how she's been helping Snuzzle with costumes for nearly everyone in the show. Jack's sparkling shorts are her biggest hit. Minty breaks into giggles when she tells me how he had to come in for a fitting and they needed to bolt the door for privacy.

Bluebell's biggest dream is to leave Magenta after her Required Service is up and design clothing for her own boutique. Even so, she admits she doesn't know how that will ever happen because she's, in truth, just a girl from a small town close to The Dusting and isn't sure if anyone will take her work seriously. But then she tells me about some person named Talia Lake who had the biggest influence on her, so if Talia could rise from relative obscurity to such heights, then so can she.

When she becomes fully absorbed by an array of selected items that she and Minty have pulled together, I take a look around their room. It's the exact same size as mine, but much more cluttered with items from both girls. It has a cozy, well-loved feeling to the chaos that puts me at ease, so I take a seat on a low tufted stool by the side of Bluebell's bed.

Beside me on a low table are stacks of red colored journals, each well-worn and full of pictures and sketches of various items of clothing and complete outfits. Her penmanship and masterful drawings take my breath away and I hold one up to her in amazement.

"These are really good!" I gasp and she snaps her attention to me.

"I know," she laughs brightly. "But thank you, I've been drawing for as long as I can remember."

"Same here," I find myself saying. "I just...haven't in a while."

"Really? That's a shame. I find it's always been very therapeutic for me," she says, her brow wrinkling in concern. She then moves to the table and grabs a blank journal, along with a collection of small colored pencils and wraps them in a very pretty shirt which she presses into my hands.

"For later," she says and her smile warms my heart.

It takes over an hour to pick out outfits for me. It's so long that I soon hear the squeals and giggles from the hallway, which I can only assume means someone is coming to find me.

Bluebell pulls an assortment of pants she has painted various decorations on, shirts dyed in all shades of purple, and a few bedazzled dresses. Minty lays them into outfits next to me on the bed. Their trunk, pushed up under the window now, still won't close from everything still inside.

Butterscotch even wakes up and donates a fuzzy white sweater she claims to have outgrown and a satiny dress made of a similar material to Snuzzle's scarf. Instead of pink, this one shines in the soft peachy color of sunset. At some point, Minty looks at my feet and disappears, only to return a minute later with a few pairs of worn shoes.

They've dressed me in a pair of faded shorts, almost paper-thin, which I'm assured is a deliberate fashion choice, and a short-sleeved white shirt from Bluebell.

"So much better than those drab outfits I gave you earlier," Bluebell says with pride and the others nod in agreement.

Minty bundles everything together, taking care to fold the scarf around my neck, and kisses my cheek. Bluebell does the same and the gestures hurl me through space and time and suddenly I'm back at Zamora House surrounded by the other house girls.

I had never given the Stage Girls much notice, only knowing what Parker had ever explained, which is next to nothing since they don't give him the time of day. Butterscotch looks like she hasn't slept in ages, the rings under her eyes dark and troubled, and while Minty is tall with blond hair that cascades down her back in loose curls, she walks with a halting limp, occasionally clamping her hand against a wall for support. Then there is Bluebell, cherub-faced with tight brown ringlets, who has the ghost of a long, thin scar that winds around her neck like a tight-fitting necklace.

No, I certainly do not know them. But I find I wouldn't mind it.

"Thank you," I whisper and give them what I hope is a grateful smile. Being with them almost makes it feel like I'm back at home with the house girls and the life I left behind in the fire. I press my knuckles into my eyes to keep from crying, but a sharp knock and Parker's chipper voice brings me back to the present.

"Dani, you in there?"

"Is that Parker?" Butterscotch asks, burying herself once more in her bedsheets.

"I think so." Bluebell giggles and pushes me towards the door. "We'll see you later, Dani. Good luck out there!"

The door closes behind me with a loud locking sound. Parker, seemingly unfazed, grins at me. Behind him, I can see Jack speaking effortlessly with a few girls and Evan looking nervous, like he's not sure whether or not to look at the shirtless girl beside Jack.

"I let Jack and Evan know I had dibs on taking you to The Baths today, but I couldn't shake them," Parker says, glancing back. "Looks like they'll be tagging along, but we could lose them if you want."

"It's fine," I mutter.

Parker and I walk past Evan and Jack, who fall into step behind us. They're already dressed and it startles me to see either wearing something more casual. In my dreams Evan is a hazy blur but always has on a lab coat, and Jack, well, he just sparkles.

I have just enough time to toss my new stash of clothes in my room and go to unwind the scarf when I change my mind. The fabric feels cool and comforting around my neck so I leave it on, but just before walking out, I pull out the flying starling brooch and secure it in place on the scarf.

Then I join Parker in the hallway for what he promises will be a memorable day. As if I hadn't had my share of those lately.

Chapter Twenty-Five

T he hallways seem quiet, but there is still an undercurrent of excitement and fun that accompanies the surrounding emptiness.

"That looks good," Evan says, gesturing to the scarf. Jack leans over to straighten the pin and nods absently, glancing around the empty hallways. I do my best to not look at either of them.

"You can thank Bluebell for that," I say, looking down to hide the redness creeping into my cheeks. "She was channeling her inner Talia Lake."

"They'll be out of swimmers by this time," Parker says, his shoulders dropping slightly. "But we can still make a day of it."

"I'm sure we can," I say brightly, trying to ignore the hulking figures close behind us. "Jack gave me some of the money I earned from working the cubby, maybe you can help me spend it on something."

Parker stops walking altogether as he stares open-mouthed at my hand when I show him my earnings, several hundred tightly rolled paper bills I'm told is quite a bit of money. Parker certainly seems to think so, and I'm glad I left the other half in my room.

"Maybe I can douse myself with some glowing paint and join you next time," he laughs, running a shaking hand through his messy hair. "Don't think I've seen someone earn that much."

"It's the novelty of seeing something new," Jack laughs and Parker waves him off.

"Well, I've never seen you earn half as much, she must do well because she's so much prettier than you. I still wouldn't stand a chance seeing as I'm only marginally more attractive."

Evan lets out a laugh that nearly causes his glasses to slip off while Jack pretends to push Parker away from my side. Parker is too quick because he latches onto my arm and pulls us into the quickly closing lift before either of the brothers can catch up.

If the land train is a dragon, then the building that houses The Salted Baths is a monster. The smooth marble surfaces glow where the sun hits white stone walls, and I have to blink several times for my eyes to adjust to the light. Manicured shrubs and small trees line the way, and various paved walkways lead towards the entrance. There must be a million pale pink butterflies flying over us, flittering from leaf to leaf and flower to flower.

"Tobias has them flown in from some farm down south," Evan says when he catches me looking at them.

A smaller stairway leads us to open front doors. From them, I can make out even more polished white stone walkways, but the many plants here are kept tightly pruned in pristine and shiny vases and planters. The sounds of water echo from afar, but while the view inside is large, you can't see anything but fantastically dressed people milling about.

"This is the main entrance," Jack says, stepping next to me. Evan pushes his way forward to my other side, but Parker seems drawn in by the crowds and floats ahead as if in a daze.

"There's another one off to the side that caters to those here for the sole purpose of visiting the pools. This is where the elite tend to enter," Evan says. "You know, those with money."

"Oh, like you?" I ask and he nods slowly.

A woman walks by using tiny steps, a man behind her leading two screaming children. Her white dress is so fitted to her body that it looks hard for her to breathe and her lipstick is red like blood. She barely spares me a glance, but the man stops and clears his throat loudly in front of us.

"Do I know you?" he asks, frowning at Evan, and then Jack. I shrink behind their forms and wonder where Parker went off to.

"You did once," Evan says and extends his hand towards the man, who drops his child's hand and immediately takes Evan's. "But we were much younger at the time."

Jack rolls his eyes.

"The Cloudspeak boys!" The man chuckles loudly, looking around to see if anyone notices his good fortune. He puffs his chest and slaps a heavy hand on Jack's shoulder. "So good to see you both here."

Evan speaks smoothly with the man, though we're soon converged on by more richly-dressed people. There are polite smiles and answers to questions on what he's been doing, studying, and working on with his father, to what his future holds—which might have to do with fund raising.

The people milling about feel suffocating and I back away to the side. Jack leans into me until we find ourselves standing aside, barely part of the conversation. I try to focus on the slight movements of his shoulders he makes with every deep breath.

"Sycophants," he whispers into my ear. "Clingers-on to the Cloudspeak name. It's a shame they don't know how he really is."

Yes, I can see how that would be true. While Evan answers their questions easily, he neglects to mention Tobias Cloudspeak is a murderer. Or maybe these people also have similar secrets. The thought alone makes my palms sweat.

"I've taken up much of your time," Evan is saying now, extracting himself from the woman in the white dress who is kissing his cheeks in an overly affectionate way. He grabs my hand and I try to snatch it away, but his grip is surprisingly strong and there is a familiarity to the sweatiness in his palms. "I'm sure my companions are famished with it being well past lunch time."

Jack presses a hand to the small of my back and pushes me forward with Evan. We have to walk through the group of people and I can feel their eyes on me. Oh friscuit, it makes my stomach hurt not knowing what they're thinking.

"Finally!" Parker says jogging back towards us. "I've seen enough of this area, fascinating but too, what's the word, stuffy? Rich? Filthy rich? You know what I mean?"

"Out of place?" I suggest, but Parker's attention catches on the woman in the white dress. I turn towards Evan and Jack. "Can we go inside now?"

"Of course," Jack says, taking my hand from Evan. The light catches his face in just the right way to make the dark rings under his eyes clearly visible, and without thinking, I reach up to rub away a small smudge of red lipstick off his cheek. The woman in the white dress got to him at some point as we passed by.

Then his other hand presses against my back and I'm flung into the present. "Come on, I'll show you a good time," he says, which immediately brings Parker bounding back to us.

"Let's go already, I'm starving!" Parker bounces on his feet and earns a hard look from both Evan and Jack.

Parker and I follow Evan to the top of the stairs and I realize we're passing by a long line of people waiting to go inside. They're all so formally dressed, but I really couldn't tell the difference between any of them if I tried. It makes me wonder why they would dress so nicely for a public pool house, but it becomes immediately clear when I take my first steps towards the main entrance.

A young woman with vibrant red hair at the front of the line takes one look at Jack and Evan and lets them through without question. She even bats her eyelashes at Jack, but Evan is the one who grins back at her.

Across the threshold is another world. The brothers take the lead because Parker and I are too overwhelmed by the sights and sounds to do much more than gawk at everything around us.

We encounter first a fountain bigger than my room on the train, so big that several people could bathe inside if there wasn't a prominent sign warning them not to. The granite has been carved into ten different lions and tigers spouting water from their mouths, and the tiles that line the bottom sparkle in blues and greens and purples.

Parker dips a hand in the cool water and splashes me, breaking the mystic trance. I retaliate and splash him back until we both earn one too many disapproving glances from a nearby guard and decide to stop.

The smell of chemically-enhanced water clings to the fountain's damp edges. But under the clean and aquatic air simmers something much more familiar. Food.

Parker must smell it too because he is turning in circles trying to find the source. Jack chuckles when he follows us from the fountain waters and towards the wonderful aromas. Evan stays busy speaking with a well-dressed woman with lilac-colored hair and has to hastily excuse himself to catch up with us.

"That was Talia Lake, I invited her to our next show," he tells me. I nod absently as Parker pulls me to a nearby seating area and we suddenly find ourselves gazing down at The Salted Baths.

The fountain's sound becomes muffled by the sounds of splashing, people shouting and laughing and eating and water pushing and pulling against itself in three large pools below. There is even a roaring waterfall off to the side that only adds to the wonder.

High above our heads must be a million windows and I marvel at how the entire space, bigger than anything I could ever imagine, is covered in glass panels. Most of the panes are clear, but every so often there is one that shines in a multitude of colors to create quilted patterns of colored light on the tiled floors around us.

Directly below are rows of seats lined along a long viewing platform and I can see some of the fancy families have positioned themselves on them, chatting away with each other while their children stare longingly at the pools far below.

"We're at the top of the world," Parker mumbles, glancing around. I can see what he means. I walk forward, ignoring the looks the elegantly dressed people give me, and go to the very edge of the polished railing before us. Just below is a second tier teeming with a livelier crowd, most wearing plain black swimmers embroidered with the large letters of "S" and "B." They make up most of the crowd and only a few of the fancier people mingle among them. Below that is the bottom level connecting with the pools and it teems with even more people, none of whom wear anything but the simple black swimmers.

The air is balmy and I inhale deeply, closing my eyes to listen to the din surrounding us. It's not the singing of birds or the quiet rustling of trees, though I think I can hear the fluttering of a nearby potted plant. No, it sings in its own melody of laughter and smiles laced with the smells of fried foods and sticky sugar.

But when I open my eyes and look around me, it seems so divided. These people around me in their nice clothes only seem outwardly happy, licking their ice cream and sipping soda from crystal clear glasses. But below I can make out one family all sharing a single soda bottle. They're passing it between themselves amid jokes and laughter.

I'm watching a mother pulling what looks like a squashed sandwich from her purse to share with her children when Jack leans against the railing next to me. We both frown at the scene below.

"I don't think I like it up here," I whisper.

"I don't either," he says, following my gaze towards the family. He turns his back to the rail and looks around the deck with hollow eyes. "The crowd down there is lucky to be able to visit The Salted Baths and afford dinner in the same day."

"Speaking of dinner, I'm starving!" Parker throws an arm around my shoulders. "I can't afford the stuff up here, let's get down a level."

I have to peel myself away from the view, but the promise of food has me and Parker hurrying down the nearest stairs to the second level. A burly attendant is positioned just after the final step. I have a feeling we will not be permitted to return the way we came.

The second level is much busier, and while there are still fancy people here, the majority of Bath customers look as if they came directly from the pools, glistening with moisture that seems to quickly evaporates in the warm air. It's much louder as well, and when I lean over this railing, I'm sometimes hit with a spray of salty water from below.

No one is wearing shoes, so Parker and I stop on a nearby bench and take ours off, but we have to take turns carrying them as we hadn't thought to bring a bag. Evan keeps his on, but Jack ties his laces together and swings them over his shoulder. After rolling up his pant legs he gives me a devilish grin as he undoes the top row of his shirt buttons. I pretend not to notice, but can't say the same for the women and some men nearby.

Parker chooses the closest food stall and the smell of sizzling sausages fills my senses completely. Shoving a few of my rolled bills into his hand, I tell him to get us something good and he runs off with a squeal of delight. I then find Evan, who has picked a quieter table off to the side, but Jack is nowhere to be found.

Evan takes his off glasses and wipes them with a clean napkin from his pocket as he considers me.

"The sun looks good on you," he says.

"As opposed to what? Fake moonlight?"

"I guess." He puts his glasses back on and runs a hand through his hair, which in the warm air remains perfectly flopped to the side in soft brown curls. "Dani, I haven't had a chance to talk to you, and I have to know…Do you hate me?"

The question is startling because I'm not sure how to answer. It wouldn't be a definite "no," but would it be a "yes"? I try to think of how Lily would answer, or even Prim, but I'm surrounded by so many foreign sounds that conjuring up their memory is an impossible task.

"I don't hate you," I start, and rather than looking satisfied, his face remains neutral. "You helped to save me. Which is more than I can say for Mother. She selfishly cared too much and Father really only wanted to save himself. I don't hate you, but I think I want to."

"You sound like Jack," he says.

"Do I?"

"I was a toddler when he was born, so I was too young to remember what they did to him. All I know is that our mother let Tobias and the Zamoras do their testing while she was carrying him, but she made them stop midway through. She died right after they handed Jack to her when he was born and had to pry him from her cold hands."

Evan's face is far away, and after a heartbeat or two, he smiles and continues.

"I got off easy because I was normal, but Tobias hid Jack at The Salted Baths and kept him in the brightest of daylight so no one knew—that is, until the right person came along at the right time. Magenta had brought her show here when he was about ten and she found him by chance one night. By the time our father and his staff realized he was missing, he was well on his way to becoming a star performer in Magenta's Magical World of Circus Curiosities."

"Then no one could touch him," I muse.

Evan looks through me as if he's thinking hard on something. "You must miss the other girls. I know Lacey went back into the fire, but I don't know what came of it. Once Tobias became suspicious of my tinkering with his plans, I had to get out of there quickly. Lucky for me, Magenta has a soft spot for Jack, so she let me tag along, no questions asked."

Parker appears in a flash and carefully sets two trays in front of us. "What are you guys talking about? You look much too serious for a place like this." While he beams happily at me, I take a moment to ponder Evan's words.

I'm not sure what to think. I knew Jack was connected to me in some way—that much was obvious with his glow—but the deepness of the connection is making me short of breath. To know he was tampered with as well makes my stomach roil with anger, and it feels like the glass patchwork ceiling above is crumbing down on me, shards of glass and light piercing my lungs and making it hard to breathe.

It's all too much, the pain I can't remember, the pain I know others have endured because of someone's science experiment. None of us asked for this.

As I think too hard on my feelings, the world begins to swim in its own salted pool and I clutch my hand to my chest, willing the spinning, whirling terribleness of everything to slow and let me catch my breath.

Just one more breath.

I just need to breathe.

So I close my eyes...

Chapter Twenty-Six

I fell off a tree once and the impact kicked all the air from my lungs. I remember laying on the ground with Tara screaming above me and Lily holding my hand. I thought I would die, but Lily's voice broke through the panic and somehow led me back to life.

Parker's chatter seems far away when I feel someone's hand on my own and another hand pressing into the skin above my heart in a firm, but warm way. It is not Lily's face I see when I open my eyes, but Jack's penetrating green gaze.

"If you can fly through the air, glow like the moon, and make flowers from the dirt, then you can do this," he says, breathing in deeply and letting the air go in a long slow breath that tickles my face. "You speak your heart and you're beautiful, nothing bothers you, you are Daniella Starling."

I claim my breaths one at a time, drawing strength from his sincere words and letting the world come back into focus and snap back in place.

"So, anyway, I couldn't decide and got you one of each," Parker is saying and I have to look at his gesturing hands and struggle to put together what he is saying about the two trays of food he's brought back to us. I'm too embarrassed to admit I wasn't paying attention.

"It all looks good," I say, moving a single white container within easy reach. Inside is steaming golden rice laced with small chunks of seared tofu. Evan hands me a fork and, smiling, takes a large bite from his own flaky pastry. Jack grabs a fork and starts stealing bites of my tofu; I let him take only a few before pushing him away and laughing so he grabs another container for himself.

"When I was in line, I overheard someone talking about one of the Black Markets happening tonight somewhere," Parker says between bites of crispy chips covered in a melted yellow goo. He offers me the second half and I nibble on them.

"They're usually held on the weekends." Jack turns his attention away from the pools and towards Parker. "And I doubt anyone who 'heard' something even knows what they heard, probably just making up stories."

"What are the Black Markets?" I ask.

"Mainly cow meat," Evan answers, wiping crumbs from his shirt. "They sell all the bits, but Father only ever bids on the prime cuts."

Jack looks at him with a slight narrow to his eyes. He must be thinking the same thing as I am: how could anyone eat a cow?

"Is he still involved in that?" Jack asks.

"As far as I can tell." Evan shrugs. "You know him, has to keep up appearances for his investors, the good ones and the bad ones. You better tell Sally to keep watch on the circus cow."

The color drains from my face. "But they're so rare and Sally's cow is so nice, why would anyone eat them?"

"They used to all the time, but these days, if you have enough money, you can eat them whenever you want." Jack swipes another bite of my tofu, but most of my hunger vanishes when I think about eating Magenta's prize cow.

We spend the rest of the meal on lighter topics and when I can't stomach any more than a few more bites of chips and a piece of cinnamon pastry, Evan asks if I would like to tour the pool floor and I hesitantly accept.

Parker excuses himself and lets us know he has to get back to the chickens, but looks incredibly crestfallen at missing out. I promise to come back with him the first chance we get and he brightens, but still looks longingly over his shoulders as he disappears out a side door.

Sandwiched between Evan and Jack, we make our way from the picnic area and down another flight of pebbled stairs. A large walkway separates us from the pool edges, but we still keep a distance from the water that seems to reach out at every turn.

We pass the largest pool, which Evan says is the shallowest while pointing out the walkway that circles around and cuts down the middle. He explains it's mainly for families with small children and we hurry away from it when the screaming becomes overwhelming.

The second pool is much deeper and set snugly in the middle of the three. Several large slides empty in from the sides, and farther on, next to a wide wall made of crystal-clear glass, are several large platforms he tells me are for diving competitions.

We stand and watch a few courageous people, and some I recognize as Magenta's tumblers, take turns leaping from the shortest platform. No one dares attempt the tallest, but I think Jack probably could if he wanted to. He flies through the air, after all.

Then we're at the furthest and smallest pool, the one with the waterfall emptying into from the side. Here the water only ungulates with small rippling waves from several couples, each serenely swimming together, their eyes glued on nothing but each other. When I notice a man and a woman entangled together behind the waterfall, I turn away blushing, realizing the top of her swimmer is completely down her waist.

I find myself looking back up at the glass ceiling. The day started out clear, but a thick haze has settled against the glass tiles and turned the cover into an opaque grey blanket. Combined with the wet heat and full stomach, I suddenly feel exhausted and have to focus on walking as I follow Jack and Evan away from the clinging couples.

"It'd be good to get out of here before everyone else," says Evan, and Jack, nodding, places his hand on the small of my back. My skin tingles under his palm and I have to resist leaning back into him. I think Evan pretends not to notice, but I can see his lips form into a thin line.

"Let's go out the same why we came in," I hear Jack say through the hazy feeling. "I don't think I can stomach going through the upper levels again."

I'm led out a set of doors that empties out into a hallway stretching from either side and that's when all the greasy but wonderful food hits me.

Suddenly.

Violently.

My stomach cramps in a twisted and painful need.

Oh friscuit, I need a toilet.

Now.

"Would you mind if we stop at the washroom?" I ask quickly, stopping and standing as still as possible to help quiet my insides. They look back at me and I give them each my best smile, hoping they don't see the beads of sweat forming above my brow.

"Sure, this way," Evan says and I scurry after him. I think I hear Jack chuckle, but I don't even care because Evan is pointing to a nearby toilet sign and I'm running into the little room all while cursing Parker's food choices.

Afterwards, I stand at the mirrors letting warm, soapy water run through my fingers. I think that perhaps I can just stay there, feeling the water, hearing the water, and pretending that water is all there is.

When I finally exit, I see them standing to the side, their attention on a small boy excitedly running up a marble staircase to the left. Above the top step is an ornate sign indicating the way towards "Aviary Wonderama, where one can experience all of earth's feathery features."

I'm making my way towards them when a large hand clamps on my shoulder, fingers digging into my flesh, and a hand snakes around my front to offer me a lollipop.

Only this time, I don't have anyone to step between Tobias Cloudspeak and myself. I turn around on shaking legs.

"Daniella," he says with a smile that does not reach the dark forests of his eyes. "I heard the rumors of Magenta's new glowing girl and wondered if that was you. What an absolute joy it is to see you again."

"My name is Dani," I tell him, but I can't even hear my voice against the memory of a sharp gunshot and Father's head laying in a pool of red blood. The same red color as the candy Tobias holds out to me now.

"Father." Jack's cooling voice breaks me from my trance and I once again feel him pulling me to his side. Evan arrives just after him, his eyes watchful.

The smile on Tobias Cloudspeak grows even bigger, if that could even happen, and he retracts his treat while taking in our trio. "Dani, that's right. It's good to see you boys, too," he rumbles. "So very, very good."

"Yes, it's been a pleasure," Evan says, "but we'll leave you to your evening. I'm sure you've got big plans happening tonight." Evan takes a place at my side so I'm between them both.

"What do you care about my plans? Neither of you ever took any interest in family affairs before. Just useless morons, the both of you. Why even have sons if they don't..."

His rant is interrupted by the little boy from the stairs running full speed into his knees with smile.

"Tobias! You said we could see the birds! You promised!" the child screams and Evan, Jack, and I take an instinctive step back.

The look on Tobias's face softens, and for a splitting second, I think I see a completely different man. It scares me knowing he can hide that darkness so well.

"Why yes I did, Miles!" Tobias laughs, roughing the little boy's hair. "I just wanted to wait for Miss Daniella here to accompany us. She loves birds just as much as you, and I've invited her along for our little jaunt. Isn't that exciting?"

I can feel Jack and Evan stiffen beside me, but Miles is all smiles, and despite my absolute terror being anywhere near the man in front of me, this child looks up with eyes full of wonder, as if he were Lily reading a new book or Tara finding a particularly beautiful butterfly.

I straighten my back and step forward, feeling Jack's hand disappear and leaving a cold spot in its wake. I smile at Miles and he smiles back, offering me his hand.

"I would love to go see some birds!" I tell him and his hand, which is sticky from who knows what, clamps around my own and he drags me towards the stairs, excitedly chattering about various feathers he's collected over the years and asking me to read every single sign that lines the walls.

The top of the stairs lets us into a much cooler section of The Salted Baths, and I'm very glad we've left the warm air behind. My encounter with Tobias, who is now only several steps behind, has left me sweaty, and I don't think I'd last long if we were still within distance of the humid air.

Jack and Evan edge further back, refusing to let me out of their sight but not willing to get near enough Tobias to elicit conversation. Miles, on the hand, dances back and forth between our three separate parties talking nonstop about everything he encounters.

I have to admit I am impressed. Despite the fear dripping down my spine, the collection is truly amazing. It's a series of several connecting rooms, each showcasing different taxidermy birds and the long-destroyed environments in which they were once found.

It's also sad, knowing that every glass display case we come across is filled with long-dead things, their glass eyes staring blankly into a world so far removed from their own.

Miles is unfazed and presses his face against every glassy surface trying to get closer looks, and as he wanders about, I notice we've drawn an audience. What began at first as a few young workers following at a respectful distance, carrying wipes and glass cleaner, no less, have now formed into a small mob and I notice Jack has moved closer.

Miles is chattering about his mother, who I learn is an assistant of Tobias, and we're admiring a group of penguins when I turn to see Evan, his face neutral and distant as he listens to Tobias explain something unintelligible in a gruff whisper. Evan lets out a sharp laugh that gets even the attention of Miles and gestures around the room with both arms.

"Just look around you, do you think you'd be able to do something like that?" he asks, and Tobias Cloudspeak's face goes red as it puffs with anger.

I take a moment to consider Evan's words, all too aware of the stares and whispers, the way Jack has moved to my side and now smiles at the people around us.

Jack is speaking with a young couple when Tobias approaches and throws an arm around my shoulders with a loud, but forced, laugh. He smiles at the crowd surrounding us and throws out his best, most winning smile.

"Hiya everyone! You've no doubt recognized our new star, Miss Daniella Starling! In case you haven't heard, she comes from circus royalty and we at The Salted Baths couldn't be happier to have acquired her for permanent residence." His voice bellows throughout the glass cases, and I'm the only one who seems to notice the veiled threat in his words, or the way his fingers dig painfully into my shoulders.

I can't even look at him, so I look down and happen to catch Miles in the act of stealing one of the stuffed birds and hiding it in his shirt. He giggles and holds a finger to his lips for me to keep quiet and I can't help but mimic the gesture and wink.

"And of course, there is her partner, the famous Jack Cloudspeak, The Flying Cloud himself, and my pride and joy. Oh, my boy Jack, I'm looking forward to having you around again as well. No more galivanting around the country, eh?"

Jack's smile is stiff as he waves at the people. Tobias leans down to my level, and for all his good looks and well-pressed suit, his words are as ugly and foul as his breath.

"Victoria was a dullard and Scarlet, while beautiful, made terrible choices for her family. Your Aunt Martha was as smart as she was arrogant and the only of those three sisters who ever got one step ahead of me—temporarily, that is. Pity she's dead, I'd dearly love to repay her tenfold for what she did to my experiment."

"*Aunt* Martha? She was related to my mother?" His statement sends a painful jolt down my spine. I have to place a sweaty hand on the nearest glass case to keep myself from falling over.

"Don't play dumb with me," Tobias says, leaning in much too close to my face. "Unless you really are as dumb as the rest of your family, though since you're the last one alive, maybe you are the brightest, however much of a dimwit you actually are."

"You're a monster," I whisper.

"Perhaps I am, but you know everything I do is for the greater good," he says with a smile. "And that includes helping Leonard to purchase you from your little circus freak of a family. I own you and always will."

"You don't own me, I—"

"Yes, I do, you little...You know what?" Tobias sputters. "I don't like you. There's too much familiarity in your spunk, it's disrespectful and you should know your place among your elders and betters. But, alas, I need you, especially now. You'd speed things up tremendously if I had full access to you back in my labs." He licks his lips and smiles at me.

"I will never go anywhere with you," I tell him, shrinking away as he lurches forward.

His breath is hot in my face as he speaks. "Martha may have destroyed her notes and our test subjects, but she made a mistake in not ensuring her ultimate success was dead along with them. If you will just come with me, I can explain..." Tobias makes to grab me again but a woman nearby thinks he's posing for a photo and snaps several pictures of us, to which Tobias transforms his face in a flash and is suddenly all smiles and kind words.

Jack inches forward and peels me away from his father's iron grip.

"My fans," he begins, raising his voice to be heard, "thank you so much for your hospitality and sweetness, but we really need to be getting back. Our new starlet needs to recharge her fuel rods for our upcoming performances." Amid disappointed but kind hearted farewells, Jack is able to lead me through the door, down the steps, and into the shadow of the beast before I can even formulate a second thought.

Evan is right behind us and when I turn to look at him, I can see the fear and what could even be loathing. He follows us inside the train without a word.

It isn't until I'm in the lift, each of the brothers standing on either side, that my legs give out and I fall to the floor, covering my face in my scarf and letting out the agonizing and painful scream I didn't realize I was holding deep inside.

Chapter Twenty-Seven

I don't know how long I scream into my scarf, but I feel arms around my shoulders and someone's chin resting on my head. I don't know which brother it is until I hear Jack's voice close to my ear.

"Let's get you back to your room," he says and I nod, all feeling gone from my body as I rise on shaky legs next to him. He wraps his arms around my shoulders and I find myself tucking my face into his chest. It's like we're flying through the air again, but we're actually just walking silently down the cool hallways.

Evan follows closely behind and is the one to open my door and close it securely behind us. Jack sits on the bed next to me and Evan sits on the floor.

"I don't know what I was expecting," I say. "I had a feeling I'd see him again; I just didn't realize it would be so hard."

"He's a difficult person to deal with," Evan says from the floor. "Always has been. You should try working for him. He's also insane, but still charismatic enough to talk people into selling their children to him. Good thing your parents changed their minds and tried to run."

"But then he had them killed to keep it quiet," Jack adds.

"I saw him kill Father," I blurt out.

"I know," Evan says, running his hand through his hair. "His people did a good job hiding that murder, so no one would believe you if you went public about it. It was the same with the Starlings. I'm not sure who helps, but he always finds someone to come in and clean things up for him."

"No one knows he's a murderer?"

"No, but I can tell you I think he suspects I had something to do with the fire, which I'd like to say again that I was in no way involved with." Evan leans back, closing his eyes tightly. "I haven't seen Lacey since that night. I ran into Milton and he thinks she was transferred to another lab, but I'm not so sure."

"He wanted me to go with him," I muse and Jack's eyes snap open at the comment.

"Go with him, where?" Jack asks.

"Some place he can drain all my blood? He also said something about my birth mother, Scarlet, and her sisters – that Martha, Mother, was the only sister who got a step ahead of him. And he mentioned Victoria... I think she was Father's first wife."

"Three brooches for three sisters," Jack says and turns to glare at Evan. "Did you know about that?"

"I knew as much as anyone would tell me," Evan answers and I feel my stomach drop at his words.

What other secrets has he been hiding from me?

"You always were such a liar," says Jack. "Even when we were kids."

"Stop it, Jack, I want to hear what Evan has to say for himself. I think he owes it to me," I say, nudging Jack's shoulder with my own. He lets out a big sigh and lays back on the bed, his eyes glued to the ceiling above.

Evan sighs, rubbing his forehead. "Like I said, I knew as much as I was supposed to know. There was a houseful of sick girls and the doctors residing there needed assistance in finding a cure. Then Lacey found some old files stored away and, well, they referenced Jack and our mother in them. We then built out the connection to this project going on at The Zamora House with the death of my mother and the alteration of my brother's blood."

I feel Jack stiffen beside me, but he doesn't sit up.

"When I heard there was a workforce going on site, I made sure to tag along to see what Lacey and I could uncover."

"The people from the white tent," I say softly and Evan nods.

"Being the boss's son has its advantages, at least for me, so I got to be very hands-on. We were putting together a report to take it public, but everything went horribly wrong before we could."

"Don't pretend this is about me and mom," Jack says from beside me. "You and I both know you're more ambitious than that."

Evan visibly bristles before saying, "It wouldn't be so bad to see that man knocked from his throne. I'd lead the company in a much better, and more ethical, direction."

"And there it is," Jack mumbles in response and Evan glares at his prone form.

"Did you know the connections between everyone when you first met me?" I ask. "And how does Magenta fit into all this?"

"Hasn't she told you?" Evan asked, cocking his head to side. I shake my head. "She probably has, but in her own backwards way. She gave you that pin, right? The starling birds? The pins are part of a set. Martha had the one you took, the nest; I noticed it the first time I met her. Your mother had one, the flying bird, I saw it on a picture of her. Even Victoria had one, the bird on the branch. It's in some of her photos. Three matching birds for three matching sisters—well, not matching like the crazy Lindy sisters, but similar enough."

"How do you know all this?" Jack cuts in.

"You should know, Jack, the Cloudspeaks keep a lot of notes," says Evan. "I found some old journals in my research that spoke of how Leonard, Magenta, and the sisters all went to school together, and then afterwards, Father employed Leonard to work for his new company. All of them were very close and Leonard had this deep obsession with Scarlet, but she ran away to join the circus with Magenta, and he settled on marrying Victoria and, later on, Martha. Maybe that's why he had to have you, because you were a part of Scarlet. I think Tobias always made fun of him for it."

My eyes wander to Lily's duffle bag. I think about the bird brooches tucked safely away and marvel at their history with my family. Maybe that's why they always brought a sense of calm, as if the metal wings and crystal eyes were always trying to connect with me.

"Tobias said something about them, the smartest being Martha, and...Scarlet and Victoria." I trail off, lean over, and grab Lily's bag to dig through it until my hands lay on the leather journal. I sit on the floor beside Evan and the love letters fall from the journal's binding, but I ignore them to vigorously flip through the pages.

And there she is, her picture placed neatly on her page of facts, diagrams pointing to her children and lots of tiny scribbled notes. Leonard's first wife, Victoria Zamora, sits unsmiling and still in her photograph. She's wearing the same bird brooch Andrea has in her photo and they both have the same blue eyes as Mother.

As I let my mind wander thinking about the whereabouts of the third brooch and the fate of my cousins, the journal slips from my hands. Jack easily catches it, bringing it up on the bed with him and flipping through the pages. Meanwhile, Evan picks up the stack of love letters and goes through them with wide eyes.

Jack leaves the journal open on Victoria's page and eyes the photos I've hung over the bed. He pulls down a photo of Scarlet and holds it next to Victoria's picture and I see it, the resemblance between sisters. When I close my eyes and think, I can see Mother's face next to theirs. Such different lives each woman had, all leading to the same fate.

"Did Tobias say why he wanted you to go with him?" Jack asks and I wonder for the first time why Tobias would only want me. He already has a glowing son to use for fame and fortune, but there is something I can do that he cannot. I can bring life.

"Because I am the success," I whisper.

Evan's attention has been on the letters, but now he meets my eyes. There is something distant in them as if he's thinking hard on something and choosing his words carefully. "They had to deem the experiment a failure since everything, and everyone, was destroyed in the fire. At least, until he found you still alive."

"I won't let him take you," Jack says. He returns the photo and his eyes rest a moment on the gate key and keychains on the shelf. He returns to the journal's pages.

"*We. We* won't let him take you," clarifies Evan and holds up the letters. "Or these, too, for that matter."

"The love letters? You're right, no one needs those."

"That's not what they are. Well, it's mostly what they are, but it's a correspondence, a back and forth between Martha and Leonard around the time they were married. They're notes, and I think the formulas and calculations in here may be correct, or close enough. This is how they tinkered with you during your embryonic stages. Not exactly the way they made Jack, but the way they made you and the rest of the girls do the things you do."

I stare at him until Jack clears his throat and catches our attention.

"Considering there seems to be a lot of, um, *connecting* information in this book, my guess is that it will be of high value to Tobias," Jack says, moving to the edge of the bed and eyeing the stack of letters. "We need to hide these from him."

When Evan gives him a questioning look, he sighs and points at the closed door to my room.

"It's no secret where she's currently residing. While her actual disappearance would be questioned, something disappearing from her room would not be. It happens more than you know."

"I'll lock my door," I say.

"A locked door is not going to stand in Tobias Cloudspeak's way," Jack says. "We need to hide them somewhere else. We need to give them to Magenta."

I feel a cold shudder as I imagine Tobias Cloudspeak sneaking into my room and going through my things. It sounds like Jack trusts Magenta and if I trust in him, shouldn't that mean I can trust her too? I think so. Besides, I can't think of any other place to hide the journal and letters.

Evan takes the journal from Jack and stuffs the letters inside. "You're probably right, Magenta it is."

"I'll take her there now," Jack says, looking at the small clock encased into one of my walls. He frowns. "Then I have to go to practice."

Evan looks at him and returns the frown.

"Do you think she'll be safe now that he's confirmed we have her?" Jack questions Evan as if I'm not even here, but I admit I'm curious to know what he thinks since he seems to have been the one most involved with Tobias in the past, but he only shakes his head.

"I don't know," Evan says. "He knows he can't touch her now. She has to perform or it'll draw suspicion which will cause trouble for his investors. It wouldn't be a smart move, but who's to say he couldn't change the show now that we're in residence and make it so he has more control? I just don't know."

"Find out," Jack says, his brow wrinkled in thought. "I'll keep her in my sight for now. We'll go someplace public tomorrow, like The Baths, and before you say it, no, you can't come, Evan. You draw too much attention with the wrong kinds of people."

"You mean the rich kind?" Evan asks, one eyebrow raised and Jack scowls at him.

The looming threat of Tobias Cloudspeak shadows my mind in thought. Maybe I'm not so good at determining my own safety. After all, it was something I never had the chance to consider growing up with so many memory-altering drugs. Now with his face fresh in my mind, I'm starting to wonder if I truly am safe within the dragon's belly.

I look over to Jack as he runs a hand through his hair. He gives me a long look that hints at the verge of exhaustion before gesturing towards the door.

"Come on, Dani, we need to go see Magenta."

Jack leads me back up to Magenta's room, but the route we take is more straightforward than the one he used when I first arrived. It's surprisingly easy to get to, just not widely used unless you're tasked with chicken or cow duty, or you happen to be Magenta herself.

We stop just before the Midnight Room so he can quickly punch in his code.

"How many people can get into to her office?" I ask, holding the journal tight to my chest.

"Just me," he says as the door hisses open. "And maybe Evan, but only because of working with Tobias when he was young. This land train was built by the Cloudspeak Corporation when I was a kid. So many different people have passed through here that you wouldn't recognize it from the generic model it once was, but I bet his stupid prodigy mind still remembers the override codes. Cloudspeaks like to leave a little bit of their legacy around whenever they do. Magenta never did figure out how to erase them."

"What about you? What's your legacy?"

Jack pauses so abruptly in the middle of the room that I nearly bump into his back. He turns to look at me.

"I haven't decided yet, but I think I'd like to take over for Magenta one day," he says with a shy grin. "I also have this itch to travel that's been scratched by being here, but I've always wondered what the country is like in the east. What it's like across The Dusting."

He might say more, but we're interrupted by the room's second door hissing open before us. It reveals Magenta, the light from her windows haloing her form, and I'm suddenly thrust into the memory of my first few days under her care.

"My dear Jack and Daniella Starling, to what do I owe the pleasure of your unscheduled visit?" she purrs, gesturing grandly to usher us inside.

I follow Jack and take a seat next to him on the same couch against the wall, while Magenta lowers herself elegantly into the couch opposite of us.

"I'm hoping to cash in a favor, Mags," Jack begins and I watch as Magenta's perfectly shaped eyebrows arch upwards.

"There are no favors among friends, there is only goodwill. What do you need?"

"Can you hide something for us? It's important it stays out of anyone's reach," Jack says and I hand the journal to her.

I watch as she holds it up, her long blue nails tapping rhythmically on its cover. She brings it to her nose and inhales deeply before setting it down in her lap and raising her large, yellow eyes to mine.

"This book smells of fire and desperation."

"It contains something very valuable to Tobias Cloudspeak," Jack answers.

Magenta's smile widens in a feral way. "I am in the habit of keeping things from that man."

"I know you are, which is why I thought you'd be the best person to hide it," says Jack.

Magenta rises gracefully from the couch and deposits the journal among a collection of similarly colored books on a shelf behind her massive desk. It blends in perfectly.

"It will be safe from him here," she informs us, striding the length of the room to the door.

"There's one more thing," Jack adds quickly and Magenta stops, though the door still hisses open before her, even as she stands there with her back towards us.

"Tobias has threatened to take Dani," Jack says, glancing at me. "Can I get authorization to assign a guard to her door at night? I can watch her during the day."

"I don't need a bodyguard!" I snap.

"You have no idea what that man is capable of," he says. "It's for the best, so just trust me."

"I actually have a pretty good idea of what he can do!" Images of Father lying on the kitchen floor come flooding back, and I feel the color drain from my face. Jack must read the agonized look because his expression softens and rests his hand on mine. I let him take my hand this time and the warmth of his skin encloses mine completely.

"I won't let him take you anywhere," he whispers.

"Granted," Magenta states from the doorway, her eyes landing on our clasped hands. "I have work to do now, but you're welcome to rest up in here. You both look like you hadn't slept any winks in any number of days. Take a nap before you go off to practice, please! I can't let my two biggest stars collapse on stage because all they do is stay up all night doing who knows what!"

The door hisses shut behind her and I pull my hands away, a deep flush heating my face. "What does she think we're doing all night?" I ask, laughing awkwardly.

"Apparently not sleeping," Jack says with a throaty chuckle while pulling his long legs onto the couch and stretching out fully, barely leaving me any room.

"I feel a little weird being in here without her," I mutter. "Isn't it her office?"

"Magenta knows I've taken more naps in here than I can count because it's a nice place to hide," Jack says, yawning deeply which I catch and yawn back at him. "She's a good boss, and she's a good friend."

Magenta is right, I haven't been sleeping well, and Jack always seems to be tired, so I'm not surprised when he's asleep in no time. It's harder for me, though. Even though the room is quiet and warm, and the couch supple beneath me, it feels strange to be sleeping here. Like falling asleep in the middle of the dining floor, or maybe a hallway.

But Jack's soft snoring begins to lure me away and I eventually stretch out behind him, but with my head and shoulders at the other end of the long couch. Tucking my feet carefully behind his back and between a cushion, I get comfortable and close my eyes.

Feeling his steady breathing feels reassuring, in a way. And although I feel out of place, I somehow find my way to sleep and for the first time in weeks, no nightmares come searching for me.

Chapter Twenty-Eight

Dragging myself from bed the next day, I splash water on my face and take my time choosing something to wear. The clothes Bluebell had given me sit rumpled on the bed, and I feel a small amount of guilt for not taking better care of my gifts.

I busy myself putting them away until I hear whistling in the hallway. I swiftly pull on a pair of billowy navy pants and a cream-colored shirt, then smooth my sleep tousled hair into a low ponytail.

There's nothing I can do for the deep circles ringing my eyes, but I hope I at least look presentable enough to pass for someone normal. Which I guess I've never been.

The whistling comes to a stop in front of my door and I open it to see Jack standing next to one of Supper's people, who's guarded my room all night. He looks like he could use a big cup of coffee, though he smiles when he sees me.

Jack winks and holds his hand out to me, but I don't take it and instead make a big deal of closing and locking the door behind me. I don't want him to notice how sweaty my palms have become. It was Jack's idea to stay out in public today, so there's less of a chance that Tobias would try anything, but I'm still nervous about it.

"We're going to blend in," Jack says, pulling a pair of hats from behind his back and offering me a choice. They're actually the same hat, the baseball kind with a stitched letter "M" front and center. One is bright yellow and the other a muted beige color with purple embroidery. I take the beige one.

"Are these to hide us from our adoring fans?"

"No, but they'll help," he says. This time, he grabs my hand and pulls me along after him, and I have to admit his warm hand feels good in mine. Laughing, he takes us into the lift and gives me a crooked smile.

"You still look like yourself. At least, *I* think you do," I tell him as the lift comes to a stop and we find ourselves stepping into a bright and clear day.

"Let's hope people don't recognize me wearing clothes." Jack gestures towards his crotch. "You see, most are focused here and I need them here." His hand travels from his crotch to his eyes as he peers down his nose at me.

"Then let's hope your crotch isn't such an attention seeker to-day," I say and immediately turn my attention forward so I can't look him in the eyes...or anywhere else.

Jack laughs. "Don't know if I can promise that," he replies and I quicken my pace so he doesn't see how red my face flushes.

Instead of taking the front entrance, Jack leads us towards a long flight of steps that are embedded in the sharp cliffside. They twist and turn on their way down and I keep a hand firmly planted on the nearby railing to keep from tipping over the edge. He assures me that going up is much easier, but I doubt anything like this phases him. The man flies through the air on ropes.

The hillside is sandy, but held together by tightly-growing vegetation blending seamlessly into tall, wavy grasses at the bottom. There's still a way to go, but Jack takes a detour and crosses over a platform of wooden planks that overlook the shore below.

The view I see when I creep up just behind him forces the breath from my lungs and makes my head spin. Far below the water churns in white ribbons and looks impossibly deep, even this close to the coast. There is no beach here. There is only endless water that undulates towards a jagged, rocky shore. I'm suddenly very glad to not be the one close to the railing; the vastness before me looks as if it could devour the world.

"Wow," I breathe and turn to him, but he isn't looking at the distant waves, he's staring at me. But in catching his eye, he turns away quickly, cheeks going red. We're silent for a moment, staring at what feels to be endless water.

"*It's beautiful*," whispers Lily, and her voice is so faint and distant that I'm not even sure I heard her.

"I grew up looking at this, but it still amazes me," he finally says. "And yet it always made me wonder what the other coast holds. Like, does the ocean look different in the east? I want to find out one day."

"I bet it looks the same, just maybe filled with slightly different creatures. Lily used to read about oceans all the time," I say.

"She was with you at the house?" Jack asks.

I nod. "She was my best friend. I was good friends with another girl, Tara, but Lily and I were closer. She was always full of such big ideas and wishes. One of her biggest wishes was to see actual, real dolphins in the sea, though I bet she would have just been happy seeing the ocean in person."

"Did she..."

"Die? Yes, in the fire. I saw her body," I answer quickly, not wanting to relive the moment any more than I have to. Without being pumped full of mind-altering drugs, the memory of Lily's cold face lingers, if I think about it enough.

Jack leans into me as he asks, "Did she glow, too?"

"We all did," I say, peeking up at him. "You know, you actually glow the same colors as her. Purple and red."

"Hmm, I like your color better," he says, bumping his hip into mine with a smile. "Better to be the color of the sun than a similar shade to Magenta's hair."

I find myself laughing. "I guess so."

We don't talk, and in the silence, I'm searching inside for what I think Lily would say if she were here. Wordlessly, Jack intwines his fingers with mine and I let him, the contact between us nice and warm. We stand like this for only a moment longer until he turns with a smile, his hand pulling away from mine, and gestures back towards the descending stairs.

"We should get going before all the swimmers are rented out," he says. "Besides, you deserve to see a lot more than just a giant tub of water."

I turn away slowly from the ocean, wanting to keep it in my sight just a little longer, but let him lead me away.

After climbing even more steps, we emerge into a large lot filled with solar cars. People mill about between them, or can be seen approaching on foot from several sidewalks feeding into the property. I stay close to Jack as the flow of the crowd leads to several booths set up before large pairs of doors that must lead inside.

He scans the booths and selects one off to the side, leading us to take a place behind an excited family. When we arrive at the front, I realize why he picked this particular booth as the extremely young-looking attendant seems oblivious to whatever connections his face and status hold. We're presented with two small tickets for swimmer rental and pointed towards large doors leading into a lobby similar to the museum's.

Jack lets out a loud breath once we're past the door. Without a glance back, we hurry to join the ever-growing rental lines. While waiting, Jack tells me The Salted Baths is one of the biggest employers for the Required Industry Service in the area. It's also popular because you get free swimmer rentals and, as long as you're currently employed, you can bring your family and friends in at half-price on your days off.

After showing our tickets to the front attendant, we're ushered toward a long table busy with people and even more attendants running back and forth among rows of folded swimmers. We exchange the tickets for a pair and use a section of curtained stalls to change.

My swimmer barely fits and I think I may have been given the wrong size, but Jack, visibly swallowing when he looks at me, assures that it looks just right. Though from the way it rides up in the back and squeezes my chest, I'm not sure I believe him. Especially not with the multiple stares at my chest as we make it out to the first of the pools. It makes me wildly uncomfortable, but Jack grabs a nearby towel and wraps it around my shoulders.

"I know there's more fabric here than my costume, but why do I feel even more exposed?" I have to stop and adjust the straps, causing more curious eyes to dart my way and Jack to chuckle lowly.

"I know a place where you can hide," he says with a wicked grin and grabs my hand.

We run, even though the signs say not to, all the way to the third pool with the waterfall. A lifeguard close to Parker's age tries to stop us, but we easily avoid him by rushing into the water. I breathe a sigh of relief when I realize the water isn't deep and Jack wades his way further in, leading me by the hand. I'm surprised by how warm the water is.

We walk further to the back and I'm thankful my feet never leave the smooth bottom. I don't feel like letting him see me flounder in the water.

We wade all the way to the back of the pool, right up to where it meets the wall where Jack finds a low ledge in the water just under the surface. A wall of windows starts just above our heads, the light illuminating the lapping water. We're away from the eyes that seem to follow our every movement, but I still step close to Jack. He's already seen me up close in a nude sock, so a swimmer isn't anything different. And besides, I kind of like the way I keep catching his eyes darting towards me every now and then.

"They stand on this when they're cleaning the windows up there," he says. "I used to come here when I was younger and just sit. If you're still enough, people forget you're here."

I look out at the other couple swimming before us, then off to the deeper pool beside us. Someone stands on one of the higher diving platforms and people are cheering him on as he makes to jump. I glance back at Jack, but he's busy stretching his long arms and yawning widely.

"Can I ask why you're always so tired?" The question seems to catch him off-guard and he stares at me for a moment before answering.

"You have to practice a lot in order to be as great as I am on the ropes," he says. I roll my eyes at him and he lets out a sigh I can barely hear over the screaming applause next to us as the diver bounces on the edge of the board. "I don't sleep very well. I never have. Even when I lived here, at this place."

"Hmm, there does seem to be a lot going on here. What was it like?" I ask, hoisting myself up and sitting beside him. "Growing up in a place like this, I mean."

"Bad enough to make me want to leave. Ran away the first chance I got, but that's just the typical story of someone running away to join the circus." He grins at me, though the expression drops almost as soon as it's formed. "I left Evan behind. We used to be close, but I don't know if he understood what it was like for me. He was never daddy's little secret."

"How strange it must be to be back here." I think on suddenly showing up back at The Zamora House, if it was still standing, and how it would feel. I'm not sure I could even set foot inside that cage again.

"Life is strange." He huffs a laugh that doesn't seem to carry any humor. "It was a really lonely life; I was only able to see actual people when I came here. Other times I had to stay inside somewhere, alone or maybe with tutors who my father threatened into keeping their mouths shut. The less people knew about my...abnormality, the better." Kicking his feet idly in the water, he glances sideways at me. "I always thought I was the only one like this, but then we found you glowing like a fallen star out in the wilds. It's been good, um, to know I'm not alone. Maybe that's partly why I like you so much."

My smile forms, easy and genuine. I can just make out Jack's hands as they clench into fists under the water lapping below his chest and take them in my own. Thinking on his words has made me realize something the same.

"Well, we're both not alone anymore."

"You're right, Dani, I..." He leans forward and stammers, his face coming near to mine. "I don't have much experience with people, so I'm sorry if I was ever, well, a jerk to you. And I'm sorry for all the terrible things you went through before you arrived, but I am glad they brought you here with me."

And suddenly, it's like I'm in one of Lily's books, a fantasy, a dream, something that can't actually be real, so I have to bring it into reality myself.

I crash my lips into his. The press is soft but firm and tastes like mint. He goes still for just a moment, and then his arms curl around my shoulders as he kisses me back and presses me against the cool tile wall. My hands fly into his hair as I feel myself suddenly forgetting how to breathe when his lips stray to my neck. His breath is rough against my throat, and my body arches into him as a low moan I can barely hear over the water escapes my throat.

It's the most glorious feeling I've ever experienced and I close my eyes to will it into eternity. And then there's a sudden enormous *splash*, the diver finally leaping off the board into the water, and the moment breaks. When we slowly draw apart, his eyes show a deep longing when he pulls away and it only makes me want more, but we smile at each other and float apart just a tad in the warm salt water.

"I want to stay here forever with you and kiss you a million times over," he says, bashful. "But it's late and we have a double performance tonight, so we better get some rest and something to eat." When I nod, he drifts on his back away from me. I wade slowly after him, not wanting to leave the quiet area and return through the other kissing couples gathered around the cascading waterfalls.

And I think I follow him because he's right about not only the time of day and the fact my stomach is growling so loud I can almost hear it above the noise, but because I can't help but follow things that glow like the moon and stars.

Chapter Twenty-Nine

I'm better prepared this time. Not only did I bring a thick jacket and pair of pants for my walk to the metal cage, but I remember to have a small snack to settle my stomach before our performance.

Sally made sure to fill a satin bag with seeds that she secured with a few pins to my sparkly sock. A quick tour of the new arena floor had shown the packed earth to be bleached bare, but if Magenta is looking for the same kind of performance as earlier, then I need the seeds for insurance. I'm nervous about purposely showing this power to so many people, knowing the target it could put on my back, but maybe the more everyone considers it as a simple party trick, the safer I'll be.

Sally smiles when I hand her my spare clothes to hold.

"Cow is in position," she says, beaming with pride. It was her idea to bring out the poor thing once the ground was thriving with greenery. She said it would be a reminder to the people of better times to come, though I think the image of a lone cow might be more heartbreaking than inspiring.

"Thanks, Sally," I tell her and mean it because I know what's coming next. The moon would be lit to the fullest and the seeds would be easily at hand, but I need the blood sacrifice to make it work.

I learned early on that Magenta's Magical World of Circus Curiosities no longer had a doctor on staff. He left them in one of the nearby cities when Magenta refused to increase his pay, and they've been in the market for a new one. In the meantime, they've been making do with what they have, and Sally was one of the people who helped. Apparently, she had a lot of experience with animals, so when it came time to have someone help administer the cut to my hand in the least invasive way possible, her name was at the top of the list.

Sally and I stand still, listening to the commotion above and waiting for the small light to change from red to yellow on the side of the cage. That would indicate it was time to get inside and be ready to be hoisted towards the ceiling.

"Nervous?" she asks.

"No, Jack will be there."

"Hmm." Sally twirls the small knife in her hand a few times. "He's changed a lot since you came along. I mean that in a good way, you seem to bring out a better part of him. I think he was...oh, I don't know, lonely before you."

Before I can reply, the red light becomes yellow.

"It's showtime! Packed house tonight, standing room only." And in one swift movement that seems so out of place for her large and intimidating hands, she slices a clean line over my palm and steps back as the door clicks shut between us.

What follows is a repeat of my first performance only with a few changes worked in to better make sense of the finale. This time, I take Jack's hand right away when he offers it, though I still squeeze my eyes shut for much of the journey down.

When we land, we keep our bodies pressed together for longer this time and I almost lose myself in Jack's penetrating green gaze when I look up at him. I feel him shift his body against mine as he slowly pulls away and I take the moment to press the seed bag into the ground with my bleeding hand. The crowd goes crazy with screaming, yelling and cheering so loudly I have to cover my ears. My right ear is slick from my bleeding palm while my mind is transported back to the white tent and Prim screaming through the air vents.

Even as the crowd's excitement tries its best to drown out the torturing thoughts, their roar becomes near-defending at the sight of Magenta's cow ambling over. But something still feels different and I cannot shake the creeping feeling that travels up my spine.

Jack takes a hand away from my ear and eyes me with a curious look as he suspends it high above our heads. We bow over and over again to our audience, but it's when we rise from the last one that I see Prim sitting between a smiling Tobias Cloudspeak and a tired-looking Lacey Kerrigan.

My stomach drops, and I squeeze my eyes shut before opening them again. She's still there, as are they.

Now the creeping feeling of the crowd's screams make sense. I've heard one of those voices before even if she's silent now. I will always remember her scream.

He has Prim. Prim survived the fire.

I must be squeezing Jack's hand hard because he has to pry my fingers away as soon as the cage enters the ground once more. I don't look, though, because I can't take my eyes off Prim until she's gone from sight and the sounds of cheering people and the smells of popcorn and sugar all fade to nothing.

Which is exactly what I feel inside. Nothing. I scream just to hear my own voice. I scream and cry and yell and scream some more. I slam my fists into the ground and the small pebbles and loose seeds sprout in green vines from my hands as my knuckles split.

Sally stands back, unsure of what to do. Jack watches, gazing at the ceiling with eyes so distant he could be thinking of nothing at all. It's only when I fall silent that he seems to pull himself from whatever trance he found himself in, and takes the gauze and sterilizing liquid from Sally.

Feeling numb, I let him tend to my bleeding hand, but I can't look at him. I can only watch the tiny flowers swirling about my knees.

"That girl," he says, breaking the silence. "Who was she?"

"Prim," I say. "I never liked her and I don't think she ever liked me, but she was at The Zamora House. I thought she was dead."

"Apparently not if you saw her in the flesh just now," Sally mumbles, kneeing beside us. She slips an arm around my body and easily hoists me to my feet.

I bury my face in her big shoulders, wanting so badly to climb back into the cage and lock out the world. But what's the use? It would only rise into the ceiling again and thrust me back into the spotlight.

Sally stays silent as she escorts us to the cubby. I can tell we're late because she leaves quickly to help her assistants load the cow into place. Apparently, they had a hard time getting her to move from the patch of fresh grass I had created. Her own little safe haven that I'm sure her natural instincts told her to stay in. I'm envious that she has such a clear-cut vision.

The dark room is already lit by a new fake moon gleaming in the corner. Someone must have purchased a bigger one to enhance our glow. Maybe one of the lookers complained they couldn't see much.

Supper is the one to close the door behind us, and after taking one hard look at me, disappears behind the curtain. He returns a few minutes later and slips a clean napkin and a small box of strawberries through the door. He doesn't smile—I've never seen him smile—but there is a sweetness to his approach that I appreciate.

I dab at the tears on my face, then glance at Jack, who nods in approval. I know I still must look red-eyed and tired, but I can't bring myself to care too much. I sit on the small sofa next to him and sip water as looker after looker comes to stare. I smile at the children and their mothers, and gently wave at the older couples. However, I ignore any single men coming in to gawk, even when Jack says that'll hurt our tip money.

Jack doesn't press for more information. Maybe he thinks we'll talk about it later, or maybe he's letting me work out my emotions on my own, but I appreciate the space he gives regardless. I will worry about it behind the safety of my bedroom door tonight, and maybe ask Evan to help piece together what I saw.

I'm only starting to feel better with my formulated plan when a group of small children, no more than five or six years old, tumbles into the viewing area and press their sticky hands to the plastic divider. I'm busy laughing at the antics of what must be their teacher trying to corral them with Supper's help that I don't notice when someone new arrives.

But when the group is finally escorted away, Tobias Cloudspeak strides to the box. Next to him stand Prim and Lacey Kerrigan.

When I imagine Lily with me, she is a ghost: unearthly white and flowing, her face illuminated by the moon, her features exactly what I always imagined of graveyard spirits. I was never one to be afraid of ghosts, even if Tara said I should because they were mere shells of who they once were and desperate for souls to fill their bellies. She called them "scary, hungry voids."

Prim reminds me of that now: alive and not dead, but not a person anymore, just a scary, hungry void. She lifts a thin hand and presses it against the partition. Her sallow skin creates a print of sweat. I touch the plastic between us and smile at her, but she doesn't smile back. I suddenly wonder if she even can.

Tobias stands behind her, a cold and calculating look on his face. This move has left me on edge, the questions swirling in my mind as to why Prim is here and how she escaped. It's overwhelming and feels like I'm being pushed underwater by one of The Salted Bath's waterfalls. All I can do is stare numbly back at Prim.

Luckily for me, Tobias is the one to break the silence. Coming forward, he puts a heavy hand on Prim's shoulder and moves her to his side so he can stand in front of me. She doesn't react, but I can see the flinch of her muscles as he makes contact and how her body sways away from him. I can just make out Lacey on his other side, but she hangs back with a haunted expression as she folds Prim into her arms and backs away.

"Wonderful performance today," Tobias starts in his typical booming voice, like we're not mere feet away. "But I wouldn't expect anything less from my son. And you, sweet child, didn't look nearly as frightened as you did that first time he flung you around up there. Then the cow at the end? What a stroke of genius."

"Wasn't my idea," I mutter, crossing my arms over my chest and taking a step forward so I can hear him better through the plastic. My body tightens in response, but I stand my ground. It's what Lily would do. She would tell me to be brave and quiet and listen to whatever this mad man has to say, if only so I can prepare for whatever he plans to do.

Tobias glares at me when I fall silent. "I'll get right to the point. I tipped well so I could get a private audience with you, but that will only buy so much time. You have quite a fan base waiting to lay eyes on a pretty young thing such as yourself." He licks his lips. "You're our own little celebrity now."

"I do not belong to anyone," I snap. "I already said I won't go anywhere with you." He grins at me with his disgustingly perfect smile that I want to cringe away from. Jack steps behind me, resting a hand on my shoulder, to remind me I'm not alone or to pull me away. Either way, I won't move.

"Is that still your answer? How disappointing," Tobias says, pulling both Lacey and Prim close. Prim closes her eyes at the contact, but allows his big arms to wrap around her while he pets her head, as if she were a pet. Lacey merely looks at the ground.

Maybe Prim really is a ghost now; the big-headed girl I remember would never put up with something like this. And while I have vague memories of Lacey, I think she was full of more vinegar than the broken person I see before me.

"Like I said before, I need you," Tobias says into Prim's hair. "So, I'm going to ask you again to come with me, willingly. I can't take you and I can't have others take you, your abduction would be too obvious. I'm not above trying, mind you, but I do have a reputation to think about."

"I will never go anywhere with you."

Tobias lets out a loud huffing sound and gives Prim a little shake that makes her head bob. "Not even to keep this thing company? I mean, her blood is still tainted, like yours, but she isn't as useful, especially as damaged as she is now. Don't misunderstand me, I can make do with just her, but the better product? *You*? That's the true power I need—that the planet needs! What Prim here needs."

"What your bank account needs," I say and think I can make out the ghost of a smile on Prim's lips.

"If that's how you look at it, yes, I would stand to raise a substantial amount of cash if I had you both." He leans in close and gestures me to do the same. I only do so because I know we're separated by the partition and he wouldn't be able to grab me. At least, I think.

"I have a feeling you have no idea about your true power, which I find most intriguing." He chuckles darkly. "Well, Daniella, here is something you should know. You have inherited the worst traits of your family and the unfortunate fascination of both my sons, but you also have something in your blood that holds true and absolute power, and if you come with me, I can help you harness it. Together, we'll be extraordinarily powerful."

His words are chilling, but I do not move and will not give him the satisfaction of looking away. I stare at him and shake my head at him.

"Ah, well, it looks like our session is up," Tobias says with a sneer, straightening his shoulders. "I'm afraid we won't be able to make your second performance tonight, but I'm sure it will go swimmingly. You have my boy here to take the very best care of you. We'll see you again soon, my pet."

"You're a murderer," I whisper and he cocks his head, somehow hearing me through the barrier.

"Perhaps, but you, dear, are the spitting image of your mother, which is even worse." He laughs coldly and begins urging Prim towards the exit, but she drags her feet and casts a haunted look in my direction.

Jack's hand rests on the small of my back, and even as I turn my body towards his, I can't raise my eyes to look at him. The nothingness inside seems to be spreading. Like a blossoming flower, it soon fills my chest and threatens to shut off all other senses.

"What is he talking about?" I whisper. "Why would I be any more special than Prim?"

Jack only shakes his head and turns his attention to a little girl now at the partition. He waves at her, smiling and tapping the plastic at her forehead, which makes her giggle. He speaks without looking up, a low whisper I don't think anyone outside can hear.

"Tobias Cloudspeak is full of himself enough to believe he knows how everyone thinks and it infuriates him when they don't do what he wants. He thinks he has you trapped, so maybe he's just making stuff up to get you to come with him. He thinks that you, and me, and even my brother, are all scared of him. That we'll listen to what he says."

"But he has Prim," I say, watching Tobias still struggling to make her walk out of the room. Lacey has edged off to the side and is watching them both closely. Prim's mouth moves as if she's screaming at everyone around her, but I can't hear what she says. "I can't let him keep her like that."

"He has us all, if you think about it." Jack's voice is distant, and even though I see him performing for the lookers before us, I know his thoughts are far away.

My head spins and I can't make sense of any of the thoughts, so I put them aside. Wrap them up in a little package and stick them into a corner of my mind.

I'm safe, I know I am. The partition is thick and locked tight, and while it might make me a prisoner for a second time in my life, it also represents safety from the outside world.

From Tobias Cloudspeak.

Jack stands by me as we watch Supper get called in to help Tobias take out Prim, who now sits on the ground, her face blank and expressionless. Everyone's eyes are on her save for one familiar set standing close by the partition, looking at me. It's Lacey and she's holding a slip of paper against the glass.

"Talk to Evan" is all the note says. I slap my hands on the partition and stare at her with questioning eyes. If there was anything more she wanted to tell me, she doesn't get the chance because Tobias rushes over and drags her away after Supper, who now has Prim slung over his shoulder like a potato sack.

And even though Lacey digs her heels into the ground and screams, the tent full of lookers simply watches him pull her roughly out, as if this is all part of the circus. Not one single person tries to stop him.

Chapter Thirty

The image of Lacey being dragged away still burns fresh in my mind when Supper finally releases us from the cubby. The instant we're outside, I can't help but be on high alert, waiting for Tobias to jump out and grab me.

I grab Jack's arm, thinking suddenly about the journal's safety as well. "Are you sure Magenta will keep the journal safe?"

"I trust her with my life. She won't let anything happen to it," Jack says carefully, taking my hand. "What was on that note?

"She said to talk to Evan," I tell him and he gives me a long look before turning away and staring at the ceiling in thought.

"You know, my brother always seemed to take after Tobias much more than me. He keeps his secrets close. I wouldn't doubt he still knows more."

"I've known him to, well, not exactly tell the entire truth of things," I say, a tinge of numbing betrayal sinking into my words.

Jack doesn't seem surprised. He lets out a big yawn and drops my hands as he says, "Come on, I need a nap if you don't want me to drop you during second performance tonight. We can talk to him tonight."

The walk back to my room is long, and I'm hardly paying attention to my feet as I stumble across the lift's entrance.

I brace my arms against the closest wall, trying to find my way back through memories of burning walls and tortured screaming, and I'm so preoccupied it barely registers when the three sisters force their way into the lift with me and Jack.

"Whew! You look awful, are you okay?" Bindy asks, putting a hand out to steady me.

"She doesn't look okay," Mindy says, peering closely at my face. "Evan is looking for you two."

"Well, he can come find us," I mumble, extracting myself from their grasp. I give the girls a weak smile, not wanting them to think I'm brushing them off, but there is just way too much going through my mind right now. Luckily, we're in a faster lift and nearly to my floor.

"Dani!" Bindy exclaims just before Jack pulls me from the lift's confined space, a groan escaping his lips at her shrill voice. "Before you go, we wanted to let you know we heard there's going to be an actual gala happening tomorrow! We haven't been hired to do one in so long, they're so unbelievably expensive these days. But Magenta is going to have some performers and said everyone is allowed to attend. It's going to be absolutely marvelous! Jack's father is hosting and I heard he always throws the best parties!"

"A gala? Is that like a party, or a ball?" Despite the heavy feeling in my chest, their words strike some excitement inside and I am suddenly ten years old again and reading books about fantastic and wondrous fairytale balls.

"It's just his excuse to get more people to give him money by impressing all his rich friends and having a fancy party," Jack says, yawning deeply.

"So, all his investors will be there?"

"Exactly," says Mindy. "We've been hired for these things before, but never something this grand. Supper will set up a schedule for a few performances to be used as entertainment, but when you're done with your act, you get to dress up and attend like a normal guest. They're so much fun."

"Dancing and food from the new restaurant they just built! I can't wait!" Bindy squeals and twirls around the marble walkway in a bizarre one-person dance. Her sisters giggle and try to stop her.

"Go find Evan!" Mindy calls over her shoulder before the lift doors close and I'm suddenly alone with Jack again.

"Have they always been like this?" I find myself asking.

Jack rolls his eyes. "Yes, ever since they learned to talk."

I pat his arm and giggle. "Someone's grumpy."

"It's been a long few weeks." He smirks and nudges me down the hall towards my room. "Do you mind if we crash here? I'll be your bodyguard and, well, I think I sleep better with you around anyway."

I blink, and then smile. "Oh, um, sure?"

"Great! Let's go!"

Jack shoulders my door open and I nearly stumble back when I see Evan already inside, sitting on my bed reading a book. It brings a sour taste to my mouth to see him in here uninvited.

"Dani," he starts, rising from my bed when I enter. He gives Jack a sideways glance just as I close the door behind us.

"Hi."

"Hi," he says back. Jack crosses in between us and sits heavily on the bed. His eyes look bloodshot, but he won't take them off Evan as he watches his every movement. I sit next to him on the bed.

"I saw Lacey," I say to him and see his cheek twitch in thought. "She passed a note telling me to talk to you."

"Probably about the upcoming gala," Evan says, and he's quiet a moment before continuing. "Everyone thinks what you can do is a magic trick. Just some...circus act. I've been talking to his investors and they haven't been happy with all his...side projects, like The Zamora Project. If he has you within his grasp, it will most likely help his case with them."

"I heard it's been a while since he's hosted a gala," says Jack. "My guess is that he'll ensure you're one of the performers and claim you as his own during the performance, maybe have those so-called investors get up close and personal with you while you stand there and make things grow as physical proof."

The thought of standing there while Tobias and people like him take turns slicing open my skin to see some plants grow is enough to make me feel faint.

"Tobias himself isn't worth much without his investors and he'll be run out without their support." Evan smiles at his own comments and gestures suddenly towards the small shelf that holds the old gate key. "Hey, I noticed this earlier, where did you get them?"

"That's the garden gate key from...home."

"Not the key, these," he clarifies as he picks the key up and dangles the keychains in front of me.

"Keychain weights, Mother or Father kept adding them on there," I tell him.

"That's not what they are," he says. "They're memory sticks and should contain information. Do you know what's saved on them?"

"No, I don't. I never paid them much attention," I answer. "Aren't they just keychains?"

"If you don't mind, I'm going to borrow them. I want to see what someone saved on them." Evan turns quickly to leave, but looks at me before he closes the door. "I'll see you later tonight, but be careful around him, Dani. Tobias Cloudspeak is a dangerous man."

"Dangerous..." I mumble back, a memory fluttering like a feather just out of reach. "Hey, are you sure there isn't anything else? Anything Lacey thinks I should know about Tobias?"

"I don't think so," he says brightly. "And if we're lucky, maybe there will be something in these that will help get him out of the picture. I know people who would be very happy to see him gone."

"I'm one of them," I mutter, my mind still working on the word "dangerous."

"I know," Evan replies and smiles. "We just need something to use for an advantage, something dangerous. We'll find it, we have to."

I turn to ask for Jack's opinion after Evan leaves, but find him fast asleep, so I lean back on the bed with my feet to Jack's head and try to rest as well. But the feather of a thought keeps drifting before my eyes and I suddenly remember the journal's scribbles calling me "dangerous."

What if I am? The smell of singed strawberries burns on the very edge of memory, but no matter how much I try to remember my sessions in the white tent, or even the majority of my time inside The Zamora House, everything is one huge blur that makes my head hurt and my palms tingle.

Later that night, I'm so preoccupied trying to put my thoughts together that I almost fall out of Jack's arms during our performance. He is able to catch me before the deadly plummet and casts a worried glance after we land, but I can barely look at him because something itches within my bleeding palm and when I press the seed pouch into the dirt, something different happens when warm sparks dance between my fingers.

The ground still erupts in the greenness that is life, but there is also the smallest curl of smoke rising from its center. The linen seed bag curls in tiny flames, and Jack, looking unsure, quickly kicks over some dirt to snuff out the tiny whisps of smoke.

I know he's speaking to me, but the words pass through one ear and out the other. I hear the crowd, the screaming and the cheering, but I also hear Tara's voice. And although her voice is but a whisper, it roars louder than the whole world.

"*I feel like a dragon*," she says. "*There is fire in my blood, and I feel as if I could fly.*"

And then I understand what Lily had been telling me, of how she believed we were something greater than what we were led to believe. I think more of what I can really do, what I was *made* to do. Even Lacey said I was more dangerous than a little fire. But what about a big fire? Could I be more dangerous than that?

I think of the house fire, of Tara, of Lily, of dragons streaking across the wilds and of The Zamora House burning in the night, and then I snap my fingers together on a small seed.

A tiny spark jumps from my hand and extinguishes quickly. I do it one more time and catch it with my other hand as it burns out in a tiny puff. No one sees, not even Jack who is leaning close as the cage lowers, our time on stage coming to an end.

"You're a thousand miles away," he says softly, his lips lightly brushing my ear.

"No, I'm exactly where I need to be," I whisper back.

The cage lowers and I watch as its jaws close above me. Jack mentions in passing to Sally that the earth around the cage tonight seemed drier than usual and Supper should have someone take care of it before any further performances.

"We wouldn't want a full-blown fire in the tent," he says and she nods gravely in agreement.

I shrug on a jacket from Bluebell. This one is silky dark blue, with just enough padding in the fabric to give definition but not become unbearably warm.

We aren't required to spend time in the cubby tonight since the performance lasted late into the evening, but while everyone hurries inside, I choose to skip eating in the dining floor tonight. Though I do make a brief appearance to fill a massive plate with mashed potatoes teeming with thick vegan butter and topped with crispy fried onions. Parker seems heavily disappointed when I excuse myself and pouts that he hasn't seen me much, but I give him a hug and tell him I'll try to make some time for him.

No one else pays attention to anything but their food and having a good time, so I escape quickly to my room and am able to chew my food slowly as I think through the most recent events of my haphazard life.

I'm debating going back for more fried onions when I see something on the ground of my room: an envelope that looks like it was pushed under the doorway at some point, and has my name painted in flowing script across the seam. It's not as practiced as

Bluebell's handwriting, but still impressive, and I sit on the bed to open it.

After breaking the seal, a small tinkling tune plays and I can hear the gears of a tiny motor inside as I unfold its contents. The paper inside, like the envelope, is a heavy golden color and the printing gleams in high-shined black. A small moon, no bigger than the tip of my little finger, lights up at the top and several glittering stars form the words "You Have Been Invited to a Gala."

My fingertips glow as I read through it carefully, looking for anything out of the ordinary in this event created by Tobias Cloudspeak, but if there are any secret messages inside, I do not find them. Instead, I find myself disgusted with how elaborate and excessive the paper is in my hands. I remember the mother from The Baths splitting a single sandwich between her family members and how large Parker's eyes had been when he saw my earnings. I bet the cost of this invitation probably could have fed a whole family and then some.

It gives me a creeping sensation that doesn't go away until I fold up the invite and shove it beneath a blanket. I consider trying my own experiment and burning it to nothing but a pile of ash, but I don't dare try to do it again, not in here. Although burning the invite from Tobias is tempting, I don't want to risk things getting out of control. All the same, I can't help but stare at my fingers and remember how they sparkled with flame.

A knock on my door and Jack's voice in the hallway calling out to Evan jerks me from my reverie.

"Just come in," I say.

Jack slips into the room, followed closely by Evan. "What was that during the show, Dani?" Jack asks and I force myself to look at him. Evan's eyes narrow at the question and he sends me an expectant look while we wait for me to answer Jack's question.

"I remembered something. Something from before I came here." I turn to Evan. "Is there anything you'd like to share with us regarding the testing I went through in the white tent? Anything at all?"

"I don't think so," Evan starts, looking away. He crosses his arms and then uncrosses them and paces the few strides he can manage in the room. He stops and pushes his glasses further up his nose, and when I don't break my stare, sighs. "Why do you ask?"

"I'll tell you why," Jack says. He turns to me and I'm lost in his eyes. Lily once read a story about beings who came from another world made of green jade and Jack's eyes look like they could be a forest made of their crystalized trees.

"Then enlighten us," says Evan.

"I didn't believe what I saw at first, but the more I thought about it, the more I realized I know what I was saw. You're the one who made the smoke, the little fire on stage. You're lucky I was able to snuff it out quickly. The damage a fire can inflict in a circus tent could be an immense tragedy, but how did you do that? I have to know."

I swallow an inappropriate giggle because it startled me to hear Jack sound so much like Evan. In this moment, there is no doubt they are brothers.

"Well," I begin, "I snapped my fingers and instead of thinking of what I normally think about, which is growth, I thought of dragons instead."

The two looks I receive each tell a different tale. Evan's eyes go wide and his eyebrows rise, causing his glasses to slip down his nose. I can tell he's thinking, going over a million things in his mind, trying to make sense of what I'm saying.

Jack's face is neutral, blank, an almost clean slate of nothingness, and even though I'm certain he's thinking *something*, it takes him a much longer time to come to a conclusion.

"That's a power I'm glad not to have," he finally says, looking straight into my eyes and taking one of my hands. It's hard to doubt his honesty as he brings my fingers to his lips and kisses them lightly. "Parker is going to be even more jealous now."

"This must be why Tobias really wants you," Evan finally says, adverting his eyes from where Jack touches me. "He and Leonard must have been up to something more, if I were a betting man..."

As if his voice has reminded Jack we're not alone in the room, he whirls toward Evan and spits, "You knew about this."

"I, uh, well..." Evan stammers, but Jack rounds on him and shoves his brother back against the door.

"Stop lying and tell her the truth."

I don't really think Jack would hurt his brother, but the pain and anger coming off him in waves is hard to ignore. I can tell Evan isn't sure, either, and after pushing Jack away from him, he straightens his shirt and lets out a long sigh.

"The Zamora Project set about creating a better world, revitalizing the farmlands and making more land habitable for more people. But it had what Leonard and my father deemed a 'profitable side effect' in that a few of the girls, Dani being the biggest talent, could harness more than just plant growth but use their abilities to summon fire. They were essentially made into vessels of both life and destruction. Weapons, if you will."

"No," I squeak. "I'm not a weapon."

"You're enough of one to be valuable to Tobias Cloudspeak," Evan continues. "Martha did her best to ensure he couldn't get his hands on any of you once the secret was out, and he only complicated things by killing Leonard, but all that just makes you more valuable to him."

"Then what is he doing with Prim?" I say, chewing my lip so hard I taste blood.

"He got lucky and got his hands on her before she died, though it looks like she may have been affected a little too deeply by Martha's drugging. He's probably using her as bait, or maybe to placate his investors until he can get his hands on you. But now that the cat's out of the bag, can I at least tell you what I found out?"

"I don't even know if I can believe anything out of your mouth," I say to him. His confession feels like it leaves a small hole in my chest, and even though I have long-since gotten over the silly crush I had on him when we first met, his betrayal still burns. I thought he had started to see me as an actual person and not some sort of fascinating science experiment gone rogue.

"I've never lied to you," he says.

"But again, you've been known to skirt the truth," I retort and he looks away. Warmth for Evan has faded to nothing more than what I think he would consider a business partnership, but I know I need his help. He's also Jack's brother, and that has to count for something. I think.

"Fine, you can make fire as well as plants and that's it. Besides, in any case," Evan says, pulling the gate key from his pocket, the weights clinking together as he holds it up. "I thought you'd like to know I was able to look into these. Well, not these ones exactly, these are blank copies for decoys; the real deal has been duplicated several times over and saved somewhere secure. These are here in case anyone comes looking for them." Evan gives me a pointed look as he hands them to me and I find my hands recoiling from his own before I put them back on the shelf.

"What did you find on them?" I ask in a demanding tone and he looks directly into my face.

"I know you'll need to see their data at some point, but I don't think you should now. The less you know or hear about them, the better."

"You're not the one to decide that for me," I say.

"*Good girl*," whispers Lily in the faintest voice.

"Fair point," he replies and seems to come to an agreement with himself. "Well, they are full of surveillance footage. Some videos seem voluntary, but given the mind-altering effects of the medications, I doubt any sane person would go along if they knew what was coming. Pretty damaging stuff, but since Leonard and Martha are dead, the blame will come on him, on Tobias. He's only in a few videos, all awful, awful acts of... let's just say he took liberties he never should have."

Jack puts his head in his hands, and after a moment, straightens and looks at Evan. They stare at each other, hard looks and calculating eyes that speak volumes to them alone.

"Dani," Evan asks. "I think I found a way to discredit him by showing these to his investors, to make it so no one will work with him again, but you need to answer me honestly: Are you okay with showcasing these videos at the gala?"

I close my eyes and tilt my head, listening for what I think Lily would tell me to do, but nothing comes except the steady breathing of the two men beside me and my own heart thundering madly in my chest.

So, because Lily doesn't come to me, I think of the dragons and I think of the wind making the flowers dance. I think of the gravestones half-buried in the earth and the ghosts hidden among the orange trees. And when Lily's face finally comes back to me, she stands silent among the wilds, waiting for my response.

"Yes," I whisper, and Lily smiles.

Chapter Thirty-One

Evan lets me watch only a few minutes of a video already downloaded onto a small device tablet. He said it was bad, but not as bad as some of the footage, and would be a good indicator if I would be okay showing it to not only Tobias, but to the world.

I almost couldn't name the girl in the video, it had been so long since I'd seen her, but Cait's dark eyes were piercing and I could see why Evan chose to show her to me. Disgust and then rage stirs within after realizing the footage is from our own kitchen table, the same table we all had meals on. Cait's face is twisted in agony from the needles Mother slides under her skin, but what churns my stomach is the blank look on her face after the final dose is administered and Mother leaves Cait alone with Father and Tobias.

After watching, I'm not surprised to find a simmering rage under my skin that boils like a pot of watcher left on the stove too long. While all three of us have decided to keep my true talents hidden - the less anyone knows, even Magenta, the better – I feel like I could set the world on fire.

Watching these forgotten events has strengthened my resolve to ensure Tobias Cloudspeak can never do something like this again, but left the door open for nightmarish fantasies in my sleep. And although one of Supper's crew hangs out in the hallway and Jack sleeps on the floor of Evan's room just across from my own, I'm tormented by dreams nearly the entire night.

At some point, I must have worn my mind to exhaustion and I finally drifted off to a fitful state only to wake sometime before dawn.

Tossing my sheets aside, the air stings my sweaty skin and my bare feet feel clammy on the floor. I force myself from bed and dress slowly, unsure of what I want to do, but the dim sunlight catches my eyes and suddenly all I want is to feel it on my face.

The hallways are cool, quiet, and deserted. Anyone Supper sent over must have left at first light, considering their duty done as the new day began.

I make my way to the closest lift, hoping I won't come in contact with anyone, and my luck holds when I find myself finally outside the beast of a land train. I turn around and press a palm to the dragon's side and think I can feel the gentle hum of the lives it holds in its belly. Unlike the white tent that heaved in single great breaths, the land train flutters with a thousand heartbeats.

I walk towards the sandy steps, thinking I will travel just halfway and stop to look at the ocean before heading back inside for breakfast. The air is salty and heavy in my lungs, but it has a delicious taste that is so different from the earthy smell of the graveyard and the crispy smell of the wilds. No, this air tastes of the ocean as if it were a giant salted cake, frosted with white tipped caps and sprinkled with glittering sunlight.

I find myself alone and staring at the water with the sun warm on my back. I still jerk at every sound, thinking it could be Tobias or one of his goons out to get me. Perhaps it was a stupid thing to come out here alone, but a greater part of me needed the space, to have time to contemplate if I truly am dangerous.

Thinking of the impossible depths of the ocean below, I can't help but wonder what the bottom looks like before something down on the shore catches my attention.

Where the waves meet the rocks, I see a very small figure. From the height and the way he runs along the sand, I know immediately it is the little boy, Miles. I can't tell if anyone is with him—if they are, they're hidden somewhere beyond my line of sight. I think he must be safe because he seems skittish whenever a wave laps too close for his liking. He's holding something and the more I stare, the more his bundle starts to make sense. I let out a gasp when he releases his treasures into a long wave and they are carried out into the surf. He begins to cheer but is interrupted when another wave comes too near and he skitters backwards from its reach.

His treasures bob in the water and drift further and further out, but I can see what they are and I smile at his bravery. The treasures he has released into the sea are birds, but not live birds, dead birds. Taxidermic birds from the Aviary Wonderama bob up and down in the water, slowly floating towards freedom.

I turn away just in case he looks up and sees me, making my way quickly back along the steps to the closest lift and hoping I make it back to my room before Jack and Evan wake up. But Bluebell finds me first as she bursts from the lift's doors and, smiling fondly in my direction, hurries over.

"Dani!" she yelps and embraces me in a crushing hug. "I wanted to tell you something!"

"Hi Bluebell." I smile at her enthusiasm and she loops her arm around my elbow and pulls me close, her eyes sparkling.

"The craziest thing happened last night after the show. Talia Lake herself sought me out and asked if I would be interested in working with her! It's like a crazy dream. It means I'll be leaving soon, but do you think Magenta and Jack will mind? It means someone new will have to help with the costumes."

"I'm not sure."

"It doesn't matter, it's happening either way. I hear Jack's brother is staying behind to help run The Baths, too, so maybe that will overshadow my loss. Speaking of which," she says and waggles her eyebrows. "We noticed you've been spending a lot of time with both brothers, alone in your room, hmm?"

My cheeks flush against my will. "What are you suggesting?"

"Sweetie, you know what I'm suggesting!" She laughs loudly. "Have you picked between them or are they still fighting it out for you? Or maybe you want both? I've read a few books like that."

"Bluebell, really, I don't think of Evan that way at all," I stammer, unsure of how much to tell her. While I really want to shout from the rooftops that Evan has a deep problem with lying, I would feel bad about speaking of him behind his back. Even if he is a jerk who can't be trusted. Now Tobias, on the other hand...

More people are venturing outside the land train, starting to glance in our direction. One of them is Supper, whose face turns red when he realizes I am alone without a brother or a guard. Bluebell does a better job at ignoring them than I do, but I can't help the redness creeping from my cheeks down to my chest.

"Sorry, little rabbit." She softens and pulls me in for another hug. "I didn't mean to pry." She lets go and smiles sadly. "But anyway, I have to go. I'll see you tonight at the gala. We're all looking forward to your performance!" She kisses me on the cheek and hurries away, leaving me alone by the lift which I quickly bolt into.

I suppose she's right. I do spend a lot of time with both brothers, but that is because I perform with Jack and Evan—well, he just always shows up.

I've thought about my future with Jack and I can see a life with him, flying through the air in different cities on different nights, the world never slowing or stopping and the sky a host of diamonds. Wearing sparkling clothes and listening to the crowd cheer as Jack clutches me close and breathes hotly against my neck. It's a glamorous, fast-paced life of freedom where your home travels with you. It's one that sounds desperately appealing.

But while we've had close moments and I get the sense I may mean a great deal to him, I'm still unsure of what the future holds for us. Maybe because I have other priorities right now, such as getting Tobias off my back.

I wonder what Lily would say?

As the lift carries me to my floor, I try to remember her face, but tears spring to my eyes when I can't see it clearly. She speaks but it's muted, and while something is being said, I cannot understand a word. I ask again and she taps at her blurry chest with what I know to be a smile on her face, but her features bleed into the rest of my memory and become a haze of nothingness.

Am I forgetting her? She would never forget me. Or is she trying to tell me something. I just don't know.

I make it back before Evan and Jack wake up and am able to slip unnoticed into my room, where I find one of my photos from my garland has fallen to the floor. It's the best picture I could find of The Amazing Starlings, my parents.

Scarlet Starling stands proudly on a thin wire strung between two boxes, while around her are the swirls and trails of a multitude of small drones flying above her head in the idea of a halo. She is breathtakingly beautiful with her small frame and dark hair, and the resemblance to the picture I have of Victoria is striking. Mother, or rather Martha, seems plain in comparison. No wonder I never saw myself in her eyes.

My father Stan is to the side, a large man with sandy brown hair and a dusting of freckles across his cheeks. He sits at a small table using a pencil to draw his wife, to capture her radiance by hand even if someone has already remembered it by photo.

I have to admit Stan isn't much to look at, but he stares at my mother with a mixture of adoration and respect. It's as if, in that moment, she is the only person in the world as he uses his creative spark to make her eternal on paper.

It makes me wish I had a picture of Lily. It was gradual, but images of her, as well as Tara, Sara, Cait, Rana, and Vera have all but escaped my deepest memory and are becoming smaller and smaller in the distance as I speed away.

I am about to press the photo back on the wall between a woman with a hairdo as tall as the man next to her and an earlier version of the purple- and white-striped tent, when there is a sturdy knock at my door.

"Miss Starling," a voice calls through. "I was hoping to have a quick word?"

Without waiting for a reply, Magenta lets herself in. She takes a look around the room, tapping a long finger against her mouth before she sighs and takes a seat on my bed. She pats the mattress next to her and smiles.

I sit down, trying to discreetly wipe my sweaty hands on the bedspread, and rest the photo in my lap. Does she know what we've been planning? I hadn't considered much of how the removal of Tobias Cloudspeak would affect Magenta's Magical World of Circus Curiosities. Then again, if Evan were to take the Cloudspeak empire, maybe it wouldn't be such a bad thing. She seems to like him better than Tobias at least.

"You know, running a show like this is hard work, little rabbit. Takes so much of yourself that you almost find you can't do it all. Sometimes all you can do is listen. And do you know what I've been hearing?"

I wipe my hands once more and go still, but instead of waiting for an answer, she plucks the photo from my fingers and holds it before her, her eyes distant as she speaks of other things.

"Did you know that I was there when you were born? It happened right on the big couch in my office," she begins and I can't help but remember that I recently took a nap on that very couch. Friscuit, that's gross.

"I remember all the lights started flickering on the ceiling as your mother was wailing, and then you came into the world screaming and hollering and with skin glowing as bright as headlights on a long stretch of highway.

"The doctor here at the time was puzzled and frazzled and dazzled by your luminescent appearance and just couldn't make out why this little thing was so bright and so loud, and he eventually handed you to your real papa and said he was very sorry, there was nothing he could do. Stan then spelled your name in the sky with his firefly drones and sent them flying through the air." Her mouth twists in a grin. "He named you after his favorite brand of battery, so 'Daniella' they cried and chased that pesky doctor out the door. What did he know, hmm? Stan then hid you away in a cloak made of stars and ran off with you and Scarlet into the night." She lets out a long sigh. "That was the last I saw of them."

"The Amazing Starlings had to die," I whisper, too stunned by her admission to say much more.

"Yes, they did, it was written in the stars. Tobias and Leonard paid to have you created, took you from your mother's belly, tinkered in unhelpful ways with your small, helpless body, and put you back in. Now I don't think in the slightest that Leonard wanted Scarlet dead. No, his own twisted mind loved her dearly. But when they took you and ran, what had to be, had to be."

We are quiet for a moment, and I imagine the couple in the picture running away into the night. When I close my eyes, I see them, bundled in old coats, driving a borrowed or possibly stolen solar car. Escaping into the wilds much like I had, but with real fire-breathing dragons chasing them. They must have trailed stardust in their wake and I wonder how they managed it.

"What was the cloak of stars made from?" I find myself asking, taken up by her tale.

"Ah, ever the child of Stan 'The Starlight' Starling, bright as the stars themselves. The stars were you, they were me, they were they. Sometimes hundreds, sometimes only a few. Some with big jobs, some with small, but all equally important and stars all the same, all working and living together. For we are the heart, the lungs, the legs, the arms, and belly of the great beast that keeps us safe from the world. And with this, we must watch after our own, dearest Daniella. Of which you will always be a part of and have a home within. Don't you ever forget that about yourself, and Tobias Cloudspeak will never stand a chance."

"You knew them all, right? Leonard, Tobias, my parents, and aunts?"

"From another life, yes," Magenta sighs as she moves to the door and her gaze drifts back to mine. "I've decided that permanent residency at The Salted Baths is not for me. This place, while beautiful and profitable, has an unauthentic spirit and I yearn to travel the wilds once more." Her gaze drifts to my window. "Besides, it stirs up too many poor memories. I've hired someone to help us make a journey like none other, and after this gala, we shall be leaving The Salted Baths and venturing to the far off and distant eastern coasts on the far, far, far side of The Dusting. I do hope you'll be coming with us. Yours is a dangerous but marvelous talent, but we could use someone like you. I know in my hair that Jack could."

Magenta looms before me and the hair that halos her head glows and spirals out of control. Her voice is strong and steady and is the mouth of the world, and I am grateful she is on my side. She smiles at me then, pressing the photo back into my hands and letting herself out. And when she is gone, the room seems smaller. As if her very presence made it as big as the dragon itself.

My fingers itch and I look down at the photo, thinking again of Lily's fading face. Then I have an idea and rummage through my belongs till I find the red journal and pencils Bluebell gave to me with my new clothes.

Trying to steady my hands, I start small by carefully penciling in a tree with a few gravestones hidden within the roots. Then the tree blossoms and sheds feathery light flowers from its branches, that drift away with the breeze towards a lonely house on a hill.

Satisfied, I move on to the next paper and draw each of the girls as I remember them. I close my eyes and open my heart, seeing Rana's big hands, Vera's kind smile, Tara and Cait looking exactly the same but completely different, even Sara's terrible cooking and Prim's smirk. Then, as my hand floats upon the paper Lily comes into view, and while I do not hear her voice, I see her smile form on the page. When I listen carefully, I sense that everything will be okay.

And once I start this madness, memories start to form like a massive puzzle, pieces fitting into places that had long since been forgotten. I can remember them now, all of them, and it is a clear picture at last. I add more and more to my art of what should have never been forgotten but what was, for a time, too painful to recall.

I look down at the final picture and find my fingers aching and my eyes burning. This last drawing is of just my hand, reaching high towards the dark sky above. My skin glows in radiance, but a single flame burns upon my fingertips, as if it were a candle lighting the darkened room of my mind.

Chapter Thirty-Two

It is the night of the gala and I was only able to stomach some applesauce during breakfast before Bluebell insisted that she needed my physical presence to create the perfect fit for my gala attire. She kept me throughout lunch to finish her masterpiece, and when I finally made it to the dining floor, Beetle only had one sandwich and a few tiny pieces of chocolate shaped into cows. Bluebell and I split the sandwich, and she tried to assure me there will be plenty of food at the event. I hope for my stomach's sake that she is right.

The gown she has constructed shimmers like an ocean reflecting the full moon. Blue, nearly weightless sequins cover the thin fabric that shines a starling gold whenever the dress catches the light. It connects with a long, hidden zipper to make it easy to slip off and reveal the nude sock I'll need to wear underneath.

To this she waggles her eyebrows at me and suggests the ease it would take to undress in a hurry. The comment makes Minty fall over laughing and Bluebell throws a romance novel at her right as the door opens and Jack steps inside.

"Jack Cloudspeak, you look almost presentable!" Minty cackles again, dodging a second book. Bluebell and I laugh when Jack looks down at himself and shrugs. He is wearing a simple beige-colored linen suit without a tie, and also without shoes.

"I look fine," Jack snorts.

"Do you like her dress? I was going for the color of the sea," Bluebell says, her eyes misting at her creation. "I was going to make her match you, but I don't think you pull off blue that well."

"She also looks fine, as long as it's functional and her costume is under there, it'll do," Jack says, giving Bluebell an eyeroll. But the instant she turns away, I can see him visibly swallow as his eyes trail down the watery blue.

"You can be the sand and she can be the ocean water," Minty struggles to say through her giggles and Jack lets out a groan.

"Goodbye, ladies!" he grumbles, grabbing my arm and pulling me out the door. I'm laughing too hard to walk straight, but pull myself together in time to look back at Bluebell before I lose sight of her.

"Thank you, I'll see you tonight!" I call and she says something I can't hear right as the lift door closes between us.

For a moment, we stand there and I can't tell if he's breathing heavily or if I am, but in the time it takes to decide, he's closed the distance and pressed his lips to my own. I wrap my arms around his neck as one of his hands tangles in my hair while the other reaches behind, grabbing hold of my dress and pressing my body flush against him. The franticness of his mouth makes me want more and more as heat builds in my core.

At last, we break apart to breathe, our foreheads pressed together. When he opens his eyes, I can't help but smile up at him, and he smiles right back. "Sorry," he says. "You just look unbelievable in that thing."

My cheeks flush despite myself, and I itch to kiss him again, but the lift suddenly clunks to a halt. He pulls away, straightening his pants and reaching over to smooth out my dress, his hands lingering on my waist.

I can only hope we both look presentable as the lift doors open and late afternoon sunlight pours in. Jack leads as we make our way to the growing crowd outside the ornate entrance to The Salted Baths.

"I don't like these things," he tells me when we take our place among whispers and poorly concealed stares. He keeps his eyes steady and forward, ignoring the people around him with a well-honed skill. It's still a struggle for me, so I find myself constantly dodging one gaze after another.

"My dear Jack!" A high pitched but musical voice washes over us and I turn to see the purple-haired Talia Lake floating over. She's flanked by several assistants, each wearing a simple black suit with a jeweled flower brooch and I wonder if this is what Bluebell has signed up for.

"Talia," Jack says with a smile and I'm relieved to see it isn't fake. It makes me feel a bit better, knowing he might like her. Maybe it means she isn't so bad.

"These functions will be the death of us all," she twitters, casting a cutting look around her. One man shrinks away from her stare and leaves the line completely, but Talia doesn't seem to notice. She pulls a slim fan from a pocket and snaps it open with a crack to wave it before her face.

"You've been to plenty of these and yet here you are, still standing." Jack tugs me close. "Have you met Daniella Starling?"

"Dani," I say, holding my hand out to her.

"Yes, I remember you..." Her words trail off as she ignores my hand to instead pat the sides of my dress, her eyes wide and hungry. I stand there with my arms raised, not quite sure what to do. I look to Jack for answers, but he only shrugs.

"Like what you see, Talia?" Jack laughs.

"This dress," she snaps. "Who made it?"

"My friend Bluebell, she mentioned she'll be..."

"This is her work?" Talia claps her hands and holds them together. When she closes her eyes, I think I might see a tear. "She is going to be spectacular, more radiant than the sun or moon when I'm done with her!" She chuckles and winks at me. "No offense to present company, of course."

"None taken," I manage.

"Lovely to see you, Talia," Jack says, "but we need to get inside and go hide in a corner until this thing is done."

Only when we're cutting through the crowd again do I eye Jack, hoping for a story.

"We grew up together," he explains as we walk. "She was the only one close to my age after they sent Evan away for school. It made things a little less lonely around here, at least during the daytime. But she can be...a lot."

Jack's expression is distant when he stops speaking and I raise a hand to trail along his arm, helping to bring him back to the now. Opening his eyes, he smiles and brushes his lips over the top of my head before letting out a weary sigh. "Let's get this over with."

I cling to his arm when we pass another line of people waiting to enter the gala. They wear stiff-looking black jackets and neckties of red and gold. Some women and a few men wear highly-structured bodices with puffed up shirts and pants that look like wet tissue paper. One lady holds a tiny dog and a few hold tightly to the hands of small children who are once again turned towards the sounds of water and play in the distance.

Heads turn our way, and though they make way for the son of Tobias Clousdspeak, the conversations do not stop as we pick our way through tall, plaster pillars painted gold and decorated with roses and leafy green vines. I reach to touch them and find they are solidly built, though not secured to either ground or ceiling. I decide to make it a point to stay as far away from them as possible.

"Nice of you to show up." Evan approaches and I'm amused to see he's wearing something almost identical to his brother.

"And nice of you to choose the same suit," Jack grumbles.

"Beige has always been our color," Evan says, and then to me adds, "I don't have words to describe how nice you look in that dress."

"Um, thanks," I say lightly, an unfamiliar smell in the air catching my attention. I take a big breath at the same time as Jack, though his results in a cutting look to Evan.

"Smells like someone purchased something good at auction," Jack tells him, and Evan nods with a grimace.

"What is that smell?" I ask.

"Cooked cow. Beef. Steak to be exact," Evan says, leading us to a small door near an assortment of fruity beverages. Someone guards the entrance, but nods when he notices the brothers and lets us pass through.

Once inside, I'm assaulted by a foreign odor that reminds me vaguely of heavy grease. Evan waves a hand dismissively about and what I see nearly brings up the applesauce and half sandwich.

Long tables have been lined with crisp white sheets, but have been since covered in small red dots and the occasional discarded piece of fatty meat tissue. Sitting among them are mostly men, but I do see a few women, each wearing an identical white bib with the Cloudspeak logo firmly stitched upon the front.

In front of them on silver plates are chunks of sweating red meat, glistening from the lights above. There are cuts both large and small, thinly seared slices with green sauces smeared across them, and even what looks like a burger but unlike the white chicken I'm used to, these have a meat that is crispy, brown, and dripping red juice.

I turn from the sight, sick to my stomach as I think of Magenta's cow and her large brown eyes, and find myself lurching for the closest door, which unfortunately leads me to a storage room for the main kitchen. Before me are tables upon tables of prepared tiny sandwiches, small cups of fruit or various vegetables, and what looks like a multitude of fried foods on little sticks. I double over trying my hardest not to think of food.

Jack is right behind me, rubbing my back and assuring me that Sally's cow is safe in the dragon, he saw it before he came to get me tonight. Evan enters a moment later, his face neutral, but I can still see the distressed and far-off look in his eyes. His reaction settles in my mind and I appreciate knowing he seems disgusted by the excess in the other room.

"Whenever you're ready," Jack says, "we should make some appearances before our turn comes up."

I stand up straight because he's right. I will not let their peculiar fascination with cooked cow ruin what we have in store for Tobias, which Evan assures me will be spectacular.

We're just turning to leave when something tacked to the door catches my attention. I pull it down without thinking and glance at its contents, realizing quickly it's the food service schedule. Someone is due to pick everything behind me up at any moment and distribute it among the hungry crowd outside these doors. In a moment of rage, I locate the section in which someone has neatly printed where each food platter should be deposited.

"Do you have something to write with?" I ask both brothers, and true to his nature, Evan produces an expensive looking pen from the pocket of his jacket. They watch in interest as I scribble new instructions onto the schedule and carefully replace it on the door.

"Not everyone is lucky enough to be able to visit The Salted Baths and have dinner in the same day," I say to the brothers before walking out.

Jack reluctantly leaves to assist one of Magenta's acts and Evan leads me to the side of the vast room. We stand, half-obscured by a large plant, and watch the people milling about before us. He points out a few important faces, but their names fade from memory as more and more personalities are introduced.

At some point, though, he points to an important-looking man surrounded by a group of richly-dressed men and women and says his name is Martin Apollo. I crane my neck to stare at him, trying to remember why the name sounds so familiar, but he moves on quickly to the next person. They all blend together, and I find myself quickly losing interest.

When Evan realizes I've stopped paying attention, he laughs and walks me through the party to a small outdoor patio. Tables and chairs have been set up and only a few quiet couples have made their way to them. None of them even look up as we take places along the railing overlooking the main pool, as if they actually intend to respect our privacy as they hope we would do their own.

Evan dips his head to whisper, "Everything is in place. Do your act and wait for the real magic to happen." He frowns. "Unless you don't want to watch. I don't think anyone would blame you."

Someone passes by and offers us tiny crystal glasses of wine, so I take one without thinking and swallow it swiftly. It burns its way down my throat as I think of what to say.

"They deserve for me to watch."

Evan downs his own glass in one quick swoop and nods. "That they do."

"What will happen afterwards?" I ask.

"I'm not sure exactly," he says, frowning into his glass. "We'll just have to wait and see."

"I thought you said this place was known for good food," sulks a portly man just to our left. His companion, a skinny woman wearing heavy makeup, pouts her lips as she trails her hand up his arm.

"Maybe it's because we're out here," she says. "Let's move inside and they'll feed us in there."

"Not likely," another man says, coming through the patio door to join the couple. "There's nothing to be had in there, either. What is the Required Industry Service coming to these days?

Someone should be overseeing those kids, the nerve to leave us without while the masses below are catered to."

"My Jimmy would never," says the woman, placing hands on her hips. "He is a model employee and I can assure you that the Required Service is a tightly-run ship at The Salted Baths."

"That's a very good idea, dear," the big man says. "Let's find Jimmy. I bet he could sort this out." With a quick nod to the newcomer, the couple slip out the door quickly as the man turns our way. He must recognize Evan, because his face turns molten.

"Master Cloudspeak, I didn't see you there," he stammers, but Evan simply smiles and holds his hand out to him.

"Please call me Evan. And I'm sure you know our newest starlet, Miss Daniella Starling?"

The man fidgets under Evan's stare, but shakes his hand and some of the trepidation melts away. "Nolan Addington, assistant chief of water sanitation. It's a pleasure to meet you in person, Miss Starling, my children will be sorry to have missed you." He gives me what looks to be a genuine smile.

"And as for the food delay," Evan says, capturing the man's attention instantly. "The Required Service isn't to blame. They work hard, and thanks to the generous contributions and support from our curated guests tonight, Miss Starling has arranged for the festivities to be shared among the people. The Cloudspeak Corporation has seen an abundance in profitability thanks to The Salted Baths clientele, wouldn't you agree Mr. Addington?"

Mr. Addington blinks, as if truly surprised, but quickly nods. "Yes, quite right. Very true."

"So, what's a little less finger food to shove into our mouths when that means more happy guests below?" Evan winks at me and takes my hand. "But please excuse us, I have to get this lovely lady backstage in time for her performance."

We're turning to leave when I happen to glance over the side of the railing. The view is spectacular with the sparkling pool below with its slick wooden decks dotted with various colored floats and happy people. Crowds of people mingle, some splashing each other and others happy to wait on the pool's edge, wading their feet in the cool water.

A sudden cheer erupts and I can hear the sound of pounding feet as server after server emerges into the crowd bearing plates of small foods. One poor server nearly falls over from a group of excited children clamoring to grab at the tiny bowls of what looks like ice cream.

Everyone on the patio has gone to the railing to see the commotion below, and more than a few snicker and make comments as to what could be happening. Even Mr. Addington cracks a smile when he looks down, and Evan and I take that as our chance to escape and push back through the door.

The room is crowded with people, most of them upset and hungry, but Evan and I walk quickly, his hand guiding me as we hurriedly exit through another door to a small lift.

"Are you happy here?" he asks as soon as the lift doors close on us. "Is this much better than feeding chickens?"

"I think I could be happy anywhere that is not under the control of Tobias Cloudspeak," I tell him, surprising myself with a small laugh.

The smooth walls of the lift remind me slightly of the steeliness of the basement lab and I wonder at how long ago the events at The Zamora House feel to me now.

My memory has done nothing but improve, but it still can't replicate the stolen memories that went up in flames along with Mother and Father. But I can't let myself be sad for them. That passage of time is over and done with, and there is nothing but the future to look forward to.

Evan shifts beside me as I'm lost in thought, and I can see why I was so infatuated with him when we first met. He is a good-looking guy, but there is something huge missing in our connection. I could never trust him to not to let me fall if we flew through the air together like I do with Jack.

"That's good." Evan's voice brings me back.

"It is," I agree.

"My brother will take good care of you," he adds quickly as the lift doors open up before us and we come into another staggeringly large room before I can even think of how to reply.

Parker is there in the corner, blushing furiously as some Stage Girls giggle at his attention. He waves to us as Evan walks with me to Jack. Magenta is nowhere to be seen.

"Just remember," Evan tells me in a low voice. "You don't have to watch the videos if you don't want to."

"I know," I whisper back. "But I have to."

Chapter Thirty-Three

The performance room is all high ceilings and huge windows and partitioned by a long red rope. With its own ominous plaster pillars and hanging vines, I assume right away it's another extension of the gala and we are just another part of the entertainment.

Benches line the walls, and upon them sit a number of women and men in formal clothes watching various tumblers doing stretches or warming up. The swings and trapeze sets used for Jack's act are high above, but scattered around are large viewing screens set to broadcast our act. Magenta must want everyone to see everything that happens on stage.

In the very center of the room sits a large structure that has been curtained off from view, and I know without looking that it is the new bird cage. It was constructed just for this show and is only big enough to hold a person or two, though it is meant for just me. Unlike in the circus, this cage won't move, and remains perched only a few feet from the ground. Jack will have to fly down to me.

When I duck inside the curtain, a mild whiff of gold spray paint someone has used on the bars fills my nose, but it's overcome by the pungent smell of the white roses, lilies, and ivy woven along the steel bars. Jack stands before the cage, and as I come up behind him, the curtain falls heavily in place to shield us from view.

He hasn't changed yet, but has discarded his suit jacket at some point and undone most of his shirt buttons. I'm at loss for words when I see his broad, tan chest and the way his suit pants gently hug his flat abdominal muscles. He's so attractive that it's almost hard to believe I'm the lucky one who gets to fly through the air with him.

He lets out a low whistle when he notices me staring at him and comes closer.

"As amazing as you look in that Talia Lake knockoff, I prefer you better in a swimmer," he says while opening the cage door and gesturing for me to follow.

I snort, unable to stop eyeing him, too. "I'm not sure which I prefer. It's just nice to have a choice."

Jack frowns. "I'm sorry you were so controlled like that."

I reach for the ivy, playing with one of the small leaves. I've never grown ivy before, but think I recall seeing it along the iron fencing back in the graveyard. "The thing is, I don't remember much of my life there. I've forgotten so much already, more and more each day. I don't know if it's just time, or maybe a lingering effect of the drugs, but my time there feels like a dream. Or maybe a nightmare."

I look up to find someone has gone to the trouble to paint a blue sky with clouds inside the upper dome. It makes me smile despite the gnawing feeling inside whenever I think of my life before the circus. I've never had a canvas that vast, and can't help but wonder who from the circus keeps painting these vivid blue skies. Maybe they would let me help.

Jack takes my hand. "Memories can be both dreams and night-mares for me sometimes, but not when I'm with the people here, or when I'm flying through the sky with you. That is home. You are, um, my home." He blushes deeply and it's endearing to see him so flustered. Now it's my turn to squeeze his hand in reassurance. "I forget things sometimes, too, but they're still there. Just stored away because I don't need them. They had to make way for good things."

"Good things," I repeat, thinking of my time with him, of befriending people like Bluebell and the three sisters, of hearing Magenta speak about my parents and how my mother danced among the stars. Maybe those awful memories will always be tucked somewhere inside, but if I can make better ones with the people here, maybe it won't matter.

"Like finding you in the wilds." He takes a breath, looking down at our clasped hands as he brushes his thumbs over my knuckles. "Dani, I don't know what you want from this new life of yours, but I want to be a part of it."

I tilt my head back to gaze at the sky, thinking of the longest day of my life traveling through the wilds in that rusty, old golf cart. Driving away from everything and everyone I'd ever known. I still don't know what the future holds for me, but... "I know what I want right now, at least," I find myself saying, and let him pull me closer with hooded eyes that are pale green slits, dangerous and sparkling like some sort of intricate and fancy cocktail.

"Show's about to start," he says lowly, his hand trailing up my spine. When I listen to the music playing behind us, I find he's right; we need to get ready. All the same, when he presses his lips to mine, I kiss him right back, the hungry itch returning fiercely.

Jack is one step ahead as the hand on my back grabs hold of the zipper. I freeze, and so does he, until I nod and let him slowly pull it down. The dress pools at my feet in its own blue ocean. It's as if I stepped off the cliff right into the ocean itself. Smiling, I undo the last few buttons of his shirt and he shrugs it off without taking his lips off mine and I help him step out of his suit pants, which we kick to the side where they'll be out of view during the performance.

We're left in nothing but our performance costumes, the sparkly shorts and nude sock, but something stops us from taking it further, even if we're both gritting our teeth at the end and panting heavily.

"Dani," Jack whispers harshly into my neck. "I don't have much to my name, but if you stay with me, I promise to give you everything that I am or ever will be. I will be your home."

Home. The faces from my past may be hard to remember, but the little things are still there. The smell of pancakes, Tara's laughter, the wood grain under my palm when I slid my hand down the stairway banister. Lily's friendship and how she always looked out for me. When I think about it, home never was an old house sitting over an even older graveyard, it was the collection of small moments I made into memories so deeply engraved in my heart that no number of drugs could ever take away.

I feel my heart open and let Jack inside so that he rests neatly among my collection. I lean up to tell him, but the music outside begins to swell loudly before I can and he parts from me letting cold air wash over my flushed skin. I find myself staggering back, dizzy, my lips tingling. Jack smiles as he steps out and closes the cage door, so we stand on opposite sides of the bars grinning at each other. His mouth opens, but a loud clicking sounds between us and we spring apart.

But nothing happens and, curious, I step forward and place my hands on the door's hidden handle and find it won't budge. Jack's eyes go wide and he jumps to the bars, muscles straining as he tries to force them open.

"He's locked me inside," I whisper without feeling the words even come out. Jack swears as the music swells again and we know he's due on stage soon. He clings to my hands through the bars and lilies rub against my skin. Even though I'm not bleeding, I can feel their vibrant and curious reaction.

"Dani," he says, like he's not sure what else to offer but my name—a reminder I am more to him than just a girl who glows.

"You have to go," I tell him and he shakes his head. "I mean it, go and pretend like nothing happened. I'll figure something out, but I don't know what will happen if you don't go."

"I won't leave you."

I squeeze his hands. "You have to, he'll want me there for the finale. If all goes according to plan, this won't be any bother at all and we'll get Sally or Supper to cut me out of this thing if we need to."

"But…"

"Go! It's the best of our current options." The comment takes him by surprise, but he straightens up, still clinging to my hands, and bends forward to kiss them softly, pressing his lips against each of my knuckles.

"All right, little rabbit," he says. "I'll see you soon."

And with that, he's gone and I'm alone.

Locked in another cage.

After Jack leaves, I check every inch of the door's frame, hoping to find a secret latch by shoving and pulling at the flowers and vines. When nothing is found, I begin to pace circles and try to concentrate on finding a way out, however difficult the music and cheering from outside the curtain wall makes it.

The cage is dark now. The lights must have been turned down low and the sun has long-since set beyond the sea, casting nothing but moonlight into the performance area. I wonder briefly if there will be a fake moon tonight or if Supper and Magenta planned for the real moon to take its place.

Slamming my hands on the bars only makes them sting, but I've run out of options. Frustrated, I can do nothing but quietly sob into my hands and try to cling to the hope that *something* will get me out.

But something breaks through my tears and I notice the ivy and flowers surrounding me have reacted as I pushed them aside in my searching. They now curl around the bars and gently caress the painted sky above, having grown twice their size. I check my hands thoroughly and finding no cuts of any kind, so I tentatively touch a small vine and feel it react with a jump at my touch. A stunning white lily sprouts from its leafy stem. As it blossoms, the surrounding lilies and roses begin to fully bloom and I'm surrounded by their sweet scents. It would be enough to make most people dizzy, but instead of being overwhelmed, I'm only more curious.

If I can do this, could I do more?

Hating to destroy any of the flowers, I pluck a single petal from the closest rose and hold it in my hand. Moving to the back of the cage, I crush it between my fingers and have to jump back as it begins to smolder and sear into my palm. I drop it quickly and use Jack's suit pants to smother the smoke before it can ignite anything else.

I then pluck a full-grown lily and hold it in my hand, but do not have time to contemplate on my discovery before the music swells once more and the cheering from the crowd grows louder as the curtain begins to rise. I bolt to the front of the cage, knuckles white as I grip the bars, pushing the flower between them and squinting as light floods the cage floor.

My eyes are still adjusting to the light when a heavy hand clamps down on my fingers and yanks one arm through the cage bars. Blinking everything into focus, I look up to find none other than Tobias Cloudspeak himself looming before me. His mouth spreads in a wide and malignant smile, and with his other hand, he holds Prim firmly to his side.

Neither of us can move. All we can do is stand there and glow.

Chapter Thirty-Four

"Ladies and Gentlemen of The Salted Baths," Tobias announces, his booming voice carrying far and wide, "it is my greatest pleasure to welcome you this evening. I hope your time here has been luxurious and that you will enjoy the upcoming decadent desserts on their way to you now. We apologize for the lack of food earlier, as we felt a brief fasting would allow you to truly appreciate what is to come."

He squeezes my hand painfully at the mention of missing food. It takes a moment for my eyes to adjust and I hope he does not take my watery stare as a sign of weakness. What must be a few hundred people fill the room watching our every move. There are too many for me to pick out anyone familiar, but I do notice a few performers from our act standing off to the side.

Prim is also whimpering nearby, but I seal my lips shut, not wanting to give Tobias the satisfaction of knowing I'm in any pain.

"Now, it's no secret why you've come. You've been dazzled by unimaginable aerial performances, tickled pink by curious clowns, and gazed in wondrous amazement at our curated circus curiosities. But now I present to you two new wonders, born for the very purpose they are about to demonstrate. A miracle of scientific discovery that I have had the pleasure of being personally involved in. This first one, oh, she's my favorite, lent on a temporary basis to Magenta and her Magical World and now exclusively under my own care. Why, with her close connection to her partner, my wonderful son, she is practically family at this point! Ladies and gentlemen, I present to you, Miss Daniella Starling!"

His words muster a round of applause from the gathered audience as he hauls my arm painfully above my head. I look out to them, but the faces I see all blend together as they stare with curious eyes. The cage's bars dig painfully into my muscles before he throws my arm back down. He doesn't let go as he raises his second arm and all but dangles a mostly-limp Prim by her wrist.

"You'll see I'm also accompanied by a second miracle today!" he bellows. "The most beautiful Primrose Helena. Another talented daughter of scientific revolution, heralded by my hands to usher prosperity for all!"

His words create hushed murmurs from the people before us, and when their next round of applause fails to meet his expectations, Tobias sneers at them and thrusts Prim's arm down as well. I think I hear her give a small yelp as he pushes her to the ground before him, her knees cracking painfully on the floor. The cry of pain causes a few of Jack's fellow performers to venture close, but Tobias's icy glare makes them freeze before reaching us.

"Sorry about this one, folks. She's a little under the weather but had insisted on being part of today's festivities. I tried to tell her to stay home, but you know how young girls are, you can't tell them to do anything!" He lets out a great belly laugh that dislodges a few strands of his perfectly manicured hair, causing one of his eyes to become partially obscured. "But truth be told, I am glad she is here with us today, because now I can show you what these two little girls are actually capable of. Their true power, if you will. Then, when we're through, I'd be most happy to speak with anyone interested in becoming more involved with this...special project of mine."

Bile rises in my throat but catches when a searing hot pain sparks suddenly on the palm of the hand still clutched by Tobias. I try to pull away, but he holds on carefully as the long knife he'd hidden up his sleeve flashes out again and Prim slumps beside him, clutching her hand to her chest in surprise.

My own blood oozes as he ignores Prim huddled on the floor and holds my hand up amid gasps and cries from the audience. Some of them exit quickly, disgust lining their faces, but more than a few stay for the show.

A commotion off to the side snags my attention and I look to see two large men holding back Jack, who is struggling to break free. Behind him, I can just make out Lacey, broken and bloody and barely holding herself upright in her chair, and Parker trying to break through the gathering crowd. Evan and Magenta are nowhere to be seen.

Time slows when I turn back at Tobias. His smile is back, but stretched too far across his face, and the green eyes he's passed on to both his sons look nothing like forests or jewels. They've taken on an intense black color that reflects the malice and greed within his heart.

"Time to show them your real power, Daniella." He raises his other hand, holding a small cloth bag that must contain seeds. I assume he wants me to set it alight, but the crackling sound of electrical static interrupts us as it roars through the air and his head swivels looking for the source.

"And now, ladies and gentlemen, it is time for our main event," the smooth baritone of Magenta rings out over the crowd. "Stay tuned, you won't want to miss it."

Relief floods through me when I realize the plan Evan created has started. True to my promise, I force myself to watch the videos playing on the screens surrounding the room. Every audience member also looks up with amusement turned horror, and like them I can't seem to turn away. Even Prim is sitting up now, mesmerized by the screens with a fixed and haunted expression.

And what plays is horrible, but also true and sad. Everything that I remember or cannot remember plays before me. I see Cait and Tara, too small and too scared to receive so many needles shoved into their skin. Rana is screaming as the strawberry plant in front of her catches fire and burns her hands. Lily stands firm as she is poked and prodded by Father, his eyes dark when he looks into her fiery expression. Sara and Vera are strapped to beds, blood pumped into and out of their veins. Prim stands outside the house wearing only a nightgown and glowing like the moon with fire dancing between her fingers as she glares at Tobias standing before her. There is a dangerous look in her young eyes and for all the power she seems to exude, I wonder if this is why they preferred me over Prim's unpredictable and livid nature. Maybe I was just easier to control.

Then there is more footage of Tobias standing alongside Father and nodding his approval. He smiles as every single one of us girls screams and writhes in torment.

My promise to watch waivers as the next few scenes focus solely on me. I see myself ripped from a small bed, and again as a baby glowing brighter than anyone else, and again as a toddler barely walking but fascinated and doing everything I can to run after a full moon high in the sky. Then I'm being sucked dry of blood, machines pumping through various other machines that are so loud they drown out the cries of one screaming little girl who has set her toys on fire. I'm being fed pills and liquids and foods to help me forget, and then going back into the testing the next day, unaware, bright-eyed and cheerful.

The performance area has gone quiet and the people not scared away begin to speak, one by one until the room is in an uproar. Shouts are hurled at Tobias, and he begins to shrink back, as if he's never received an insult before. As if he is astounded that anyone would call him a monster or even dare suggest he'd be a business liability.

He curls his lip at them and, straightening to his full height, looks down his nose at me. His breath smells like lollipop candy when he leans close to the cage bars.

"I'll burn you alive for this, Daniella Starling. You and those worthless sons of mine."

"My name is Dani," I snarl back and thrust the lily in my free hand at him, aiming for his heart. I push with all my might, my palm making contact with his shirt, and the sickening stench of burning flesh envelopes us as his clothes catch flame.

He screams, stumbling back and nearly tripping over Prim as he tries to rip off his burning suit jacket. People in the audience start to scream as well, a few of them running towards the exits. But still some stay, perhaps convinced this is all part of the show.

With the jacket discarded on the floor, Tobias stomps the fire out and turns to me, his eyes no longer black pools but infernos. He presses down on a small remote that he takes from his pocket and the clicking sound of the lock disengaging fills the cage. He kicks Prim to the side and in several quick steps, he's reached the door and flung it open. His hands clench and unclench as he struggles to maintain composure. One hand pushes back his hair but it flops out in resistance and, for a moment, I can see the resemblance to Evan and Jack.

"This is all your fault," he begins, his hands held up in mock defense before him. I know he isn't scared, though I think he should be. Rage boils inside my blood at what this man has done to not only me, but both the family I grew up with and my newfound family among Magenta's people. It makes my whole body shake in anger.

"How would any of this be my fault?" I spit back at him. "You're the one who helped make me this way."

"No, I simply provided the funds and helped facilitate. If you had come with me when I asked, then you could have been stored safely away. A danger such as yourself needs to be controlled, caged up, observed, and tested. Now that you've been let free to cause such as spectacle, it'll be much more difficult to gather funds for continued research. It would have been hard enough without Leonard, but this extra damage control is really going to drain not only my resources, but my time and patience as well."

"Then maybe you shouldn't have killed him," I say and the corner of his mouth twists up in another sneer.

"Maybe it did create a hassle," he says, stalking toward me, leaving Prim's unmoving body behind. For every one step forward he takes, I take one step back. "But with him and Martha out of the picture, that's two fewer people to share the spotlight with." He pauses to sigh heavily. "But then my two idiot sons had to get involved. Now Jack, he's always been a thorn in my side, but Evan? I expected better from him, even if I'm mildly impressed by his designs to replace me. Although, I'll admit, I did hope he could see the big picture."

"He just saw a different picture than you. All you care about is power."

"You're right about that," Tobias seethes. "What's the word you girls always liked to use? Friscuit or something stupid like that, right? Oh friscuit, you're in trouble now, *Dani*. Am I using that word correctly?" Tobias is close now and I have since ran out of space, my back pressed against the wall.

"There's a better one," I say. "You, Tobias, are bad gravy."

"Bad gravy," he repeats, malice dripping from his lips. "Well, I've had enough of this bad gravy and will take my chances with Prim. You, Daniella Starling, are more trouble than you're worth, and I won't be needing your services any longer."

Tobias lunges for me, but right as I feel his fingers curl around my neck, something happens and he staggers back. His eyes, once wide with anger, are now wider in shock. One hand travels to his heart, and he seems surprised to find something sharp protruding just under the singed fabric of his shirt. The projectile's end smolders red, and small wisps of flame lick the bloody skin around the puncture. Tobias stumbles back with his hands scrabbling at his chest as more and more sharp projectiles sprout out of his chest, each making a terrible squelching sound.

His steps backward are followed by Prim screaming something I can't make out and a sudden, sharp *CRACK*. I look up and realize what the sound is and dive to the back of the cage as one of the huge pillars comes crashing in a column of fire.

It slams into the side of the cage with such force that huge chunks of hard plaster and curling steel shoot out around us. I huddle in the back, tucking my head under my arms and trying to hold my breath until it's all over. When I open my eyes, I see the front of the cage has been torn clear open, almost as if someone had sliced it in two by a huge knife. And all around are red and angry flowers, their vines set ablaze where they wrap around the pillar. It's only as they twist and twitch around the gilded stone that I realize they are responsible for bringing it down.

My hands pat down my hair, then arms and legs and I marvel that I am virtually unscathed, only a few slices caused by errant plaster. It only takes one quick glance to know that Tobias wasn't as lucky. His mangled and bloody form lies before me, and much like I saw with Father, a pool of dark, red blood pools beneath his still body.

I reel backwards, my palms pressing hard into the debris-laden ground. Tilting my head back as I catch my breath, I stare blindly at a bit of painted blue sky until I feel Jack's presence and his strong arms wrapping around my shoulders. He pulls me away from the wreckage as the fire around us is quickly extinguished and cooled by strong streams of water pumped from the pools below and through a multitude of faucets set high in the ceiling.

A small chuckle escapes my throat because I realize he's still only wearing his sparkly shorts. And it sounds crazy that the first thing I can think of to say is "I think your pants are ruined." My voice is raspy and weak and the words feel wrong, but I cannot think of anything better.

"That's too bad, they were my favorite pair," Jack whispers back, pressing his forehead against mine. "You know, when we first met, you were the one not wearing pants."

I laugh, loud and free, and cling to him tightly as salty pool water cascades all around us. It's like we're back inside the big waterfall in the pool. Then something releases inside me and my laughter is replaced with tears, as if they are washing away all the pain and anxiety I've kept in my heart for so long.

It's finally over, Tobias and the Zamoras won't be able to hurt me, or any of us, ever again.

Chapter Thirty-Five

After the rain makes short work of any flames, Jack helps me to stand and we make our way out of the mostly-empty performance room. My legs shake and it takes most of my concentration to put one foot in front of another. The shock of everything seeps into my mind like melted butter on toast, and while it blissfully clears my head of anything other than static numbness, it makes moving an almost impossible task.

One of Jack's performers rushes over to help but disappears again after Jack shakes his head and waves at the mess on the ground. He says something I don't really pay attention to, but think it has to do with cleaning and salvaging what they can. The words are nothing but a distant rattle as I work to process my new reality.

We have to walk by Tobias and I turn away from his prone body in disgust, but then my eyes fall on Prim's still form beside his own and I hide my face in Jack's shoulder.

Everyone is dead now, even Tobias, but I am not. I am alive.

"Jack," I hear Sally's deep voice rumble once we're out of the room. "Let me help, please."

Only then do I feel another strong set of hands slung around my shoulders as Jack allows her to assist him. The three of us—Jack and I still wearing nothing but our performance costumes—walk carefully down the marble stairways and back towards the lumbering land train that waits for us in the twilight.

We don't stop until we reach a lift I've never used before and Sally props me up against its wall and gives Jack a once-over with a critical eye.

"I need to make sure no one touched Magenta's cow," she says, then fondly smooths down my hair. "Take care of this one."

The lift takes Jack and me to a deserted floor, and he leads me down a plain hallway to what he tells me is his room. He mumbles that I'm the first person to see it, since Magenta gifted it to him when he left The Salted Baths to travel with the circus. I don't know exactly where we are, but I think we're near the dragon's heart.

He helps me to lay on his bed and takes my bleeding palm into his hand, but I can't even stay conscious enough to watch him wrap a clean bandage around the wound and am asleep in seconds. No dreams come to harass me in my sleep and I am forever thankful for it.

Then the passage of time speeds back up and suddenly I am opening my eyes, startled awake by someone pounding on the door to Jack's room. Jack rises from his place beside me on the bed and opens the door slowly, breathing out an almost agitated sigh when I see Evan standing in the doorway.

I can tell from the light streaming through Jack's window that it is barely morning. More like the crack of dawn. I want nothing more than to go back to sleep, but Jack has let Evan inside and he strides over to me on his long legs.

"Tobias is dead," he says simply and Jack narrows his eyes as he considers the news.

"I thought that might affect me much more, but it doesn't," he says, leaning against the wall. Evan regards him with a sour look.

"I wanted him discredited, but not dead. Though I guess either way works out for us."

"For you," says Jack. "I don't think being alive or dead matters to me, but for Dani's sake, I'm glad he's gone."

"And now it appears we're the last of the Cloudspeaks."

"No, you are. I want nothing to do with that name ever again," Jack tells him, grabbing the closest pair of pants he can reach and pulling them on before adding, "I'd prefer to be a Starling." He tosses another pair my way and they're comically big, but I'm thankful for the extra coverage, even if they don't hide the way my face flushes at the thought of Jack taking my last name.

"Well, that's a good thing because, well..." Evan stalls and runs a hand through his hair before continuing. "Seems like the old man didn't leave you anything. He didn't leave me squat either, but luckily, I made sure to get name into the trustee's hands this morning. You're looking at the new commanding officer of The Cloudspeak Corporation and proud owner of The Salted Baths."

"But not the circus," Jack says, crossing his arms.

"No, even if I held to the contracts, I don't think Magenta would listen. Everything that's happened has certainly made a name for this place, and I doubt you'll lack additional venues, or people wanting to run away and join."

Jack nods absently, gazing out the window before replying.

"We'll be parting ways then, brother."

"I figured as much." Evan holds out his hand for Jack to shake, but Jack lifts an eyebrow at him and clasps his hand heavy on Evan's shoulder instead.

"Hope you can manage to be a bit more honest with this place," he says, and Evan gives him a wan smile in return.

"I'll do my best." He then turns to me. While this man may have saved my life several times over, I don't think I'd ever be able to fully trust him. But knowing he did save me from Tobias, twice, I think I can at least trust him to steer his father's company in a better direction.

"What happens now?" I ask, barely able to cover the huge yawn that follows.

"Right now? Absolutely nothing," Evan says. "I think we all need a little bit of rest. Besides, I have arrangements to make." He turns to leave, but spins at the door to look towards Jack. "Martin Apollo came around asking for Magenta. I sent him to find Supper, figured he could lend a hand."

Jack nods and stares at the closed door behind him.

"I know I've heard that name before," I mumble, trying to pinpoint where I'd heard it before.

"Martin Apollo takes caravans across The Dusting," says Jack, and a few memories of reading about his exploits with Tara come drifting back. "Magenta has hired him to help take us across."

My mouth drops open. "You mean we're going to cross The Dusting and travel to the Eastern Coasts?"

"Yes," Jack says softly. "That is, if you're coming with us. You haven't said—"

I cut him off by pressing my lips against his in the kind of kiss that belongs in the wilds.

"Of course I am," I say when the kiss breaks. "This is my home." I truly mean it and we're smiling at each other until I can't help but let another big yawn escape, which causes him to yawn in return and we're both left laughing at our absurdity.

"I don't know about you, but I'm exhausted," he mumbles, dropping onto the bed beside me. He pulls me down next to him and leans his head against mine.

"Me too," I whisper. "But I still can't believe it's over. I can't believe that he's dead, that Prim...is also dead. That they all are." My voice cracks with a shuddering sob as I twist into Jack and clutch my arms around him. Without the pressing weight of an unknown future, the pain and muddled memories have nothing to hold them back. "I just miss them all so much."

"I know you do," he murmurs into my hair. "What's that thing Magenta says, something about how we miss the dead when they are gone, so who is to say they do not miss us in return? She doesn't always make sense, but maybe that one's true. That the dead still think of us even though they're not here. We're a part of them and they're a part of us."

I sniff and give him a watery smile. "I guess so."

He smiles right back. "I'm always here if you need to talk. Tell me what you remember of them and I'll help you never to forget."

"Thank you," I whisper.

"But now I think we both need some rest. Let's take a nap, then we'll go find something to eat," Jack says, pressing his lips softly on my own. I'm too tired and shaky to take it any further and he seems to sense that, so after a slow, burning kiss, he tugs me down into his arms and together we fall into a deep and dreamless sleep.

I am thrown away by the normalcy I encounter when Jack and I come to breakfast the next day. But like Sally once said, it is the circus way not to pry, and while I have no doubt that everyone in this land train knows every detail of every event that has occurred in the last two days, no one says a word.

After breakfast, Jack excuses himself and lets me know there is something he needs to take care of, and I find myself alone for the first time in ages.

Without the threat of Tobias looming over me, I wander the hallways of the train, glancing into old and forgotten rooms to see what's inside and running my hands along the many books stored in the library rooms. I even find one about dolphins, which I pick up and hide quickly in my room.

I then make my way to the entrance of The Salted Baths. It's still early and not open to the public yet, but the woman with the vibrant red hair is there speaking excitedly with Lacey, who looks much better after a few visits from a doctor, and I'm let inside without question. Miles is by their feet playing with what I think might be a taxidermy blue jay, but I keep his secret and don't say anything.

My feet barely make a sound on the cool floor, but I am alone wandering the hallways, looking for signage that could help me find my way.

I finally find it, a placard set into the wall indicating which way to turn towards the business section of the huge complex. It takes several minutes, but I finally emerge into an empty office. No, not empty, someone has been busy stacking boxes of personal belongings in the corner. What seems like a once-cluttered and dusty room is being transformed into a bright and cheery place. Through the windows, I can see the ocean on one side and a giant stretch of green grass on the other. People already move about upon the field, trimming and measuring the lawns.

The door opens behind me and I turn to see Evan standing there. He doesn't seem surprised to see me and gives me warm smile.

"You asked if I was into golf once," he says mildly, walking over. "Well, I'm still not, but enough people are, and I figured we could profit from it and make a course here."

"Did you get some new golf carts, at least?" I ask and he chuckles as we stare silently out the window together.

"Magenta came to see me," he says, breaking the silence. "It's always hard to fully understand her, but she did pass off the remainder of my Required Industry Service. She knows I'll have my hands full here. I already started, you know. Lowering the cost of admission was the first thing, my fool of a father kept making it higher and higher just so he could fund his elaborate parties and, of course, invest in certain scientific endeavors. I promise you that nothing like that will happen under my watch."

"Can you do all that?" I ask, unable to keep the hope from my voice. It never occurred to me that Tobias could have been investing in other Zamora Houses out there.

"I'm a Cloudspeak, I can do whatever I want," he says dryly.

"I guess you can." And oddly enough, I believe him. It occurs to me, perhaps belatedly, that Evan is one of the last few people alive who would remember my former life.

"I'm sorry I wasn't able to save more of you," he says, as if reading my thoughts. There's a real tinge of honesty in his words and I know he's not lying.

Maybe if things had worked out differently, he and Lacey could have saved us all. But I have no reason to wonder about what the past could have been, I can only hope and move towards the future.

And to do that, I have to forgive him like I've forgiven myself.

"I'm sorry I never thanked you for saving my life," I say and he gives me a small smile as he holds the door open for me.

"I'm glad I was able to. Someone needs to keep an eye on my brother," he says. "But now I need to get some work done, so I'll see ya around, Dani. Take care."

"Yeah, see ya around, Evan."

When I leave The Salted Baths, I gaze up at the sleeping dragon before me. She is full of chickens, all plump and well cared for by Parker, and wonderful friends like the cookie-stealing Lindy sisters, and Sally, and even Supper and Beetle. She rests before the long flight across The Dusting, and I stand gazing up at her steel frame and wonder again if she is a train or a living thing. Perhaps, with all of us inside, she is both.

"Saying goodbye?" says a familiar voice from behind me and I turn to see Bluebell, pulling behind her an overstuffed suitcase. Nearby are Butterscotch and Minty, each hauling similar suitcases, though Minty's looks as if it could burst open at any point.

"Are you really leaving?" I ask and she smiles widely.

"I am, and Minty and Butter are coming, too. I asked Snuzzle to come, but he said no. People born into this place rarely ever leave. It's easier for those like us, born or raised elsewhere. Besides, I need to share my talent with the world."

"I'm staying with the train," I say, surer than I've ever been. "Even though I was brought up on a hill overlooking a graveyard and not into a circus life." Visions of the house girls I grew up with flash through my head and I hope that, wherever they are now, Tara, Cait, Rana, Sara, Vera, Prim, and Lily are happy.

"Hmm, that sounds like the perfect inspiration for a winter fashion show," she sighs dreamily. "Hills and graveyards! Promise me that you'll stop by and see me once you're back in the area."

"I promise," I tell her and she gives me a big hug before collecting Butterscotch and Minty, who has resorted to carrying half her clothes over her shoulders. Together, the three of them disappear into The Salted Baths.

The morning has quickly bled away and it's near lunchtime. I trail my fingers along the dragon's scales toward the closest lift. When it arrives, three familiar faces light up, and the sisters wrap their many arms around me.

"Rabbit! We almost left without you!" Bindy screams.

"We wouldn't have, though. Jack would have made sure we waited," Mindy says, making kissing sounds and laughing.

"We would make sure Magenta waited, too," says Cindy, giggling at her sisters and helping to pull me inside with them. They press a series of buttons and the lift lurches upwards and outwards and I feel it propelling me to a future that I both do and do not know. The sisters cling to me and chatter endlessly, but it's soothing, in a way. The emotions they bring no longer eat away at my insides, but are instead a happy and bitter sweetness. They bring memories of a house on top of a hill overlooking a graveyard.

We arrive on the dining floor, and I find myself trailing after them, thinking of my first time here, when Parker falls into step with me.

"I'm glad you're staying with us," he says, his face flushing pink. "It'll be nice to have help with the chickens—that is, when you have time."

"Shush, Parker," Bindy says. "She'll be spending that time with Jack and we have priority of anything left over." Her sisters all laugh and Parker's face goes scarlet until Cindy smiles shyly at him and touches his shoulder.

"Don't worry, you can also come visit us sometimes," she says softly and Parker's eyes grow wide as he looks at her with new appreciation.

"Speaking of Jack, where is he?" I ask Parker.

Beetle answers for him from his perch at his table: "Saw him earlier, said to tell you to meet him up top. Has something for you, I guess." He spits off to the side.

"Up top?"

"Take the middle lift." He gestures with one intact finger. "Either that or get your book out if you want food."

I thank him and make my way through the crowds coming in for lunch. We've started moving and the dragon lurches under my feet as I pass by Sally and Supper, sitting by each other and discussing the purchase of an additional cow, and some newly-appointed Stage Girls running from table to table with napkins.

When I get to the lift, Magenta of Magenta's Magical World of Circus Curiosities is the one to exit. When she looks down at me, it is not her hair that catches my attention as it did so long ago, but her amber eyes as she considers me, really considers me. When I smile and step into the lift, she follows me.

"You're just the person I've been looking for," she says and I wonder if she means now, or in general, and from a deep pocket of her navy coat, she takes out the worn journal and hands it to me.

"The little man in my hair said to give this to you," she says and I tuck the journal tightly against my chest. She then pulls out another familiar velvet bag which hands to me.

When I open it and drop the brooch into my palm, my breath catches. It's a starling sitting on a branch. Victoria's lost brooch.

"I thought you might like it to complete the set," she says, the knob in her throat bobbing as she swallows visibly. "I hate to part with it, but I shouldn't have hidden it away. It belongs to you."

"How long have you had this?" I can't help but ask.

"Ever since my best friend, Victoria, died, and the hospital shipped me a box of her belongings. I think Martha and Leonard were too ashamed, or too nervous about suspicion, to pick it up, so they sent it my way. I've kept it hidden in my hair all these years, even when Martha eventually wanted it back. Only then, when you appeared as if you yourself were a starling taken flight, I took it as a sign that it should be returned to the family. An heirloom, if you will."

"I'm sorry you lost your best friend. I know that can be hard," I say, swallowing painfully at my words. She gives me a genuine, non-showmanship smile and taps her chest.

"Little rabbit, I don't dwell on her death because it leaves less time for my future. But I will always have a special place set aside for her in my heart and she will travel with me in this life and into the next."

Before I can say a word in response, she steps out just before the lift door shuts.

"Thank you," I whisper to the door instead, then drop back against the wall and hug the journal to my chest as the lift rises and rises. When the door opens, Jack's there, leaning against a door.

"Took you long enough," he says. "Come on, we only have a few minutes before this thing picks up speed and we'll be blown off into the wilds."

"What are you talking about?" I ask, but he's opened the door and the sound of rushing, whirling wind swallows my voice, and I realize we are about to step foot on the very top of the dragon.

Jack holds out his hand and I take it without question, following him into the bright afternoon. We come out just behind the head, wedged between an iron rail that protrudes from either side, and while I'm in no danger of falling off, I grip the rail until my knuckles turn white. Jack laughs and turns to face downwind, gesturing for me to do the same. He pulls me against his chest so we're both facing the dragon's tail, and then from his pockets, pulls out a bag of ash. There would be no way for us to talk, but there's no need.

A sob catches in my throat. He's brought Prim's remains. He helps me open it, and I release her into the wilds. I close my eyes and whisper into the wind that I'm glad she's no longer in pain.

Then I bring the journal up in front of us and press my fingers once more into its thick pages. I think of nothing but Lily's mischievous smile as I set the book on fire and hastily throw it out before us, watching the flames twist and turn among its secrets until it is nothing but an ashy blur in the wind.

It's all over now and it makes me feel like I'm closing one of Lily's books after reading the final chapter. Everything that once happened is still inside my mind, tucked safely inside in case I need it, but now I can start a new story. My own story.

The dragon picks up speed, so we hurry back inside, Jack's hand never leaving mine. His grip tightens as we enter the lift in silence, leaning against the wall with our heads dropped back. When the door opens, and I realize he's brought me to his room, that same hungry itch builds in my core. He glances at me, as if making sure it's okay, but I don't answer with words. Instead, I sway toward him, smiling wide. The door closes behind us and he presses my back against it, his body warm against mine.

"Dani," he breathes. "Stay with me, please. I need you here with me."

"I'll stay," I promise and pull his face towards mine so I can look into the green depths of his eyes. "This is my home. *You* are my home and I want to fly through the sky with you forever as *The Amazing Starlings.*"

His eyes grow wide in excitement just as he throws his arms around me and we tumble to the bed. Our closeness comes naturally from already knowing each other's bodies after being so close to naked in our costumes. But this time, the sparkles that come are not from our glowing skin. They're from the way my vision goes fuzzy knowing he's this close, that he is mine and I am his.

In the small moments later, I remember Tara telling me anything can be true if I believe it, so I believe in my newfound freedom and in my hope for the future.

And then as the great beast bellows into the night and we careen through the wilds tucked safe inside her belly, I stay quiet and listen, believing that I can fly.

After all, it's in my blood.

THANK YOUS FROM THE AUTHOR:

•To my wonderfully kind editor, Katie, for being so nice when helping me polish my first draft.

•To my cats who sometimes had to wait an extra ten minutes for their supper because I was busy writing (IYKYK) and all the veterinarians I've been to in the last three years.

•To all my family and friends for putting up with me ghosting their texts or declining invites so I could stay home and work on this beast of a novel.

•To you, dear reader, for taking the chance on a new author and letting me share Dani's story with you.

•And last, I'd have to go very far back in time (the 90's, I believe) to thank the teacher who had the biggest impact on my writing. That was Mrs. Mars, my 5th grade teacher, and it was her praise for the picture book I created in the school's computer lab that made me believe I too could fly.

Interested in leaving a review?
It would mean the stars to me if you shared your thoughts on Amazon or Goodreads.

You can also follow me on Instagram!
@Marie.Indigo.Writes